Charles Henry Ross

The Pretty Widow

Charles Henry Ross

The Pretty Widow

ISBN/EAN: 9783337044527

Printed in Europe, USA, Canada, Australia, Japan

Cover: Foto ©Andreas Hilbeck / pixelio.de

More available books at **www.hansebooks.com**

THE

PRETTY WIDOW.

A Novel.

BY

CHARLES H. ROSS.

New Edition.

LONDON:

TINSLEY BROTHERS, 18, CATHERINE STREET, STRAND.

1868.

LONDON :
SAVILL, EDWARDS AND CO., PRINTERS, CHANDOS STREET,
COVENT GARDEN.

CONTENTS.

iv

THE PRETTY WIDOW.

CHAPTER I.

A MYSTERIOUS STRANGER.

If thou my secret guess,
 Speak of it never ;
Nor let thy lips express
Scorn of the deep distress
Which on my heart must press
 Ever and ever.—GABRIELLE CARR.

ONE dusty July afternoon a threadbare-coated gentleman and a very shabby brown leather portmanteau arrived together at the hotel of the " Three Crowns," in the Little Place of a certain dull old town in Picardy. Under the name of Polyblank this same portmanteau and its proprietor had been booked at the diligence office at Calais, from whence they had started that morning at daybreak. The former wagging loosely on the roof, and the latter packed tightly in the *rotonde,* they had bumped and jolted many weary leagues ; and, in the end, much travel-stained and very dusty, they thus reached Madame Gobinard's hotel door.

Time out of mind the heroes of romance have made their entrance into the realms of fiction as interesting travellers. When Mr. James was master of the ceremonies they generally came on horseback. Under Mr. Cooper's guidance they usually arrived on foot, and in

1

mocassins.   Other popular novelists have sent them to us
by coach and rail, and now and then a lucky one has
come in his own carriage.

It certainly is rather mortifying, when one has got a
hero to do what one likes with, to be obliged to bring
him under the reader's notice as a traveller in that " re-
ceptacle for dust and bad company" the *rotonde*; to be
compelled, by troublesome considerations of probability or
veracity, even to dispense with that wild and stormy night
which romancists ever have at their command; and to be
fain to introduce him to you in a natural common-place
manner, without as much as a single flash of lightning or
a distant peal of thunder to give *éclat* to his entrance on
the scene.   More mortifying still is it to have to record
that Mr. Polyblank, from slipping his foot in alighting
from the diligence, signalized his arrival in Saint Babylas
by sprawling on his hands and knees before the assembled
landlady, guests, and waiters, after the manner of the
Norman Conqueror's first descent on British soil; only
that, alas! as the sequel will show, our Polyblank's subsequent career was anything but triumphant.

He was a spare man, of middle height, of a mild aspect,
with an intellectual dreamy expression, which seldom
failed to interest those who observed him closely.   His
nature was evidently timid and retiring, and that little
accident of the fall was not calculated to set him at his
ease.   His knowledge of the language, too, appeared to
be rather limited; and failing to understand the at-
tendants, or to make them readily understand him, a kind
of contest ensued respecting the porterage of the brown
leather portmanteau, from which he emerged temporarily
triumphant, but much flustered and out of breath,
and staggered with his prize up the passage of the
hotel.

The mean appearance of this Polyblank and his luggage, had there been any other travellers to honour Madame Gobinard with their company, would not, probably, have attracted much attention ; but being the only arrival, everybody stared at him very hard, and indeed stared him quite out of countenance.   It was therefore an unpleasant promenade he had to make all the length of the hall before half-a-score of grinning idlers, bumping his legs with the edge of his portmanteau when he tried to drag it, and tripping himself up with one of its loose hanging straps when he endeavoured to carry it with both hands in front of him.

The " Three Crowns" is, as everybody knows who is acquainted with the ancient town of Picardy, which is the scene of this history, the most expensive of its hotels ; and as the English traveller's appearance seemed to indicate that he was not as wealthy as continental landlords usually give his countrymen credit for being, it is not to be wondered at that he tried to get his board and lodging for the night at the most reasonable rates obtainable ; or that he was desirous of conducting the necessary negotiations for that object in the lowest possible tone of voice.   In this endeavour, however, he was signally frustrated by the landlady, who, on receiving his inquiries in a whisper, repeated them with variations at the top of her voice ; at the same time replying thereto with such ready loquacity that even if Mr. Polyblank had not been— as he was—overwhelmed with shame and confusion by this undesired publicity, he would never have been able to follow her meaning.

Had he been alone he would, probably, have ventured on a bargain.   As it was, if he could have managed it, he would at once have turned tail and fled ; but what could our poor hero do with half a hundredweight of

portmanteau knocking about his heels ?   There could be
no doubt that he was very poor ; but it is more than
probable that he would have allowed himself to be robbed
of his last farthing rather than have revealed the dreadful
secret of his impecuniosity before the genteel company
there assembled.

Surrendering his luggage, therefore, to a nimble
person answering to the name of Alexander, he followed
that blithe domestic up a remarkably slippery staircase
to a room on the third floor, where he seated himself on
his luggage to take breath.

Not that there was much breath to be got in this
apartment, for the window was closed, and the nature of
its fastening remained, after he had investigated it, an
unfathomable mystery   The sun's rays, throughout the
day, had poured into the chamber uninterruptedly, and
there was a choking smell of dry cedar-wood, with a faint
suspicion of stale cigar smoke, a puff of charcoal, and a
whiff of garlic, making up, altogether, that peculiar and
indescribable perfume which every English traveller with,
as they say at the theatre, a " practical" nose, must have
experienced in most continental bedrooms on the third
floor, and in many on lower storeys.   As Mr. Polyblank
sat there, in moody meditation, he could not help thinking that the aspect of affairs in general was anything but
comforting.

This was the first time he had crossed that Channel
which, looked at from a Briton's point of view, is entirely
British property ; and he did not as yet agree with Sterne,
that they manage these things better in France.   He
could not, for instance, understand how it was better to
have a hearthrug by the side of the bed instead of a carpet
all over the room.   He could hardly reconcile with his
insular notions of cleanliness a pint-and-a-half water-jug,

for washing. And as the bear of famous memory observed, "What, no soap?"

The strangeness of his surroundings was not, however, that which caused him the most uneasiness. He was, perhaps, one of the most bashful men alive, and, at the same time, and perhaps for that reason, very awkward. He had hurt himself more than a little when he fell on his hands and knees at the hotel door; but the concussion had not bruised his body as the laughter did his spirit. His imperfect French and his abortive attempts at economy, had also, he well knew, afforded considerable amusement to the lookers-on, and, to crown all, he had slipped his foot again upon those horrible polished stairs when following Alexander, and the titter of the spectators still tingled in his burning ears.

He was miserably poor and very lonely. He knew not a living soul in the country to which he had come to work for his bread. In his thirty-sixth year he was about to begin life afresh. He had begun it ever so many times before, and had made as many woful failures. The prospect now before him was not very brilliant. He had come here in answer to an advertisement, to take a situation as teacher of English in the Imperial College, and his salary was to be fifty pounds per annum. Nor had he any hope of a rise. He had, indeed, no particular hope of the affair generally, further than that he trusted to be able to keep the place he had obtained. Twenty years ago he was very sanguine. There was a time when he supposed, as the saying is, " he had all the world in a string." Since then he had grown wiser, growing meanwhile older and greyer, creeping nearer and nearer to that common abode in which we all at last, be we simpletons or sages, must mingle dust with dust.

His was to the general eye an emotionless face, but to

the observant it seemed as though beneath the placid surface, fierce tempests of passion might have raged, all unsuspected. A poor commonplace, harmless sort of creature he seemed to be, with a worn and wearied look at times about his blue eyes, and a hungry one about his pinched and fleshless cheeks, which would have frightened a boarding-house keeper.

"At what hour is the ordinary?" he had inquired of Alexander, when the waiter, having deposited the portmanteau on the floor was about to retire, continuing the air which he had been humming to himself throughout the upstairs journey.

"At five, sir," he replied.

"Thank you," said Mr. Polyblank; "thank you. At five? Thank you." Then, with a desperate effort, and in as careless a tone as he could manage, "How much is it?"

"Three francs, sir," answered Alexander; and, having waited a moment for another question, he resumed his tune at the point he had dropped it, and retired leisurely.

"I wonder," murmured Mr. Polyblank, uneasily, "whether he'll mention downstairs what I have been asking. I wish I had not spoken. There's a disagreeable smirk about the fellow. I certainly don't like these foreign waiters. I wonder whether they all hum in that way!"

He got off his portmanteau, presently, and opened it to take out the necessary articles from the poor little stock it contained; for its great weight was occasioned almost entirely by shabby old volumes very much thumbed and very weak in their backs. From among these he drew out a small paper parcel of clean linen, and having selected a collar he fastened it on with a little manœuvring, chose the best part of his blue satin scarf for the outside fold, and fixed it with a neck-pin of bygone fashion, the head of which contained a speck of something about the size of a pin's point which its owner gratified himself by supposing to be a diamond.

Before his toilet was completed the loud ringing of a bell below stairs informed him that dinner was ready, and so, with a final wrench at the collar, a throttling tussle with the scarf, and an unexpected stab in his thumb from the jewelled neck-pin, he pulled himself together, and made up his mind to face the company. What, however, with the delay caused by these arrangements, and the time occupied in the perilous descent of the shining oak stairs, he did not reach the dining saloon until the soup had been disposed of.

Through a hot mist he saw a long table crowded by hungry gentlemen, who evidently regarded the meal as a matter of business, from the earnestness with which they devoted themselves to it. He could see no vacant place, and meandered vaguely behind the guests' chairs until the blithe Alexander taking him into custody led him to a seat and fixed him between two very fat farmers, who squared their elbows while eating, like winning jockeys passing Tattenham Corner.

"You're all behind," said Alexander, nudging him with a soup plate; "you must be quick! Here, take some of this. It is good."

"I can choose for myself," replied Polyblank, with English dignity, and in the best French he was capable of.

But Alexander was not so easily routed, for he seemed to have resolved on taking the poor foreigner under his protecting wing, and, in the innocence of his heart, never for a moment dreamt that his kindly-meant suggestions

could be deemed offensive. He therefore pressed upon
Polyblank all those dishes which he thought he would
like, but which Polyblank persistently refused. At other
times Alexander energetically warned him off certain
other dishes of which the misguided gentleman obsti-
nately insisted on partaking, very much to his own disadvantage.

Owing to this petty warfare, and also to the circumstance of his having, while running his eye helplessly
over the wine list, ordered a higher priced vintage than
he wished, or had any occasion to do, this dinner was not
a very pleasant affair. He was glad when the appearance
of the roast fowl and salad indicated the end of the
meats; and Alexander having borne down upon him,
unsuccessfully, with grapes, green figs, plums, peaches,
Gruyère cheese, and "lady's fingers," left him to regale
himself upon almonds and raisins, which, perversely, he
pretended to prefer to the rest of the dessert.

While he sat munching and sipping he listened to the
company conversing, though without being able to make
much out of it. There were two persons whom he took
to be commercial travellers, and there was an officer in
uniform with one epaulet whom, afterwards, he knew to
be a sous-lieutenant in a foot regiment then quartered
in the town. There were one or two small farmers with
dull, heavy faces, and loud, harsh voices. There were
half a dozen fat and affable little men, natives of Saint
Babylas, who probably enjoyed small independencies, and
came to dinner at the table d'hôte for the sake of the
society. Other persons there were, besides, of whom,
from the place in which he sat he could not obtain a
clear view; and directly opposite to him was a mysterious
stranger.

This person probably did not strike those around him

as being particularly mysterious; but to him, from the first moment, Mr. Polyblank's eyes had been attracted by a curiosity for which he could not account to himself. A well-made, handsome young man he was, though with a sort of affected weariness about his expression and manner, more often to be met with in England than in France. Evidently a young man whose existence was a burden to him, although he seemed to enjoy robust health, and to have an appetite which some of your delicate, finnikin eaters would have thought enormous. It was not, apparently, worth this young man's while to enter into conversation with those around him, or to listen with any attention to what was said to him, or even to be commonly polite.

One of the affable little men, before alluded to, having caught this gentleman's eye, in the course of a long story he was telling, weakly supposed that he had awakened his interest, and continued to address him, but, presently, the young man yawning in his face and turning wearily away, the affable little man was overwhelmed with confusion, and found the climax of his tale so embarrassingly remote that he was obliged to wind it up prematurely.

The young man sat sipping his wine, frowning now and then as though in deep thought, and biting the ends of his moustache. Evidently he was a hero of the romantic school, and, hero like, had weighty matters on his mind ;—a dark intrigue, perhaps—the honour of a noble house—a half-arranged murder—the unburied body of a victim weighing heavily on his conscience ! Which was it ?

To poor Polyblank he seemed a prodigiously fine gentleman. He was handsomely dressed. He had good jewellery.. That supercilious withering manner became

him mightily, though perhaps not fully appreeiated by
the withered.   As for the Englishman, the mysterious
stranger seemed to be unaware of his existence, although
he sat direetly opposite to him.   When first of all Polyblank had blundered into his seat, the other had not
raised his eyes.   Now and then, during the eourse of the
dinner, he seemed not so mueh to stare at Polyblank as
at a highly-gilt eloek upon the mantelpieee behind him,
in the manufaeture of whieh the time of day had been,
as it were, swamped by elaborate allegory.   There eer-
tainly was a mystery about the stranger, in the eyes of
Polyblank at least, who, munehing his almonds and
raisins, fell into a reverie respeeting his probable name
and position in life, wondering as he did so whether it
was likely they would ever see one another again.

It was not probable.   During the last twenty years,
passed as usher and tutor in many English sehools, Polyblank had more than onee felt an interest in and formed
an attaehment for some pupil who going away had easily
forgotten his tutor, or if remembering him at all, remembered him only with a laugh half pitying and half eon-
temptuous, as that poor devil who led sueh a life of it at
old So-and-so's.   In time he had eome to think it quite
in the nature of things that some persons should leave
sehool, live happy ever afterwards, forgetting all about
other persons; and that the other persons should go
grinding on with an ever lessening interest in life, taking
their kieks and halfpenee with beeoming humility, and
praising the Lord the while that the halfpenee were no
fewer and the kieks no harder.

Well! well! it had been a weary life whieh he passed
in those hateful English sehool-rooms, and doubtless as
wearisome a prospeet lay before him; but he eould bear
it better now, beeause he had buried his old hopes and

ambitions. Yes, buried them very deep, and well trampled down the earth. All that was gone and done with. He scarcely retained anything to remind him of the unhappy, wasted time that was gone, unless it were those dog-eared volumes upstairs in the battered portmanteau; in some of which Monsieur Polyblank, traveller to St. Babylas, figured as P and Peter Polyblank, accompanied by a date that was nearly thirty years old; for the books had been his when he himself was a schoolboy, struggling over that asses'-bridge across which he had since coaxed, and dragged, and driven so many reluctant learners.

Only these humble records of the past remained, together with one or two ragged bills, which it had pinched him sorely to pay; one or two testimonials to his moral character and his learning; the certificate of his mother's marriage pasted upon calico; one of her wedding cards, stained blue and brown with damp; and her portrait, in faded water-colours, which some heartless young rogue years ago had decorated with a pipe and moustaches, that no effort upon Polyblank's part had been able wholly to efface.

But while he sat pondering upon these and other matters which somehow unaccountably at the sight of the mysterious stranger came crowding on his memory, the other guests began to rise one by one from the table and take their departure. The sous-lieutenant rising first went buckling himself up down the passage and across the courtyard, until his face assumed a crimson hue. The heavy farmers stumped out, and fell to screaming over the harnessing of their lean beasts of burden, and presently went jolting in their carts over the Little Place as only those were ever jolted who have travelled without springs across Saint Babylas's boulders. After them the affable little fat men began to drop off one by

one, as so many over-ripe plums may drop from the
parent bough, as some one else has somewhere said.

It was then that Polyblank in his turn began to think
he ought to be going, though he did not exactly know
where to go to.   He had no business on hand for that
evening.   He thought it would be time enough to call
on the following morning upon the Head of the College,
since it was not until the day after, as had been arranged,
that he was to begin his duties.   To-morrow, too, he
would be able to find some lodgings.   He did not think
it would be wise to go to a café, because it might be
contrary to the college rules for a teacher to enter one
of these establishments.   Neither did he want to walk
about the streets until it should become dusk, when he
thought he might venture out and reconnoitre without
fear of being noticed; for perhaps the less that was seen
of him before he was regularly installed as a " professor"
the better.   While he was hesitating what to do Alexander
came once more to the rescue, and this time Polyblank
was fain to take the waiter's advice.

" You can go anywhere you like, and do what you
please," said Alexander, waving his hand grandly, as
though he were making a present of many acres.   " The
courtyard is at your disposal.   You are at liberty to
enter the garden beyond, or you can go for a little walk
and take your half cup at a café, or you can take it
here."

Mr. Polyblank would take it there if Alexander
pleased, and Alexander pleasing, it was brought to him
and set upon a little marble-topped table by the side of
a window looking out into the courtyard with its white
walls and its green shutters, its row of plants in wooden
boxes, and its distant view of madame in her bureau, and
of the flower-garden beyond—beginning on the house-

top and going up steps into the sky. Alexander by this time had cleared the table ; for all the guests, with one exception, had now left the salon. The mysterious stranger still lingered. He had risen the last from dessert, and had stood a long time at the window on the opposite side of the room, looking gloomily out upon the grass-grown street.

Disturbed by a hurricane of tablecloth, which arose beneath Alexander's nimble fingers, he sauntered away with a scowl into the courtyard, and meditatively picked his way across and across the flagstones, taking especial care to avoid the cracks. But growing, in due course, weary of this exercise, he wandered back again to the salon, called for writing materials, and began laboriously to fill a large sheet of paper with very small crabbed writing. Meanwhile Polyblank had reached the dregs of his coffee, and was wondering whether or not it was the custom of the country to leave any of the brandy in the little two-go decanter in which it had been served to him ; finally he decided that it was, though at the same time he wished it was not.

And now he endeavoured to amuse himself with the reports of the Tribunal of Correctional Police in the Saint Babylas local journal; but he was unable to keep his eyes off the mysterious stranger, or to avoid listening to the scratching of his pen, which was distinctly audible in the heavy silence that had fallen upon the hotel. Afar off Alexander was faintly melodious, warbling one of the immortal Soap Bubbles of the great Charles Paul. Occasionally was to be heard the clic-clac of a sabot in the street, or a sing-song voice, raised suddenly and as suddenly subsiding again. The twilight was gathering in the corners of the room. Surely it was too dark for the penman to see what he was about where he sat, for

even at the window the faint brown printing-ink began
to dance before the reader's eyes.   The stranger, however, went on a little while longer, then made a dash and
a flourish, indicative of an imposing signature, and walked
away to the window looking on to the street, to read
what he had written.   But soon Mr. Polyblank heard
an exclamation of impatience, and the crumpling of
paper, and then the stranger was tearing up the result of
his labour into a thousand atoms, which he threw upon
the floor and trampled under foot with a muttered oath.
Then throwing himself upon a couch, he lit a cigar and
puffed at it despondingly.

"A very strange gentleman," said Mr. Polyblank to
himself, as he rose and put on his hat—"a very strange
gentleman, who has evidently something on his mind."
And thus reflecting he made his way towards the street.
It happened, however, that when half across the court-
yard he came to a standstill, to feel in his pockets for the
key of his portmanteau, which he fancied he might have
left upstairs; and, while feeling for it, he stood near
enough to Madame Gobinard's counting-house window
to overhear a portion of a conversation between that lady
and the wife of Mr. Pomponney, the chemist round the
corner, of which the mysterious stranger was the subject.

"Oh yes, he's here," Mr. Polyblank heard the landlady say; "he's been here close upon a month.   He may
go away, too, as soon as he chooses, for me.   I shan't
ask him to remain, I promise you.   He's writing a letter
in the dining-room, and I hope it's to tell his friends
he'll soon be back with them."

"There's not much chance of that, though, is there,
Madame Gobinard?"

"No, indeed! not much while somebody remains in
the neighbourhood."

" Unless somebody dismisses him."

" I am afraid that somebody is too tender-hearted to do that. Poor little angel! Good little heart! Oh, the good-for-nothing; and oh, what fools we women are!"

While thus Madame Gobinard was exclaiming, and while Mr. Polyblank was still fumbling for his key, the mysterious stranger, himself, came lounging out, and slowly approached the speakers.

" Will you prepare me my bill, madame?" he said. " I shall leave Saint Babylas the first thing in the morning."

Not altogether without a guilty blush, good Madame Gobinard answered that she would do as he desired, and seemed upon the point of adding something in the shape of an apology when a carriage came rattling across the Palace and drew up at the door. The window of this carriage being lowered, Mr. Polyblank caught a momentary glimpse of a dainty little black bonnet and a dear little round pink-and-white face with big, brown, wondering baby's eyes, with a low forehead, which a cluster of light brown curls made even lower still, with a dimpled chin, with decidedly a wide mouth, with very red lips and two rows of teeth, white though not very regular. In point of fact, he caught a glimpse of a very pretty woman—one of that sort whom men turn round to look after, and all other women pull to pieces.

That mysterious young man who had something on his mind, who had written the long letter and torn it to pieces and given himself up to despair, came eagerly forward at sight of this pretty woman's head, to clasp the plump little tightly-gloved hand which came out of the carriage window to meet his. Then, as he stood talking to its owner, and Madame Gobinard and her friend whispered furtively together, Mr. Polyblank having found his key, took his way slowly across the Little Place. He had not gone very far when the rattling of wheels behind him warned him of the carriage's approach, and, as it passed him rapidly, he caught one more glimpse of the pretty head with the brown curls and the wondering baby's eyes which, as long as possible, were fixed upon the figure of the mysterious stranger standing in front of the hotel door.

" I wonder," said Mr. Polyblank, as he walked away, " I wonder whether that is the Somebody they were talking about."

While he was yet in the Place, and lingering in front of a shop window, he heard a brisk footfall behind him, and a merry voice humming a tune. Turning, in expectation of seeing Alexander, he found instead, to his astonishment, that it was the young man of mystery ; no longer gloomy and despairing though, but instead having such a radiant countenance as must surely have belonged to one of the happiest men alive.

" I wonder, now," said Mr. Polyblank, as he walked onwards, " whether that is Somebody's work."

And actually it then for the first time struck him as being odd that there had never been a Somebody in his case. Certainly there never had been ; and was it likely there ever would be ? At any rate, he had got through his first thirty-six years in safety. He was now in the prime of life—such a prime as it was. He had not over much flesh on his bones, or hair on his head, and he was of but little use at diamond type without his spectacles. The clothes that covered him were threadbare and frayed at the edges ; but his brain was stored with classic lore. He did not know much about life, but you could not easily have puzzled him with a Greek verb. Yes, he had got through six-and-thirty years of toil and trouble ; and only to think that all his troubles were yet to come !

CHAPTER II.

THE MARTYRDOM OF THE NEW PROFESSOR.

Non diable au front cornu, mais un diable d'enfant
Comme en donne le ciel sans qu'on les lui demande.
                                        RAYNAL.

A PERSON of consequence, who was staying at the hotel, opening his chamber window very early one morning, and looking out upon the still sleeping town of Saint Babylas, smiled a pitying smile as he said :—" How in the name of wonder do the inhabitants of this humdrum place pass their lives ?"

And truly such an inquiry might naturally suggest itself to the mind of a person of consequence who lived somewhere else ; for Saint Babylas was indeed but a poor little town stuck in the middle of a bare, bleak country of uninviting aspect.   A very quiet, orderly town it was, which went to bed soon—shutting up the most dissolute cafés by half-past ten ; got up very early, caught its little worm, and took it to the best market, where, however, it frequently happened that a very few pence rewarded a great deal of labour.

The richer portion of the population of Saint Babylas was for the most part made up of worthy citizens with an income of from eighty to a hundred pounds a year—good souls who grubbed on somehow not less happily or unhappily than the rest of the world which never heard of them.

A very poor place indeed : yet it had once been strongly fortified, and cannon was still mounted on its grey old crumbling walls ; and on these ramparts any fine day the Saint Babylas children and their nurses might be found sauntering beneath the somewhat niggardly shade fur-

2

nished by the double row of lime trees there growing.
Rather a bare, naked look had Saint Babylas, the streets
of which ofttimes lay so silent in the midday sunlight
that had it not been for the inevitable idle dog panting
in the white heat, it might have suggested the idea of a
city of sleepers.

Now, if you had entered Saint Babylas by Saint
Abraham's Gate and, traversing the street of the Soul-
which-mounts-to-Heaven,* turned sharply to the left,
where, at the corner of Sucking-pig-street, is the tobacco
shop, standing outside which that little wooden military
man with the weather-beaten nose has smoked the same
pipe these fifty years and more, you would have found
yourself, once upon a time, in Louis Philippe-street.
But a few years afterwards, pursuing the same course,
you would have found no such place in existence, although
the same houses still were there, and apparently kept by
the same people; but the name had been changed, and
it was then the street of the Republic. There came a
time, however, when that name was also discarded; and
now-a-days, the street of the Emperor will conduct you,
by Boiled Potato-street, to the street of the Martyred
Saint, where stands a building that was once the Royal
School and the Lyceum, but is now the Imperial College
of Saint Babylas.

This Imperial College is at the present writing an ancient building, which would be gray with age if it had
not been recently whitewashed; which would be venerable
had it not lately been subjected, at great cost, to hideous
modern improvements. It would be difficult now to say
what style of architecture it belongs to; it has been so
knocked about and undergone so many changes since the

---

* *It may perhaps not be unnecessary to state that these names are real.*

days when Titus Oates was one of its parlour boarders. A noble old building, doubtless, it had been, before brick-layers, plasterers, and painters made wild work with its mullions, billet mouldings, trefoils, lancets, pinnacles, and flying buttresses, and sacrilegious whitewashers fell foul of its architecture, generally.

"We have here, Monsieur Paulyblon," said M. Roustoubique, the proviseur or chief of the Imperial College, indicating with a graceful turn of his hand a large assemblage of dusty urchins screaming and scrambling in the great courtyard; "we have here that which, rightly moulded, may some day be their country's ornament and pride. Who knows, Monsieur Paulyblon, but we see in these our future senators, our future field-marshals, our great authors, our famous artists. Here, Monsieur Paulyblon, we have them in the rough (there was no mistake about the rough). Let us do our best to mould their plastic minds. This is the raw (raw enough) material. Let the finished work bear the impress of the master's hand."

But here a small portion of the raw material coming unexpectedly full butt into the proviseur's stomach, knocked all his breath and the remainder of the allegory out of him, and though the urchin certainly bore the impression of the master's hand—and foot, too, for that matter—for some hours afterwards, there is no reason to believe that he felt particularly grateful for it. Professor Polyblank found out, before the first day was over, that a teacher of the young who tried to do his duty in the College of Saint Babylas, would earn every halfpenny of his twelve hundred francs. It was a tough job, and not without its dangers; indeed it was a wonder how he lived through all his sufferings.

Besides a settled determination from the outset to

badger him out of his wits, there were not wanting among
his pupils some who plotted together to do him grievous
bodily harm.   How otherwise shall we account for the
pin in the seat of his chair, the pepper mixed with his
snuff, the train of gunpowder in connexion with the
cracker artfully concealed under the leg of his table?
He had to deal with some rough customers in his time,
had Mr. Polyblank, and it had been his lot to lick or half
lick some very awkward cubs into shape.   He knew, too,
to his cost, that boys would be boys ; but until he came
to the Imperial College of Saint Babylas he had no notion
what a mischievous French boy was.

For fifty pounds a year the professor was expected
to teach eight hours per diem, and on some of those hot,
thirsty, restless July afternoons young France became a
trouble to him.   He began at nine in the morning, and
stopped till twelve.   Went home to dinner, and returned
at one ; then worked till six.   The scene of his labours
was always one or the other of two rooms overlooking a
dreary courtyard, the gravel of which was, here and
there, partly worn, and partly scooped, into holes, as if
rabbits had been burrowing in it.   The two apartments
where the new professor taught closely resembled each
other.   They were both spacious and dingy, and had
been whitewashed long ago.   Their ceilings were decorated
with coloured wafers ingeniously stuck thereon by boys
who threw them up on two-sous pieces, the upper surface
of the wafers having been wet in order that they might
adhere when they came in contact with the ceiling.
High up on one of the walls was a small leaden crucifix.
There were two windows to each room, strongly guarded
by iron bars.   Round the room were several cupboards
or lockers, each bearing a number.   Along three sides
of the room ran a long desk, with three forms which
were fixtures in front.   On the fourth side was a small

raised platform, with a chair and table for the professor. In the middle of the room a stove. They were not pleasant places, these two school-rooms, to pass long summer days in; and it must be confessed that while waiting till his pupils had perfected themselves in their lessons, Mr. Polyblank occasionally covered his eyes, and snatched portions of a never to be completed period of forty winks. From that raised platform a professor gifted with ordinary powers of vision might have raked the entire class with eagle glance; but Mr. Polyblank's range of sight being limited, the young Français were not slow to avail themselves of this optical defect. The young gentlemen delighted in playing off various schoolboy pranks.

A paper warfare, taking the form of pellets, was waged almost continuously during the hours of Mr. Polyblank's class, and wagers were sometimes laid as to who would first succeed in hitting the professor—an unprecedented outrage in Polyblank's scholastic experience. For this and other offences of graver or lighter turpitude, he allotted to the culprits certain hours of Retenue or Arret, the former punishment signifying stopping in during play time to write from dictation, the latter that the culprit should stand with his face to the wall in the playground whilst the other boys played; a position which certain of the blackest sheep frequently maintained, during play-hours, for a month or six weeks at a stretch.

During the winter months the stove in the middle of the room offered, under the supervision of a short-sighted professor, peculiar facilities for the cultivation of some of the lighter branches of the culinary art. The manufacture of toffee was a flourishing business, and a brisk trade was done in roasted chestnuts and potatoes. Deprived of these pleasures during summer, the young

gentlemen found compensation in the pursuit of horti-
culture and entomology. Sickly crops of mustard-and-
cress were grown in desks upon strips of flannel.
Silkworms were reared in large numbers, and small
happy families of lizards, May-bugs, and black-beetles
were kept in cardboard boxes. As the nurture of
these pets demanded constant attention upon the part
of their owners, and as it was not unusual for a pupil's
head to disappear for some ten or fifteen minutes at a
stretch, within his desk, the professor was frequently
obliged to demand an explanation of these prolonged
burrowings.

One day, after he had been about a week at the
college, Mr. Polyblank, seeing that six heads in a row
had disappeared, and hearing from behind the upraised
desk lids the sounds of angry contention, bore down upon
the young gentlemen, and instituted a rigid search; and
then, oh, what a discovery was made! In the desk of
one Bardajos was found a frog. One Bourdichon kept
crickets. Coquillard was evidently a dealer in May-bugs,
Pepinet had a lizard, and the brothers Moineau silkworms. Stores of paper pellets also came to light, as
well as offensive weapons in the shape of pop-guns and
toy cannon. To seize the latter articles seemed to Mr.
Polyblank the proper course of action; but how to deal
with the live stock? Unhappily, making a snatch at a
cardboard box, the lizard it contained ran up his sleeve.
The professor, in some alarm, pulled off his coat, reckless
of the condition of his flannel-shirt, the elbows of which
were repaired by patches of a brighter coloured stuff.
A roar of laughter saluted his appearance in shirt sleeves,
and was a signal for a general riot. All the May-bugs
were immediately launched in the air. A shower of
pellets rattled about Polyblank's ears.

Fixing upon the one whom he supposed to be the leader, the new professor seized Bardajos by the collar, but that young gentleman being extremely strong and nimble, slipped between his legs and tripped him up. And at that moment, in the midst of a demoniacal shout, M. Roustoubique strode into the room and gazed about him in astonishment.

"Is this the way, sir, you conduct your class?" he inquired, in icy tones; and, before Mr. Polyblank could explain, he added hastily, "Put on your coat, sir, put on your coat. It is not to teach *le boxe* that your services are required."

When they talked the matter over afterwards in private, M. Roustoubique made a passing allusion to the patched elbows which was not wanting in severity.

CHAPTER III.

THE POMPONNEY'S FIRST FLOOR.

Shrinking from each rude gaze or jesting word,
A hidden fire within his lustrous eyes,
Telling of musings deep; and pale thin cheeks,
Bearing their witness of the midnight watch.—PLUMPTRE.

"FELICITE," said Mr. Hippolite Pomponney, pharmaceutical chemist, of Saint Babylas, "you will see."

When thus he spoke, Mr. Pomponney was standing outside his shop upon a chair, which Madame Pomponney was holding steady for him, and he was knocking a nail into the wall by the side of his private door. In case of accident, Mr. Pomponney's forethought had provided Madame Pomponney with another nail, which she held at the same time that she held the chair, and she furthermore had charge of a loop string, attached to which was a small parallelogram of pasteboard, bearing an announcement respecting a furnished room to let in Mr. Pomponney's establishment.

The first nail, however, having done all that was required of it, Mr. Pomponney, passing down the hammer, called upon Félicité to give him the card, which took both hands to hang up. The card thus disposed of to his satisfaction, Mr. Pomponney called upon Felicité to concentrate her energies upon the steadying of the chair, and having made the descent with safety, he stepped back into the road, with his head on one side, to contemplate the result of his labours.

" Felicité," Mr. Pomponney repeated, " you will see."

Mr. Pomponney was a large man, and Madame Pomponney was small and spare. He was bland and clean-shaven. He wore trim mutton-chop whiskers. Moustaches never were popular in provincial France. He was what women call a very fine man, and indeed his figure and mien were not wanting in a certain grandiose air which he mistook for dignity. Perhaps his shirt-sleeves and slippers somewhat marred the effect ; but then that was an accident, for it was to be presumed that some time or other he put his coat and boots on. A fine figure of a man he seemed in the eyes of poor little Madame Pomponney, who was herself a mere whisp of a woman, with a fluttering, half-scared way about her. Not only a fine man, though, but a sage, whose word was law and whose prophecies were infallible. Thus was it that when the question of how the first-floor front was to be disposed of first came upon the back parlour carpet, Mr. Pomponney had said, right off, " We'll let it furnished." Although Madame Pomponney had a passing doubt with respect to where the furniture was to come from, and when it had come where the tenant was to be found, yet as Mr. Pomponney said it was to be let, and knowing that when Mr. Pomponney said a thing he, in point of fact, said it, she, as in duty bound, came presently to look upon the matter as as good as settled.

How to furnish the room fit for the purpose was the first point to be considered; but with this detail it could not be reasonably expected that Mr. Pomponney should trouble himself. One thing was certain, no money could be expended upon upholstery; and so the poor little woman took a mental inventory of the furniture of the other rooms, and set about selecting from them the articles which could best be spared, in order to furnish the first-floor front. There was, to be sure, a kind of a bed in the room, with a sort of a mattress. There was, also, something in the shape of a table, and one or two other things in the form of chairs; but all were old and ricketty. These things, however, could be replaced by others. Mr. Pomponney would never know if he were robbed of his under mattress and one of the worst from the first-floor furtively substituted for it. The invalid table would do as well in the back parlour as the sound one: the latter being used only as a sideboard on which to display the gala-day service of coffee-cups of white and gold. As for the crippled chairs, one could be mended, and the other might take the place of a sound one, and stand in a quiet corner of the parlour, venturesome visitors being warned off it as skaters are warned off from a weak place in the ice.

And now came the decorative department. There was a fine engraving, in a handsome frame, of the great Napoleon, galloping over the Alps on a high-spirited steed, which could easily be spared from the hall, together with two smaller pictures of sanguinary engagements terminating in French victories. Next the lavatory arrangements had to be seen to, and the swivel of the looking-glass attached to the washhand-stand tightened, to guard against the mirror unexpectedly intervening betwixt the washhand-basin and the head of the lodger, who might otherwise butt at it unthinkingly when his eyes were closed. With a bright strip of carpet for the side of the bed, with its clean polished floor, its clean painted walls, and its clean white window-curtains, the little room looked, surely, worth every sou of the modest twenty francs a month which it was Mr. Pomponney's decision should be asked for it. And now that the apartment was ready, all that was wanted was the lodger.

"I wonder," Madame Pomponney said, timidly, "when we shall have an application."

"To-day," replied Mr. Pomponney, decisively.

"To-day!" echoed the little woman, almost (if such a thing had been possible) incredulously.

"Felicité," observed Mr. Pomponney—a fact, indeed, already twice recorded—"you will see."

It certainly has a handsome card, beautifully written, with an astounding delicacy of upstroke; and when it was not fluttering in the wind, was distinctly legible nearly a dozen yards off. Having sufficiently admired his handiwork, Mr. Pomponney followed Madame Pomponney—who, after the manner of good wives, carried the chair, the hammer, and the other nail—and taking a seat in the back parlour, folded his hands across his stomach, as though he meant to sit there and wait until the first-floor front was satisfactorily disposed of.

Now, looking at probabilities, it would have seemed that, like John Leech's Yankee young lady, there was a danger of his sitting on till he "took root" before meeting with a chance customer in Saint Babylas; for there were no chance customers there.

Strangers either settled irrevocably or ran away at once. Murray warned off the marauding Briton. There was no show church. There was no foot pavement. Except at fair time, nobody ever thought of making holiday in the dull little town, and then the holiday-makers, for the most part, were the heavy-heeled rustics from the neighbouring villages—clumsy louts in blue blouses and wooden shoes, long-limbed matrons, shrill of voice and scraggy of shape, and thickset maidens with swollen fists and shiny elbows, bashful and coy, and as awkward as so many calves in petticoats.

The chance of letting the first-floor front, therefore, seemed rather remote, unless the one solitary stranger who had come to Saint Babylas by diligence the previous evening, and who it was said intended to reside in the town, should take it into his head—but really that was too improbable. As, however, it often does happen—to the great confusion of your wiseacres, who, if they had only time and tape enough allowed them, would set the world straight without the aid of a two-foot rule—the most improbable thing that could occur did occur, and the new professor, walking down the shady side of the Street of the Priests, crossed over into the sun on catching sight of Mr. Pomponney's caligraphy, and rang the private door bell.

" Felicité," Mr. Pomponney observed with a triumphant smile ; " you see !"

True enough, looking in at the corner of the next shop-window, belonging to a book and music seller, and pretending to admire the cover of a new waltz by Leduc, or a new romance by Elie Berthel, Felicité saw a shabby-genteel and slender man who, thinking himself unobserved, was making one of the panes of the window do service as a looking-glass, while he adjusted a diamond pin in a very much be-pinned, black satin stock.

Mrs. Pomponney knew him at a glance.

" It is the new professor, who put up last night at the ' Three Crowns.' "

" To be sure it is," said Mr. Pomponney—as though Mr. Polyblank had come according to order. " Go, my dear, and make the necessary arrangements. We will take the professor."

Felicité only waited a moment to arrange her little corkscrew curls and to pull off her apron, and then tripped lightly to the door. She was not used to strangers, and was all in a flutter and a tremble ; but her confusion by no means equalled that of the professor, who, however, was very much pleased with the room, and more so with the rent, which was lower than he had expected. But besides being bashful and tongue-tied, owing both to his modesty and his limited knowledge of colloquial French, this poor Polyblank had a great notion of strategy, and thought it wisdom not to appear as well satisfied as he really was. Therefore when Madame Pomponney told Mr. Pomponney that the professor had gone away without deciding, saying that if he wanted the room he would come back in an hour's time, it must be confessed Monsieur was a trifle disconcerted ; nor was the hour passed by the head of the Pomponneyian household without some small amount of uneasiness.

" Perhaps," said Felicité, " if the gentleman should take the apartment it would be as well, as he is English, to change the big picture for another, since he might feel uncomfortable with Napoleon in the room."

All the world over they are not under the impression that the English had it all their own way at Waterloo.

At the end of the hour, however, the professor returned,

bringing with him that rusty brown leather portmanteau with which he had grazed his shins in the hotel passage, and, paying a month's rent in advance, took up his resi- at once under the chemist's roof.   It was very pleasant to sit there at the open window those calm July evenings, book in hand, with the choice of reading the book or looking out into the street.   Though it was the dullest street of a dull town, there was nevertheless a great deal for a foreigner to look at.   Over the way was a washer- woman's shop, outside which hung a little board bearing an inscription that was in itself a never-failing cause of wonderment, for it said—

> Ici on maingle
>
> Le Linge.
>
> MANGLED.

This evidently was intended to catch English residents. There was also a milliner's a little distance off, where there was a dark-eyed apprentice who seemed to look twice out of window for every three stitches she made. And there was a barber's apprentice at another shop who came out into the street under various shallow pretences many times a day, but who never by any chance did so without looking up at the dark-eyed young milliner, who for her part never by any chance when looked up at failed to toss her head disdainfully.   There was a long- haired cat which slept for hours together in the barber's window ; and a shaved poodle at the milliner's, which puss treated with as much contempt as the milliner's girl did the barber's clerk.

At a certain hour every fine afternoon a certain old lady from one of the houses opposite went out for a walk with her bonne.   At another hour, with equal regularity,

a young man went out of another house in a great hurry
and walked rapidly out of sight. Two days a-week, and
always at the same time, a rosy-faced priest, carrying an
umbrella and a prayer-book, paid a visit to another house,
and if kept waiting at the door read his book upon the
door-step. There was an unseen female on the professor's side of the way who sang snatches of songs pretty
regularly every evening; and an unseen invalid next
door who as regularly groaned. And there were many
other matters calculated to arrest the attention and excite
the curiosity of a new-comer in Saint Babylas who had
nothing better to amuse him. But there was an almost
grave-like silence at nightfall, and an impenetrable obscurity in the Street of the Priests.

To improve himself in the language, the professor,
though by no means an admirer of works of fiction, hired
a few volumes from the library next door and perused,
in French, Charles Dickens's " Nephew of My Aunt;"
and Thackeray's " Livre des Snobs," and " Memoirs of a
Footman." Mr. Polyblank was a perfect model of a
lodger. The Pomponneys could never make sure whether
or not he was at home, unless they went out into the
street and looked for the light in his window. It was a
lesson to the careless to see how, when he came home of
an evening, he scraped those ricketty old boots of his
upon the scraper, and polished them upon the mat. In
the morning Madame Pomponney served him up a frugal
repast of coffee, and milk, and bread and butter; and at
night, in lieu of supper, he had tea in the English fashion,
with more bread and butter. When first he came Felicité
had asked him whether he would dine at home, thinking
that perhaps he might not like to dine in the college.
He answered in the negative, with some slight confusion in
his manner, of which she took but little notice at the time.

One day, when he had been with them about a fort-night, Mr. Pomponney met him strolling under the lime trees upon the ramparts, about half an hour after noon. As this Mr. Pomponney knew to be the hour at which the Imperial collegians took their meal, he was somewhat surprised.

" You don't dine there then to-day," said the chemist, waving his hand in a northerly direction.

" Dine where ?" asked the other, innocently.

" Where ?   In the college."

" In the college!   No.   Why ?"

" Why ?   Why I thought——"

" I never dine there.   I dine—that is—I never dine there."

The conversation ended thus, and probably, the pro-fessor having much more important matters to think of than mere vulgar victuals and drink, soon forgot all about it.   However, one day, Félicité, arriving again at the subject, either by accident or intention, asked the pro-fessor point blank where he *did* dine.   Mr. Polyblank seemed to gasp a moment—then replied, " At the ordinary."

" At the ordinary ?" repeated Madame Pomponney.

" Yes."

" At the hotel ?"

" Yes, yes."

" At the hotel of the ' Three Crowns ?' "

" Yes, yes, yes."

" Really now, but don't you find that very expensive ?"

" No, I don't," cried the professor, in an excited, almost angry tone.   " Not more expensive than I can afford.   And if it pleases me to spend my money so, I don't exactly see, ma'am, what you or anybody else has to do with it !"

Upon this Felicité fled in terror, and it was the very next morning after this dialogue that Mr. Pomponney made the discovery that the professor must be a most extraordinary glutton !

Madame Gobinard's table d'hôte enjoyed a sort of small celebrity in Saint Babylas and its environs, and for many years past its praises had been sung by those fat, little, independent gentlemen who dined at it regularly, as well as by the chance travellers who arrived by the diligence, and partook of a single meal.　Decidedly Polyblank must be a lover of good cheer when he every day regaled himself with such an extravagant repast ; for three or four shillings a day is a good deal to spend on dinner out of fifty pounds a year—which statement please to verify by the aid of your slate and pencil, and you will not find a large balance remaining for breakfast, supper, and bed.　But of course, as Madame Pomponney argued, Mr. Polyblank knew his own business best ; and, after all, might he not have private means of his own beyond his scholastic earnings ?

It was only a question of extravagance, until next morning when Felicité, with the pardonable curiosity of her sex, opening a neatly folded paper packet which, when Polyblank went out, he had accidentally left behind him on the breakfast-table, made a remarkable discovery. This packet contained a quantity of Lyons-sausage skins, and the bones of what the English humbler classes term a " trotter." The facts of the case, together with the skin and bones, having been laid before the chemist, Mr. Pomponney was compelled to search for a solution of the mystery among the hairs of his mutton-chop whiskers, and to seek a satisfactory explanation in the depths of his bandanna.

" Felicité," said Mr. Pomponney, when he came at last

to the surface, holding tight on to an idea, "the man with twelve hundred francs a year, who not only in public regales himself like a prince, but subsequently in secret gorges himself like a pig, is unworthy of the name—in fact of any name but pig. How can he get through it all?"

"There certainly seems skin enough for a foot of sausage," said Madame Pomponney.

"I cannot determine with anatomical accuracy," said Mr. Pomponney, "how many bones go to a trotter; but I should say that there are the remains of at least all one pig ever walked upon."

"It does not make him very fat," said Félicité, after some moments' reflection. "Il est sec comme un clou."

"It isn't likely to make him fat," observed the chemist. "Food eaten by stealth is not likely to do anybody any good. One thing is very certain, though. He is ashamed of what he does, and hasn't the manliness to let us see the fragments."

When, however, the Pomponneys came to think the matter over, a doubt arose in Mr. Pomponney's mind. They never before had come across any remains. Perhaps this was quite an exceptional feast on the part of Mr. Polyblank. There might by chance have been a bad dinner at the "Three Crowns." Thus matters stood, until one day Mr. Benoit, the pork-butcher from Onion Soup-street, dropping in, on the part of Mrs. Benoit, for some pills and a mixture, asked Mr. Pomponney whether the new English professor did not lodge at his house.

"To be sure he does," replied Mr. Pomponney, "and he is a customer of yours, too, if I don't make a mistake."

3

" You make no mistake, sir.   He is as good a customer as any I have got."

" You don't say so ?"

" At least he is not one of the worst.   He looks in every day for something or other.   A Lyons sausage, perhaps a pig's foot—a morsel of spiced beef—in fact, all sorts of things, according to his fancy."

" And he comes every day ?"

" Every day he spends his ten or twelve sous."

Decidedly the professor gorged in secret.   However, let him go on gorging.   Mr. Pomponney had something else to think about, and therefore abandoned the subject with appropriate contempt.   About a month after the thrilling events above recorded, Mr. Roustoubique one afternoon sent by a messenger a letter for Mr. Poly-blank, marked "immediate" upon the cover.   The letter arrived at the chemist's shop at half-past five, and had been sent under these circumstances : Mr. Roustoubique had gone into the country for the day.   Polyblank feeling ill had asked for two hours' leave of absence of the next in command.   Mr. Roustoubique, returning earlier than was expected, was indignant at the proceed-ing, and invented an excuse for sending to the new pro-fessor to return at once.   Mr. Pomponney, thinking that the letter was of importance, took charge of it, and carried it himself to the " Three Crowns," at which he knew the ordinary was then in progress, and where he expected to find the professor ; not being aware that Polyblank left off work of an evening not earlier than six o'clock.

" Mr. Polyblank ?" he demanded of Madame Gobinard.

" Mr. who ?"

" Mr. Polyblank, the English professor of the Imperial College."

" I don't know such a person."

Mr. Pomponney was taken aback.

" Do you mean to tell me he does not dine here regularly every day ?"

" Certainly he does not. Now I think of it, he did dine here one day—the day he arrived by the diligence. A meagre man, is he not ? With a tout-ensemble quite rococo—altogether English ?"

Thus in some barbarous foreign parts they actually liken guys and Goths, and human scarecrows generally, to the natives of that island which, as all the world knows, or ought to know, is first on the Blazoned Scroll of Fame, et cetera, with a chorus.

" That is the man," said Mr. Pomponney, recognising the truth of the description. " And so you know nothing about him? He must be dining somewhere, though."

It did not exactly follow. There was indeed no other ordinary in Saint Babylas than that at the "Three Crowns," unless you counted as one a small establishment close to Saint Abraham's Gate, which was frequented by the pipe-makers from a neighbouring manufactory, and where for eight sous the regular customers certainly got all that was good for them—if not more. It was not likely that the professor would go there in search of his meal; besides, the fourpenny dinner took place at noon precisely, and it was not until close upon half-past twelve that he could sometimes get away from the college. Where then did he go? It certainly was no business of Mr. Pomponney's where he dined, and yet both he and his wife felt rather curious upon the subject.

" Here is a letter that came for you, sir," said Mr. Pomponney, when the professor came home in the evening. "As you said that you dined at the 'Three Crowns,' I went there in search of you."

The professor blushed. "I am much obliged—I am very sorry that you should have had the trouble—I ought to have told you that I don't go there now."

"It was not the least trouble; but perhaps if I did know where to find you at some future time——"

"Yes—yes," stammered the professor; "yes to be sure. We must arrange about it—I did not think that such a thing was likely to occur."

But in spite of all this Mr. Polyblank beat a retreat without giving any particulars.

"Felicité," said Mr. Pomponney, "mark my words; if that man has not some reason we have no notion of for deceiving us, I am very much mistaken."

The mystery grew gradually darker as the shades of night gathered over the Pomponneyan domicile. A council was held in the back parlour, and it was decided that Benoit, the pork-butcher, should be lured into the house upon some pretext, and suddenly confronted with the man of secrecy The only difficulty was the pretext. During the evening the worthy couple kept a close watch upon the object of their suspicion. Without their shoes Mr. and Mrs. Pomponney relieved each other in their vigil at his keyhole; but they only inflamed their eyes without making any discovery. About ten o'clock Mr. Pomponney, feeling much fatigued and business being slack, thought he would poison the summer air outside his shopdoor by way of relaxation. With his slippers on his feet, his pipe in his mouth, his hat on the back of his head, and his hands under the tails of his coat, he strolled out into the middle of the street, and gazed upwards at the window of his lodger's room.

As thus he gazed, however, the sash was noiselessly opened and the professor's head cautiously protruded. In a very cat-like fashion then did its owner peer to the right and to the left, while Mr. Pomponney, creeping back into the shadow of a doorway opposite, watched his movements with trembling eagerness. Apparently satisfied that he was unobserved the professor retired for a moment, and then returning to the window, raised his arm and flung something violently out into the street. With an exclamation of terror Mr. Pomponney staggered back against the door; for the object ejected had actually struck him on the chest. The sound of his voice and the bumping of the back of his head against the door had evidently been heard by the professor, for he instantly closed the window. As for Mr. Pomponney, he groped about upon the pavement for the unknown object, and having found it, hurried into the house in a state of strong excitement.

" Felicité," said he, " in the name of the three hundred and sixty-five saints in the calendar, here are the skins of more sausages and the bones of more trotters."

" Where on earth did you get these from ?" asked Madame Pomponney.

" They were hurled at me, Felicité; whether by accident or intention I am not in a position to say. At any rate they reached me in the form of a projectile. There seems to me to be but one course to pursue. You, Felicité, shall take them upstairs at once, and lay them before the perpetrator of the outrage. Yes, it will be best for you to be the messenger, Felicité; and we had better lose no time.

A few moments afterwards Madame Pomponney tapped at the professor's door and entered the room with the packet in her hand.

" Beg pardon, sir, but, Mr. Pomponney says that this parcel fell out of your window—"

But here she stopped in wonderment at the face before her. There seemed to be a mixture of half a dozen expressions struggling together for the mastery upon the professor's countenance. There were rage and wounded pride. There were mortification, confusion, and unspeakable shame, and there was withal a desperate and despairing effort to appear at his ease. He made no answer to her speech, but stood as though he were transfixed, his fingers clutching nervously at the table edge. Gradually she approached him, still holding out the disgraceful little parcel of bones and scraps. When it was within reach he suddenly made a snatch at it. Then with a jarring laugh—

"I am much obliged," said he. "It must have blown down with the wind. I am very glad—that is—I'm very sorry. I am very much obliged, though it was not of any consequence, as I intended to throw it away ; and —and——"

But he broke down here and smiled painfully, and fidgeting with the parcel thrust it into his pocket. There was something like a tremble in his voice that rather frightened little Madame Pomponney, and something, too, she fancied she saw glistening in his grey eyes. And then all the mystery was at an end, and the miserable truth struck a sudden pang into her woman's heart.

"Oh, sir," she cried, as the tears welled up into her own eyes,—"oh, sir," she sobbed out, catching at one of his long, thin hands, "we never dreamt. If we had known—but we had no idea. Oh, I am so very, very sorry !"

"Thank you, my dear madam," he answered in a hoarse voice. "I know you had no idea how poor I was. How could you know ? I ought to be able to live well on what I get from the college, but—but I

have calls on me which I must attend to before everything, and—and———. But don't distress yourself, my
dear madam. I can get on very well indeed if—if you
will please not to notice me."

" It's my opinion, in spite of all that," said Mr.
Pomponney, " that what he tells you is only a fable, and
that he is a miser who hides his money up the chimney
and under the floor. I shall certainly keep my eye upon
him."

CHAPTER IV

AN ACTRESS'S HUSBAND.

> Ami, vieillard, enfant, fille ou femme adorée,
> Quel est le corps glacé qu'un marbre va couvrir ?
> Sous quel toit la douleur est-elle encore entrée ?
> Qui va porter le deuil, et quels cœurs vont souffrir ?—MANUEL.

THE Baroness de Grandvilain was a widow, was nineteen
years old, and had been a widow two years and six
months, and enjoyed an income of a hundred thousand
francs per annum, which—to save the reader unnecessary
trouble—may be roughly reckoned four thousand pounds
a year. Five years before the date of this story her
yearly gains were forty-eight pounds, which she earned
in the corps de ballet at the Châtelet Theatre, where the
baron fell in love with her, from the first gallery. Now
she had for a residence the rambling old château of
Longanna, situated half a league from Saint Abraham's
Gate, Saint Babylas ; and she had another château, more
or less dilapidated, in the neighbourhood of Prély le
Chétif, in the Department of Cher ; but in the days of the
Châtelet she lived on a fourth-floor in the Rue Charlot,

which, as any Parisian can tell you, is anything but aristocratic.

He was a miser and enormously rich—this baron who fell in love with her—and had she inherited all his property she would herself have been as rich as an Eastern princess. But this was not to be. By reason of sundry legal quips and quirks—with which it were perhaps as well not to overload this narrative, firstly, because the reader might be bored by them, and secondly, because the writer, in his ignorance of the terrain, might by chance fall into one of those quagmires into which some of his literary betters have ere now taken fearless headers and come to signal grief—the young baroness lost more than three-fourths of the property.

It is just within the limits of possibility that pretty Manon de Grandvilain was a good deal cheated. You can easily imagine when the gay young bachelor (he was seventy-two) married the poor little actress from the Châtelet that some virtuous indignation manifested itself among the gay young bachelor's relations. Had he made over his millions of francs to any one of a numerous family, all of whom, severally and collectively, he had all his life vowed that he hated, no one for a moment would have questioned his sanity. Had he given all his property to a public institution to the exclusion of his relatives, however loud the outcry which the act might have occasioned, it is doubtful whether the officers of the institution would not have triumphantly vindicated his sagacity. But when he married that young person from the Châtelet, straightway the faculty was consulted, every word and deed of the venerable simpleton closely scrutinized and disparagingly commented upon, and the whole seventy-two years of his life were passed under review in search of early indications of lunacy.

Insane they would have proved him to be, there is little doubt, had not that actor woman, with what her enemies very happily called the artfulness of her class, adopted a course of proceeding that in the end saved her some of the property and kept the baron out of an asylum. This was what she, or rather her mother for her, did. She induced her husband to subscribe towards the repairs then in course of progress in Saint Babylas Cathedral. Hitherto the clerical party had not been backward in their condemnation of the baron's conduct. Father Mathias had unhesitatingly pronounced the bridegroom to be a lunatic. Father Tristepatte was of the same opinion, while Fathers Gimbecque and Grégoire in a general way agreed with them, and all four, in speaking of the bride, referred to her as " that person." But just about the time—perhaps a little later—that the baron, who had been a sabbath-breaker and scoffer at things holy from his earliest youth, repented him suddenly of his evil ways and paid over to Mother Church sixteen hundred thousand francs, it oddly enough happened that doubts arose in the ecclesiastical mind respecting the rights of the case. And so on until in due course what little doubt remained gave place to a positive conviction that no saner person existed in all Picardy than the Baron de Grandvilain, and no truer and better woman breathing than the baroness his wife : at which conclusion who shall cavil ?

You, reader, of terrible experiences, have no doubt formed your own opinion upon the latter head, so that it would be waste of time to try and persuade you that the conclusion arrived at by the fathers was the correct one. With you, ladies, it is just possible that those insular prejudices, which all right-minded persons honour you for, may to some extent, and very properly, obscure your judgment respecting the sprightly Floreska. It has long ago been settled on this side of the water that Paris is a sinful city (though some recent disclosures about what is going on among ourselves should teach us to be charitable), and you remember what Gozlan says on an English lady's opinion of a Parisienne. " Impossible de la reproduire. Les lois de la décence et celles de Septembre s'y opposent "—the joke in which you doubtless perceive and appreciate. The Floreska besides was an actress, and therefore all but actresses will at once acknowledge was no suitable match for a baron. When she was the Floreska—she by the way was born simply Manon Dubois—she became at one time the talk of all Paris—that Paris which is always talking and so quickly exhausts its topics. It was in a highly successful *cocasserie* that she first attracted public attention, and her carte by Pierre Petit had an enormous sale.

It was in this amusing piece that the baron first fell a victim to her bewitchments. He was the last of a long line ; but his ancestors had been poor and proud. There was, however, very little pride about our baron. He had gone into commerce heart and soul, and made more money than all his ancestors together had ever possessed. One other merit had he over his predecessors—what he made he kept a tight hold of. Some of his speculations were gigantic, but he was not above a little quiet money-grubbing on a small scale. One day he would be buying up the shares of a copper mine, and the next driving a hard bargain for a waggon-load of secondhand shoes to be adroitly renovated and foisted upon an unsuspecting public as bran-new misfits by the best makers. While too he was making money he wasted none. When he could not dine at another person's expense he chose the cheapest cookshops. He did not often trouble the omnibuses, and was never known to hire a remise in his life.

He wore clothes which no weather could injure, and by way of change in summer time would leave off his waistcoat. When it rained he turned up the collar of his coat and the bottoms of his trousers, the latter of which he often enough omitted to turn down again for a day or two. But in due course there came a night when he went with a free admission to the first gallery (which by the way is not the same as the lower gallery of one of our theatres—over there called amphitheatre or *paradis*), and from it he fell in love with the Floreska. Was this to be wondered at, when all Paris was raving about her talent and beauty? Mind you, she was not beautiful; but oh how becomingly she was dressed! As for her talents, the part in which she displayed them was not a very long one. But in spite of her rather large mouth, and her nonsensical little bit of a nose, there was what they call a *chic* about her which was too much for the over-susceptible.

Yet, the fact of the baron's falling in love with her was rather extraordinary. He was not an admirer of the drama; perhaps because he had had no opportunity of becoming one, not being in the way of going to see it for nothing. This order for the first gallery had been given to him for the purpose of appeasing his wrath, by a defaulting debtor; and he had used it because he did not like to throw anything away, and did not know how to turn it into money. Having an admission for two he had prevailed upon a friend to defray the expense of a dinner in return for a seat, and they had gone together, taking their places in the queue at the door long before the time of opening, and staying until the lights were turned out before they thought they had quite had their order's worth. Very much astonished next day was the defaulter upon receiving a visit from the baron. He had half promised to give a week's grace; but here he was again in less than twenty-four hours. At sight of him the debtor began to stammer out some excuses.

"I haven't come about that," said the baron. Then correcting himself as a bright idea occurred to him— "You can keep it a little longer, and I shan't charge you anything. Let's see—what shall we say? (here the defaulter quaked inwardly). Suppose you get me a few more of those ticket-papers for the theatre?"

The debtor was astonished; but as he had a large circle of friends in the theatrical line he answered readily enough, "I'll get you some with pleasure. What house would you like them for?"

"The same, of course," replied the baron.

"The same, eh! You want to see the piece again, then? Well, I can get that without any trouble."

"That's all right then," said the baron, snapping him up greedily. "How many can you get me?"

"How many do you want?"

"As many as you can manage."

The debtor reflected. "Will an admission for four do?" he asked.

"Four all at once?"

"To be sure."

"I'd rather," replied the baron, "have four admissions for one, on separate nights."

About this time the baron's commercial associates began to think that there was something wrong with the millionaire. Some capital specs he neglected to take advantage of. Several of his debtors were astonished at not finding themselves sold up after they had neglected to meet their engagements. He made some alterations in his toilet too; purchasing clothes which, though second-hand, were much smarter than anything he had

before been known to wear. One never-to-be-forgotten
day he was actually seen strolling down the Boulevart de
Sebastopol with a pair of real kid gloves on.

Who could pretend to describe the extraordinary revolution which the tender passion effected in the heart of
this sordid old curmudgeon? An old man's love has
formed the theme for the exercise of much satirical talent,
and perhaps it will be best to settle the matter at once
by setting down the baron for a silly old fool, and saying
no more about it. Youth, we know, is the season for
love, and the loves of youth are never ridiculous. He
went—this foolish De Grandvilain—every night of his
life to see the bewitching Floreska; getting gradually
nearer and nearer to the object of his admiration, and
arriving at length at that pitch of infatuation that he
absolutely paid five francs hard money for a fauteuil
d'orchestre for a week running.

He began to be remarked before long, and the persons
connected with the theatre wondered what on earth could
bring him nightly to see the same piece. All sorts of
wild conjectures were hazarded upon the subject, and he
even formed the topic of a facetious article in *Figaro,*
where he was called, in consequence of an unusual display
of starched linen round his face, the Man with the Collars. At length he accidentally heard that it was sometimes the custom to throw an actress a bouquet. That
night he came with an enormous " posey," and to the
wonder of all beholders flung it upon the stage at the
feet of the beauteous Floreska. It was not after she
had done anything to call forth applause, but upon her
first entrance on the scene, and this unusual proceeding
caused much amusement and some surprise both upon
the stage and among the audience, and considerable confusion also to the object of the ill-timed honour. But it

solved the mystery; and next day *Figaro* informed its
subscribers that—

Paris had spent a sleepless night.

Trade was at a stand-still.

The discussion of politics was suspended.

One topic alone occupied the public mind.

The great fact then riveting the attention of high and
low was that the Man with the Collars was in love with
the Floreska.

The worthy baron knew nothing of this harmless
pleasantry Neither did he dream that his floral offering
had not been over acceptable ; but next night, armed with
another prodigious nosegay, presented himself at the
theatre door, and once more hurled his posey. You can
easily suppose that the astonishment of the audience was
equal to that of the previous evening ; but who shall picture the sensation which the repetition of the daring act
caused upon the stage, or what was said when it happened for the third time ? But on the fourth evening a
startling event occurred which put an end to the little
comedy.

When the baron got to the theatre at the customary
hour he was surprised to find it unusually crowded.
Perhaps the fact of its being Sunday might account for
it, but decidedly it was more crowded than usual. He
was further astonished when the curtain drew up, to miss
the familiar costumes and landscape. He sat and stared
and listened in blank amazement. Then he fidgeted
and wiped his head with his pocket-handkerchief. He
never bought a programme, so he presently appealed to a
neighbour. " What were they doing?" he asked; for
his own part he could make neither head nor tail of it.
The person addressed gave him the name of the piece,
and handed him the paper. The baron ran his eyes

down it with an expression of dismay. In a voice tremulous with agitation he said, as he handed back the programme: "The Floreska! When does she come on?"

"She does not play at all," replied the other; "she used to play here in a piece that was acted for the last time last night."

The Baron rose without another word and left the stalls. In the passage he addressed himself to the box-opener, and learned that, if successful, the new farce would probably be played for some months, and that, to the best of her belief, the engagement of the Floreska was at an end. Upon this he went away in despair, with so blank an expression, that a stranger seeing him would have thought he had met with some calamity. And so he had. The loss of a few thousand francs would have been a trifle to this. With the termination of the Floreska's performance his romance had come abruptly to a close. The only real happiness he had ever known was lost to him. The heavens had closed again, and hidden for ever that radiant vision of the goddess in the satin boots. Entering the café next door to the theatre he called for the Entr'acte and searched vainly for the deity's name. Then he wandered about reading the bills posted upon the pillars in the Palais Royal; and at last worn out with fatigue, crawled back to his shabby lodging and went to bed.

He did not sleep a wink that night; but an idea occurred to him. He could see the Floreska no longer upon the stage. Could he make her acquaintance off it? How was it to be done? Would any amount of money purchase the privilege? You see he was an innocent old gentleman in these matters, though very knowing in such cases as that of the renovated boots. For seventy odd years he had been grovelling and grubbing, and

really had not had time to amuse himself. He had kept aloof
from his fellow men, except in the way of business, and now
there was no one in the world with whom he was acquainted
who could give him the necessary information, except—
except that person—the St. Peter who had given him
his first glimpse of heaven.   The debt had not yet been
paid.   Pierre Raynal, the debtor, had been in the country
for some time, and thus had avoided his creditor, whose
importunities for tickets had become almost as troublesome as his demands for the repayment of the loan.

Strange to say, the baron ran against his young friend
the very next morning in the street.   " I don't want the
money," were the old man's first words, shrewdly gues-
sing from the other's long face what was passing in his
mind.   " I don't want it yet awhile—not for a long
time—not at all, perhaps ; but I want you to do me a
service."

" Some more tickets ?" said Raynal involuntarily.

" No."

" Tired of the drama, eh ?"

" Yes."

" I always wondered what on earth you could want
the tickets for.   Share in the profits, I suppose, eh ?
And went there on the cheap to count up the heads."

" Ye-es—ye-es.   Exactly.   That was it.   But I want
you to do me a favour."

" Name it."

" Well, I want you then—I have a particular reason
for wishing—in point of fact, I want to be introduced
to an actress called the Floreska."

At the mention of this name Pierre Raynal started
slightly, and stared very hard.   Then smiling to himself,
as he traced figures on the pavement with the end of his
walking-stick, " I think I can do what you wish," he

said; "but I must ask her permission first. She lives in rather a quiet way, for her salary is not large and she has a sick mother to take care of." It is surprising what a many sick mothers there are attached to the theatrical profession.

Walking away, Raynal several times stopped to think the matter over. "Why does he wish to know her?" the young man thought. "Can it possibly be—but no. That's too ridiculous."

The baron on his side stopped to rub his hands and chuckle, "A sick mother and poor!"

Three months after these events Manon Dubois, otherwise the Floreska, became the wife of the Baron de Grandvilain, and the rest of the world cried with one voice, "the man must be mad!" Long before this he had been grievously neglecting his commercial pursuits, and now he gave them up altogether. "I've money enough," he said, when reasoned with upon the subject. "I've worked hard all my life, and now I'm going to enjoy myself."

He was seventy-two, as has been already stated, and surely it was not too soon for enjoyment, if he could afford it. But it was not to be. Six months after his marriage, death laid his hand on the happy bridegroom. He died with his affairs in some confusion. The legal vultures alighted, screeching, upon the carcase of his estate, scuffled and fought over it furiously, and flew away at last gorged with the prey. The baroness found herself at the age of nineteen an orphan and a widow, possessed of a yearly income of one hundred thousand francs.

So far so good.

4

CHAPTER V.

RICH, YOUNG, PRETTY, AND VERY MISERABLE.

I see the angry blood flush in your cheek :
Ah, child ! I thought you strong, and you are weak.
                                        DONALDSON.

THE château of Longanna was one of those queer, old-fashioned, ugly, dear delightful places such as you may find a few of even now-a-days round about our town of London, in spite of the fell machinations of railway projectors and building societies. The exterior of the château, as seen from the high road, was not commanding. It had something of the appearance of a brewery in a poor way of business. Its green Venetian blinds were almost always closed. Its porte-cochère was almost always open, and through it could be obtained a view of one of the dreariest courtyards imaginable.

In summer time, several hours a day, might be seen seated at the door of the porter's lodge an old woman, gently dozing her life away in the broadest patch of sunshine obtainable ; and in winter she might still be seen, seated and slumbering ; but this time by the side of the lodge fire. Always at her feet, whether indoors or out, summer or winter, reposed a plethoric tom-cat, who thus got through the autumn of his existence ; going to bed of a night with his old mistress, where they slumbered together with their heads on the same pillow.

The interior arrangement of the château was awkward, and in some parts unsightly. Beams crossed the ceiling of the drawing-room. The floors of some of the bed-rooms were composed of a kind of cement, brown and speckled, like oatmeal porridge congealed ; while others were formed of red tiles, and others again of oaken planks, all highly polished and slippery as glass, though so irregularly placed that when the feet of the heedless stranger were not slipping from under him his toes were for ever tripping over the projecting ends of the boards. At the entrances to the various rooms were unexpected steps, about the position of which much uncertainty prevailed; so that when acting upon past experience a visitor made preparations for stepping up he found, too late, that he ought to step down, and *vice versá.*

All the apartments were panelled, and abounded in cupboards, the doors of which, looking exactly like the doors of the room, a timid visitor was occasionally overwhelmed with confusion by opening one of them in a mistake, and coming unexpectedly upon such of the family skeletons as might have been hastily stowed away there upon his arrival. There was a dark staircase leading from the hall to the landing, out of which the bedrooms opened, and from that landing another dark staircase led to the kitchen; so that the bewildered stranger, mistaking his way, was apt to find himself in the company of the cook when he believed himself to be approaching the lady in the drawing-room, and had to be escorted across a back yard, and through a scullery to reach the desired spot.

The furniture of the quaint old house was mostly in keeping with the singularities of the building. There were bedroom chairs you had to use both hands to lift, and arm-chairs in the sitting-rooms which a good many people could not have lifted at all. In one gloomy chamber there was an awful bed, a gaunt erection of tall posts and heavy faded curtains, surmounted by nodding feathers black with dust; and in this the old baron had died. "As well he might!" Montandon, wine merchant of Blanquefort, remarked when first he saw the lugubrious

4—2

piece of furniture. This Montandon of Blanquefort was a remote relation of the baron, and, for reasons best known to himself, supposed he was heir to the baron's estates—an erroneous idea dispelled in the course of litigation. Strolling through the house, with his hat on the back of his head, and his hands thrust deep into his trousers pockets, Montandon took his measurements with a mental foot-rule, and decided, to a nicety, where he would make a new door, where he would pull down one wall, and where he would build up another; but as the property never came to him these improvements were not practically effected.

Sarazin, of Pont l'Evech, was not so particular about the house, but made up his mind for sweeping reforms in the garden and grounds. According to him, there were to be paths where there were now beds, and beds where there were now paths. There were to be several fountains; the shubbery was to be cleared away at once; a new carriage-drive must be laid down, and the back of the house turned into the front.

"We shall soon set all this straight, sir," said Sarazin, of Pont l'Evech, striking with his cane as he spoke the pedestal of the chaste though weather-beaten Diana, who for the last thirty years had been flying from Actæon through a little forest of brambles and briars. "You shall see, sir, what you shall see." Unluckily, however, Sarazin did not come into the property; but retired crestfallen and purse-lightened to his native town, and subsided as quietly as might be. A dear old garden was this which would have been sacrificed to Sarazin's taste—a hundred years old at the very least; with a high red brick-wall, convent like, surrounding it; with old fruit trees with moss-grown trunks and gnarled branches, which in the fruit season drooped beneath their load of peaches, apricots, figs, apples, pears, and plums ;—a garden abounding in sheltered nooks, where there was deep shade upon the dark green grass at hottest noon ; a garden in which to dream away a lifetime, secure from intrusion, hidden from sight : a sleepy, lotus-eating spot—a little paradise on earth some would have called it, and among their number its reigning deity, Manon Baroness de Grandvilain. She dearly loved this old house, with its straggling garden and grounds; and the life she passed there, though rather too monotonous maybe for some ladies, was not, for a time at any rate, without a certain charm for the ex-actress of the Châtelet.

Quite early in the morning she would awake of her own accord—at that preposterous period, in the days of infancy, when the bloom was on the rye, when the early bird was coming down to his worm ; so early in the morning—so very early, that among town-bred folks none but sweeps, market gardeners, policemen, coffee-stall keepers, wicked people, and—strange association !—the élite of society going home to their beds, can be expected to know anything about it except by accident and under abnormal circumstances—well, at something like five o'clock in the summer, and as soon as it was light in winter, our pretty Manon would arise, and in any kind of weather plunge boldly into her cold bath. Rachel protect us !—what rubbings and scrubbings were then self-inflicted with coarse sackcloth towels, to be followed presently by a more careful desiccative process with a variety of soft linen cloths, which, with their elaborate fringes and fantastic red and blue borders, looked more like pocket-handkerchiefs or d'oyleys than the things we make use of over here.

That business over, what a work of time awaited the pretty baroness and her tiring woman in the selection and arrangement of snowy white raiment, the number and nature of which it is but for the learned in such matters to specify! And then—following a long and elaborate process of braiding and plaiting, quite thrown away upon a rebellious head of hair which an hour afterwards was all rough again—came the great question of whether it was to be the brown holland, with black-velvet band, cuffs and trimmings, or the blue or brown-spotted Swiss cambric or the white piqué, et cetera and so on; which being decided satisfactorily, the fair dame came downstairs singing as blithely as the lark.   As for singing, though she had been singing ever since she got out of bed, with only such brief pauses as her occupations necessitated.   That good soul Madame Dubosq, the baroness's lady companion, was not an early riser, and probably had not yet made her appearance in the breakfast-room.   But there was plenty of time for that; and other breakfasts had first to be looked after.

Three cats, by name Mimi, Bibi, and Dodo, were always a-hungered at early dawn, and at sight of their mistress cried aloud for their rations and their rights. These having being disposed of, or sometimes before their repast had been prepared, plaintive whinings from the kennel announced the fact of Ponto the house-dog's emptiness, and his anxiety respecting the coming of his turn.   Hollow pretenders were these Mimi, Bibi, Dodo, and Ponto, whose selfishness any one in the world but their young mistress might surely have seen through from the first; but they were successful in their imposture. Round her came the three cats, mewing, with their tails erect, rubbing their deceitful old heads against her frock, and making the most palpable cupboard love; and when they had got all the wanted retired to spread themselves before the fire, or went out to sleep in the sun, and dream of future feasts or past repletion.

A loud boisterous humbug was that Ponto the house-dog, roaring and rattling his chain at the first faint sound of his mistress's footfall in the court-yard, bounding and bellowing as she approached, and thrusting his great wet nose into one of her little hands—keeping his eye the while upon the plate of food she carried in the other ; but which he would have her believe was a matter of great indifference to him as long as he could enjoy the superior delight of the baroness's society. When Ponto's little farce was acted out, and he himself replete and sinking into a torpid state of felicitous indigestion, an aged raven would come hopping out of the stable with a peculiarly knavish expression of eye and a general double dealing, backsliding demeanour, indicative of any amount of moral turpitude. This hoary-headed hypocrite having run through his two or three hacknied phrases and received his reward, would give place to the poultry clucking at their mistress's heels, the rabbits thrusting their twitching noses through the bars of their hutch, the sleek chestnut horses whinnying at her approach ; and so on down to the ancient tortoise, supposed to be a century old, hobbling towards its benefactress with clumsy alacrity as she entered the garden. And now this part of the live stock disposed of, the old portress, invariably accompanied by her cat, would present herself to wish her mistress good day, bob her curtsies, and pay her may be some artless compliment.

But by this time Madame Dubosq was certain to have come down and to be waiting breakfast with perhaps a little pardonable peevishness, caused by five minutes delay. Not quite at her best did madame look thus early in the morning. At the best, however, Madame Dubosq was not very attractive. A general scragginess of figure was not redeemed by the harshness of her facial outline ; added to which a peculiarity of complexion, bearing some resemblance to the skin of a freshly-plucked fowl, rendered it necessary—when she wished to create a favourable impression upon those unthinking ones in whose estimation the beauties of the mind hold an inferior place to mere evanescent outward charms—that she should cull roses from that branch of science which has ere now lent its aid to so many other fair ones within and without the pale of society. As these roses did not show to advantage the first thing in the morning, they were not assumed until later in the day, and it was probably an injudicious peep at herself in her nightcap immediately upon getting out of bed that had produced a depressing effect upon the good lady's spirits, and sent her downstairs very grim and grumpy.

It was her wont to greet the baroness in tones of gentle melancholy, and, at intervals during breakfast—to which she uniformly did justice—to heave sundry doleful sighs ; although when questioned respecting their cause she was either unable or unwilling to give any satisfactory explanation.

" I'm so glad to see you so light-hearted," the good lady would say sometimes, with the aspect of an undertaker condoling with the departed's nearest relative. " I wish I had your spirits," was another favourite remark of hers. Or, " Bless you, my dear, if I could only laugh as you do !"

" Why not try ?" Manon retorted one day. " It does not hurt half as much as you would think."

" Ah, I shall never be merry again," said the Dubosq, with a mournful shake of her head ; " the memories of past sorrows press too heavily for that. Yet I was light-hearted once. Oh yes, I was a giddy thing !"

It was rather difficult to realize the notion of the Dubosq

at that volatile period of her existence. She must in her giddiest maidenhood have been rather long of limb and large of joint; and as the ideal picture of her coy gambolling in search of buttercups and daisies presented itself to the baroness's mind it required almost a super-human effort to keep serious. Once when the lady housekeeper was expatiating lengthily upon the sorrows of her wedded life at the period when the dead and gone Dubosq was at his worst, and going on, as the cant saying is, anyhow, Manon mildly intimated that she, too, had had her troubles, but that the recollection of them made her more thankful for her present happiness; which remark madame taking as a reproof, burst into tears and sobbed long and persistently, refusing consolation upon the ground that she was of no use to any one in the world, and wishing herself out of it as soon as might be, and economically but comfortably interred.

This course of conduct may seem somewhat unreasonable, and it may create suprise in the reader's mind that the baroness should willingly have suffered under such companionship. But are there not many others amongst us who suffer silently? If all the couples who have at some time or other wished themselves divorced were at this present moment separated, what a revolution there would be in our London households! If all our wicked wishes had been fulfilled, what would ere this have befallen our near relations and distant kinsmen? Why the entire globe would some fine morning be swept clean of human beings at one fell swoop if some evilly-disposed persons had their way, which luckily for him who writes and him who reads, they haven't.

Our pretty Manon, then, bore patiently with the Dubosq because her life through she had ever been the victim of a peevish old woman. The sick mother pre-

viously alluded to had been a wearing old soul in spite
of many excellent qualities more or less imperfectly de-
veloped. Propped up by pillows, she lay a-bed and
prosed long hours together upon the subject of her divers
aches and pains. When others were wakeful she slumbered, and when others would have slumbered also she
was wide awake and loudly complaining. A regular old
woman of the sea had been this mother of Manon, who
not only kept her child down in the depths of poverty,
but did her little best to make the burthen of her support
as painful as possible. In this, however, she was un-
successful, for the burthen was never felt, and her death
sincerely lamented by the young girl left behind. There was
no doubt that had it not been for the old lady's persua-
sions somebody else instead of the Baron de Grandvilain
would have been Manon's husband. But that was all
past and gone now. There is more than one young lady
in the world who has fancied herself in love and thought
better of it.

When these two ladies had eaten their breakfast, the
meal concluded, there were various household duties to
perform, directions to be given about the dinner, a tour
of inspection to be made round the garden, the newspaper to be read (not a long job in the case of the Saint
Babylas local journal), then lunch to be ordered, and the
baroness and the Dubosq to make their toilets for a promenade en voiture. A very bright and pretty little
lady did the Baroness de Grandvilain appear when she
was fully attired, with her wondering baby's eyes, dimpled
chin, and bright red lips, so often arched in a joyous
laugh.

And her toilet—but how can that be described, when
every day it varied? Well, one day out of the three
hundred and sixty-five she was thus attired—and will

not the description seem to be absurdly old-fashioned, though it was *the* fashion of a short time ago? Her rebellious curls that morning had been tied back and bound down and forced pell-mell into a delightful little bonnet of violet aerophane, with a bavolet of white blonde covered with black lace, a small plume composed of two black feathers, fixed in front by a coquille of black lace, with quillings of black blonde on the forehead, and white at the sides, and strings of broad velvet ribbon with black velvet edgings. Her dress, a rich violet moiré silk, falling about her in ample folds; the corsage high, slightly pointed at the waist, and fastened up the front by small black velvet buttons. A little turn-down collar of black velvet, with a black velvet neck-tie, fastened by a plain gold brooch. Her sleeves loose at the ends, with broad mousquetaire cuffs, trimmed with three rows of black velvet, beneath which a plain white linen cuff, fastened by gold studs to match the brooch. A handsome shawl of white China crape with a deep fringe. The closest-fitting violet kid gloves, to match the dress, and the tightest-fitting stockings of dead-white silk. Little bronze leather boots, laced up the front, peeping from beneath layers of white petticoats, knee-deep in embroidery, and seemingly numerous as the leaves of a full-blown white rose. "On a remarqué que de tous les animaux, les chats, les mouches, et les femmes sont ceux qui perdaient le plus de temps à leur toilette," says Nodier.

As for the Dubosq, her style was more staid. She had left off colours for ever when she put on weeds for the dear departed. She had not the heart, she said, for reds and yellows. She wore, in spite of all remonstrance and many offers of other dresses, a tumbled black silk which smelt of lavender, a scanty shawl, and a bonnet of evidently home-manufacture. In this raiment she seemed to take a mournful pleasure, by reason of its general dinginess contrasting strongly in the sunlight with the baroness's gay attire, and reminding her that she was only a poor dependent, and ought to be shabby and humble. The object of the drive which these ladies took together was to visit certain pensioners of the baroness, who, in their way, were perhaps upon much the same tack as Mimi, Bibi, Dodo, Ponto, and Co.

First of all, at a cottage up a lane, leading out of the straggling main street of Longanna, was to be seen, any day you might have taken it into your head to go and look for her, a suffering female, who was in a very small way a purveyor of cakes, who also had purveyed for herself a ne'er-do-well husband and a large small family which did not thrive. Piteous were the tales which this afflicted soul always had ready for the baroness's ear, and loud were the promises of future amendment upon the part of the worthless male parent, and of improvement on that of the unlikely olive branches. Unbounded was the gratitude of the whole household when the of course wholly unexpected pecuniary assistance was forthcoming, and boisterous and prolonged the orgies thereupon consequent. In the same lane lived a lone widow, even more grievously afflicted with an endless history of lumbagoes, sciaticas, catarrhs, influenzas, and tic douloureux, whose piteous case necessitated a constant supply of something cheering. Round the corner, down another lane, was a blind man, providentially in possession of the full powers of locomotion, and capable of telling his pitiful tale with a lavish profusion of language, which perhaps to some extent consoled him for his misfortune.

" Did you make yourself some tea as I told you, mère Corbeau ?" the baroness asked a pensioner.

" Did I cook the black leaves you left me ?" asked
mère Corbeau, rather shily. " Oh yes, we cooked them,
Madame the Baroness, but we couldn't drink any of the
liquor. Indeed I and my old man were well-nigh
poisoned with it, though we supped only a little spoonful."

" But it was beautiful tea, such as the Miladies drink
in England."

" Droll tastes those ladies must have," snorted mère
Corbeau.

" Not at all. I drink it myself, and very nice it is.
But I suppose you made some silly mistake."

" Oh no, ma'am, there was no mistake. I boiled it
ever so long."

" You should not have boiled it at all. However,
where's the remainder ?"

" There's none left."

" But you don't mean to say that, after all my directions, you used half a pound all at once ? Did you eat
it like sorrel soup ?"

" Well, ma'am, we tried it every way, but we couldn't
get it down."

Upon receiving which reply the baroness retired in
much vexation, having, as she said, done for good and
all with the Corbeaus and their perverse folly ; which
meant that in a week's time the worthy woman would
again be the object of the baroness's charity Not unfrequently would the pretty lady lose patience with the
wooden-headed rustics, and stamp those little bronze
leather boots with anger and mortification upon the floors
of the cottages in which her gifts were wasted.

" There are some old women," the baroness said one
day, " who are really and truly unbearable."

At such outbursts the Dubosq only smiled in the
gentle, long-suffering way which was natural to her.

She seemed to think it strange that Manon should show such airs. They were not ladylike.

Some days the baroness was more angry than others, and she complained of everybody. "How is it, père Gros, you have not had your window mended, when I gave you the money to do it? As I live, there are Margot's children still without shoes and stockings! Why does not your son, mère Dory, wear that velveteen waistcoat I gave him? What in the name of wonder, maître Grognard, have you got on your neck? Oh, it's the cravat I gave you, is it; and it doesn't fit—and so you are making a martyr of yourself, are you? It's extraordinary, but nothing ever does seem to fit that man; besides, now I come to look at him, he's got the stock on upside down. And listen to me, mère Baldayroux, if you persist in drinking that camphor lotion, instead of rubbing it in outwardly, you never will get rid of your lumbago, and never· ought. And as for you— but I can't be troubled with any more of you this morning. Please drive home, coachman; I quite lose all patience."

You, like Madame Dubosq, would rather have had your heroine less hasty. Is it not so? She ought to have borne with the vagaries of these poor creatures, and not have petted them one moment and scolded them the next. Did they love her the less for those angry heel stampings and clenchings of a plaything fist in a violet kid glove? Perhaps, to tell the truth, when she had gone away in a pet they would scowl after her and comment, among themselves, upon her shortcomings; saying with many defiant chuckles that they could get on well enough, they would be bound, without any of her high and mighty assistance and her condescending airs and graces; which the most satirical of the cloddesses would sometimes mimic in a boorish fashion, stamping an uncouth sabot and doubling up a fist like a leg of mutton, suggestive of a baboon posing in burlesque of the Venus de Medici. But when our little baroness overcame her anger or forgot its cause, and returned to her pensioners laden with cake and wine and small silver money, these worthy people would crawl out and fawn upon her, kissing her hand as Mimi, Bibi, Dodo, and Ponto were in the habit of doing when, as sometimes happened, this pretty impulsive little lady thumped them all round.

After all, perhaps it is a mistake to have imperfect characters in one's books; because, you know, the good ones are as easily manufactured as the bad. It's only a question of so much ink, and so many up and down strokes : and why should not all one's *dramatis personæ* be brave, wise, beautiful, and noble-hearted, as we all are in real life, present company not excepted ?

Returned home from their drive the ladies soon afterwards would take their places at the dinner-table, and the meal ended, one would read while the other worked at faldidals in embroidery ; or they played cards together, say at Boston, écarté, piquet, double dummy, except sometimes when visited by Fathers Mathias and Triste-patte.

The life which these two women led may strike you about this time as being rather dull and monotonous. The lives of most women are dull enough, and a change of condition is not very often easily effected, particularly that sort of change upon which one of these sometimes meditated rather seriously. Staying at Madame Gobinard's hotel of the " Three Crowns" was, as we have seen, a certain handsome and mysterious stranger, whose name was Raynal. Now it is not divulging any secret—for all the chattering womankind in Saint Babylas said as much—to state that had this Mr. Raynal pressed Manon de Grandvilain to be his wife she would very probably have consented. Public opinion said also that Mr. Raynal was in love with her. But he did not ask. Why, the chattering womankind aforesaid could not explain. Tired of asking herself the question, our pretty baroness—after sore provocation from Mimi and Co., and the grievous ones in the village—would lock her bedroom door upon the Dubosq and cry herself to sleep.

At such times that good gentlewoman, thus debarred from offering sympathetic aid, would, after knocking vainly for admittance, whimper at the door in a fashion that might have made some angry people angrier. One night Manon said, after a long interval of silence, during which she had sat gazing into the smouldering embers on the hearth, " I think I shall shut this place up and go away somewhere for a year or two."

" Where will you go ?" asked Madame Dubosq, with some astonishment and uneasiness.

" I don't care where it is," replied the other, " as long as it is hundreds of miles away. But I'm tired of this dreadful village and that wearisome old town, and I should like never to see anybody in the place any more."

After which remark she went to bed and cried herself to sleep. But next morning she was up with the lark, and as blithe and gay as ever.

" Did I say I'd leave you, my poor darlings ?" she said, kneeling down to embrace that shaggy impostor Ponto : " and you, too, poor dear," she added, as that ancient villain, the tortoise, waddled towards her wagging his wicked old head.

65

CHAPTER VI.

"YOU CAN GO."

Wide's the world, and men will give
Ample room to let him live,
If his sharpened wits can find
Fortune blowing in the wind :
In the curtain of the sky
Solid roof to keep him dry ;
And for clothing warm and gay
Fleecy clouds and sunny ray ;
For his bed the flint stones bare,
And for food the plenteous air.—UNDERWOOD.

THE world wagged thus within the walls of the Imperial College of Saint Babylas. At half-past five o'clock in summer (six o'clock in winter) a bell rang, and five minutes afterwards, the collegian who was not out of bed found in all probability his bed during the next five minutes several degrees too warm to hold him. At forty minutes past five the usher, having scrambled into his own clothes, called upon his young friends to fall into rank, and towel in hand they marched to a long tank, at the end of the room, provided with a number of small taps, one for each collegian, where, with soap, if they had any, or without, if they had none—the use of soap being optional—such ablutions were performed as were practicable during the space of two minutes by the clock. Then falling into rank again, wet or dry, they marched back up the room. At ten minutes to six they were marched downstairs, and prayers were read to the French Catholics in Latin and to the English Protestants in French. One of the eldest boys read aloud, the others kneeling on the floor in a circle, with their caps or pocket-handkerchiefs between their knees and the red tiles, their faces turned towards the reader and their arms folded.

5

Prayers over, followed two hours of study, and at eight o'clock the young gentlemen fell in again and marched off to the refectory for breakfast. In winter breakfast meant a basin of warm milk and water and a hunch of bread, for which it was optional to buy butter, had those inclined to do so the halfpenny requisite for that purpose. In summer breakfast took place in the playground, and consisted of the lump of bread and no milk; but water was procurable at a small cistern in the yard, to obtain a drink from which the boys formed a queue, and each in turn putting his mouth under the tap took as many gulps as the pushing of those behind would allow of. Sometimes, however, it would happen that there was no water, and at other times one of the young gentlemen having satisfied his own wants would fling a handful of earth into the cistern, with the view of preventing those who came after him, if they were at all fastidious, from drinking.

After an hour's recreation, the study-master's voice was heard calling out—"In rank! in rank!" Then, again—"Make ready! March!" And then—"Slower! Faster! Not so fast! Keep step! Halt! Find your books! To your places! Sit down! Silence!" An order, in fact, preceded every movement throughout the day. From nine to ten the collegians were in class. Then from ten to eleven, and eleven to twelve, with occasional falling in and marching between while, and then followed dinner. Dinner consisted of soup, rather thin, a course of vegetables—potatoes and butter, perhaps, or haricot beans—and, except on fast days—that is to say, every Friday and Saturday—a course of meat three inches by four and one thick. After dinner recreation until one; then class until four, and tea in the play-ground. This meal, called tea for want of a better name, consisted of a lump of dry bread, with an opportunity of buying butter or pennyworths of very dry figs, and apples which tasted extremely like potatoes. After an hour's recreation, study followed until half-past seven. Then prayers. Then supper—the dinner without soup—and then bed. Five minutes allowed from the time of entering the dormitory to the time that every boy was to be between his sheets, and woe betide the slow coaches! These were the arrangements observed in the college.

The terms, including all expenses for board, washing, repair of clothes, loan of books, paper, pens, pencils, &c., and medical attendance and medicine, were twenty-six pounds per annum. No additional charge was made for boarders left at the college during the holidays, which consist of ten days at Easter, and two months in the autumn, besides a day once a month. A collegian might bring with him and wear in the college any clothes he had in use, but it was necessary that they should be provided with one full college uniform, without which he was not allowed to go out walking with the others on Sunday afternoon. The price of the uniform was three pounds ten shillings. Or, if the parents thought fit, by paying twenty pounds down and thirty shillings a year extra, the collegian was provided with all clothes, linen, sheets, and towels (which otherwise must be bought by the collegian and left behind on his departure) as long as he might remain in the college.

There were nearly four hundred pupils, about ninety of whom were day scholars. The boarders were arranged in classes according to age and acquirements; and of these classes there were eight, each containing about forty pupils. Two classes slept in one dormitory, which contained nearly a hundred beds. The youngest pupil was ten years old, and the eldest nineteen. All which par-

5—2

ticulars, though found in a work of fiction, may be relied
upon as correct, and have been here written for the benefit of English parents with sons to educate.   The writer
would premise that in the descriptions of school-
life which follow there is very little exaggeration, though
the reader is, of course, at liberty to believe as much or
as little as he may think fit.

"It seems to me, Mr. Polyblank," said the Proviseur,
one Saturday morning, after reading through the professor's report of the conduct of his young friends during
the week—a document in which the disorderly behaviour
of Messieurs Bardajos, Bourdichon, and Coquillard,
though but faintly reflected, yet failed not to suggest the
idea of anarchy and disorder—"it seems to me that your
class is growing more and more insubordinate."

"They are rather unruly," stammered the professor;
—"some of them."

"All of them, I should say," retorted Mr. Roustoubique.   "Anyhow, twenty out of twenty-five.   Let me
see, now, why you have punished them. 'Bardajos, five
hours' dictation for cutting his desk.' Do you mean to say
that he cut his initials?"

"Well, sir," said the professor, with some hesitation,
"it was rather more than that.   In fact it was the table
leg."

"The table leg!" repeated Mr. Roustoubique.   What
did he do to it?"

"He cut it off."

"C-u-t it o-f-f!" cried the Proviseur; "and you gave
him only five hours?   Why it's monstrous.   He should
have had twenty.   He should have been sent to the dungeon.   I don't know that he ought not to have been ex-
pelled. At all events I'll take a note of his case and think

it over. And now what's this about Bourdichon. 'In-
subordination : one hour's dictation. Impertinence : two
hours' drill. For bringing animals into the class : two
hours' dictation. For flying an insect : two hours dictation. For drawing a portrait. For leaving class without
leave. For making faces through the window and refusing to come in again. For resisting authority and kicking.'
This is a fine picture of scholastic life, Mr. Polyblank."

"He is rather troublesome, sir, sometimes," said the
professor, "but he is very clever with his translations."

"Bah !" said Mr. Roustoubique, "I'll take a note of
him too. And Coquillard. What's this ? 'For cooking
during the class.' Cooking what ? Do you mean to say
that there are culinary operations in progress during the
time that your pupils are supposed to be receiving your
instruction ? Haven't you got a nose, Mr. Polyblank ?"

"Yes, sir," replied Mr. Polyblank, simply, laying as he
spoke, his hand upon the organ alluded to, which, to tell
the truth, was not the least prominent of his features ;
"I smelt something peculiar, and found out what was
going on."

"And what was that ?" asked Mr. Roustoubique, with
suppressed indignation.

"In my country," said Mr. Polyblank, unconscious of
the brewing storm, "we call it hardbake. It is a preparation of sugar and butter."

"A thousand thunders !" roared the Proviseur,
springing from his chair. "Has it come to this, that
confectionery is to be carried on during the hours of
study—that menageries are kept—that half the class is
out at play and their professor out after them, giving
chase—that windows are broken and table-legs cut off,
and the professor and pupils practice le boxe ? Mr. Polyblank, you're a fool !"

"Sir!" cried Mr. Polyblank, turning white and trembling, "I cannot submit to such language."

"Do as you choose," retorted the other in a towering passion; "you're utterly useless in this establishment. Go back to England if you like. I don't require your services another hour."

Like as it were one in a dream, but trembling with agitation so that he could scarcely hold his hat, Mr. Polyblank walked to the door. With the handle in his hand, he turned and said—"I'll take you at your word, sir; I'll leave your college to-day."

"This minute, if you wish," replied the other, with a brutal laugh. "The sooner I see the last of you the better I shall be pleased."

But when Mr. Polyblank had left the room Mr. Roustoubique began to reflect and to repent of his hasty words, and his reason for regret was this. The object of Mr. Roustoubique's life was to distinguish himself among Proviseurs. How was that to be done? There was only one way, and that was to increase the revenue of his college. He thought of a plan, and hoped to work it with success. He asked permission of the Board to advertise in some of the English journals for English scholars. Permission was granted, but the funds refused. He didn't like the idea of spending his own money. What was he to do? The Board had no faith in the idea. It had been tried at other colleges without success. The Proviseur's scheme seemed likely to go to the wall, when chance helped him. One of the boy's parents wrote to request that his son might learn English. Seizing upon this idea, the Proviseur canvassed the collegians to learn who was desirous of acquiring a knowledge of this language.

A great many young gentlemen were only too eager

to do anything for the sake of novelty ; and these he told to write to their parents to tell them that there would be no extra charge on that account, and to induce them to send him a formal letter to the desired effect. The letters thus obtained he submitted to the Board, and suggested that an English professor should be obtained. The Board consented to the appointment being made, but only on condition that his instruction should be considered extra, and paid for at such a rate as would defray the expense of his hire. This arrangement did not daunt the Proviseur. By dint of perseverance he obtained the consent of a large number of parents to the extra charge, and making a calculation found that their payments would amount to the ordinary salary of a professor, with a very decent balance to spare. In that case, why not spend the balance in advertising for English pupils ? Indeed, why hire a professor at so large a salary ? There must be plenty of men of talent to be picked up cheap.

The Proviseur advertised, and picked up Mr. Polyblank at a slight reduction. He also advertised for English pupils with considerable success ; and things had gone on tolerably smooth until this day on which Mr. Roustoubique and Mr. Polyblank quarrelled. Mr. Roustoubique had been a good deal put out that morning. He had come to the conclusion that the English professor had not sufficient strength of character to manage young France, and he did not know how to better himself at the price. That morning, too, Mr. Roustoubique had received an unpleasant visit from the resident English clergyman respecting the conduct of the English boys at church the previous Sunday. A fortnight before, in consequence of a letter received from an English parent, Mr. Roustoubique had determined upon sending the Protestant boys, thirteen in number, to the English church.

Hitherto it had been the practice for the eldest English student to read through the Morning Prayers on a Sunday, while the French boys went to the chapel attached to the college; but this primitive arrangement had been objected to, and led to the sending of the before-mentioned letter. The parent in question had threatened to remove his son, and Mr. Roustoubique had decided upon sending the English boys to church. This, how-ever, would be attended with some difficulty. Who was to take them ? One of the ushers was ill. Another had left in a huff. The professors could not be asked to undertake such duty. There was nothing for it the first Sunday, if the boys were to go at all, but to let them go by themselves. That, however, was contrary to all pre-cedent. It was one of the oldest rules of the college that every pupil's parents who did not reside in or near to Saint Babylas should appoint some person to act as their agent, or, as it was called, *corréspondant*, with whom the principal of the college might at once communicate in case of emergency.

Unaccompanied by this agent, or some person authorized to act in his stead, no pupil was allowed to leave the college on the monthly holiday, when all those whose friends approved of the arrangement were at liberty from eleven A.M. until seven P.M. ; and thus it was not an unusual sight to see a fine young man of eighteen years, or thereabout, walking home in charge of a little bonne who had seen at most seventeen summers. If found walking alone in the town during the day, a collegian was liable to be immediately sent back into the college, though this rule was rarely enforced, unless the pupil happened to be found with a cigar in his mouth, when the choice was given him of getting within the walls in five minutes or of stopping out for ever.

With such rigid rules as these in force, how could Mr.

Roustoubique contemplate such an innovation as that above alluded to ? But then the English parent said— "If my son is not sent to an English Protestant Place of Worship (all with capitals) on the coming Sabbath, I will remove him immediately from your college." Upon receiving this letter, Mr. Roustoubique seized a pen with the intention of sending back a stinging reply ; but upon consideration did not carry it out. He then determined to send this pupil by himself ; but two days after the receipt of the first epistle came two others from other parents, containing a similar threat. Mr. Roustoubique had an engagement which he did not want to break. No one could conveniently be sent, and so he determined to let the young gentlemen go by themselves, with what result will be presently seen.

During the next week arrangements were made, and Captain Ponson, professor of calisthenics and sword exercise, accepted the duty of marshalling the English boys to church. "They behaved well enough of themselves," thought Mr. Roustoubique, quite erroneously as it happened, "or I should have heard something about it before this. However, I had better let the captain take charge of them, and screw the expense somehow out of the quarterly accounts." The captain was a worthy man, but pompous. He wore the ribbon of the Legion of Honour upon his broad chest. He had a perfectly bald head, and a fierce white moustache and beard à l'Empereur.

That Sunday he had evidently got himself up for the occasion. He was in his Sunday best—blue shaven and buttoned up to bursting in his military surtout. He wore a new pair of white cotton gloves, and carried a cane with a massive silver knob. On leaving the college gates he cried in stentorian tones, "En route !" and marched by the side of his young friends, flourishing his cane after the manner of a tambour-major. For about half an hour his young friends marched very steadily, and being occupied with his own thoughts, the gallant captain paid no particular attention to the road they were taking. All at once, though, he drew up short and looked about him. It struck him forcibly that they were describing a circle, and were at that moment within but a short distance of the spot from which they had started. The captain's visage assumed an expression of anger. The ear of the foremost young gentleman was within easy distance, the captain took hold of it and inquired—" Where are you going to ?"

" I don't know," replied the young gentleman, in a tone of suffering.

" Don't know ?" repeated the captain in indignant surprise. " What do you mean ?"

Then taking possession of more available ears— " Don't you know either ? And you ? And you ?"

It turned out that nobody knew. One of the smallest boys professed to have a glimmering of knowledge on the subject, and was put at the head of the column, but he proved to be impracticable. The captain began to storm. How had they found the way the previous Sunday, and how was it that they had forgotten it ? What did it all mean ? But they could give no explanation, and the captain raged impotently. Time was getting on, though, now. They had been marching for nearly an hour. The captain made inquiry at a shop, and found that they were at the end of the town which was furthest from the church. " Right about face !" he cried, and away they went again at a quick march. The fact was, as it subsequently transpired, the young rascals had never been to church at all upon the previous Sunday, but had repaired in a body to an estaminet outside the town, where they had smoked cigars, drunk sour small beer, and played at bosquet with much enjoyment.

The English church was up a bye-street, on the first-floor over a wine merchant's store—a long, narrow room, furnished with a pulpit, half-a-dozen pews, sixty benches, and an organ. Attached to this establishment was a red-nosed reverend gentleman, who, contrary to the practice of Protestant clergymen in England, wore a black satin stock, which, unaccompanied by shirt collar, had not a very clerical appearance. There was no clerk. About fifty persons composed the congregation, and they were rather astonished when the collegians made a boisterous entry in the middle of the communion, and marched with measured tread up the room. More astonished still when the captain—the worthy creature never before having been inside a Protestant place of worship, and was wholly ignorant of its forms and ceremonies—gave orders in a ringing voice for his young friends to prepare themselves for sitting down, to sit down, to prepare themselves for rising, to rise, to observe silence, to pay attention, to prepare for sitting down again, to sit down again, and to take care what they were about. Most astonished when, misled by one of the young gentlemen, the captain rose in the middle of the sermon, before the Reverend Mr. Backshiver was half way through his thirdly, and shouted—

" Prepare yourselves. In rank. March !" and marched away triumphantly at the head of his chuckling young friends, who drowned the remainder of the clergyman's discourse in the thunder of their blucher soles.

Mr. Roustoubique, however, was in his turn not a little surprised on receiving a letter from the Reverend Mr. Backshiver, complaining of the unhappy Ponson's unseemly conduct, and threatening harsh measures should he come again to disturb the service. What was to be done now ? he asked himself, and paused for a reply. If such goings on were repeated, the fact might reach the

ears of the Board, and then good-bye to all the Roustou-
biquian dreams of greatness. The boys must go to
church, could not be trusted by themselves, and yet there
was nobody to take them. Nobody unless Mr. Polyblank were pressed into the service. But after what had
occurred how could that be managed ? Mr. Roustoubique was not the man to be easily overcome by difficulties. When he had made up his mind that it would
be to his advantage to keep the professor a little longer,
he determined that he should not go, and springing up
rang the bell at once.

" Send Mr. Polyblank to me."

" He has just left the college, sir."

" Run after him."

While the servant was gone Mr. Roustoubique
rehearsed a conciliatory speech or two. Presently the
door opened and the man re-entered, somewhat out of
breath.

" Well ?"

" I told Mr. Polyblank you wanted him, sir."

" Well, where is he ?"

" He thanked me, sir, and—he walked on."

" You mean to say that he is not coming, then ?"

" I should think not, sir. Anyhow I left him walking
hard in the opposite direction."

When the door was closed upon the servant the Proviseur had an opportunity of swearing at his ease.
Presently he put on his hat and set out for the Street of
the Priests.

" I don't see how I can do without him," said M
Roustoubique, pausing on Mr. Pomponney's door step·
" At least not yet awhile. When I can, though, I'll
make him smart for this."

He found the professor seated in front of a cup of

cold tea in his modest apartment. He held a book in
his hand, but he held it all on one side, and was evidently
lost in thought. The Proviseur's eyes travelled rapidly
round the room, taking in its various details—the jumble
of odd furniture, the battered old portmanteau standing
open and revealing the poverty of its owner—the frugal
meal, and the professor himself sitting in his shirt-sleeves
to save his coat—a coat which Mr. Roustoubique had
disapproved of upon account of its shabbiness.

"He's as poor as a rat," thought the Proviseur, with
an inward chuckle. "He'll be glad enough to stop if
I'll keep him." Then he coughed loudly to attract Mr.
Polyblank's attention.

"Ah, Mr. Roustoubique," exclaimed the other, involuntarily, and in some confusion because of his shirt-
sleeves. But having shuffled on his coat he recovered
himself, and bowing stiffly continued—"I did not expect
this honour, sir. Pray be seated."

"Pardon the intrusion," said the Proviseur, taking a
chair, assuming a careless air, and crossing his legs.
"The fact is, I wanted to speak to you with reference to
our conversation a short time ago. I am afraid I was
too hasty and said what—what I really did not mean.
Pray do not attribute my visit to any motive but the
proper one. Understand, I have no wish for a recon-
ciliation ; but I make it a point through life to act fairly
if I can. I know I was wrong in speaking to you as I
did. I had no intention of discharging you, but—but
you have no idea what things occur to harass a man in
my position. I beg to withdraw all I said that may
have been offensive to you. I beg your pardon. Here
is my hand."

He spoke in such a frank and manly way that the
guileless professor was caught at once.

" Pray make no excuses, sir," he said, hastily ; " I—I was annoyed, I confess ; but after this explanation—I certainly thought that you treated me uncourteously, but after you say—that is, when you say——"

" Let us say no more about it, Mr. Polyblank."

Mr. Polyblank was very glad that it should be so. He was one of those persons—and there are many of them—who are shamefaced when they are doing right, who bungle when they should triumph, and only long after the crisis is over perceive what they should have said, and when they should have said it.

" I'd be the last man in the world to do you an injury, Polyblank," said the Proviseur, " because I am sure that you do your best, although you are not at all times very successful. I said just now that I hated to be unjust, and I hate to be misunderstood. Hardly had you left me when a letter arrived, bringing me an intimation that the number of my professors must be reduced. I was afraid that when you came to hear of this you would think that I knew it before, and had picked a quarrel with you to make your dismissal easier."

Mr. Polyblank bowed and murmured something, and felt rather uncomfortable.

" Yes," continued Mr. Roustoubique, " it has been determined that the professor of English shall be removed, and in his place a gentleman engaged who, besides his duties during the week, shall also give a portion of his Sundays to the superintendence of the English boys during their religious exercises."

Mr. Polyblank's jaw fell at this news.

" But—but," he stammered.

" I beg your pardon ?" said Mr. Roustoubique, smiling blandly.

" I—I thought you meant me to stop," stammered Mr. Polyblank.

"I should like you to stop; I should like nothing better, but I don't ask you to do so. If I did, it would seem as though I wished you to do more work for less money. By the way, did I mention that the gentleman who is to be engaged is to be paid a hundred francs less per annum than you receive? It is really a great shame. A hundred francs less; but I am told that at Douay and Boulogne the colleges do not give even as much."

Mr. Polyblank sat silent for a minute or two. His first idea was to say that he would go. But this idea very soon gave place to another. Where was he to go to? He had turned the matter over awhile ago, sitting in front of his cup of cold tea. If he went away, what was to become of him? He could hardly hope to get employment in any other French college with the character he would take away from this one. And if he went back to England?—but he had given up England in despair when he came out here to make a fresh start. No, he could not go back. He must earn a certain amount of money, somehow, for a time, and if he left his present situation he would be penniless. Mr. Roustoubique, twirling his thumbs, waited for a reply. He was pretty certain that the professor would come to terms, and he was not disappointed.

Next Sunday, Mr. Polyblank accompanied the young gentlemen to church, and he found the task thus imposed upon him anything but agreeable. The professor's character as a person to be got over had spread through the college; and though this was the first time the English pupils had been brought in contact with him, they had been well coached, and were prepared. This Sunday, although they knew the way, they repeated the joke of the previous week, and arrived at church by a circuitous route after the service had begun. As they came stamping upstairs an old woman, who acted as door-keeper and pew-opener, pointed out some benches which had been kept vacant for them near the door. It was a very hot day. The window stood open, and upon the window-sill all the young gentlemen piled their uniform caps in the form of a pyramid. The professor having produced his prayer-book, and found the place, half-a-dozen young gentlemen eagerly inquired what Sunday it was, in order that they might find the collect, and, being informed, half-a-dozen other young gentlemen wanted the same information. To avoid unnecessary noise, Mr. Polyblank passed his book, which going down the bench and turning the corner, disappeared mysteriously, and was chased, to the great scandal of the remainder of the congregation. in the style of hunt-the-slipper.

The book having at length being restored to its rightful owner, nothing particular occurred until one of the most audacious of the young gentlemen, producing his cap, which he had retained, asked permission to go out into the air upon account of a sudden faintness. Indignantly refusing the request, for which he felt sure there was no just ground, Mr. Polyblank ordered the boy to put his cap upon the window-sill; upon which the young rogue violently launched the cap in question at the pyramid, and, striking it at its base, sent most of the caps out of window. The excitement of their owners occasioned a general movement and murmur, to quell which, Mr. Polyblank sent out the cause of the mischief to pick up the caps. Some time elapsing without his reappearance, it became necessary to send out another young gentleman to look for him, who in his turn had to be sought for by another. Mr. Polyblank waited helplessly for their return, afraid to leave the church to go and look for them himself lest those left behind should misconduct themselves. The sound of suppressed laughter, and the shuffling of feet on the stones in the street below, drove him at length in desperation to the door, where he hoped to find the old woman, but she was nowhere to be seen. Going downstairs he saw her in the street giving chase to the young gentlemen, who were playfully pelting her with caps.

With as dignified a tone as he could assume, he bade the culprits go in. They obeyed, but on ascending the stairs the professor found the door bolted, and as the young gentlemen inside were resolved not to hear the professor's gentle tapping, and he was unwilling to knock louder for fear of attracting the attention of the congregation, he was obliged to remain outside until Mr. Backshiver's discourse reached a conclusion.

Then some of the congregation having unbolted the door, the professor rejoined his lambs, vowing vengeance. Vengeance, indeed!—when to tell Roustoubique what had occurred was to own himself incapable of performing his duty. As he was leaving the church with his promising young flock, Mr. Backshiver stopped him.

"Excuse me, sir," said he in French, " but when I last drew attention to the misconduct of your pupils I thought I should have no further occasion for complaint. I trusted to gentlemanly feeling and a sense of what was right; but I see I was in error. I shall now seek protection in another quarter."

With that speech, accompanied with a freezingly polite bow, the clergyman left the unhappy professor, who walked homewards by the side of the lambs, frolicsomely disporting themselves by the way, treading on each other's heels, and playing other pranks which were productive of much amusement to a select audience of rag-tagish St. Babylasians following in the rear.

6

CHAPTER VII.

A CLANDESTINE PIC-NIC.

It is a day to rest from toil,
  To lie upon the grass and dream ;
To bid life's beating pulses stay,
To bid life's beating pulses stay,
Through a'l the hours of one bright day,
  Beside the murmur of the fal.ing stream.
                                        ANDREWS.

ALL through the week Professor Polyblank had now but
little time left for recreation except it was upon a Sunday
afternoon.   There was then little rest to be got in the
Street of the Priests, for business being slacker than
usual on Sundays at the chemist's, Mr. Pomponney was
apt to walk upstairs for a gossip, and had been known to
take his pipe in the lodger's room under the pretence of
the lodger finding his time hang heavily on his hands.
It came to be the main object in the poor badgered
schoolmaster to get away—to escape from society at any
price—to burrow his head and hide himself.   For some
time past he had been rather shy of the ramparts, for
there the vagabond boys of the town mostly congregated :
a lawless race, prone to derision, and even capable upon
occasions of resortihg to overt acts of violence, such as
pelting with pebbles and bits of clay.

The streets of the town and the public promenades
were affected by the other professors, whom he hardly
liked to meet while wearing the same suit he wore on
week-days.   His only hope lay in long distances—so
getting out of the town with all the speed of which he
was capable, he had placed half a league between him
and it before he began to feel at all comfortable.   A long,
hot, dusty road was that which he had to traverse,

stretching across the flat marshes; but there was rest and happiness to be found at last in the shady garden of the little cabaret on the outskirts of the village of Longanna, where refreshment in the shape of sugar-and-water—a tipple not inebriating, if cheering,—cost but one sou the jorum. Some cool places, too, were to be found by the side of the river, where, squatting between the pollards, indefatigable line fishers sat sedately bobbing the live-long day, happily content to wait for that which came not. And with lengthened contemplation of these anglers Polyblank would sometimes catch something of their feeling of drowsy contentment; while at other times he persuaded himself that he shared their desire to secure the fat trout that wagged their tails and would not be caught.

Of all spots, however, that he had visited, there was one particular little wood, or rather copse, by the water-side, of which he was fondest. It was a kind of neglected plantation at the bottom of a garden belonging to an old-fashioned house standing at the entrance of the village of Longanna, by the side of which the canal ran. The front of this house was white and mournful of aspect, as it is the nature of most French country houses to be; and there were large green wooden gates in the centre of the wall in front which when open afforded a glimpse of a stony-hearted courtyard—such as you might expect to find in connexion with a jail—always sad and cheerless by reason of the high walls surrounding it, and into this courtyard a number of windows looked. But on the other side of the house was a large irregular old-fashioned garden, beginning with a grass plot surrounded by a box-hedge clipped into a semblance of birds and beasts, with —in the centre of the greensward—a statue of chaste Diana, very much the worse for wear and tear. Beyond this a wild growth of flowers—the common choking the choice. Beyond, again, an eruption of cabbages running fast into walking-sticks. After this a little forest of apple and pear trees with wondrous twisted and knotted trunks, which of a moonlight night took the shape of crouching giants—spindle-legged and distorted. After this, the copse running down to the water's edge.

Of course Mr. Polyblank was perfectly well aware that he had no right to force his way through a weak place in the hedge which divided one side of this plantation from the high road, or to recline by the water-side beneath the grateful shade of the overhanging trees. To begin with, he knew that he must be doing wrong in trespassing on another person's property. Besides, there was a board with an inscription, very old and weather-worn, but yet for the most part legible, by which tres-passing was forbidden under penalties none the less terrible because they were not easily to be deciphered. The fact was, however, that the first time the pro-fessor ventured upon this highly improper proceeding the sunbeams had been pouring down on his head all the length of the long, white, shadeless road from Saint Babylas. He was panting under the heat. The gap in the hedge was temptingly large. The river trickled past through the trees. There was half an acre of cool green grass to spread himself out upon. And lastly, there was nobody looking. Climbing through the hedge, then, he luxuriated by the water-side for a good hour and more before he set off home again. The second time he passed that way there was the same gap—the same delicious shade, and nobody to see him. And then came the third and last visit, upon which, as will be seen, something very dreadful occurred to him.

He came away from home upon this ocasion—this

desperado—with the settled determination of trespassing.
Long impunity had given him courage, as is the case
even with the most timorous of spirits—though, to tell
the truth, he had come to the conclusion that the old
house was unoccupied, because upon his previous visits
he had never seen or heard any sign of life about it.
While panting up the dusty road he had, when a mile at
least distant from the place, in his mind's eye, climbed
through the gap and stretched himself out at full length
upon the mossy bank. He had started earlier than
usual, so as to have a much longer rest; and he took
with him one of those famous sausages, a hunch of bread,
and a cracked tumbler. The last he intended to fill
from the canal, for he meditated a small thing in picnics, and he had also got a little red wine in a physic
bottle, with which he purposed taking the rough edge off
the canal.

This was to be a gala day, you see. It happened to
be his birth-day, not that that ought to have been any
occasion for rejoicing, for surely he had been about as
poor a spec as mother nature ever ventured on. However, he was going to rejoice for reasons best known to
himself—if known at all—and had come provided with
the requisites on a limited scale. If ever there was a
day all the year round when the sun poured down its
fullest heat upon the long road from Saint Babylas to
Longanna it was that particular Sunday; and more than
once by the way was the perspiring Polyblank fain to
shelter himself in streaks of shade, a foot wide at the
utmost, which the lanky lime trees with their lopped
branches cast spectre-like across the highway. He was
well nigh fainting with heat and fatigue when at length
he reached the long-coveted journey's end. But he
found that something had occurred during the week

which he was very far from anticipating. The gap had
been made up.

Poor professor! It was with a very woful countenance that he noted this new arrangement, and stood
scraping his chin with his hand, while he considered
what steps he ought to take under the circumstances.
A good many steps would be required if he made up his
mind to go back again. Half-a-dozen and a good long
stride if he decided upon surmounting the little difficulty
of some wooden palings by the side of the hedge which
had just been repaired. It was not at all the sort of
thing for a teacher of the young to do; but only think
of the temptation. It was one hundred and twenty in
the sun! The palings were so easily to be climbed, and
there was no one to see him. It was anything but
right; but then, you others,—if there never was any
one to see you? Mr. Polyblank thought the matter
over. He peeped through the palings and listened. He
could hear nobody about, and he yielded at length to
the promptings of the tempter—without a very hard
struggle. Indeed, if there were a struggle at all, it was
on the top of the palings.

The difficulty surmounted, oh! how delightful it was
to be here in the cool shade, and watch the wanton sunlight playing bopeep among the floating branches, beneath
which the barbel slept securely in the deep shadow. On
the other side of the water a grey-headed angler, crouching among the feathering grass and bobbing bulrushes,
was dozing under an umbrella whilst the frolicsome
gudgeons sported round his trembling float, and the less
venturesome roach looked on at a safer distance, warily
watching the bait. A soft, refreshing breeze coming
from the surface of the water fanned the schoolmaster's
face, and the turf on which he lay was as soft as velvet.

There was not a sound to break the stillness of the peaceful scene save the occasional splash of a fish, or the chirping of a bird, or the faint murmur of summer air rustling amongst the topmost branches of the trees. This was rather different from the playground at the Imperial College, with its ceaseless clamour of shrill voices, and its clatter of heavy boots upon the rugged gravel. Suppose it possible to get one's living by lolling all day on the sea beach, or under the shadow of the trees by a river side ! But there's not much money to be made that way, unless the brain be hard at work while the body lies idle ; and that does not sound much like making holiday.

There was nothing wanting to render his happiness complete, the professor thought, as he lay there in a state of dreamy contentment. Presently, however, an improvement suggested itself. His feet were dreadfully hot, and he thought it would be heavenly bliss to lave them in the cool water. Why should he not ? He peered round coyly, as Dorothea might have done. The angler over the way could not catch sight of him from the place where he sat even if he woke up. There was no one else about. Polyblank hesitated no longer, but forthwith relieved himself of his socks. The water was deliciously cool, and there was surely nothing now left to wish for, unless it was lunch. He produced the paper parcel containing his sausage and bread, and the physic bottle full of wine, and began his repast. He had forgotten to bring a knife with him ; but he did not allow the want of it to mar his pleasure. He had brought his favourite author in his pocket, and read a line or two between the nibbles.

It was quite a picture to see him sitting there, ankle deep in the water, his book in one hand and a hunch of bread in the other, with nothing in the world to

trouble him but the gnats.   All at once, though, something of a very terrible nature happened.   In the
middle of a mouthful he heard a rustling behind him
among the bushes, and pricked up his ears like a timid
hare to listen.   There was a rustling of leaves and a
cracking of twigs, accompanied by a sort of half-hissing and
half-scraping sound, which those who are used to pay for
such things might have recognised as that which a silk
dress might make in sweeping past brushwood.   This
idea, however, did not immediately occur to the professor,
for his mind was running rather upon gamekeepers ; but
presently he heard the sound of a woman's voice, singing
softly, and then a thrill of terror ran through his frame.
He dropped his favourite author, flung away his hunch
of bread, and began to struggle with his half-Wellingtons.
This was not a moment to think of such trifles as wet feet
and want of stockings. He got one boot on somehow, being within an inch of falling head over heels into the water
in the process, and began to tear away at the other one. But
in his agitation he tore off a tab ; the boot was refrac-
tory, and shame and humiliation stared him in the face.
In another instant he was confronted by the proprietor of
the rustling silk—a black moiré trimmed with violet
velvet and bugles.

" I beg your pardon, madame," gasped Polyblank,
dancing an involuntary hornpipe among the fragments of
the small thing in picnics, to the utter annihilation of the
physic bottle full of Saint Etienne.   The lady regarded
him with silent wonder for full a minute.   Then the
state of the case, with the evidence of the half-off boot,
the stockings and broken victuals, became apparent—the
truth dawned upon her, and a twinkle in her eyes began
to show through the would-be sternness of her pretty
face.

" May I inquire, sir, what you are doing upon my grounds ?" she asked. He looked at her hopelessly. Had he been a boy thief caught in an orchard with his cheek stuffed with pippin, he could not well have worn a more sheepish look under the farmer's threatening horsewhip.

" I—I—I," he stammered. He was trying to stand upon his stockings so as to conceal them from view. He had just kicked one of the sausages riverward, but it had cannoned off a pollard and was gambolling shamelessly in endless evolutions out in the open. If he could have taken a sudden spring, dived to the bottom of the water, and remained there for an hour or two without drowning himself !

" Well, sir ?"

This to him, with an impatient stamp of a beautiful little bronze leather boot. No further delays were practicable. He must make an excuse. But oh, ye gods, what sort of one ? It was a goddess helped him at last —the goddess in the black moiré.

" Perhaps, sir, you did not know that this was private ground when you landed from your boat ?"

At last our poor booby plucked up courage, and, as no truthful-looking lie occurred to him, ventured on the truth itself:—" I do not know how to apologize, madam, for the intrusion. I thought the house was uninhabited. I did not intend to do any harm, but I—I climbed over the palings."

" I accept the explanation, sir," said the lady with the calmest and most self-possessed manner in the world. " And now nothing remains but for you to climb back."

" Before going, madam, if you will allow me to ask your forgiveness, I will retire with——"

" As much haste as possible."

" Yes, ma'am."

Decidedly, thus far, the professor's position was any-thing but dignified; but the worst part had yet to come. Presently he would have to stoop lower still—to pick up his stockings for instance. And how about the scraps of newspaper littering the grass, and the broken victuals? And after this there were the palings! Is there any little episode in the past life of any one of you which sets your ears a tingling when you look back at it? Such passages occur in the lives of even the highest-placed. There is an undress rehearsal to every grand performance —there is weakness in strength—some trumpery details under the most splendid effects. Humans are human, in short—more's the pity!—and it is no use our pretend-ing to have souls above sausages: at least it was with this reflection that the professor having disposed of his stockings fell to scrambling after a polony which would not be caught. The owner of the moiré, after watching him a minute, was troubled with a cough, and Polyblank resumed the perpendicular with a scarlet countenance.

"I am afraid," said the lady, "you must have found it very difficult to climb over those palings. If you will follow me you can pass out through the garden."

"You are too kind, madam," said the unhappy tres-passer, catching eagerly at the chance of her leaving him for a moment. "I will follow you immediately." Then, as she passed out of his sight behind the bushes, he fell with fury upon his obstinate half-Wellington, dragged it on, and kicked the remainder of those miserable frag-ments far away among the rushes. After this he stood for a moment panting for breath. If he could only escape now, he thought. A bound or two and, if all went well, he would be over the palings in the road, a free man. He took a step forward, but the lady's voice ar-rested his progress—

" Sir, are you coming ?"

" I beg your pardon, madam ; yes, madam."

He gave himself up for lost and followed passively. Surely there never was a more comical object than that poor professor, blushing like a girl and looking very much as though he would have liked to cry. He carried his hat in his hand and shambled by her side, as the boy in the orchard before mentioned might have accompanied the farmer to the place of execution. Yet she was not a very terrible-looking lady, this, who had taken him prisoner. She was, indeed, rather small and slim, and was one of those pretty-faced women, with small noses and big eyes, who have some trouble in looking fierce, though they may have tempers of their own for all that. Until now, however, the professor had not summoned up sufficient courage to look at her fairly. She might have been old or young, plain or pretty, for what he knew. She wore an extensive robe of silk or satin which rustled portentously—this much he knew, but after that nothing. When, at last, he ventured upon a peep, it was the dearest little round face, rather sun-burnt though, and with the brightest eyes the professor had ever encountered.

" I think I have seen you before," she said, " though you are a stranger in the town. To be sure—I have seen you walking with the collegians."

" I am a professor at the college, madam."

" A professor ! Ah, then, you are English. I thought so from—I thought so."

But she did not say why, which made the succeeding pause rather awkward.

" I wish I hadn't disturbed you," she said presently, with quite a childish, innocent sort of manner. " You did seem to be so enjoying yourself. But (with determination) you'd no right to trespass."

" I—I should never have dreamt of doing so if I had known——"

" I am afraid I broke in upon you in the middle of your lunch. Let me offer you some before you go."

" Oh no, madam, I could not think of intruding, and I had quite finished, thank you. I am quite certain—thank you."

" You know best, of course. It was at the hotel of the 'Three Crowns' I first saw you, now I remember. And so you teach at the college—what ?"

" English, madam."

" English? Really. And so there are people want to learn English. I have some property in England, but it never occurred to me to learn English. This is the way out—if you will not let me offer you some refreshment."

" No, thank you, madam. I am very much obliged to you, and I beg a thousand pardons."

" There is no occasion. Good day, sir."

He sidled out and bowed and shuffled round the corner, thanking Heaven for his escape. She, still holding the door, looked thoughtfully after him. He cut a comical figure in his seedy old clothes, but, strange to say, the humour of his threadbare knees and glazed elbows was lost upon her.

" Poor man !" said Manon de Grandvilain, with a sigh. " He looks half starved, and I have robbed him of a dinner. Teaches English, too ! I wonder how anybody can take the trouble to learn barbarous English !"

CHAPTER VIII.

PLAYING AT LESSONS.

Si vous l'aviez vu, c'te jeunnesse,
All' était gentille à croquer,
All' était belle à rend' malade
Jusqu'au greffier du jug' de paix.—CARRÉ.

"FELICITE," said Mr. Pomponney, "you will see."

She was always on the point of seeing, according to Mr. Pomponney, whose habit it was to make predictions which were not often verified. Not that that mattered much. Very few persons in the world were blessed with as short a memory as Felicité, and when Mr. Pomponney's predictions were unfulfilled he said nothing, and she recollected nothing about it ; but when, by some extraordinary chance his words came true, loud was his self-glorification, and sincere the admiration his sagacity excited in the wife of his bosom. Now it can hardly be supposed that Mr. Pomponney would meanly take advantage of this shortness of memory on the part of Mrs. P. even if he was aware that it existed ; and it is therefore to be presumed that his own recollection sometimes failed him, for it is very certain that he was not unfrequently in the habit of congratulating himself upon the success of predictions which he had never made. Indeed, according to his own account, nothing ever happened in his small circle that he had not anticipated, though it must be owned that upon some occasions— such, for instance, as when putting up the shop-shutters, one of them fell down on and bruised his head—he found it somewhat difficult to explain why, if he was aware of coming events of an unpleasant nature, he did not avoid them.

" Felieité," said Mr. Pomponney one day, whilst spreading a blister, " I'm very sorry for your friend Polyblank, and I should like him to get on, but I feel an inward conviction that he wont. Please to recollect my words, Felicité. I say so, and you will see."

An oblong piece of white cardboard in the window had led to these remarks. Mr. Polyblank had written in French—in his best large hand, and with his most imposing capitals—" English Lessons," and had timidly begged Mrs. Pomponney to allow the announcement to lie in the window, where accordingly she had placed it, and where it had caught Mr. Pomponney's eye as he returned from his café in the forenoon. A question had then arisen respecting the advisability of allowing it to overlie and cover up two boxes of capsules which had been lying there unnoticed for the last two years. The point to be decided was whether it would not be pre-judicial to the sale of the capsules which, though they had been a long time on hand, might yet be asked for at any moment if seen. If moved from the capsules would it be best to cover up the pulmonary wafers, swamp the leech label, or partially eclipse the show blister? It was not—Mr. Pomponney was anxious to explain—that he grudged Polyblank the favour he had requested, if any good could come of it, but who on earth in Saint Babylas could possibly want to learn English ?

" What is England ?" said Mr. Pomponney, abandon-ing the blister for a moment to wave his hand. " A place without a climate, and peopled by savages. A nation without music or with any knowledge of cookery ; who sell their wives, steal our plays, and caricature our fashions. Why should we care to know any more than we know already of that abode of prudery, pomposity, fog and doleful Sundays ? When our William hundreds

of years ago went over and conquered them he took his
language with him, and when presently we go over and
conquer them again we'll do likewise. Why then trouble
our heads about their barbarous gabble?"

To which remarks Felicité having nothing to say,
Mr. Pomponney went on with his plaster, and just at that
moment the Baroness de Grandvilain's carriage drove up
and stopped in front of the shop. The chemist immediately ran out, cap in hand, to open the carriage-door, and
followed the two ladies bare-headed into the shop. They
had come to purchase some scent and soap, and to have
a prescription made up for one of the pensioners; which
articles it seemed as though Mr. Pomponney would never
have done folding up, so many wrappers did he employ
for the purpose, fastening each with sealing-wax, and
descanting the while most genteelly upon local topics, the
weather, and the wares in his shop.

All this while the announcement about the English
lessons had been lying upon the counter, and once when
the Baroness stretched out her hand intending to take it
up, Mr. Pomponney, misinterpreting her motive, and
supposing she was desirous of looking at some pomatum
pots and tooth-brushes underneath, hastily snatched it
away. When at last the articles purchased had been
wrapped up to Mr. Pomponney's satisfaction, the younger
lady rising and walking towards the door had again
approached the piece of pasteboard, and this time succeeded in getting possession of it.

" What is this?" she asked.

" That, madam? oh, nothing! I am sure I don't know
why it is lying about here. A new perfume, this, madam.
All the rage in Paris. The ' Theresa.' "

" Thank you, thank you. Do you teach English, then,
Mr. Pomponney?"

" No, madam ! On the contrary."

" You are learning ?"

" No, madam, I assure you. Heaven forbid !" And he was going further to express his sentiments on the point when good little Felicité stepped forward with an explanation.

"He lodges with us, madam—the new professor at the college. A gentleman of much learning. On the first floor, and gives no trouble."

" Certainly, to be sure," said Mr. Pomponney, very grandly; " he is our lodger, and—behold him !"

Even as he spoke the professor came up to the private door heavily laden with books, and was in no small degree confused by finding himself confronting the baroness with his hands full, so that he was unable to raise his hat. But who shall picture his misery when trying to shift the books from one hand to the other he let some fall, and in endeavouring to pick them up dropped others; so that had not Felicité gone at last to the rescue there is no saying how the painful scene would have ended. At length, however, he made his escape, but not before he had heard Mr. Pomponney's explosion of mirth. That worthy tradesman's risibility was indeed so intensely excited that he would not very soon have been restored to his usual sobriety of demeanour had he not happened to roll up against and break some of his own physic bottles during one of his convulsions of laughter; upon which he suddenly became as solemn as a mute, and with a long face picked up the pieces.

It may seem strange, perhaps, that the baroness did not even smile at the misadventures of the clumsy professor. She might have done so, perhaps, had she not chanced to notice the expression of almost agony upon poor Polyblank's face, and then her eyes filled with tears.

"Poor man! poor man!" she muttered, half aloud. Pomponney, holding his sides, rolled at that moment among the phials, dealing out destruction right and left, at which she broke into quite a savage laugh, and to judge from the way in which she clutched the handle of her parasol, one might have fancied that she had been seized by a sudden and almost irresistible desire to smash the rest of the bottles that had escaped the chemist's ravages.

That evening there came a note from Manon to the professor, inviting him to call at the château next day to make arrangements about some lessons, which she was desirous of receiving in the barbarous tongue. No time was named for the visit, and so he went in the evening after he had finished his duties at the college. Manon was in the garden when he arrived, and he was received by the Dubosq, with respect to whom the poor man committed the fatal error of mistaking her for the baroness's mother. Bungling again, this Polyblank rushed to the conclusion that it was the Dubosq who wanted to learn English, and actually began to explain the rudiments in the usual scholastic style, which only caused the good lady to bristle up in silent indignation. From the first hour that they met the Dubosq conceived an antipathy to the simple schoolmaster, which he never succeeded in entirely removing, and she treated him with a chilling haughtiness.

The fact was, she wanted to keep the baroness as much as possible to herself, and resolutely set her face against intruders. Not that her motive perhaps was, as the world goes, so very mercenary. She did not expect or wish to get any of the baroness's money in case of the baroness's death. She was very comfortable in the situation that she held, and as happy as she could expect

7

to be in this world (earthly bliss and the lamented Dubosq having perished together), and she wished things to remain as they were, if possible. That notion of travelling, which had entered Manon's head the other evening had made the good lady feel very uncomfortable.

She did not wish to travel. Long ago, without being so foolish as to take the trouble to go and look at other countries, she had come to the conclusion that there was no place like home. There was much wear and tear, and much worry and fatigue, she had been given to understand, in travelling, which might suit a parcel of Englishwomen, but which no French lady in her senses, who had been properly brought up, would willingly undergo. All this she represented to Manon, who thereupon, with a prodigiously serious face, proposed that they should immediately begin to learn to climb, practising upon the garden wall and the apple trees, in order to get their heads steady for the Grands Mulets. But these annoyances, upon which she lengthily dilated, did not form the chief objection to travelling in Madame Dubosq's eyes. How was it possible that she could take her pretty lamb about in the world, without some prowling wolf crossing their path and snapping her up? Even here, hidden away in this tumble-down old château of Longanna, she was not safe.

Certainly the rakes of Saint Babylas were not a very dangerous race, and were easily enough sent to the right-about. The marrying men were not on the whole attractive, and though they might do well enough for the marriageable maidens of those parts, were scarcely formed to inspire a passion in the heart of the ex-actress of the Châtelet, even had she not been a baron's widow with four thousand a year. But there was danger from one quarter, the Dubosq could not help fancying. Although he made no sign, that young man Raynal meant mischief, she felt convinced. What puzzled her was his going on shilly-shallying; and she would dearly have liked to question him respecting his intentions, had she not feared either that he might question her right in so doing, or that such a course of conduct would offend the baroness.

Gradually, however, as time rolled on, although Raynal still visited the château, yet no talk of love having, as far as the Dubosq knew—and she watched them closely—passed between him and Manon, the housekeeper began to feel more comfortable, and at length persuaded herself that things would go on thus until the end of their lives. Yes, they would thus pass away their existence. The pretty young widow of nineteen would be content to carry her weeds to the grave. The Dubosq would ever remain her valuable friend and companion, and keep the keys of the wine-cellar and grocery cupboard under the stairs. Raynal would call two or three times a week, and lounge about, and talk in his vague, dissatisfied way of things in general; his remarks acquiring piquancy from an under-current of irony which pervaded his conversation without being pointéd enough to offend the persons addressed. Yes, he would come and go as heretofore, and would humour and banter the Dubosq, as was his wont, until, she showing some signs of restiveness, he would grow of a sudden preternaturally deferential. And thus the good lady had settled it; the world was to go on until her further orders. But are we not for ever reckoning without our host?

Suddenly Manon expresses a desire to travel. She is reasoned with, and apparently convinced of her error. A few days afterwards she mentions England, and wonders whether it would be a nice place to go to. Raynal, con-

7—2

sulted upon the subject, says decisively " no," particularly
if the intending visitor does not know English. The
Dubosq, listening to this opinion, is joyful, and Manon
is silent ; but in less than a week she engages our professor to instruct her in the unknown tongue. One person, at least, gained by this arrangement, and that was
Polyblank. Manon had proposed her own terms, which
amounted to rather more than double what the professor
had thought of asking. Then she paid a quarter in advance, allowed him to fix the time for instruction most
convenient to him, and the lessons began.

The lessons ! Surely since the art of teaching was
first invented no living professor of it ever entered with
such zeal upon the task allotted to him. At the book-
seller's next door to Mr. Pomponney's he purchased
Chambaud's dictionary, published near a hundred years
ago, chez A. Millar, dans le Strand, also the " Traveller's
Companion, or Dialogues in Six Languages," by Madame
de Genlis, wherein, as their author observes, " shall be
found all the expressions of politeness wich (*sic*) are made
use of in society." Also " Paul and Virginia" in English, to be re-translated, a grammar and a book of exercises. To these he added half-a-dozen plain paper books,
which with great care he himself ruled and labelled ; and
with the lot in a great brown-paper parcel, he one evening took an inside place in the diligence, and nursed the
packet on his knees from the door of Mrs. Gobinard's
hotel to the White Stag in Longanna.

Who could pretend to picture the almost infantile
delight with which the pretty baroness turned over the
contents of that brown-paper parcel ? How she straightway ordered to be dusted a certain corner-cupboard,
thenceforth to be devoted solely to these works of instruction. How she wrote her name in every book, with the

date and a flourish ; having, however, first got out her
desk, filled afresh her inkstand, and selected a new pen
and a spotless piece of blotting-paper. How she secretly
looked for " love" in the dictionary the very first evening, committing it to memory, pronouncing it to herself
as though it rhymed with grove, and feeling highly gratified by this acquisition of knowledge. Lastly, how,
having spread out and smoothed down her skirts and
folded her little hands, she compressed her red lips, fixed
her large innocent eyes with an expression of concentrated attention which was quite comical upon the professor's face, and waited for him to begin. Perhaps
never in his life before had Polyblank found himself
placed at greater disadvantage than he did then ; with
the baroness thus regarding him, and the Dubosq's cold
spectacle-glasses glittering in the background. But he
was equal to the occasion, and acquitted himself, all
things considered, with distinction.

When, however, she had had her mind improved for
half an hour or so, it occurred to Manon that it was
supper-time, and that the professor had better have supper
with them, an arrangement against which the professor
protested mildly, to yield, however, in the end, and took
his departure in due course, having set certain exercises
to be prepared for his next visit. But of all sights in
the world the best and most delightful was that afforded
by the pretty baroness when she sat down after the professor had gone—oh so seriously !—to her work, and
made such a lot of blots and blunders.

CHAPTER IX.

OUTSIDE THE DOOR.

Grands aboyeurs tant qu'ils sont à la porte,
Et muets dès qu'ils sont entrées.—LAVALETTE.

OH how the sun used to shine when we were all youthful and happy! Oh the days when we were young! Those happy days before Strephon grew bald and Chloe began to lose her symmetry. But all the world is terribly changed for the worse since then, and time must e'en have used ourselves rather roughly, for you must candidly own that you hardly make the impression now that you did in those days—do you remember, when we went gipsying a very, very long while ago. Polyblank, poor soul, had never gone gipsying—never having had a holiday and the money to spend, conjointly. His highest jinks had been such very small jinks withal. His youth had never been more than lukewarm at its hottest. He had never "gone in" for anything, and had never "broken out" like other young men.

It had never occurred to him that he was a genius, and it must be owned he was not one. Yet he was no fool, for a fool could not have earned his living, as he had done these twenty years past, as a teacher—he began to teach at sixteen, while he himself was learning. There was a time when he could command a tolerable salary, and was looked up to in the public school in England where he was employed as one of its brightest intellectual lights. Through a certain misunderstanding, in which he was not to blame, he lost his place, and since then had gradually sunk—not because he was less capable, but because other rising men appeared in the scholastic world and pushed him towards the wall; and there was not wanting, either, a certain dead weight to pull him down and keep him under, with which incubus this story, also, will very shortly be encumbered.

At thirty-six years of age, then, the sun—which had never shone for him as it did for us when we were hay-making in the happy era aforesaid—burst suddenly over his head in all its glory, and Polyblank was a boy again, if a person can be again a boy who skipped that period of his early life under the pressure of more important business, and went from childhood, at a jump, into stick-up collars and a tail coat—the emblems of full-blown usherhood. He had a hard life of it at the Imperial College, it is true; but the hours of his martyrdom over, there was now much happiness in store for him.

What a delightful walk was that over the marshes through which ran the stream that skirted the baroness's garden, spangled with broad-leaved water-lilies, and edged by round-headed pollards, leaning over the water. At eventide no sound was heard to break the stillness reigning over the broad expanse of pasture land save the uncertain tinkling of distant sheep-bells, the far-off lowing of cattle, the soft drone of the ever restless insect tribe, and the lulling murmur of the water, flowing gently onwards. Arrived at the copse of firs and hornbeams where the baroness had, upon that never-to-be-forgotten day, surprised him, and through which the sun at noon-day could scarcely penetrate, he would often pause to peer wistfully through the tangled branches of the hedge into the wilderness of garden beyond. Very beautiful, too, that garden seemed to him, in spite of its rank turf, its choked-up fountain, its wild and rugged flower-beds, its neglected vines flinging their long sprangs across the moss-grown path, its old trees strangled by unruly climbers, and its stagnant pool, dark and motionless beneath the boughs of a weeping willow, through the leaves of which the faint summer breeze whispered softly, as though evil-doers were plotting mischief in its deep shadow.

But a light gleaming through a hanging wood of hazels, which almost hid the house from his view, would warn him that the lamp had been lit in the oak-panelled parlour, and that the ladies were ready to receive him. What happy evenings were those when the ladies listened to the worthy professor's accounts of the manners and customs of "ces barbares!" During these lengthy narratives, the Dubosq, who was perhaps just a little bit bored by them, would stitch vigorously, while the pretty baroness—as idle a young lady as ever lived—lolling back in her soft, luxurious chair, listened with a sympathizing smile, and sometimes broke into a low musical laugh, which was evoked either by the professor's native wit or some failure in his French. He was so eminently successful as a story-teller, and met with such a warm reception as a humorist, that it can hardly be wondered at if he occasionally talked a little too much, and to the extent of half an hour or so sometimes outstayed his welcome.

When thus transgressing it was not unusual for the Dubosq to yawn at him in an alarming fashion, and then apologize in a stately style for so doing. Oftentime she would light the bedroom candles very slowly and deliberately. Then, placing them side by side upon the table at which he sat, stand on guard over them, fixing the prolix Polyblank with an unflinching eye. Once indeed, the professor failing to take the hint, the Dubosq went even as far as to bring him his hat and put it into his hand, upon which Mr. Polyblank, covered with confusion, and language failing him, turned and fled without even saying good night. But his welcome next evening from the young hostess was none the less gracious in consequence of this little incident, and he was even more successful than usual in amusing her.

Encouraged by his success, he even ventured one evening to bring with him certain Latin verses of his composition, which with very little persuasion he was induced to read to the ladies. Sort of epigrams he said they were, and upon the same authority there was reason to suppose they were witty. He had an idea, he told the ladies, of adding a few more to them, and trying some day whether he could not find a publisher. From what has been stated the reader will already have arrived at the conclusion that as far as the English lessons went the lady's progress was small. She generally forgot to do the exercises her teacher set her, or she cribbed in a shameless and transparent way after promising faithfully not to look in the book. She would listen to his remarks with the demurest and most attentive face, and forget every word he had said five minutes afterwards. Her pronunciation was the most hopeless thing you ever heard ; and she argued seriously in support of a supposed difference in the formation of English and French jaw-bones. But then she was the prettiest little dunce that ever the sun shone upon, and gibberish from her seemed to her tutor the sweetest discourse he had ever hearkened to. The Dubosq looked somewhat coldly on these visits, and more than once ventured upon an opinion respecting their frequency and their small value, regarded from a commercial point of view ; but the baroness would reply, "I don't care what it costs. The poor creature wants the money badly I know, and I don't want to learn anything. I'm sure it's not his fault if I can't learn. After

all too he amuses me, and I'm dreadfully bored sometimes, my dear, I am really."

The Dubosq it must be owned was not the liveliest
company in Christendom. She was one of that class who
make themselves disagreeable upon principle ; who persistently set wrong right, when by so doing they annoy
all the rest of the community ; who, having their cross
to bear, take particular care to bear it, so that it barks
the shins of other pilgrims on the road. Upon the subject of the dead and buried Dubosq, she was apt to be
discursive, and it was a peculiarity of the departed one
that he was all that was bad until you called him bad,
when he as it were turned into a different person in his
grave, and was all that was good, with a few odd virtues
to spare. Upon other subjects, however, she was not so
fluent, and the conversation flagged a little for lack of
interest during the long days and nights which the two
women passed together at the château of Longanna.

He was quite a god-send then, our poor professor, and
came out for the first time in his life as an agreeable
rattle. There never was wanting a hot supper and a
bottle of good old wine upon the baroness's table some
time during the evening, which meal often very considerably curtailed the famous lessons. Sometimes, in the
excitement of talk, Polyblank would take a glass more
than usual, (worthy soul, water was his drink when he
drank at his own expense !) and then a flow of language
would come to him which secretly excited his surprise
and admiration, and on his way home across the marshes
he was wont to repeat with a chuckle some of the remarkably good things he had said over the supper-table.
He was very happy, and though he had the most limited
notion of harmony ever portioned out to human being,
yet going home beneath the shining stars he would often

enough sing snatches of bygone melodies as near the tunes as he could manage them.

After all he thought life was not as hard as he had hitherto supposed it to be. He was beginning to get on famously. What with his salary at the college, and his lessons at the château, he was now in receipt of really a tolerable income, and was actually able to buy new boots without pinching their price out of his saucissons. Perhaps presently, if he looked about him, he might get some other private pupils in the town, and be able to give up the imperial establishment. Who could say, the baroness was so kind and good she might start him in a school of his own! There was no knowing what would be the limit of his good fortune. When luck does come, it comes sometimes in bucketfuls. Above all, though, that dead weight over there in England, which has been before alluded to, had fallen off his back at last, and seemed to be removed for ever. For the first time in his life he had got a fair start, and he felt ten years younger now the load was gone.

Coming home, however, to Mr. Pomponney's one evening he received a severe shock. He was lighter hearted and more joyous than usual, for he had made several great conversational hits at Longanna, and almost surpassed himself. He, therefore, came along singing as blithely as a bird, and skipped, quite fawn-like, up the door-steps. But while in the act of closing the door a sudden panic seized him, and he staggered back against the wall; his jaws dropping open as he did so. Somebody else in the house was blithe and gay. A familiar voice smote upon his ear—apparently a jovial voice—which he knew very well. The owner was evidently making himself extremely agreeable in Mr. Pomponney's parlour, and Mr. Pomponney and his good lady were laughing heartily at some droll story he was relating. Pressing his hand upon his heart the professor crept noiselessly forward, and, with a ghastly face, peeped through the crevice of the door. Sure enough there was the dead weight come back to settle on him—the dissipated prodigal, the curse of his life, rosy cheeked, and robust as ever.

"God forgive me!" groaned Polyblank; "but I had hoped never to set eyes on him again in this world."

CHAPTER X.

THE CURSE OF HIS LIFE.

But hast thou wholly,
In sin and strife,
Forgot for ever
Thy childhood's life?—Höedt.

CATCHING sight of the professor's countenance the jolly man within sprang eagerly to his feet, and gave him a boisterous welcome.

"Peter, old son," he cried, in Whitechapel English, "how are you by this time? Tip us your fin, old fireworks. Let's have a claw at you. Why, you look bluer than ever, Peter. Blessed if you don't;" and then, turning to the others, he added, in Brummagem French, "he looks as if it didn't agree with him. Don't he? What have you been feeding him on? Is it frogs?"

"We cannot talk here," said the professor, in a faint voice. "Let us go to my room."

"If the lady here will excuse me, with great pleasure," and, promising to return soon, the jolly man followed Mr. Polyblank upstairs. Not until he had lit a candle, and they were seated by the little table, did the professor break silence, and then he exclaimed, in a despairing tone, "What, in Heaven's name, has brought you here, Joseph? What do you want with me now?"

The jolly man had not quite as jolly a manner about him when alone in Polyblank's company as he had downstairs, and, indeed, seemed rather to avoid meeting the professor's eye. Therefore, in replying, he kept his gaze fixed upon a red finger of a large red hand with which, as he spoke, he practised ba-ba black sheep on the table. "That ain't a very overkind way of putting it, Peter," said he. "Excuse my mentioning it; but it ain't, strictly speaking, hardly up to what one could call brotherly—now is it?"

The other answered with an impatient gesture:

"You're not the person, Joseph, to talk about brotherly behaviour, are you? You've not been a very good brother so far. But let that pass—what do you want now?"

"You take a chap up so uncommon short, Peter, and after such a long journey, too, when one hasn't even had time to have a good sit down."

"What do you want?" repeated the professor.

"Well, Peter, I want such a precious lot of things," said Mr. Joseph, smiling good-humouredly; "I don't know how to give a name to 'em, but——"

"You want money?"

"You've hit it," cried Mr. Joseph, finishing ba-ba with a flourish: "I am awfully hard up, and must have some tin somehow."

"When last I heard from you, you said that you wanted only a few pounds to buy clothes, so that you might make a respectable appearance at the hospital of some county town where you had been appointed housesurgeon, and I sent you the money."

" You did," responded Joseph, heartily ; "and it was devilish good of you ; only I didn't get the berth for all that."

" Didn't get it ?"

" Filled up when I got there, Peter, although I had been promised it for a dead certainty. It was deuced disappointing to a fellow, you know, but I'm used to that. I'm used to roughing it, I am."

Mr. Polyblank, however, did not appear to think that he was the only person in the world who had had a hard time of it ; and it was with a struggle he stifled his rising anger and continued, though not without emotion :

" If you wanted money and expected me to give you any, you have not acted wisely in coming here. I have had rather a disagreeable time of it in the college, but I—I am happy to say I have found—found friends, and am getting on pretty well."

Here Mr. Joseph broke in warmly—" I'm deuced glad to hear it, Peter."

" My only hope," pursued Polyblank, " lies in my good name. If I can establish a reputation as a decent scholar——"

" You've a head like an almanac," put in Mr. Joseph.

" And a respectable man, I may make a good living as the master of a scholastic establishment of my own, but——"

He could get no further before Mr. Joseph had clutched him by the hand and was working him like a pump.

" Don't be down-hearted, Peter," he cried, enthusiastically. " We'll pull it off yet, old man, or I'm very much out in my reckoning. We'll square 'em, sir ; make no mistake. We'll ketch 'em a-live—alive O, or my name ain't Joe Polyblank."

The professor, however, did not respond very cordially —" I'm afraid, Joseph," said he, " that you may spoil my chance if you go on in the way you always have gone on as yet. You ruined me once, you know, and—and— I think it would be best for all parties if you were to go to some other place. The world is very large, you know. This is only one out-of-the-way corner, but it is big enough for me."

" Why not big enough for both, Peter? You asked me why I came, and I'll tell you. I got a chance of going in charge of an invalid to Paris. Being at Paris, I tried my luck at getting something to do, and found my luck as unreasonable as usual. Coming back, I thought I'd give you a look up. Don't think I've come to beg of you, though, Peter; nor to rob you, for if I took any more of your money, old fellow, it would be nothing short of robbery ; curse me if it would. I've got enough to get back to London, and then I can do the same as I've done before, I daresay. Good-bye, I'm off."

Mr. Joseph rose as he spoke, wiped something from his eye, and moved towards the door. As he reached it his brother, with an effort, called upon him to stop.

" You are not going away like that," said he. " I have managed to save a pound or two lately which I thought I might want presently, but you can have them. You can repay me if you get on. You must go back to London, though, and try once more, and I'll manage somehow to let you have something to keep you going. Here—here's the money."

" Upon my soul I don't like taking it," said Mr. Joseph, with manly emotion, at the same time pocketing the gold. " But you shall have it back—every penny— with interest. At any rate I wont stop here to be in your way. I'll leave the town this very night. I suppose there's a coach. No, Peter, you need not fear that your brother will come between you and your good fortune. I'm a poor unlucky devil, but that can't be helped. It's my own fault, perhaps. Some people say so, anyhow. Well, good-bye. I'll be out of the town in an hour's time."

" Stop," said the professor, " I will show you an hotel where you can sleep for the night. The diligence goes to-morrow afternoon. I will see you between this and then, and we will have some conversation about your future prospects."

" As you like, Peter," replied Joseph. " It ain't a cheerful subject. Don't let me drag you out, though, to-night."

Mr. Polyblank had some misgivings, however, respecting the prudence of allowing Mr. Joseph to see any more of the people downstairs, and therefore saw him off the premises, and only left him when safely lodged in the " Three Crowns." Next day the professor was unexpectedly detained at the college, and did not reach the hotel until just after the diligence had started. He went into the booking-office, and as the list of passengers was lying upon the desk, referred to it without asking any questions. Indeed there was no reason why he should make useless inquiries. There, sure enough, was the name of Polyblank ; and with a sigh of relief, with which was blended no small amount of grief and remorse at having sent his brother away so abruptly, and, as it might seem, unkindly, he slowly retraced his steps. He had suffered severely from Mr. Joseph's little games, and there could be no doubt that he would have suffered again had he remained in the town.

Unlike his brother Peter, this gentleman had been born a genius, and could not be expected to work and plod after the style of ordinary, every-day sort of people. From his birth upwards great things had been expected of him, and were in certain circles expected still; although, thus far, he had never exactly arrived at any result calculated to justify the expectation. Not that Joseph was destitute of ability, but irregular habits and want of application generally prevented him from turning his talents to any account. Nor was he without a certain amount of scientific knowledge, but it was unmethodized and undigested, so that he could rarely turn it to any practical purpose : in this resembling a man who, possessing a collection of useful articles, keeps them jumbled together confusedly in a room, and is never able to find any particular one when he happens to want it. Joseph Polyblank was never more happy than when he had an opportunity of performing some daring feat in his profession of a surgeon, and would gladly volunteer his assistance, which sometimes proved useful, in cases that presented features of a novel character; but as to regular and constant application to business, that was what Joe never condescended to.

He was a great projector, and had been connected with several public companies, which, somehow or other, had come to grief. While Peter had been labouring hard, Joe had been launching into grand schemes from which a colossal fortune was always just about to be realised, when unforeseen circumstances occurred which nobody could possibly have guarded against. There were times when Joseph had been almost too fine a gentleman to associate with Peter. Indeed, Society demanded, as it were, that as a rising man he should maintain a certain position, which connexions like Peter would to some extent have jeopardized. At other times, however, he was most affable, and even condescended to accept small loans from his humble relative, which were not repaid with remarkable regularity. There were actually persons who did not scruple to call the jovial Joseph a heartless scoundrel; and other hard words had been broken over him by those who had fallen victims to his joviality.

To Peter, of all others in the world, he had probably behaved the worst, and yet for all his faults there was still something very much akin to love for him in his brother's heart. Therefore was it that sitting that night in his lonely bedroom, the schoolmaster felt very sad, drank his tea with anything but a relish, and was wholly unable to settle down to his English classic. The English classic was, under ordinary circumstances, rather a dry old person, though with a style of diction allowed to be faultless, and this evening the Professor hardly felt equal to grappling with him. Somehow, as he sat there book in hand, a young face rose up between him and the page. It was the face of little Joey—long years ago—when he was only just beginning to develope into a genius, and singed off his own and Peter's eyebrows by daring experiments with gunpowder in the back yard of their home in Church-walk, Lambeth. Throwing down his book, he walked about the room, and, opening the window, leant upon the sill and watched the stray foot-passengers as they went clattering past in the dim lamp-light on the pavement of the street below. But here the sound of a child sobbing again recalled to his mind the young brother he used to play with in that dear old time so long ago, and he closed the window with a sigh.

"Poor Joe!" he said; "poor Joe, I am very, very sorry we parted as we did. I am sorry I did not give him some more money, too. I might very well have spared a little more by just pinching a bit."

Under the circumstances he thought he would go to bed ; he felt so low-spirited and unsettled.

" Joe would take a pipe if he felt dull," the Professor reflected : " but I was always, as Joe used to say, too much of a milksop to learn to smoke, and it would only make me ill if I were to attempt it now; so instead I'll try and go to sleep."

He undressed himself thus pondering, and paused before the looking-glass to contemplate the reflection of his thin face, garnished with a long-tasselled night-cap.

" I've. not acted like a brother," he said half aloud ; " Joe's had his troubles, poor fellow, as well as I have. Perhaps, after all, he might have done well here if he had been steady. If I could have been sure he would not break out again and drag us both down, as he had done before—God grant he may get on well where he has gone."

The Professor blew out the candle and got into bed after this, and laid his head upon the pillow. But as he did so the sounds of harmony from the streets below smote upon his ear. It was harmony born of strong drink, and a loud but not unmusical voice was chanting words familiar to his English ear. " We wont go home till morning " was the burthen of the minstrel's song, and his voice was not unknown to Mr. Polyblank, who sat up in astonishment to listen.

" Bong swore," he heard his brother Joe bawling out in his celebrated Brummagem French. " Bong swore, mussoo. Vows bong ongfong. Moy aussy bong ong-fong. Faites pas erreur. Bong swore, et donnez mes complimong à madame voter bong dam."

He was bidding good-night to no less a person than Mr. Pomponney, whom he had brought home somewhat

the worse for spirituous refreshment.   After all, then,
he had not gone by the diligence, and the brothers need
not be parted.

CHAPTER XI.

MIRACLES, ETC.

Cependant je ne saurais croire
Que tous les hommes sont ainsi ;
Il en est d'autres, Dieu merci !—Houssot.

THE rise and progress of the jovial Joseph were as surpris-
ingly rapid as his unlucky brother Peter's were slow and
painful.   To begin with : he, right off, had become the
bosom friend of Mr. Pomponney.   "A man, of talent,
madam," was Mr. Pomponney's expressed opinion, when
talking to the wife of his bosom—"a man of undoubted
talent combined with social qualifications of a surpris-
ingly high order—a thing utterly incomprehensible to
me in a native of his country."   Under the influence of
these qualifications, before the two gentlemen had known
each other forty-eight hours, the worthy chemist was led
into unwonted excesses at the "Café Leduc," upon the
Little Place, where Joseph, almost from the first hour he
crossed its threshold, became a notability.   "Ohé, garçon,
du punch !" he was wont to cry in those days of magni-
ficence which shall presently arrive, and when he shall
have made rapid strides in the French language.   "Un
punch flamboyant et soigné—un punch au kirch."

Yet further off, however, in the misty future, the now
radiant waiter shall observe, with a disparaging shrug of
his shoulders, and he talks in confidence to the "patron,"
"Quelle fichue pratique," meaning none other than the
erst jovial—and shall add with a contemptuous smile,

" Il a trouve un jobard qui lui paie un Boek." By which it would almost appear as though Joseph would be seen through, in those bad times coming. Be that as it may, he was at starting a great success, and his name and fame soon spread far and wide ; for before he had passed a night in Saint Babylas he had effected a miracle. After all was it to be wondered at ? He had ever been on the point of doing the desirable something, had not some untoward event occurred to prevent it. The world would have been upside down before this, and the Thames long ago burnt out, if he had had half anybody else's luck. However, it now seemed as though his luck had come at last.

The very first night he passed under Madame Gobinard's roof one of that lady's most esteemed guests had an apoplectic attack. The nearest doctor, Tominet by name, who was sent for in a violent hurry, came running to the scene of action half dressed, and three-parts asleep, forgetting in his hurry to bring his case of instruments with him. While he was giving directions to Alexander to run to his house with all speed for a lancet, Joe Polyblank abruptly broke in with a suggestion.

" Why not throw some cold water over him ?" he said.

" Because it would do no good," replied Tominet, impatiently.

" I'll show you whether it wont," said Joe, and rushed for a bucket.

" You'll kill him," said Tominet.

" I'll cure him," said Joe ; and sure enough to Tominet's disgust, and the wonder of the lookers on, he was as good as his word.

Next day another miracle. One Lardois, a master builder, having mounted to the highest point of the

scaffolding outside a house in course of erection, while
swearing himself black in the face at the want of skill
in his workmen, tripped himself up, and came down
from the first floor into the street, where he lay among
the soft mortar very white and bloody.   Picked up insensible, he was carried into the " Three Crowns," which
was close at hand, and medical aid immediately called in.
This time Tominet, who came under protest, brought his
lancet with him and let blood in profusion, but without
restoring the builder to consciousness.   Doctor Cancoin
also, assisting, felt the patient all over, and pinched and
poked him back and front, as connoisseurs at a cattle
show do the prize beasts, finally pronouncing his bones
unbroken.   But yet Lardois remained insensible. Under
these circumstances, blood-letting doing no good, other
more or less violent measures were resorted to without
any satisfactory result.

At this stage of the proceedings Madame Gobinard
suggested sending for the English doctor, upon which
Cancoin, rising with a shriek, and Tominet rising speech-
less, they moved towards the door. Having been pacified,
however, they kindly stayed to make further experiments,
retiring at length with a promise to return shortly, and
leaving behind them strict orders that the patient should
not be disturbed ; though if by that they meant he must
not be brought back to consciousness, there seemed but
little chance of such an occurrence.   But when they
were gone, the jovial Joseph chancing to stroll into the
hotel court-yard, cigar in mouth, Madame Gobinard could
not refrain from asking him his opinion. Joseph listened
attentively to what had been done, then flung away his
cigar, and went and stared hard at the patient.   After
which, says he, " Send for the barber."

" The barber !" echoed Madame Gobinard, who thought

perhaps these words signified that Lardois' case was hopeless, and nothing remained but to prepare the toilet of death.

" To be sure," continued Joe, without noticing her surprise. " I want to have his head shaved, so that I can have a good look at it."

This proposition rather startled the good lady. With his head shaved there would be no concealing from the other doctors the fact that the patient had been meddled. with by an interloper. However, she determined that it should be done, having some vague notion of afterwards concealing the deed in a nightcap. But there was no occasion for this, as things turned out. The great Joe, when the barber had done his work, applied himself to making a very minute examination of Lardois' bare cranium, and with the aid of a pair of nippers effected the second miracle ; for scarcely had he withdrawn his hand than the master builder, with a deep sigh, opened his eyes, and presently, to the relief of all beholders, began to swear again as naturally as ever. It was a splinter which had penetrated the skull, and just reached the brain, and, being removed, Richard was himself again, and Joseph partook of liquor at his expense.

The third miracle, though, was yet to come ; and this time no less a person than the Mayor of Saint Babylas benefited by Joe Polyblank's science. A worthy man was Monsieur Tête, a bachelor and bon vivant, whose only fault, perhaps, was a want of self-restraint in the matter of eating and drinking. Chancing upon the second night of Joe's stay in the town, to give a little dinner to two other bons-vivants, he ate, among other trifles, three parts of a goose, and went to bed about eleven, saying his head felt heavy. Just before one, he began to cry out in his sleep, and to struggle, and pant, and claw at the bedclothes. At last, with a hoarse cry, he fought his way back to consciousness, crawled out of bed, and staggered across the floor.

" I'm choking," he gasped, tearing at his neck-band as he spoke.

With difficulty then he helped himself to a glass of water, but having raised it to his lips was unable to drink. He seized the bell-rope, and, dragging at it furiously, brought it down in his hand. Yet nobody seemed to hear him. With an overwhelming fear upon him that he would die there alone in the dark, he made for the window, and in his dressing-glass on the table, reflected by the faint moonlight, caught a glimpse of a purple and swollen face, bearing a horrible and distorted resemblance to his own, from which he started back in terror. His legs seemed to bend and give way beneath him, but he managed to reach the window somehow, and with what strength yet remained to him, got it open. One o'clock was a very late hour for Saint Babylas, and the most irregular were accustomed to seek their couches shortly after midnight, whilst the really good folks were abed and snoring at ten. Rolling up the street, however, upon that particular occasion, was a bacchanalian, musically inclined, to whom Mr. Tête cried out, in a choking voice, for medical aid.

This bacchanalian was, of course, the jovial Joseph, returning to the " Three Crowns" after seeing safe home his esteemed friend Pomponney. Responsive to the call of Monsieur Tête, he made a violent assault upon the door-bell; explained to the sleepy porter that there was an old gentleman upstairs, in his nightshirt, bawling for a doctor; and, after a desperate struggle, reached the Mayor's bedchamber just in time to save his life. It was a great stroke of luck this, and jovial Joe, considerably to his own surprise this time, found he was on the high road to fortune. No longer after,.indeed, than the following day, the master builder, shaking hands with him, left a bank note in Joseph's palm, which was so extremely liberal in amount that the doctor thought the builder must have made a mistake, and passed the next hour or two in an uneasy apprehension of his wanting it back again.

Two days afterwards, the Mayor sending for Joseph asked him whether he was open to an engagement, and upon that gentleman's professing a general openness for anything, offered him the appointment, then vacant, of medical superintendent of the Imperial College. The result of this interview was that our professor, walking meekly next day along one of the vaulted passages of the abode of learning, met his brother Joseph swaggering as though the place belonged to him; and then, for the first time, he heard the astonishing news—hearing which he groaned inwardly, for he knew a good deal more than Monsieur le Maire about his medical relation, and knew also that he could kill as well as cure. To begin with, however, surely nothing could have been more gratifying to Joseph's brother than Joseph's progress in popularity. Mr. Roustoubique, it is true, regarded with some distrust the advent of the new doctor, fancying that there was a conspiracy on the part of the Polyblanks to obtain entire predominant power in the college. But, in spite of Mr. Roustoubique, Joe, in his loud-voiced, blustering style, carried all before him. He was the jolliest doctor there had ever been within the school gates. He ordered wine for boys in the infirmary, and prescribed roast chicken and rich soup, as though he had been dealing with no more expensive food than hasty pudding and skillygolee. Coming, for the first time in his life, upon the famous tisane*— the panacea of the ailing of all classes among our lively neighbours—he smelt at it, sipped at it, pulled a wry face over it, and flung the contents of the basin out of window into the yard.

"Cochonerie !" he called it, which was as near "pigs' wash" as his knowledge of the language enabled him to get.

His views upon things in general rather startled the infirmary nurse, as indeed did the frequenters of the "Café Leduc," his wholesale denunciation of what he called the antiquated bungling of Martinet, Andral, Meckel, Morgagni, Rouchoux, and indeed most other well-known authorities. Out of doors he worked several cures more or less surprising, and, fortunately for him, all his patients lived through the somewhat desperate experiments which he remorselessly carried out at their expense. As he worked for poor people gratuitously, there was a mania for doctor's stuff in some of the back streets, and consequently Joe, who had no idea of ruining himself, went in heavily for bread pills and bottles of a mixture of which aq. pur. formed the staple. As this course of medicine killed nobody—nature lending a helping hand at the same time—quite as satisfactory a result was arrived at as though the mostly costly drugs had been employed. Every now and then, by sheer good luck, our jovial friend effected a fresh miracle, which Mr. Pomponney—now the friend of his bosom—duly recorded in the "Faits Divers" of the *Saint Babylas Gazette,* to which he was an able and esteemed contributor.

Notable among these cures was the case of the wife of a cabaretier, without the walls of the town, who had unfortunately swallowed some aquatic monster in a draught from the pump, which monster in due course attaining

---

* Tisane ; a decoction of which the chief ingredients are Spanish liquorice, barley, and dog's grass.

alarming proportions, became the torment of an otherwise tranquil existence.   Mr. Joseph having fortunately
succeeded in delivering her from this unpleasant companionship, his fame spread, through the medium of the
Gazette, far and wide ; and Tominet, Cancoin, and Co.,
gnashed their teeth with envious rage at Joe's success.
Besides physicking them gratuitously, he won the hearts
of the poor of Saint Babylas by one or two highly dramatic episodes, in which he showed himself a true artiste.
One market-day an old beggar-woman was knocked
down by a countryman's cart and killed on the spot.
Joe was fetched from his café hard by, and came running
up in his usual impetuous manner, dropping down upon
his knees on the ground reckless of the mud, and calling
to the people about to stand back and give the woman
air.   But when he had glanced at her face and felt her
pulse he dropped her head, looking very serious, and
rose slowly to his feet.   A little girl also, regardless of
the mud, knelt by the dead woman's side, looking frightened and crying noiselessly.

"Is she your mother ?" Joe asked.

Being answered in the affirmative, and furthermore
informed that she had no other relatives in the world,
the doctor exclaimed, "We'll see what can be done for
you, then."   With that he thrust his hand into his
trousers' pocket, and dragging out a handful of silver
and copper flung it into his hat, and straightway went
round amongst the crowd begging for contributions, a
proceeding which though to some extent distasteful to the
uncharitable in the front row, to whom escape was out of
the question, gained the doctor enormous popularity after
it was over, particularly among those who were not there
at the time, and had not been called upon to give anything.

All this was very delightful, but yet the professor was

uneasy in his mind.   As has been previously observed, he knew Joseph.   He had seen him set sail before to-day with the fairest winds and brightest of skies, but before long a squall had invariably sprung up.   Upon this occasion, as we shall see, a regular hurricane was preparing, but in the meanwhile the jovial Joseph was in the best of spirits.

CHAPTER XII.

WHAT MIGHT HAVE BEEN.

Ere yet she spak I could espy
  A flutterin' at her breast;
But whether 'twas wi' grief or joy
  I gat nae time to guess't.—YOUNG.

THE sufferings of Professor Polyblank were not over, but just beginning.   In the college affairs began to assume a gloomy aspect.   Ronstoubique's hatred for the jovial Joseph daily increased, and his wrath falling harmlessly upon the doctor, rebounded again with redoubled force upon the head of the unhappy Peter.   Surely never " since Adam was a lad" were boys to be found so imp-ishly inclined as those young gentlemen in the imperial establishment, and the amount of ingenuity expended in preparations for the professor's torments rivalled, on a small scale, the diabolical contrivances of the Inquisi-tion.   Even those famous evenings at Longanna were not quite as happy as they used to be, for reasons hereunder given.

During the course of the first half dozen or so of les-sons there never was a more diligent scholar than the pretty baroness, and the quantity of cream-laid notepaper consumed in the copying and re-copying of exercises quite astonished the Saint Babylas stationer at whose shop it was purchased. But after a time Manon very naturally grew tired of her new employment, and when the professor asked for an exercise, he got instead some shallow excuse, so prettily spoken though, that no living male creature could have hesitated to receive it. And when these excuses coming at last to be a matter of everyday occurrence, the professor looked grave and shook his head in gentle reproof of such blackslidings, the prettiest little penitential expression in the world compelled him to forgive the fair young culprit, who promised amendment with a readiness which was only equalled by her systematic neglect when Polyblank's back was turned. But though he might pretend to look severe, and in reality felt somewhat hurt at this wholesale neglect of his instructions, yet when the make-belief lesson was over he never failed to regain his good humour at the supper-table, and many a time, as we have seen, went carolling homewards across the marshes as merrily as might be.

Meanwhile, however, the thunderbolt was forging and fell thus:—Coming in one evening more quietly than usual, the professor unintentionally overheard a small portion of a conversation between Mr. Pomponney and his Félicité.

" It certainly is a strange fancy of the baroness," said Félicité, " to want to learn English."

" It's absurd," said Mr. Pomponney; " but as far as Polyblank's concerned, he probably has no objection."

" Of course it is his business to teach those who wish to take lessons," said Félicité.

" To be sure it is," said Mr. Pomponney; "and whether they learn or not I suppose it doesn't much matter."

" But don't you think——"

"I don't think anything; but one thing I am certain of."

"And that is——"

"Polyblank is not nearly as thin as he used to be."

The professor noiselessly mounted the stair, carefully closed his door, and sat down with his head in his hands at the table. Was it possible that people could thus misinterpret his motives? Was the cruel slander prompted by malice, or was this the view of the case which would most naturally occur to anybody's mind? Was it the general opinion that he went to Longanna only for the sake of what he could get to eat, pocketing at the same time the ill-gotten gold which Manon gave him out of charity? Was that what people thought—and was it far from the truth? He went at once to look at himself in the glass. He certainly did not seem to be quite as thin as he had been once; but his figure even now would not have struck a casual observer as by any means robust. No, in all conscience he was yet sufficiently lean to furnish a refutation to the slander.

But though he knew that Pomponney's statement was a libel, a blush of shame suffused the honest schoolmaster's face when his mind reverted to those gay little suppers at which he had, it must be confessed, never failed to partake freely of the good cheer provided. There was one thing, however, about which he soon made up his mind. That very night he would tell the baroness the lessons must cease unless——But no, there was no chance of that. She never would learn anything. It had all along been a game of play, and it would be disgraceful on his part to pocket another napoleon or eat another supper. He had no appetite for his tea, and was in a fever until the time arrived for him to set out. All the way to Longanna he rehearsed the speeches he intended to make, and half a score of times at least buttoned and unbuttoned his threadbare body-coat in his agitation.

"I must have been as blind as a bat. I must have been a dolt and a fool not to have seen it all before this," he said to himself. "She has asked me there out of charity, and fed me because she thought I was starving."

His face flushed with rage and shame when he thus reflected. The crime of poverty is such a disgraceful one; it cannot be defended. Excuses may perhaps be found for manslaughter or robbery, but how are you to explain that you can't afford to have your boots mended, or buy new ones?

"I am a poor fool," he went on thinking; "I know nothing of the world—nothing of human nature. I am as helpless as a child. I'm all thumbs. I know nothing —nothing but what is useless. I can't get a living out of teaching. Now, Joe would not have been so blind; Joe would have seen through the whole affair at once, and——" However he did not care to pursue this train of thought, for past experience told him that if the jovial Joseph had once got his nose into such snug quarters, and therein taken root, it would have been as difficult to get rid of him as a ten years' growth of horse-radish from a kitchen garden. When the professor arrived at the door of the château he was all in a heat, but his mind was made up, and his sentences prepared. Only the worst of it was that Manon, on that very identical day, was a great deal prettier and more bewitching than usual. When he arrived he found her sitting under the shadow of a far-spreading yew-tree in the garden, and wearing a lovely little straw hat trimmed with blue ribbon, which made her look like one of those pretty shepherdesses Watteau painted. She rose up to meet him with a bright smile, and a flutter of dainty white petticoats, suggestive of a gale among the sails of a fleet.

"Ah! you cannot think how glad I am to see you, Mr. Polyblank," she said, in that frank child-like way she had—after all she was hardly anything but a child, in spite of her being a widow. "I had no idea it was so late, and I do so want something to amuse me."

Perhaps she might have used other words which, as a schoolmaster, he would have preferred to hear; but of what value are words? A pretty woman talks, and who among male listeners cares for the sense, or notices that she trips in her logic? The music of a sweet voice is pleasant to hear, whether the song be in high Italian or low Dutch. The professor, indeed, scarce heard aright the words she uttered. The sunshine of her bright eyes bewildered him. He knew just this much, that she was glad to see him, and he was very happy in her presence. She had that morning purchased a glass case of ugly aquine monsters, with very hard names, to add to her already large stock of domestic pets, and she now took the professor to look at them, and to beg him to tell her what they were called. Much information upon the subject he very eagerly furnished, and she repeated each name after him with that profoundly serious expression which she was in the habit of assuming upon such occasions, declaring herself highly gratified by her recently acquired knowledge, which flew out of her head five minutes afterwards.

The water creatures disposed of, some newly-purchased bulbs demanded the professor's polite attention, and then something else; and after that other things; and then a sudden twinge of conscience seized him, and he said—

"About the lesson?"

At this, Manon laughed merrily.

"To be sure," she said, "about the lesson. But I've been learning Latin to-day, haven't I? Let me see now, what was it? Anemo-thingembobs, zoophy-whats-their-names! Why, I feel already quite half as learned as M. Louis Figuier."

"But," said Polyblank, weakly struggling, "we are to have a lesson in English to-night, are we not? A short one?"

"It must be very short if it is to take place before supper," snapped the Dubosq. There was nothing in life that vexed this worthy woman more than the postponement of meals; for she possessed, in common with every well-regulated female mind, a rooted antipathy to the derangement of the great business of life for other less important matters, such as reading the last page of an interesting chapter, or employing the last available five minutes in writing to catch the post—as it is the habit of the superior animal to do when he has his own way. At the mention of supper, however, the professor felt his face grow red.

"I—I am afraid you must excuse me this evening," he stammered, in reply to the baroness's invitation.

"Excuse you!" she repeated, in surprise.

"I—I promised to return early."

"It is very early yet. Besides, you just now were going to stop to give me a lesson."

This, of course, was the opportunity which you would have seized on, had you been in the professor's place, to give this absurd little ex-actress a piece of your mind. But the worst of Polyblank was his being so slow. He felt that the time had come when he ought to speak, and the only difficulty was what to say. He felt afraid of rashly saying anything that might offend or be misunderstood. The sentences which he had rehearsed upon the road would not fit in well under existing circumstances. Hesitating, he was lost, and—oh! that it should be

9

written, and this pen have to write it—he stopped to supper! But going home he made his mind up.

He rehearsed no more sentences, because that would have been waste of time. Now he had formed a much more sensible plan. There were such things in the world as pen and ink and paper. In his own room, when her eyes were not upon him, he could be "bloody, bold, and resolute," and he would write the baroness a letter and resign his appointment as instructor. You must allow that this was a very proper determination to arrive at, and we will not, if you please, insinuate a doubt that he would not have carried it out, had not an unforeseen and extraordinary event occurred to prevent him.

On the doorstep of Mr. Pomponney's house he met his brother Joe. His brother Joe was a constant visitor at the chemist's. Very often, for hours together, he and Mr. Pomponney would be closeted in a little upstairs room, which the chemist grandly called "the laboratory." They were supposed to be on the point of arriving at some highly-important chemical results, and their operations had occasioned more than one explosion, which filled with terror the unscientific Felicité, who devoutly hoped Joe would not get her Hippolite into trouble.

"Well, Peter," was the jovial Joseph's remark, "you're earlier than usual, aren't you?"

"Than usual!" repeated the professor, rather uneasily. "I didn't know that I was earlier."

The jovial Joseph looked at him very hard and laughed, tapping the professor lightly on the chest as he did so.

"You're all there, Peter," said he; "and not bad either, for such a quiet old card as you are."

"I don't understand," said the professor, more uneasily still. "What do you mean?"

"Come, I like that, Peter," retorted Joe; "but you can't deceive me, you know. Besides, everybody says so. Ask Pomponney there."

"I don't understand," repeated the Professor.

"Oh, you lamb and mint sauce!" continued Joseph, with playful raillery; "as if we didn't know all about it. Lessons in English, eh! Not such a bad game either. She has ever so many thousands a year, though, mind you, and it would be rather a better spec. than school-mastering. I only wish she had taken a fancy to me."

"You talk like a fool," cried Polybank, in violent agitation, and left him without another word.

Presently he found himself in his own room, though whether he performed the upstairs journey on his head or his heels he would have had some trouble in determining for the next half-hour or so. For half-an-hour good he sat bolt upright in the dark, his eyes fixed upon a swaying lamp in the street below. Who shall say what was the nature of his thoughts! Peter, the wild boy, was doubtless much surprised when first he met a lady. A gentleman who had spent the first thirty-six years of his life filling his head with stores of Greek and Latin, and neglecting sentiment and the ladies, was necessarily unprepared for such an emergency as the present.

"Nonsense!" he exclaimed aloud, when he had sat there silently staring at the oil lamp, as before stated, for a period extending over thirty minutes. Then he arose, lit a match, and went to look at himself in the mirror. "Nonsense!"

There he was sure enough, much as he expected to find himself—that is to say, rather grim and worn; not exactly the sort of person you would have supposed a rich and pretty young lady likely to fall in love with. And yet young ladies, often enough, have conceived a tender

passion for their elders, and Mr. Polyblank had read of
such cases in ancient and modern history. Why she
should have selected him, when the wide world was over-
running with others who would have been only too
eager to secure her favour, was a problem difficult of solution; but, after all, what mattered the why and where-
fore? He, Peter Polyblank, was beloved by a baroness—
had probably been beloved ever so long; and, like a bat
and a dolt and a fool, had never perceived it.

"If it had been Joe, now," he reflected. But again he
did not choose to follow out this train of thought, for he
did not like to think of Manon as Joe's wife, which, without a doubt, she would have been long ago, had she given
that energetic person a hundredth part of the encourage-
ment it was now evident she had vouchsafed to his brother.
Was it true, though? He felt very uncomfortable when
he put the question to himself point blank, and—pinning
himself, as it were, in a corner—argued the matter out
with a determination to stand no nonsense. Certainly,
it was much more reasonable to suppose that this was the
motive which prompted the baroness to invite him so frequently to the château than that she did it out of charity.
It was certainly more gratifying to think that his society
was agreeable than that he was an object of commise-
ration. But how to be assured on this delicate point?
To what quarter could he turn for counsel and instruction?

His favourite Horace had remarked on the desire that
every piâ mater feels for the enlightenment of her offspring,
and perhaps Peter's mother might have given him some
good advice if she had lived long enough. Now, had he
gone in for some of those exciting French novelettes
which he saw so many of in the window next door,
"format in 18-Jésus," he might have acquired some know-

ledge on the subject. But then did not Seneca, or some one in his name say :—

> " —Quis sapiens bono
> Confidat fragile ?"

He had his subsistence to earn, and never expected to have a young, pretty, and rich French baroness, fall in love with him ; and so, as the saying is, " had not come provided." Now, could he have managed it, he would willingly have foregone a little of his classical learning to acquire some knowledge of the rudiments of the language fo love. But these remarks need not be prolonged, for has not this same story been already told, over and over again ? The poor professor, however, was not aware that he was only acting a part in a silly old drama with which the world had long ago grown weary. Of course silly boys and girls may be excused for indulging in some absurdities when first they find out that they have got such things as hearts ; but better things surely might have been expected of a man of intellect, thirty-six years old, who earned his bread by the instruction of youth.

He went to bed that night and rolled and tumbled, but never slept a wink. " Fiends in shape of boys " strove vainly next day to arouse him from his dreams. He walked about, all unconscious, with a long paper tail dangling behind him, and a toy cannon, let off in the middle of his class, scarcely awakened him from his reverie. Somehow, though, things went smoother that day than they usually did. It was hot, idle weather, and the insects hummed in the air at the open window, suggestive of lassitude and repose. Young France was drowsy, and lay with his head upon his desk. The professor's thoughts were elsewhere, and with his chin in his hand he sat and pondered, all unconscious of the progress

of time.   There was no Roustoubique that day, and so
life, on the whole, was endurable.   Yet when school hours
were run through the professor was very glad.

He hurried home and made a most elaborate toilet,
pressing into the service a long-ago forsaken Kerseymere
waistcoat adorned with monstrous sprigs.   For the first
time in his life, it occurred to him that perhaps he was
a little out of date in the cut of his coats.   Then, having
brushed himself scrupulously, he set off for the château of
Longanna.   He did not exactly know what he was going
to do when he got there ; for it was not one of his regular nights.   Half way there he pulled up short to ask
himself whether it were wise to go uninvited; but you
may be sure he found a sufficient excuse for doing so.
If things were as they were represented to be, she would
be   glad   to   see   him.   If   not,   he   could   make   some
excuse for having intruded, and retire.   Oh, it was all
admirably planned ;   and   he was—don't you think ?—a
very ingenious gentleman.   When he reached the house
he was shown into the drawing-room.

Left alone, he gazed around upon the articles the
apartment contained like one who had recently come into
possession of the property, and he regarded with quite a
new sort of interest the pictures hanging on the walls—
the   terrestrial   " Paradise of Prud'hom," Meissonier's
" Dancing Lesson," and a forest piece by Theodore
Rousseau.   He sat down upon a soft velvet couch and
contemplated at his ease the costly elegance surrounding
him, and while so occupied let fall his hand, which rested
accidentally upon an object lying by his side.   He took
it up and examined it.   It was a cigar case very beautifully worked in beads, which, now he came to think
about it, he had seen Manon engaged upon some days
ago.   On the side of it was embroidered the name of

Pierre. Now you who know that Pierre is the French of Peter can imagine what must have been the feelings of our Peter upon making this discovery.

It is true that he did not smoke. He had never had time to waste in that way, or no doubt he would have acquired the habit; but it made his heart bump violently to think that those dear little fingers had been so busy on his account. Had she made instead a pair of skates or a pair of stilts he would have tried to make use of them, and what could be more easy than to learn to smoke? It certainly was an odd gift when he came to think of it, because he distinctly remembered telling her he did not indulge in the fragrant weed; but then it was evident she admired smoking in men, and had determined that he should share her taste; which he resolved he would do, cost him what agony it might.

Presently, as he sat there, smiling contentedly, he heard Manon's voice in the garden, and walked towards the window to meet her. She was coming across the lawn towards him; but was not, as he at first supposed, talking to Madame Dubosq. A tall, handsome young man occupied that lady's place, up into whose eyes she was looking with an expression which somehow seemed quite different from any he had seen upon her face before when she had looked at him. This young man did not seem altogether unknown to him, although at the moment he could not call to mind where they had met before. As the couple drew near, however, the truth flashed upon him. It was that mysterious stranger he had met at the "Three Crowns" upon the night of his arrival in Saint Babylas. At the same instant he recollected that he had several times heard the ladies speaking of a Mr. Raynal, who must certainly be the person now before him.

While the professor stood spell-bound, hidden from their sight behind the Venetian blind, the young couple came to a standstill within a couple of yards of him, and once more was the unhappy Polyblank doomed to hear a portion of a conversation not intended for his ears.

"And what have you been doing all day?" asked the young man, Raynal.

"I have been working very hard, sir," replied the lady.

"At what?" he asked.

"At something for you—you recollect—but, no, you recollect nothing. However, whether you remember or not, I promised you, long ago, a cigar-case of my own manufacture. I have been toiling, sir, like a slave, to finish it, and it is done; and presently, sir, if you are good, you shall see it; and, perhaps—but that's not likely, for you are sure to do something to offend me before the evening is over—you may take it away in your pocket."

"It is very kind of you to think of me when I am away," said Raynal, sinking his voice. "I don't deserve it."

Her eyes were fixed upon the ground, and she did not raise them when she spoke again, which was not, this time, in the playful tone she had used a moment ago.

"I hope I shall never forget my old friends," she said.

"Sometimes I wish to Heaven I could," he rejoined, with a slight tremor in his voice. "It makes me hate myself, and all the world, when I think what is and what might have been."

"Oh, Pierre!" she said, looking up to him with tears in her eyes, "if you would only tell me what makes you unhappy. If you would only let me help you. I don't suppose I could help you much, because, you know, I am not very clever; but, if you are in trouble, I might share your grief, and that always lightens sorrow, they say."

Oh, so earnestly she looked up into his face, as she spoke—his eyes the while averted! For just a moment he seemed hesitating, and as though about to reveal his secret; but quickly changing his mind, said, with a short laugh—

"My dear Manon, I have nothing to tell you. Don't fret about me, because I don't deserve it. I always was a miserable dog, and always shall be, I suppose. Never mind, let us go and look at the cigar-case."

The last words aroused the professor from a sort of trance into which he had fallen. Seizing his hat he made for the door, and, passing through, closed it behind him as they entered the room from the garden. As he crossed the court-yard he heard the Dubosq calling to him in the distance; but he made no reply. The old portress bobbed a curtsey to him; but he took no notice of her. Like one in a dream, he walked down the straggling street, and paused irresolutely when he reached a place where two roads met, one going to Saint Babylas, and the other due east—the way to England. While he stood thus the diligence approached, and the driver, supposing he wanted to get in, stopped his horses; but the professor, thus appealed to, stared at him unconsciously, and the driver, after taking in vain the names of a pipe and a dog and a little good man, whipped up his horses again, and laughed as he drove away. Polyblank observing his mirth, but being at a loss to account for it, cast his eyes down, and seeing the famous sprigged kerseymere, hastily buttoned his coat over it, and tramped away with his nose pointed westward.

CHAPTER XIII.

HAPPY AT LAST.

C'est l'amour, l'amour, l'amour,
Qui fait le monde à la ronde,
Et chaque jour à son tour
Le monde fait l'amour.
                              Les Orgues de Barbarie.

IT is often very difficult to trace a rumour to the fountain-head, and this appears to have been the case with one particular rumour, now to be treated of, which circulated in the town of Saint Babylas. At the chemist's shop the Dubosq had first heard it.

" So, madame, the baroness is going to marry Mr. Raynal."

Mr. Pomponney was sealing up a small packet of medicine which the Dubosq had purchased, and, as he dropped the boiling wax, he looked up with a beaming smile, and addressed the lady in the words just quoted. But the smile faded fast enough as his eyes encountered the look of indignant wonder upon that good lady's countenance.

" Who dares to say such a thing?" she demanded, in so awful a voice that Mr. Pomponney was seized with a trembling, and sealed his fingers instead of the packet. But it was necessary for him to reply to her question.

" Everybody," he answered.

" Who is everybody?" she persisted, with her spectacle glasses fixed unflinchingly upon him.

" Well, then, I heard it at the café."

" Who dares to make the Baroness de Grandvilain the subject of café talk?" the Dubosq inquired, growing more and more terrible.

" Nobody would venture to do such a thing, I'm sure," said the chemist soothingly, " in my presence. I should not dream of allowing it; but my friend Polyblank——"

" So, the professor told you, did he?"

" On the contrary—no," cried Mr. Pomponney. " It was the doctor I referred to—the brother of the professor, you know, and——"

" Enough!" exclaimed the Dubosq, and, rising, she swept out of the shop, leaving Pomponney dumbfoundered behind his counter. As for the Dubosq's private thoughts, had the cathedral of Saint Babylas suddenly turned a summersault and regained its position without displacing a single brick, she could not have been more startled than she was by the news she had just heard. Everybody said so, did they? while here was she, the lady's bosom friend—living under the same roof with her—who had never heard of it. Of course, it was wholly untrue—at least she hoped so, for it must be confessed that when she came to think the matter over, she did not feel quite comfortable. Therefore, determining to know the worst, she said, as soon as she got home, " My dear, do you know what everybody is saying?"

" No," replied Manon.

" I hardly like to tell you."

" Do tell me."

"Well, then—that you are going to marry Mr. Raynal."

Manon blushed and dropped her eyes; then looked up and smiled; then ran and clinging round the Dubosq's neck, kissed her again and again—then said, half crying and half laughing—

" How dare everybody say so, when it ought to have been kept a secret? Oh, my dear Mogador, I always meant that you should be the first that I would tell it to, and here actually everybody seems to know it as soon as I do myself."

The tears of joy which sparkled in pretty Manon's eyes somewhat obscured her sight, else must she certainly have noticed a surprising elongation of the good Dubosq's expressive countenance, while this communication was being made. Feeling that some such course of conduct was called for, under the circumstances, she bent her head forward and bestowed a short, sharp kiss on the baroness's forehead, which sounded not unlike the uncorking of a pickle bottle, and then jerked herself up straight again. But she did not say a word. She dared not venture upon a single sentence until several moments had elapsed, lest the tone of her voice should betray the rage and disappointment which possessed her. Luckily for her Manon required her to say nothing, but went on, eagerly telling the story of Raynal's proposal, and the probable date of the wedding, with the arrangements *in futuro*. In all she said she used the word " we ;" but that might mean her husband and herself, and the Dubosq listened in some anxiety, and at last managed to gasp out—

" When you are married, my dear, you wont want me."

" I shan't want you?" Manon cried in astonishment. " You are very much mistaken, my dear. I shall want you then a great deal more than I do now."

" No, no, my dear," replied the other in a tone of gentle resignation. " You think so now ; but you wont. No, I'm only in the way. Don't mind me, my dear ; I should be the last person in the world to stand between you and your happiness.

That was scarcely a wise speech, and, for the first time during the course of their friendship, a suspicion entered Manon's mind that her companion was not quite as unselfish as she might have been. At that moment, however, there came a loud, imperious ring at the bell, betokening Raynal's arrival, and so the conversation ended. What everybody had said was, upon this occasion, true enough. Raynal and Manon were to be married. Whatever reason he might have had for his former reserve existed no longer, and so Manon, at last, was to be wedded to the only man she had ever loved. But how describe this happy period, when all doubts were removed and the love she had so long coveted was hers! It is the general opinion that lovers are more interesting to one another than to a third person, and in the present case we labour under the extra disadvantage of having a widow for a heroine, which is, one would suppose, rather an unpopular character among unmarried lady readers.

Both the lady and gentlemen readers would, perhaps, hardly thank the writer were he to repeat verbatim all the sentimental speeches of the happy couple; and although some of their utterances must, of necessity, be introduced into this veracious history, it will be sufficient now to state, in a general way, that they loved one another and were happy. Somehow, though, the world is so constituted that everybody cannot be simultaneously in the enjoyment of unlimited bliss. Just at this identical time, when Manon was happy, mère Corbeau's rheumatism set in worse than ever.

While Manon dreamed away the joyous hours, mère Baldayroux lay groaning in her bed, sciatica having fast hold of her in its grip. Though the folks were usually in a bad way up the back lanes of Longanna, they never before were in such a very bad way as they were at this time, when Manon's sun shone brightly, and now she actually began to neglect them and stop at home, love-making, instead of going her usual rounds with wine and soup and such like—offering timely assistance, and listening to the long and harrowing tales of woe which were always in readiness for her ear. Just about this time, too, a circumstance occurred which much damaged the baroness's popularity. As the chief actors concerned do not figure in this story, the facts of the case may be thus briefly stated. A certain native of Saint Babylas had obtained permission from the baroness to erect a small manufactory at Longanna, it having been represented to her that its establishment would greatly benefit the poor population of the neighbourhood. She heartily gave her consent, and for some time, sure enough, the inhabitants of Longanna thought that they were all on the high road to make their fortunes; and, indeed, many families came from Saint Babylas and settled amongst them under a similar belief. But presently the factory was accidentally burnt down, and the proprietor, having neglected insurance, was ruined, and the speculation failed. Some unknown person set afloat a shameful rumour that the baroness had profited by this transaction. In reality she had been a great loser; but beyond the limits of the domestic drama virtue is not always triumphant. Half-famished men scowled at her from the doors of their hovels as she drove past in her carriage. There are times when it is a sufficient crime in poverty's eyes for a person to wear good clothes and go by smiling. And so this pretty lady came to be what is called " unpopular."

CHAPTER XIV.

CASTLES IN THE AIR.

But even as babes in dreams do smile,
And sometimes fall a-weeping,
So I awaked as wise this while
As when I fell a-sleeping.
Hey nonny, nonnoy, O.
The Shepherd Tonie.

You may be sure this was not a very happy time for the professor. For more than a week after that dreadful day of involuntary eavesdropping he kept away from the château; nor, indeed, was it very improbable that he would thenceforth have kept away for ever, had he not been specially invited. A great change had come over the spirit of the dream, he fancied, when again he entered the handsome drawing-room. He found a pair of men's gloves lying on the table, and to the owner he was presently introduced. Raynal was not, perhaps, as polite as he might have been. He knew English well, Manon said, but he did not attempt to converse in that language.

Polyblank watched him uneasily. Maybe it is somewhat difficult to see the merits of one who has cast us into the shade. The loved one's other lover it is as hard a matter to judge fairly of as it is to strike the happy medium respecting one's friend's wife—between absolutely hating and liking too well. What could she see in him? Polyblank asked himself, as he walked slowly home, reaching his door at last with the question yet unanswered. He did not sing on his way home that evening, and he did not return to Manon's until another invitation was sent to him. In the meanwhile rumours reached him, through Pomponneyian channels, of gay doings at Longanna—of the inauguration of the snipe season, by the arrival of some of the baroness's Parisian friends—and at last the professor was asked to meet some literary celebrities, whose acquaintance, Manon said, she was anxious the professor should make.

Of course, there are many tens of thousands of persons in the world for whom the eyes of society have no terrors —who are quite at their ease in the presence of their betters, or who perhaps acknowledge the existence of none better than themselves, and are, in their own true, honest, unbiassed opinion, as good as anybody—if not better; who keep the best of company, and yet keep their countenance. But there are other persons—poor-spirited creatures these, though, and hardly worthy of the notice of the superior class aforesaid—who are differently constituted; whose hearts palpitate in the company of strangers : who tread with timid and uncertain step when they go out into the world, and who are by nature so shame-faced and self-depreciatory, that they endow with a factitious superiority all who are unknown to them, and thus sometimes mistake shallow simpletons and impudent pretenders for wise men and high-bred people.

It is unnecessary to acquaint the reader, who by this time must be familiar with the character of a certain professor in the Imperial College of Saint Babylas, that sensations such as those last described agitated Mr. Polyblank's breast, when one evening, returning to his lodgings in the Street of the Priests, he found there awaiting him a little note in the handwriting of the baroness, which requested the pleasure of his company to dinner on the following Sunday, to meet certain brilliant stars from the literary and theatrical spheres of Paris. Nevertheless, he must go, and then came the question of wardrobe. If painful to you—well-born and wealthy reader—

a description of the pitiful makeshifts which poverty compelled our professor to resort to before he could resume the appearance which he felt to be necessary for the occasion, how humiliating to the writer of this history to record the petty contrivances to which his hero had recourse—the glazed edges secretly inked, and frayed edges skilfully pared, and so on.

Let us then be satisfied with the information that Mr. Polyblank sought the privacy of his own apartment, drew down his blind, did his little bits of tailoring, tinkering, and cobbling, and what not ; and in due course emerged into broad daylight, the wonder of all beholders—those beholders being Madame Pomponney, rolling pill-paste in the shop, and a blue-bloused urchin playing in the gutter. When Polyblank reached the château he found the stars already shining there.

First and foremost was the great Oscar Max, the world-famed theatrical critic of *Duchesne fils*—a prodigiously stout gentleman, with silvery locks and flowing white beard, who said but little save in the way of flattering comments upon his pretty hostess's wines and viands ; but laughed heartily at others' jokes. He had made his way, had Oscar, and was well to do—rarely using his pen now-a-days except in the deletion of excessive exuberance on the part of younger members of his staff. He was content with the crop of laurels which he had gathered, and over his excellent dinner every day listened, not unkindly, to the sanguine talk of the aspiring unfledged, who had yet their worlds to take by storm, and their societies to regenerate.

Very different from this well-fed philosopher was Alexis d'Abligny—tall, thin, sallow, back-bearded, and long-haired —the celebrated author of " Les Premiers Amours de M. Satan," a drama, which over there in the gay capital,

10

made its author's fortune ; although, over here, considerations of propriety precluded all idea of translation.
Wonderful was it to see the d'Abligny rolling his eyes and
his cigarette.   He lived almost entirely upon smoke.   It
was, he affirmed, meat and drink to him ; but it must be
confessed that it was not fattening.   It was interesting to
observe his proceedings.   A cigarette was manufactured,
with a snatch and a twist of his long fingers, and, while
smoking one, he was busy with the preparation of another
to follow, puffing away the while like a factory chimney.
An incredibly small number of hours would exhaust the
little Book of Job he carried with him in his waistcoat
pocket.   At his bachelor dinners he smoked between his
soup and fish, and so on between the other courses.   Occasionally he ate and smoked together.   He usually fell
asleep at night with a cigar in his mouth, and it was
popularly supposed that he went on smoking long after
slumber had overtaken him.   Besides smoking, however,
he did other things—for instance the "Premiers Amours ;"
also a long string of novels and novelettes, and some
brilliant articles in the newspapers.   Indeed, his consumption of ink almost equalled his consumption of
tobacco, and there were few subjects too vast or too
insignificant to escape the withering sarcasm for which
Alexis was so justly famous.

The third star was, more properly speaking, a little full
moon of a man, Paul Cherami, the farce writer, a jovial
spirit, who ate and drank and made merry, and knocked
off his couplets and calembours when he had nothing
better to do—who had always two or three things on at
two or three theatres, and two or three more in preparation ; but who, to all appearance, had nothing in the
world to employ his time, and to whom you could do no
greater service than bid him come and play, morn, noon,

and night, for all he seemed to want was some other idle
rogue to kill time with him.   Yet he too must have had
his working hours—this Cherami ; for jokers generally
find joking by the yard laborious.

The fourth celebrity was an Englishman, and it was
chiefly to meet him that the professor had been invited,
for though a very great man indeed in his own country,
his knowledge of the French language was limited.   He
was a London theatrical manager, who had made his
fortune by some lucky hits and long runs, and had come
over to Paris to look out for fresh pieces.   He was a very
important person this, though, owing to lingual difficulties, not quite as great over here as at home.   The
Parisian authors, knowing that he had made his fortune
in a theatre, not unnaturally perhaps imagined he must
be a man of histrionic talent ; and hearing that his line
was comedy, supposed that he might be humorous off
the stage as well as on it.   But in this they were quite
mistaken.   The manager was, indeed, a very common-
place person.   By some fatality, whenever he did try a
piece in which he himself performed he did it to empty
benches.   Upon some grounds, best known to himself,
he believed he was one of the most able because he was
one of the luckiest of London managers ; but yet it cannot be denied that after his first hit, and before achieving
his second, he tried very hard indeed to do something
else, about the success of which he himself felt quite
certain ; but being at the last ·moment prevented from
carrying out his intentions, the piece in question shut up
another person's theatre at which it was produced, and
forced the lessee to Basinghall-street.   Yet, in spite of
this, our manager had every confidence in himself, and,
to hear him talk, anybody would have been led to suppose that he really knew what he was talking about, and

10—2

that it was not by the veriest " fluke," he had become a
man of fortune, instead of remaining the third-rate actor
he had been for twenty years or so.

Mr. Polyblank found the gentlemen assembled in the
drawing-room, and almost immediately after his arrival
the servant announced the dinner, which was served in
an apartment with windows opening on to the lawn.

" I know we ought not to dine by daylight, Mr. Max,"
said the fair hostess; " but it is such a pity in the
country to send the sun to bed so many hours before his
time."

" That is more to favour the dinner than the diners,"
Max replied.   " Some rural roses put the sun to the
blush."

He bowed to the baroness as he said this and smiled
his sweetest.   His manner, though, struck the professor
as rather too familiar.   That of the other two French-
men also seemed open to the same objection.   Who were
these old friends he had never heard tell of, and how
long did they mean to stop ?   These reflections somewhat marred the pleasures of the table, as far as Mr.
Polyblank was concerned.   It was, however, a dinner to
be remembered.   The profusion and novelty of the dishes
were an unfailing source of wonder to the humble schoolmaster, who cast furtive glances towards his next-door
neighbours in order that he might, by their example,
regulate his own course of action with respect to unknown
" plats."

The wonders began with half-a-dozen native oysters,
which he found lying on his plate, and the elaborately-
folded napkin, which latter was of itself an incident that
nothing short of the wonders to come could have driven
from his thoughts.   It was a thorough French dinner
this ; not in the latest Anglo-Parisian style, but accord-

ing to high provincial etiquette, quite en règle, and had been carefully planned by the Dubosq. First there was potage au Compte de Paris, which gave place to the inevitable boiled shreds of beef served with slices of melon ; after which came ragouts à la Cardinale, tendrons de veau aux petits pois, epigramme d'agneau aux con-combres, filets de poussins à la Maréchale, suprême de volaille aux truffes ; while at intervals were handed round' radishes, anchovies, red herring, salad and gherkins. Then came haricots verts à la poulette, flageolets à la Provençale ; then a leg of mutton and endive salad ; then miroton de homard and jambon glacé à l'ananas ; then macédoine de fruits, corbeille de ratifia à la Chantillie, meringues à la crême, peaches, grapes, green figs, and Roquefort cheese. To this wondrous repast the wines served were, to the first course, Maçon, followed by Clos Vougeot ; then Pic-Pouillie and Château Grille ; then Barsac, Segur, and l'Ermitage ; at dessert, champagne and Arbois ; and with the sweets, Grenache, Malvoisie, and Alicante. Each of these wines was in turn gravely handed to Mr. Polyblank by the servants in attendance, and of many the professor partook with becoming gravity, wondering, as he did so, what amount of practice would be required before an inexperienced person could distin-guish one from another.

But if the things upon the table surprised him, how much more did the ladies and gentlemen seated round it —who talked a language which, though he was now no mean French scholar, was almost incomprehensible to him, it being the chit-chat of the Paris green-rooms and the latest dialect—if one may apply that phrase to written language—of the Parisian journals.

It was more than probable that Madame Dubosq was as much in the dark as the professor, although she smiled very affably, and looked very knowing.   Mr. Polyblank strongly suspected that she was much out of her element, and once glancing at her when the rest were all laughing and talking, and she thought herself unobserved, he saw her yawning fearfully, and looking very worn and weary. No, she was not happy, and he sympathized with her.

As he sat in silence, timidly sipping his wine, he was wishing himself back in his humble lodging in the Street of the Priests.   Never before had the baroness seemed to him so beautiful as she did then, in her pretty evening dress, which scarcely concealed her plump white shoulders.   The sparkling Aï had perhaps imparted just a suspicion of extra roses to her cheeks, without detracting from the lustre of her eyes ; and she laughed and chatted more gaily than he had ever heard her do before. The English manager was not altogether happy.   He ate and drank vigorously, though ; missing nothing.   He made hay while the sun shone, as far as the feast was concerned ; but he did not make merry.   He was obliged to play second fiddle—an instrument to which, when at home, he was not accustomed.   He would have liked to engross the conversation ; but it was as much as he could do to slip in a few words edgeways, for little Paul and the great Alexis monopolized the talk, while Mr. Max encouraged them from time to time by his good-natured laughter.   They were evidently very witty fellows these gentlemen from Paris, and Raynal and the baroness seemed readily enough to appreciate their jokes ; but while the poor professor sat vainly striving to catch their meaning, he could not help asking himself how he could ever have been so mad as to suppose that beautiful and clever woman had fallen in love with him.   Thank Heaven he had discovered the truth before it was too late—before he had spoken the never-to-be-recalled words, at the bare thought of which he now flushed crimson. In love with him, indeed! A pretty sort of host he would make in such company.

"The French nation is not properly understood," the great Alexis was at that moment observing. "My dear friends, we ought to go abroad and sow the seeds of truth. Let us gather up our beds and assume our staves, or at any rate our walking-sticks, and go to all quarters of the world to enlighten the minds of the ignorant."

"I object to enlightening minds upon principle," said Max, "but I don't mind you, dear boys, doing it."

"I object to being absent from Paris for more than a very limited period," said little Paul.

"My friends," continued Alexis, in a tone of remonstrance, "shall we allow paltry personal considerations to stand in our way? Shall we sit down contentedly and allow the world to underrate us? Is it possible, Paul, that in such a case you would refuse to die for your country?"

"And I'm killing myself with its good things as fast as I can. You don't want any more of me, surely?"

"Ah, he is like me!" put in Manon. "He has given up ambition, and instead of a laurel wreath is quite content—

"Couronné par Jeanneton
D'un simple bonnet de coton."

"Only I haven't got a Jeanneton," sighed little Paul.

"Look at us," continued Alexis, "whom they affect to regard with contempt! Look at our men of science, quoted by all other nations! Look even at our mobs! Have you any mobs over there, Monsieur Brownjones, where Policeman A 1 single-handed routs ten thousand Chartists?"

" Voilà un chose que vous n'avez pas, Mossoo !" exclaimed the manager ; " et cela est un Shakespeare."

" Your only original dramatist, retorted Alexis. " We know all about him. Our great Alexander has written us his history ; but after your Williams what have you ? Come, Mr. Raynal, you have lived in England, and ought to be an authority."

" To be sure," said Manon. " What is there now, Pierre, worth going to see ? The horses, eh, and the Meese Anglaises ? "

Somehow, Raynal seemed by no means pleased at the turn the conversation had taken, and no way inclined to communicate any of his personal experiences.

" I brought nothing away with me," he said.

" Ah ! but what did you leave behind ?" asked Mr. Paul, waggishly—at which Raynal's face for a moment flushed and darkened.

As the professor sat silently whilst this and similar talk was going on, his eye rarely wandered from the faces of his hostess and her lover. He certainly did not like this Mr. Raynal. Endeavouring, to the best of his ability, to regard him without prejudice, there yet was something about Manon's lover—although he could not determine what it was—which inspired the professor with a feeling of distrust. One thing, however, was very certain, and that was that Manon loved him. Little as Polyblank knew of the language of love, he was sure of that much : and having heard that they had known each other for several years, he wisely concluded that they were themselves better judges than he could be of their chances of future happiness. It was once when Polyblank's eyes were fixed upon Manon's face, that she suddenly said to him—

" I hope you did not forget to bring those very clever

Latin verses, Mr. Polyblank?" (There had been a P.S. to the Baroness's invitation asking him to bring them.) "I have been speaking to Mr. Max about them, and he is anxious to see your work."

It must be confessed that Mr. Max took some pains to make his face express the amount of anxiety attributed to him, though he succeeded but indifferently nevertheless. Probably anybody else but the author of the verses would not have failed to notice the circumstance. He, however, saw nothing, and produced the MS., twitching it nervously in his fingers.

"They are epigrams after the manner of Martial," said Manon. "Is it not so, Mr. Polyblank? Women don't know anything about those sort of things; but you, Mr. Max, who know everything, ought to be a judge."

"Are they Latin, sir?" asked Mr. Max.

"Yes," replied the deluded professor. "They do not possess any great merit, but I thought the notion a novel one."

"Very novel," said Mr. Max, sipping his wine.

Poor unhappy Polyblank. The pretty baroness was eager in her championship, and would insist upon our author reading one or two pieces aloud. He felt a little bashful about doing so, but of course he did it, after the gentlemen smiled approvingly—all but the manager, who having no particular object to gain by conciliating a schoolmaster, contented himself by observing when the reading was over—

"Je ne sais pas parler Latin."

"Only French," observed the professor, at which Mr. Max laughed prodigiously, attributing his mirth to a joke in the epigrams which he had hardly comprehended at the moment he heard it.

"I am very glad you think they are so clever," and

the baroness, though the beautiful young lady knew
well enough why he had laughed. As she spoke, she
passed over the manuscript to Mr. Max, adding, as she
did so, " You understand now, Mr. Max, you must do all
you possibly can with them, and a word from you to the
Paris publishers will effect anything."

Under any other circumstances Mr. Max would probably have repudiated the possession of such powerful
influence ; but he did not want to offend his pretty
hostess, and he thought, perhaps, that it would be more
gracious to say he had tried to serve the professor and
failed than to refuse to try at all ; so he promised to do
his best, and pocketed the verses. The poor professor's
epigrammatic achievements are yet unprinted. They
were not very brilliant affairs. He was indeed, as we
shall see, of that opinion himself when he came to read
some of the MS. over in cold blood, some time afterwards, and he did not break his heart at the disappointment. Not having got into print, he brought himself to
believe that he had acted wisely in keeping out of it.
We are all of us much more witty till we show up in
type, and then somehow we never do half what is expected of us. Now if we would only leave the world
expectant of what we might do if we tried, no one would
find us out, and we might pass through life with our
little shallownesses never plumbed.

The professor, however, was not of this way of thinking at the time of which we are speaking ; and fancying
himself, worthy man, already well started on the road to
fame and fortune, his conversation became animated and
amusing, and would perhaps have been even brilliant, had
he been able entirely to overcome his natural timidity.
Altogether, his efforts were very successful, and, when he
took his departure, he walked with quite a rollicking air

across the marshes, with his hat, actually, a good deal on one side, and, more than once, he stopped to laugh at some good thing that somebody had said. If—it once occurred to him—he had only gone in for epigrams, ever so long ago, instead of wasting his time at the scholastic business, he might now have been a jolly devil-me-care sort of fellow, such as those he had been dining with.

"Merry dogs," he said to himself. "It is fortunate that I have made their acquaintance."

The other guests were to return to Saint Babylas in a carriage which had brought them, and there being room for only five besides the driver, they were unable to accommodate the professor with a seat. Polyblank had started first, and, indeed, had reached home long before the others set out from Longanna. He was humming a tune as he walked up the Street of the Priests, and he skipped nimbly up the steps of Mr. Pomponney's house. But the shop door opened suddenly, and Felicité appeared upon the threshold.

"Oh, Mr. Polybank!" she said. "If it would not be asking too much—oh, it would be so kind of you! Oh, it is so dreadful.

"What has happened?" asked the professor, suspending his music in the middle of a bar, for his thoughts immediately reverted to his jovial relative ; of whom, as a matter of course, he expected to hear some bad tidings.

CHAPTER XV

PLOTS AND PLANS.

Dead faces in my visions floated.—AARESTRUP.

"A poor Englishwoman," said Félicité, in great excitement—"a poor Englishwoman is at the point of death,

over there, opposite, at the laundress's," and looking in
the direction she pointed, the professor saw a faint light
glimmering in the third floor window of the house from
which hung the announcement of " Le linge mangled."

" Your Protestant priest has been sent for," put in
Mr. Pomponney, " but he is not at home.   We thought
she was dying, and went for him.   She cannot speak a
word of French.   Will you go over and see her?"

Mr. Polyblank would have much preferred stopping
where he was, but he could not refuse to go.   It was, to
be sure, a rather startling request to make to a man who
was neither a doctor nor a clergyman.   He was, however,
soon persuaded.   The idea which Félicité's description
conjured up of the lonely woman dying up there, on the
third floor, among strangers, jabbering in an unknown
tongue, filled him with pity, and very soon he was ascending the stairs of the laundress's abode.   A very hot,
close-smelling room was this into which he was conducted.
A tallow candle on the mantelpiece cast a dim light upon
a small table littered with plates, basins, and bottles; the
rest of the furniture consisting of a couple of chairs, over
the backs of which hung some dingy old garments, and
a squalid bed, in which lay the dying woman—undoubtedly a dying woman, but very unlike what the professor
had pictured to himself.   Félicité had not said whether
she was old or young;   but Mr. Polyblank had somehow
come to the conclusion that it was to be an old woman.
She was twenty, at most.   Her face was of ashy white-
ness, and her hair jet black.   Her bare arm lying outside
the bedclothes was wasted, and quite bird-like was the
appearance of her thin fingers, clutching the coverlet.
Her features appeared to be contracted by pain.   She
rolled her head slowly from side to side upon her pillow,
and her eyes were turned upwards, so that the pupils

were scarcely visible; yet might be observed, in the poor suffering face, traces of a faded loveliness which years of trouble had failed to obliterate. Who and what was she? It was impossible to form any conjecture from the contents of the squalid room and the few ragged garments hanging limply over the chairs. The landlady could give but little information, except that the lady called herself " Smit."

" What's the matter with her?" asked the professor, in a low voice.

" My dear sir," replied the laundress, thumping her own chest with her closed hands, " very bad here."

" How long has she been with you?"

" About ten days."

" And ill all the time?"

" Came ill."

" What does the doctor say?"

" She would not have one. We wanted to send for Dr. Tominet; but she would not see him. Then she's too poor to pay doctors' bills. We know what they are."

" I think I can get some advice gratis," said the professor, and promising to return immediately, went in quest of his brother Joe. As a general rule that hilarious practitioner was not very difficult to find when off college duty, for he spent all his leisure time in the Café Leduc, of the most quiet of the regular frequenters of which he had now become a sort of bête noir. Upon this particular evening, however, he was not to be found at the usual haunt, but as he was expected there soon the professor sat down in a quiet corner to await his arrival. He had sat there more than ten minutes, and was just thinking of leaving a message and taking his departure, when the café door opened and three gentlemen entered the room, talking and laughing loudly. Polyblank looked up and beheld some of his late companions of the dinner table—Alexis, little Paul, and Pierre Raynal. They had been drinking freely, it appeared, since he saw them last, and their high-pitched tones drew the attention of the other occupants of the café upon them. Now it was not that he was ashamed of being claimed as their acquaintance—for, tipsy or not, they had the airs of very fine gentlemen—indeed it would be difficult to explain his motive, if one existed; but some inscrutable impulse caused the professor, while in the very act of rising, to sit down again, and shade his face with the *Saint Babylas Gazette*. For some five minutes or so he sat thus, wishing himself well out of the place, though, stupidly, ashamed to rise and depart openly. Meanwhile, the three gentlemen continued to laugh and talk as loudly as before; not forgetting to grumble at the quality of the liquor supplied to them. Presently, however, they arose, upon Raynal's proposing an adjournment to Madame Gobinard's. With much jingling of glasses and knocking about of chairs, they paid the score. Before going, though, a cigar had to be lighted. The waiter supplied a match which would not burn, and Raynal diving into his pocket searched for a piece of paper.

"Here is some," said little Paul, producing a small packet, and tearing off a sheet amidst the laughter of his companions.

"Poor professor!" said Raynal, as he screwed up the paper and thrust it into the flame of the gas jet nearest to him. Then, the cigar being lighted, the three took their departure. Before they had passed through the doorway, however, our professor was groping underneath a billiard table for the fragment of burnt paper which had fallen to the ground. A glance at it was enough, and then, white and trembling, he followed in pursuit.

" M'sieu has forgotten to pay," the garçon cried, excitedly catching his flying coat tail, but the professor shook him off. With a bound he had reached little Paul's side, and laid his hand upon his shoulder.

" Give them back to me," he said ; " give them back— the verses."

Paul Cherami produced the same little packet, somewhat sheepishly, and murmured something about Mr. Max having asked him to show them to a publisher.

" Don't trouble yourself, sir," said the professor, stowing his literary valuables away in his breast-pocket, and buttoning his coat over them, "I've changed my mind."

With this he turned upon his heel, and the three gentlemen walked on less joyous than before; for there was something in the poor schoolmaster's white face and gleaming eyes which was not altogether provocative of mirth.

" I will tell her how her friends keep their fine promises," Polyblank said to himself, as he retraced his steps. But hardly had the words passed his lips before his mind was altered. " No, no," he thought, " it would vex her if I did so. It was very kind of her to speak to them about my verses. She shall know nothing about it, unless they tell her themselves ; and I do not suppose they will do that."

As he was paying the waiter at the café door on his return, the jovial Joseph came up, and they walked back together to the Street of the Priests. Then the professor found the sick woman, in much the same condition as that in which he had left her an hour ago. Yet had she the same look of pain—yet did she roll her head to and fro, with the same weary motion he had observed before. Joseph approached the bed, and took her hand in his.

"What is the matter?" he asked, in English.

She lay still and silent for a minute, with her large eyes fixed inquiringly upon his face. Apparently she had not caught the meaning of his words; but when, after looking at her earnestly for a while and feeling her pulse, the doctor was turning away she caught at his sleeve, and cried in a weak voice : "Where is he—where is he?"

"Where is who?" asked Joseph.

But she closed her eyes again and made no answer.

"Is she dangerously ill?" asked the professor in a half whisper.

"It's a case with her," replied Joe, in the same tone. "Wont more than last the week out."

Gently as they spoke, it seemed that the purport of their remarks reached the woman's ears, for she called upon the doctor in a low, plaintive voice to stop.

"Don't let me die," she pleaded. "Not yet, not yet. Don't let me die before I've seen him!"

"Whom do you wish to see?" asked Joe.

"Who?" the sick woman repeated, with a wondering stare. "Who but my husband, that I have travelled so many miles to find—hundreds of miles—hundreds of miles. Nearly all on foot and half starving. Don't let me die before I see him."

"Tell me his name, and where he is, and I'll telegraph for him," said Joe.

For a moment the woman lay still as before; then broke out again, in the same low, pleading tone. "No, no, you must not write. He would not like it known. I want to see him myself. I must live to see him, now I'm so near. I must live——"

But her voice died away with these words, and again the heavy rolling motion of the head was resumed; while a pang of extreme pain contracted the features of the thin, white face.

" It's a chance if she does see him," said Joe, " unless he comes precious soon. It's a pity we can't find out who he is." And he began to make inquiries of the laundress respecting the sick woman. But the laundress knew no more than she had already told the professor. She had come there ten days ago, had paid her rent for a month in advance, and had written her name " Mary Smith" in the official return called for, in the usual manner, by the police. Only one thing the laundress knew, which was that in a little shabby leather portfolio desk the sick woman had locked up certain papers which might perhaps throw light upon the business. Had not the gentlemen better open it and see whether they could not find out something about the poor creature's friends ? the worthy woman suggested— she herself being devoured by an anxiety to know what secrets the leather case might contain. Joseph was inclined to take the same view of the case; but the professor objected.

" Not yet," he said ; " we must not do so without her consent."

"Very well," said Joe; "we shall know all after it's over."

" Can you do nothing for her ?"

" Not yet. I'll get some physic made up if you like. It wont be of much use."

Just as they reached the door the sick woman, restored to consciousness, again cried to them to stop, and they once more approached the bed.

"You must not send for him," she said, closing her thin fingers upon Joseph's hand. "Not yet—not yet, I say. But remember the name if anything happens—remember Mr. Raynal, at the hotel of the ' Three Crowns.' "

11

When the woman ceased speaking there was for a moment deep, unbroken silence. The landlady stood at the door, too far away to catch the name, which was uttered in a tone scarcely above a whisper. Both the brothers, however, heard it distinctly, and stood there motionless—a wondering, half-frightened look upon their faces. Not until they reached the street did they speak, when the doctor said :

" If it is true, the marriage may never come off, after all."

" He is a villain !" the professor muttered to himself, scarcely heeding the other's words.

They had crossed the street now, and stood outside the door of Mr. Pomponney's shop.

" Good night," said the doctor.

" Good night.—Joe !"

" Well !"

" How long did you say it was possible for her to live ?"

" I'll give her a week at the utmost."

" You must mention this matter to no one, Joe, till we've talked it over together. Do you hear ?—to no one."

" I hear," said Joe. " Good night."

" I'll sleep upon it," said the professor, as he extinguished his bedroom candle ; and, having come to that determination, he rolled and tossed from side to side of his restless couch until the morning. Then he arose and shaved himself with an unsteady hand. He was obliged to be at the college at half-past eight o'clock, in accordance with Mr. Roustoubique's latest regulation ; but, before going there, he hurried round to Joe's lodgings, to impart to him the result of the night's reflections. Early as the hour was, however, the bird had flown. Mr. Polyblank turned away from the door, feeling anything but comfortable. Somehow, he had always a secret misgiving as to what mischief Joe might be about when he was out of his sight.

A long, hard day's work awaited Peter in the imperial establishment—one of the longest and hardest he ever remembered to have passed within its walls; during the course of which the vagaries of Bourdichon and Co. well-nigh drove him to distraction. As soon as he could get away, without going home to tea, as was his custom, he went straight to Joe's lodgings, and, not finding him, proceeded thence to the café, where, wonderful to relate, the doctor had not been seen all day. With a fast increasing feeling of uneasiness, the professor set off for the house of the sick woman. He found her in a seemingly unconscious state, and incapable of holding any conversation; but it appeared, from the statement of the laundress, that Joe had been there the first thing in the morning, and had had some talk with the invalid. Could it be possible that he would use the secret as the means of making money? Polyblank shuddered at the thought, and, when it first occurred to him, rejected it with indignation. But, do what he would, the idea returned, again and again. Joe's nearest and dearest relative could not disguise from himself the fact that that distinguished disciple of Esculapius was rather unprincipled.

Without taking any refreshment, Mr. Polyblank once more set out, but this time upon the road to Longanna. Since Raynal had been publicly declared Manon's future husband, the professor had not been a very frequent visitor at the château. Those famous lessons were woefully neglected during the progress of Love's young dream, and the professor having once or twice come and gone, without the pretty baroness as much as opening a book, he began to feel ashamed of making his appearance. It was not to be wondered at, if she neglected her education under the influence of the all-mastering passion. Young ladies without number, since the world began, have put aside their crochet, and abandoned their Berlin wools at such a time; and instances are on record, even of grave philosophers abandoning severer studies for the cultivation of the graces, in the hope of rendering themselves more acceptable to the objects of their passion. Can we, then, blame Manon for not seeking to perfect herself in the barbarous language at such a moment?

The professor of course had, in the dinner party, an excuse for calling at the château; and he was most anxious to ascertain whether Manon had heard anything of the sick woman in the Street of the Priests. He walked so quickly across the marshes that he was almost out of breath and somewhat excited when he reached the château. The old portress and her cat were there as usual, and the sight of them seemed to reassure him. The old woman's first words, though, brought his heart to his mouth.

"Madame la baronne is not at home. Madame and Madame Dubosq have been out since eleven this morning."

Such a thing had never occurred before during his experience, and this unlooked-for disappointment fell upon him like the presage of some heavy misfortune. But worse was yet to come.

"I thought they had gone to see you, sir," continued the portress. "Monsieur le docteur came to fetch them."

The professor made no anwer. He leant against the wall, and put his hand to his head. The old woman thought he was ill, and toddling into her little sitting-room, brought him out a chair to sit upon, and a glass of water to drink. Polyblank took the proffered glass and carried it to his lips, but he was unable to swallow.

"Good heavens ! he could not be such a villain," muttered the professor. "I cannot—no, no—I will not believe it of him."

Presently a faint hope dawned upon his mind ; and he inquired, "What doctor ?"

"I think he is your brother, sir ; so the ladies said, Monsieur le docteur Peau-le-blanc," she answered, smiling, for the name seemed to her such a very droll one she seldom pronounced it without a smile. The professor scarcely noticed her reply. He had foreseen what it was to be, and had only hoped against hope when he asked the question. He rose to his feet with an idea of returning to town and waiting for Joe at his lodgings, so that he might know the worst as soon as possible ; but while passing the threshold, a sudden weakness came over him. He staggered, and would have fallen had he not hastily clutched the door-post.

"Monsieur is ill," said the portress, with feeling. "You must not think of going away yet awhile. Will you go into the drawing-room, and wait for Madame's return ?"

The professor said that he would. He was all bewildered and in a maze, and scarcely knew what he said or did. He had worked very hard during that day ; he had gone without food and sleep, and overtaxed his strength, and was shaken by agitated feelings. The windows of the drawing-room were shut, and he moved painfully towards them, with the intention of unfastening one of the sashes. But, before he could do so, the same giddiness under which he had just now suffered seized him again, and he sank down upon one of the sofas, with a deadly sickness at his heart. How long he remained thus he could hardly form a notion. It might have been one hour or two hours. He did not heed the lapse of time. Twilight was gathering when he entered the room, and it was quite dark before any one came to disturb him, but at last there was a loud ringing at the outer bell. Presently, footsteps and the rustle of silk skirts. Polyblank rose to his feet in dread anticipation of the interview to come. Next moment the door opened in a blaze of light, and Manon entered the room radiant with smiles, and prettier than ever. As yet, then, she knew nothing of the terrible truth. As yet, she was happily unconscious of Raynal's villany, and Joe, after all, was not as bad as he had supposed.

" Hallo, Peter !"

Why, as sure as there was a sky above, there was Joseph in the flesh. Yes, actually, Joseph ; and, as sure as in the sky there is a moon, a broad-faced simpering moon, which smiles benignly down upon all true lovers here below, Madame Dubosq was hanging fondly upon that Joseph's arm, in such a way, mayhap, as she had once hung on the arm of another, long since dead and gone.

" Hallo, Peter !"

CHAPTER XVI.

JOE'S LITTLE MISTAKE.

Mais le monde est un vrai tyran.—De Varennes.

WHY do we not all die when we have done it ?   When after long struggling, hard fighting, frequent repulses, we gain the topmost round of fame's precipitous ladder, and the mob below (the same who used to hoot us once ; but that is no matter) are vociferously cheering, why don't we, then and there, finish our career gloriously, with a bang, as it were ? But we don't. We stay there, swinging our legs and chuckling ; we stop on the top round as long as we can hold on, then we slip to the second. We are mighty proud even of that lower round, and our self-esteem does not entirely desert us when we have sunk down further still—to the third, and fourth, and fifth—although the cheering of the mob has grown very feeble by this time. Is it not always thus? After the Queen of Song has bidden us a last farewell, does she not return, when her voice is merely a memory? Has the once agile Jack Pudding never lingered on the stage long after his limbs have lost their elasticity? Are there not faded beauties in our drawing-rooms, clinging, with drowning desperation, to the wreck of good looks; and a hundred and one heroes who, having outlived the fame of their exploits, still revert to the old battle-fields, long since ploughed up and sowed with turnips?

There was a time when, if that Joseph Polyblank had only had the good luck to die, he would have left a repu-tation behind him which might, perhaps, have endured for a generation or two among the poor people of Saint Babylas. Unhappily, however, for his fame, he lived long enough to scatter to the winds all the fruits of his first successes.

Upon the road to Longanna was to be seen, fair weather or foul, a certain whining beggarman, horribly knock-kneed, and otherwise deformed, who was a source of everlasting terror to the little vagabond boys of the village, between whom and him was carried on a sort of guerilla warfare. A most unclean and unsightly creature was this man; with matted red-hair, bleared eyes, blotched face, and other bodily ailments which need not be parti-cularized; who shambled after the diligence, and endea-voured by the display of his baboon-like antics to wring a few odd sous pieces out of passengers. Why this hideous creature had not been drowned like a blind puppy

at his birth, was a question which the least tender-hearted
among the passengers asked themselves ; but all wondered
why he was allowed to thrust his physical horrors upon
the public eye, and to carry on his illegal trade of begging
with impunity.

Somehow, the municipal authorities of Saint Babylas,
all-seeing in other respects, overlooked him.   It would
have been lucky for Jean Gin had Joseph been equally
short-sighted ; but it was not to be.   One fatal day, as
the English doctor passed, *summâ diligentiâ*, Jean Gin's
knock-knees caught his eye, and from that moment Joe
longed to have a knife in him.

" I should like to have a go in at those legs of yours,"
Joe mentally remarked as he rode by.

When he came the same road again, he once more regarded Jean Gin's deformity with a wistful eye.

" Now if I could only persuade that crooked wretch
to let me have a cut at him," thought Joseph, " supposing it were successful, the news of the thing would be in
everybody's mouth in Picardy."

He never paused to think what everybody in Picardy
would say if he did not succeed.   From that instant he
marked the unhappy Jean Gin for his own, and straightway set about the misshapen creature's allurement.   He
began by flinging a handful of sous at him, some of which,
striking tender points, caused him to bellow like a bull.
Subsequently, when passing by on foot, he soothed the
savage with more sous, and some tobacco.

" Were you born so ?" he asked, pointing to Jean's legs
with his walking-stick.

" Ugh !" grunted the beggar, munching at a mouthful
of caporal which Joseph had just given to him.

" Wouldn't you wish to look a little more like a
human being ?" Joe inquired, persuasively.

"Ugh!" grunted Jean Gin, to whom the notion seemed never previously to have occurred.

Joseph presently put the matter to him more plainly. He would give him twenty francs if Jean would let him operate on his legs. Jean stared very hard, chewed his tobacco, and scratched his head; but would give no definite answer. A few days afterwards, Joe, coming by again, or more accurately speaking, having gone there expressly, invited Jean to drink at the cabaret, and regaled him with a couple of quarts of the sour beer of the country; then laid a bran new ten-franc piece upon the table. To see the hideous monster's eye sparkle, and his great gash of a mouth water at the sight of the bright gold, was a thing to shudder at. Joe thought the business as good as settled; but Jean, stroking his ugly limbs with his great hands, shook his head, chuckled, and said he would rather be as he was.

"Be as you are?" cried Joseph, wrathfully; "an object like that, only fit to scare away crows, when you might walk as straight as I do? Why, man, if you'd only anything like legs the women would all run after you."

At this the scaramouch grinned like an ape. They say that the most hideous male creature upon earth can find one of the other sex who will look upon him not unkindly. Even this Quasimodo might hope to achieve a conquest among the fair maids of Longanna. The doctor seeing that he hesitated, ordered another quart of sour beer, and while he talked, played with the golden piece in his fingers. But the crooked beggar only got stupidly drunk and savage, and, at last, inflamed by some imaginary insult, was for challenging the doctor to mortal combat. "Eh! Bogr-r-r'i!" he cried, working his arms like the sails of a mill, "je veux te montra que

Jean Gin n'a pas froid aux yeux. Nom d'un nom! Aligne toi que je te cogne!"* Joe, warding off the blows with his walking-stick, besought Gin to be calm.

"You ought to be grateful to me, you fool," he said; but Jean responded indignantly, "J't'en baillerons récompense d'la main gauche."†

Joe saw that it was useless to argue further, and turned upon his heel, when Jean's intoxication taking a maudlin turn, he whined out, "Bonne gent! baillez-moi cinq franes et je serons quittes."‡ Upon this Joe came back, and producing a written paper from his pocket-book, induced Jean to affix his mark to a promise, therein made, to forfeit fifty francs if he refused to have the operation performed after the receipt of twenty francs. Then, having had Mr. Gin's blot properly witnessed, the doctor paid ten francs on account, and took his departure; leaving the scaramouch and his friends to the enjoyment of a select orgie which they prolonged far into the night.

"But you'll have to be cut," the landlord said, as they sat swilling beer together.

"He'll never have his knife in me," Crookedshanks replied. "We'll drink his good health, though."

"That we will, brave heart," responded mine host, slapping the entertainer, blithely, upon the back. "On voit ben que t'a été z'à à Paris, gars!"§ He was an awkward customer to deal with—this Jean Gin—and it is more than probable that, had not others assisted him, Joe would never have succeeded in prevailing on the cripple to allow him to operate upon his knock-knees. Perhaps, when he made Jean sign the agreement he had

* Je vais te montrer que Jean Gin n'est pas lâche. Mets-toi en garde, etc.
† Je ne te recompenserai pas.   ‡ Donnez-moi cinq francs, etc.
§ On voit bien que tu as été à Paris.

a vague notion of proceeding against him before the civil tribunal for breach of contract, in the event of his refusing to submit to the knife; but whether he was likely to have succeeded in getting the forfeit or not, it did not seem very probable that he would get hold of Jean's legs. When, however, the news spread about that the doctor had given Jean Gin twenty francs to be allowed to straighten his limbs, everybody naturally observed, " How kind of the doctor, and what a good thing for Jean Gin." Indeed, so it was; and Jean Gin ought, properly, to have felt grateful and eager for the doctor to begin to operate; only the poor wretch could not help thinking how it would hurt when the doctor's knife was hacking its way through muscles and tendons. As the rest of the world was not disturbed by these apprehensions, not a day passed but somebody urged Jean Gin to be a man and have his legs altered. Passers-by would stop and put it to him, forcibly. The driver of the diligence daily inquired when the affair was coming off. The postman took the liveliest interest in the operation—having made a bet upon the subject. The frequenters of the cabaret at Longanna every evening addressed him, at length, upon the advantages which would accrue from this cure; and when, as it sometimes happened, he ventured as far as Saint Babylas, the whole town attacked him, and drove him well nigh out of his wits by their friendly suggestions. But the poor creature could not screw his courage up to the sticking point. He lay awake of a night and quaked with fear. After a more than usually indigestible supper, he would be troubled with nightmare, in the shape of the doctor sharpening a knife upon his breast, and, at other times, Joe had him by one leg, and, struggle as he would, he could not shake himself free of his perse-cutor. To finish all, the Baroness de Grandvilain, also, attacked him; and at last Jean Gin's obstinacy was overcome, and the poor wretch gave himself up to the tormentor. And now is the time for a few words of explanation. It was upon the subject of Jean Gin's legs that Joe had called upon the baroness. For once his brother had cruelly wronged him. Instead of trying to trade upon Raynal's secret, Joe had been working in the cause of science—in other words it had occurred to him that, as Manon was so kindly disposed towards the professor, she might be inclined to help him also. In that case, the way to help him was to exert her influence upon the knock-kneed Jean, and induce him to submit to the operation. Our good friend Joe had, as has been shown, what in the vernacular is termed the gift of the gab, that is to say, he spoke fluently. To him pretty Manon listened with interest, and having, like many kind-hearted women (God bless them!) small reasoning powers, she was easily convinced that the luckiest thing in the world that could happen to Jean Gin was to be experimentalized upon by Joe Polyblank. Straightway she paid Jean a visit on the highway, and laid the case before him, and among the advantages which she enumerated as likely to result from his compliance, were forty francs, which she promised to pay immediately the operation was performed. The previous day Joe had used a little quiet influence with the police authorities, and just before the baroness spoke to Jean, he had been given to understand that he must forthwith abandon his mendicant habits, or look out for himself. Dreading the withdrawal of the baroness's protection, and the wrath of the gendarmerie, Jean Gin at length cried peccavi, and Joe sharpened his knife. The feat, which it was confidently supposed would immortalize everybody directly or indirectly concerned in it, was to be performed at the hotel of the "Three Crowns," that being chosen as a locality easily accessible to the doctor and Mr. Pomponney, one of the principal agents in the business. From the first day of his arrival in Saint Babylas, Joe had found a staunch adherent in the worthy chemist, who had, far and wide, prophesied for him a glorious future.

This is not intended to be a medical work, or the history of the famous knock-kneed case might easily be drawn out into ten times the length I purpose allotting to it, if I were to insert only one-half of the articles which appeared upon the subject in the columns of the Pas-de-Calais press. A new era in science had arrived, one writer remarked, and the old-fashioned doctors—the Tominets, Cancoins, and such-like—reading these words, tore their hair and gnashed their teeth. It was rumoured that there were legs in the most elevated circles which were not as straight as they might be, and, consequently, the operation created a decided sensation among the highest as well as the lowest of Saint Babylas society. Jean Gin was accommodated with a light and airy apartment in the front of the hotel, where the very pattern of the wall-paper was at first a source of unbounded wonder to him. He was told that he should eat of the best, sleep softly, and drink and smoke in moderation; but that he must be upon his back for ten days. When first these conditions were named to him he laughed to scorn the absurd notion of anybody's growing tired of such luxurious indulgence. He would lie on his back for three months, the unhappy object declared, with a hoarse laugh.

A little crowd gathered round the hotel door when it got about that the doctor had been seen to enter with a small mahogany case under his arm. Those who saw him shuddered as he passed, and listened, with pale faces,

for any noise that might come from the chamber of mystery, the door of which Alexander jealously guarded.
Anon, the silent echoes of the Little Place were awakened
by a dismal howl, then succeeded a death-like silence,
and then a howl and a series of groans.   Then silence
again, and then the doctor came forth arm-in-arm with
the chemist, but smiling blandly.

That evening Joe and Mr. Pomponney sent a flaming
article of their own composition to the *Saint Babylas
Gazette*.   One short week afterwards, and the whole
business was publicly denounced as the work of a dangerous madman.   Yes, dreadful to relate, the grand
theory had failed.   In a fortnight's time this was the
state of affairs : Joe Polyblank stigmatized as a quack
and an impostor, whom no man in his senses would
allow to cross the threshold of his door; Mr. Pomponney
declared to be an imbecile, and unworthy of further consideration; the Baroness de Grandvilain set down as the
chief cause of a fellow-creature's barbarous mutilation,
the promoter of all sorts of preposterous schemes and
frauds, and the harbourer of lunatics who cut and carved
other persons' bodies with as much indifference as they
would exhibit in slicing a melon.   Finally, Jean Gin
minus his legs.

The doctor's theory with respect to knock-knees, which
had so lamentably broken down, was somewhat similar
to one in vogue a few years back with regard to squint-
ing eyes.   Some scientific surgeon then discovered that
the extra turn of the eyes towards the nose which amounts
to a squint, was occasioned by the too powerful action
of some muscle or tendon, which drew the eyes out of
their natural position.   " Sever the attracting power,"
said he, " and the patient will see straight before him."
So Joe Polyblank maintained, that all that was required
to set a knock-kneed man straight on his legs was to cut

some tendons, which he described, on the inside of each leg and thigh. Joe had long ardently desired to have an opportunity of proving the soundness of this theory, and lo! one unluckily presented itself in the case of Jean Gin, and ended in the way just described.

Dreadful as all this may appear, there were not wanting persons—Doctor Tominet among others, who said that it might have been worse.

" It is a wonder they did not kill you among them," said he to Jean.

" I wish they had, instead of leaving me this figure," said the monstrosity, as he woefully contemplated his wooden props ; " but, curse them, I'll be even with them before I die !"

He lay a-bed and cursed all concerned in the business with a vigour and persistency that astonished his auditors, and when, at last, he was able to resume a perpendicular position in the world, he stumped about, cursing still, and imparting his woes to all who would listen to him. Against the doctor who had curtailed him of what certainly could not be termed his " fair proportions," it was only natural that the creature should bear some enmity, and the same might be said of the chemist who, when he had him down, had dosed him with the nastiest of nasty physic ; but for some reason or other, his resentment was directed chiefly against Manon. " She egged me on," he said ; " I'd never have stood it if she hadn't made me. I'm a cripple for life, I am, and all on her account. Curse her for it !—may she too know what it is to be afflicted !"

Thus would the wretched man exclaim as he hobbled over Saint Babylas's uneven roadways : surely the awkwardest town in Christendom for the owner of wooden legs to take a walk in.

CHAPTER XVII.

THE AFFAIR OF THE YELLOW BASIN.

———— When bloody mouthed
The dogs had tussled o'er the reeking game
Forgetting ties of friendship and of kin.
                                                ARTHUR BROWNING.

A HAPPY time was it for our pretty Manon when Raynal, having told his love, and the day having been fixed, the coming marriage was almost as much a fact as if it had really occurred.   Surely never since she was born had the young baroness ever tasted such happiness as she did in those long peaceful days when the birds sang love, and the flowers bloomed love, and it was bright, glorious summer weather every day, to be loved in.   Bah! how such nonsense grates upon the ears of those among us whose poor old bones are aching—who are trying to ward off scarching draughts with insufficient wrappers—who have none to love them, and who are half disposed in return to hate everybody.   But every one is not as wise or cold as we elders have become.   That dear, old, sadly used-up comedy of love will still be drawing crowded houses hundreds of years after the worms have done their worst for us.

Our dear Manon—little dullard—saw nothing ridiculous in being in love.   She had for some years been secretly loving the same handsome gentleman ; but had heretofore never ventured to show it.   Even if she had not been afraid of her affection not being returned by its object, she would have dreaded the fact coming to the knowledge of the terrible Dubosq.   Therefore she kept her—as she supposed it—hopeless passion a profound secret.   Alas, we have seen how everybody knew.all about it.   We have seen, too, how the Dubosq received the tidings of the betrothal.   It will be remembered there was no excess of rapture upon the worthy creature's part, nor, indeed, for some time to come did she manifest any great amount of sympathy with her friend's happiness.   Strange to say, however, from the day when the jovial Joseph first set foot in the château a great change took place in her demeanour.   Hitherto the Dubosq was always a woman with a grievance; but just now she appeared to be not nearly such an afflicted soul as she used to be.   A sort of subdued sprightliness was, at times, observable in her manner.   She was heard to hum.   It was also noticed that when the doctor was expected she put on a smarter cap.

There was something rather diverting in all this, to those who remember how, in days gone by, she had disparaged the tender passion.   She had aimed at being a woman of sense—a strong-minded woman.   A praiseworthy enough ambition for those who are large of joint and harsh of feature; but as to you pretty ones, you know perfectly well that your mission upon earth is to love and get married.

Yes, it was very clear that the Dubosq had also fallen a victim to a passion of which the jovial Joseph was the object, and it must be confessed that the baroness was not sorry for it.   Not, however, because there was a chance of the good lady's being thus comfortably disposed of, for in spite of a thousand and one provocations, Manon loved the grievous relic of the departed Dubosq, and would much have preferred that Mogador should remain to keep house.   But she was, in this time of her own great happiness, unspeakably glad to see all the world happy around her, and would have spared no pains or money to obtain that result.

12

Alas, though, there are some who will not be comforted; and at this time, which should have been a period of uninterrupted felicity, there was a more than ordinary amount of bewailing and bemoaning among Manon's pensioners in the back lanes; and, worse than all, there was the creature with the wooden legs, who stumped about all day howling out his wrongs in the public highways. Yet, though everybody else knew all about the way he had been treated, and how he laid his misfortune at the door of the Baroness de Grandvilain, she herself for a long time remained in ignorance of it. The fact was, the great Joseph for some time brought glowing accounts of the patient's convalescence, until the symptoms grew so alarming that he dare no longer falsify his reports. Then he became suddenly silent upon the subject, and the Dubosq learning something of the real state of the case, did all that lay in her power to screen Joe's misdeeds from her friend.

At last, however, the truth suddenly plumped out. The baroness met Jean Gin with his wooden legs on. She was utterly dumbfounded at the sight; but he, after the first moment of surprise, shook his clenched fist at the carriage window, and called down such a fearful curse upon its occupant, that the poor girl went home white and frightened, and burst into a passionate fit of tears upon the Dubosq's deceitful bosom. But, when she had somewhat subdued her agitation she asked for a true account of Joe's proceedings, and not feeling well satisfied with what she learnt, determined to ascertain the facts of the case for herself. But how? Whom should she apply to? She thought the matter over during the day, and after dinner ordered the carriage.

"Going out again, dear?" inquired the Dubosq.

"Yes."

" Shall I come with you ?"

" No, never mind ; I shan't be long gone."

And thus bidding her friend rather coldly good-by, Manon set forth for Mr. Pomponney's shop.

Manon found the chemist's establishment in confusion. Mrs. Pomponney was making a liqueur in the parlour. On one table stood an earthenware jar. On another six bottles, into which she was filtering her cassis, through blotting paper. Three young lady nieces in brown holland pinafores and black coburg trousers, who had come on a visit, were assisting. In the middle of the room was Pomponney, holding in one hand a large yellow basin, and in the other the car (with head attached) of one Coquillard, recently a pupil of the professor's at the college, now apprenticed to the chemical trade.

" What is the matter ?" asked Manon.

" The matter, madam—the matter !" cried Pomponney, in great excitement. " Oh, nothing—positively nothing ! —a trifle not worth mentioning. The possible death of a family of six. Absolutely no more than that. This young gentleman here, when sent for a basin applicable to culinary purposes, goes and brings it before our very faces out of the laboratory—out—of—the LABORATORY !"

The apartment thus designated was that in which the important experiments were conducted under the supervision of the great Joseph. The laboratory, therefore, was a sacred place, from entering which the youthful Coquillard had hitherto been deterred by Pomponney's warnings and denunciations ; but he had now as we have seen, intruded upon the hallowed ground, and brought down a basin until now used only for profound scientific experiments, to be defiled by its application to mere household purposes.

" A boy capable of such an act," said the chemist, magnificent in his wrath, though labouring under some disadvantage as regarded stage effect on account of his
apron, short sleeves, and slippers—" a young man who
could do such an act, would do—yes, by heavens, would
do—" but as no simile occurred to him at the moment,
he added, after an impressive silence—" anything."

" Pray calm yourself, Hyppolite," entreated poor little
Mrs. Pomponney.

" Oh, my uncle," cried the youngest of the young
ladies in coburg trousers, clinging to his coat-tails.

" Release me," cried the chemist, growing momentarily
more terrific.   " Take a basin from the laboratory !—
what next ?   Take the mortar for a pie-dish; roll the
paste with the pestle ; break the bottles, burn the blisters;
let loose the leeches !   The world's at an end !"

And he flung Coquillard from him against the wall,
and waved the basin aloft.

" Will you be good enough to tell me, sir," began
Manon, who was growing impatient.

" Unhappy youth," continued Mr. Pomponney, without heeding her, " do you know what might have been
the result of your conduct ?   Did you happen to observe
what stood on the shelf by the side of that very identical
earthenware basin ?   Speak, if you still retain the use
of any of your faculties ; say something, or I'll pull
your ear off."

" I—I—don't know," bellowed the miserable Coquillard.

" Oh, you don't, don't you ?" said the chemist ; " well,
then, I will inform you.   You saw a blue bottle filled
with white powder, on which was written the word
' Poison ;' and do you know what was the name of that
poison ?   You don't ?   Well, then, I will inform you.

Arsenic is its name, and this identical vessel of earthenware was beside it, and you fetched it down-stairs for
culinary purposes!"

"Arsenic!" cried Mrs. Pomponney, who having to
keep a sharp eye on the filter, had not been able to
follow the chemist's discourse very closely. "We shall
all be poisoned in our beds."

At which dreadful prophecy the three young ladies in
the coburgs set up a roar as though they already felt the
first pangs in their little insides.

"Poison us! what does he care?" cried the chemist:
"he will poison the customers next. I may be tried and
guillotined upon the Great Place for some of his doings;
what cares he? He'll come early to get into the front
row to see me."

"Will you have the kindness," began the baroness
once more.

"Dear me, Hyppolite," said Mrs. Pomponney, "you
don't observe that you are keeping madame."

But he had not quite run himself out yet, and went
on talking.

"Take this basin back, sir; away with it—cleanse
it—replace it—let such an act never occur again
beneath this roof. Never! never!" Taking Coquillard
by the ear, as though with the intention of swinging him
thereby from the apartment, he shook out from under
the young gentleman's waistcoat an illustrated romance,
in a coloured paper cover, upon which the chemist
pounced.

"The Two Corpses!" he cried aghast. "What is
this? And then with a sepulchral laugh, "But this is
only two, and we should have been five. Enough, sir;
it is thus that you poison your mind previous to poison-
ing my family and my customers. But we will destroy

this work, sir, at once; and without loss of time I will visit your boxes and cupboards, to see how many more corpses you may have secreted upon the premises."

"But, Mr. Pomponney," broke in Manon at this juncture, out of all patience with the tiresome scene, "can you spare me a moment? I came to ask you whether you knew anything of Jean Gin?"

"Jean Gin? Yes, madame, certainly. He's dead."

For a moment, the baroness stood in consternation before him, unable to utter a word. Presently, she said, impatiently, "Do you know what you are saying, sir? I saw him myself this morning."

To tell the truth, the chemist had not quite got the yellow basin and the "Two Corpses" out of his head. Recalling himself, however, with an effort, he begged Manon to accompany him to another apartment, and leading the way up a lofty flight of stairs, opened the door of a dusty, close-smelling little room, which was none other than the laboratory about which so much had been said.

"That is the shelf where the poisons are kept, madame," he said, not yet quite able to drop the subject. "And that is where he took the basin from."

"Yes, yes!" cried Manon, stamping her little foot impatiently. "Will you please to tell me about Jean Gin?"

"Ah, madame!" said Pomponney, with a long face, "that's a sad affair."

"What is? What has happened? Will you explain?"

"I always was opposed to Dr. Polyblank trying the experiment," continued Pomponney, "I really did not see my way clearly; but he would do it. I always said what would be the result."

"What has been the end of it?"

"Wooden legs have been the end of it, as you have

seen," said the chemist, sadly. " At least that has been
the end as far as Doctor Polyblank's new theory is concerned. I always said there was nothing in those Polyblanks, from the first beginning. But poor Jean Gin
has suffered heavily for others' faults."

" For Heaven's sake, explain yourself !" said the
baroness, trembling with impatience.

" Certainly, certainly ; I was coming to the point.
Mr. Raynal's dogcart, you see, this afternoon—the horse
having got the bit between his teeth——"

" What ?"

" It was no fault of Mr. Raynal's, of course, and Jean
Gin, being drunk, got in the way—and being flushed
and not having the use of his legs, could not get out of
the way again, and so—and—so——"

" Well, well ?"

" And so—in fact—Jean Gin was knocked down and
killed."

CHAPTER XVIII.

GONE !

But you are wandering—who knows where ?
A wan, wild face under drenched black hair,
With terror I search 'neath midnight skies
For altered eyes.
Is it your ghost that I dread to meet,
Gladys, my sweet ?—MORTIMER COLLINS.

THE jovial Joseph, as you may recollect, prophesied that
the sick woman at the laundress's would not live more than
a week ; but a whole month passed away, and she was yet
alive. At his brother's request, Joe visited her, more or
less irregularly ; for the Jean Gin business had so disturbed him he was unable to give his serious attention to

anything, and the consequence was, that such few patients
as he had left were put through a course of treatment
which, to say the least of it, was very eccentric.   A
dreary life it was which this lonely woman was painfully
wearing away in the little third-floor room.   For many
hours together she lay so silent and motionless, that the
laundress's little girl, her usual nurse, would sometimes
come, all in a tremble, to the bedside, to listen for the
faint sound of her breath—fancying that, in her sleep,
her soul might have passed away.

This was the quietest and most patient of little girls;
mostly occupying herself with the manufacture of her
male parent's shirts.   She wore a white cap and large
gold ear-rings, blue worsted stockings, a black stuff frock,
and a great apron up to her chin; and she usually sat
perched upon a high straw-bottomed chair, with plain
deal legs, round and straight, like broom-handles; her
own little blue legs dangling in mid-air by reason of
their wanting another five years' growth to reach the
floor below.   But she had the staidness of a person
of mature age, and a wonderful knowledge of sick-room
requirements, which it would be impossible to account
for, unless one could suppose it came by instinct.

At rare intervals, the sick woman recovered sufficiently
to hold a few minutes' conversation with her little guar-
dian; but as her knowledge of French was limited to a
few words, and the little girl's ignorance of English was
absolute, they were able to exchange but few ideas. Not
that the woman seemed to feel acutely the deprivation.
She appeared to have but little interest remaining for
earthly affairs.   She lay there still and motionless, as
though she were waiting for death, and indifferent whether
it came now or a month hence.   Her complaint was one
under which the sufferer may linger a long while—may

even seem to be getting well again—but which will, sooner or later, surely kill.

We must not, therefore, blame the doctor beeause he was somewhat out of his calculation. Of eourse the general publie, after that sad knock-kneed failure, denouneed him as wholly ineompetent; but his brother, whose knowledge of him dated from an earlier period, did not judge him so harshly. He knew that, speaking generally, Joe was a elever fellow in his profession: but he was not to be relied on from one day to another. If he treated a patient aecording to his knowledge and experience, all would probably go well; but it was always the toss up of a halfpenny whether he would not try some madeap experiment, more likely than not to prove injurious, and, it might be, fatal to the objeet of his tentative seienee.

From time to time the professor also visited the sick Englishwoman, and upon several oeeasions attempted, though without success, to gain her eonfidenee. It would, however, be almost impossible to convey any distinet idea of the various and eonflicting emotions of his mind at this period. What, he asked himself over and over again, was the eourse of eonduet an honourable man, under the eireumstanees, should pursue? Was he aeting properly in allowing a woman, to whom he owed a heavy debt of gratitude for her great kindness to him, to blindly marry a man who had a wife living? The marriage was fixed to take place in a few weeks from the date when Polyblank diseovered the wife's existenee. Joe had then predicted that she would not live more than a week. Had she died within the time specified, Raynal would have been free to eontract another marriage. In that case, why should he disclose a seeret whieh would only oeeasion unnecessary unhappiness?

With respect to Raynal's conduct, was he aware of this woman being alive? Had he known it, would he have proposed to marry Manon? Some time ago, Polyblank felt certain that Raynal was disturbed by some secret sorrow. At that period, Raynal never, by word or deed, betrayed his sentiments with regard to Manon. But all at once his whole manner underwent a change. He declared his love, and asked her hand in marriage. It would seem from this, Polyblank argued, that Raynal, at the time of his change of conduct, had received false news of his wife's death.

Supposing all this to be the case, how was it that Raynal had been living separate from his wife? What had led to the separation? How was it that his marriage was a secret? Supposing the sick woman lingered on, and the wedding-day arrived, should he, Polyblank, stand quietly by and allow Manon to go through a marriage ceremony which would be but a mockery? No; he felt that when that time should arrive, it would be his duty to come forward and speak openly. Yet suppose, after he had done this, and caused an exposure and a scandal, and inflicted much misery on Manon, that, on the very next day, the first wife should die?—suppose she were not really his wife after all? Although she called herself so, she might have no legal claim to the title. Polyblank was only a poor schoolmaster, whose good name was three-quarters of his stock-in-trade. Might he not get himself into trouble if he stirred in the matter? Excepting a few words spoken by a woman in a fever, what evidence had he to go upon? The laundress had referred to a leather case containing papers. The case was there, sure enough, and the question was, what papers did it contain? Suppose he should find, too late, that the result of his meddling was only the discovery of a mare's-nest, and that he had exposed himself to an **action** for slander, which would probably compel him to leave the town, and at any rate would cost him his post in the college ?

Thus he argued the case, coolly and disinterestedly, he tried to make himself believe; but never since the world began was there a more shallow pretence than this same cool and disinterested argument—and, struggle as he would, the truth at length forced itself upon him. He was himself hopelessly in love with the pretty baroness, and if she married Raynal his future existence would be one long scene of misery. But though he was madly in love, he was not mad enough to suppose that there was any chance for him. He felt positively certain of two things: one was that Manon loved Raynal; the other, that she never would love him. If he kept the secret, she would surely marry Raynal; and if he divulged it, time alone would show the result.

In a fever of excitement he struggled with his daily occupations. When these thoughts took possession of him in his lonely room at night, he often would catch up his hat and rush hastily out of the house; then wander about the dark streets, or upon the unfrequented highway across the marshes : and coming back at last exhausted by fatigue, he was able to rest and forget his troubles in sleep. But during school hours there was no escape, and sometimes his sufferings were almost more than he could bear. Thus things went on from day to day, until one Sunday evening, as he approached the sick woman's bedside, she slowly turned her head upon the pillow, and said in a low earnest tone :

" Fetch me the English clergyman. I want to see him."

Polyblank stood silent; his heart beating fast, his tongue refusing to move.

" Yes," he stammered at last, and left the room.

More than once he had expected this would come.
She would want to see the clergyman. She would tell
him all, and he would at once communicate with the
baroness. Polyblank hurried along, never pausing to
ask himself a question. He would have thought himself
a criminal had he failed to execute the dying woman's
orders ; and he did not venture to inquire what his own
feelings were, and whether he was pleased that any other
should be the instrument of doing what he felt would
have been wrong had he done it himself. He delivered
his message, returned home, and locked himself in his
room, afraid that any one should speak to him or see his
face. He ventured out no more that night; but, sitting
by the window, watched the door of the opposite house.

It was so dark that he could with difficulty discern the
faint outline of the passers-by ; but a fitful gleam of light
from the swinging street lamp fell upon the laundress's
door, and presently it showed him the clergyman's face
as he stood there waiting to be admitted. A few instants
afterwards a man's shadow crossed the blinds of the sick
woman's room. Then there was a long pause, and presently
the shadow crossed again, and a minute afterwards the
clergyman passed out into the street. A moment, and his
figure was lost in the gloom. Had he the secret ? How
would he use it ?

The professor caught at his hat with an idea of running after and questioning him; but his constitutiona
timidity intervened, and, standing irresolute for a few
minutes, he sat down again at the window, and after
watching an hour or two longer, went weary to bed.

It wanted now only a week of the day fixed for the
marriage. What would happen between now and then ?
He proceeded next morning as usual to the college, and

went through his ordinary duties like one in a dream, scarce knowing what was going on around him. Hurrying away the moment the hour of release arrived, be sought for Joe, to obtain tidings of the sick woman, but unfortunately that distinguished practitioner could not be found. He left a message, and went home. He waited impatiently until one in the morning, and at last went to bed and obtained some feverish sleep. Next morning he hastened to Joe's lodgings before going to the school, and learnt that Joe had gone to endeavour to obtain an important medical post then vacant in a town about six leagues distant, and would probably not return until next day. He did not return that night. The professor, though tormented by anxiety, yet refrained from making inquiries, deeming it prudent to leave the business in the clergyman's hands.

Watching at the window that night, he saw the clergyman's wife enter the laundress's house.

"If she tells her, it will not long remain a secret," thought Polyblank.

Wednesday was the day when Joe ought to pay a visit to the college to inspect the pupils, and the professor gave up his hour's recreation at twelve o'clock to wait for him.

"Have you been to see the Englishwoman?" were the first words he uttered when his brother appeared.

"The Englishwoman?" said Joe; "no! I have had something else to think of. Bless the Englishwoman! What a wonderful interest you take in her!"

"I do take a great interest in her. You will see her to-day, Joe, wont you, and tell me how she is?"

"Yes—all right; if I've got time. By-the-bye, the wedding day is drawing near, isn't it?"

"Ye—es."

That evening Joe called upon his brother to report progress.

"It's an extraordinary thing, but she is much better than on the first day I saw her. For what I know, she may now live another three months."

" Was she alone ?"

"No; there was a middle-aged woman there—very stiff in the back—English : who said, with a toss of the head this way, ' A friend of the Baroness de Grandvilain, I believe ?' "

" And you said—— ?"

" I have that honour, at which point the conversation concluded."

The next day passed without any incident worthy of record. The professor, watching at his window, saw the clergyman's wife leave the laundress's house during the evening. On the Friday, Joseph, after paying the sick woman a visit, reported that she was much worse again. Saturday came, the day before the wedding. The hours crept slowly along within the college walls until noon, and then Polyblank felt that he could endure his imprisonment no longer, and, seeking out Roustoubique, begged for a half-holiday. The Proviseur laid down the newspaper he was reading, and regarded the professor with astonishment. " A half-holiday ! What do you mean?"

" I hope you can arrange it somehow, sir. I am very unwell, and—and—I cannot attend this afternoon."

" Cannot ! You *must*, my dear sir," replied Roustoubique, smiling pleasantly. " A half-holiday ! Impossible." Then he went on reading the paper.

There was a heavy volume on the table, with a massive wooden binding, with which it might have been possible to split any cranium of ordinary thickness. Polyblank looked towards it with an angry glitter in his eye—

something of the ugly look a sheep assumes when goaded into a rage of terror—but without a word he turned and left the room. Outside in the passage his heart beat tumultuously, and the hot tears sprang up in his eyes; but overcoming his emotion, he left the college, and proceeded towards his home through the back streets, not without engaging in his hundredth skirmish with his old enemies, the street boys. Arrived at his lodgings, he threw himself into a chair, covering his face with his hands, scarce knowing where he was or what he did. During the last week he had suffered indescribable torments, although it would have been impossible for any listener to his abrupt exclamations to have guessed at half the mad thoughts that were passing through his brain. Sometimes he gnashed his teeth and heaped curses upon Raynal's head; sometimes Manon was the object of his rage; and then, in a moment, he would sob out fervent prayers for her future happiness. What was the true wish of his heart, poor wretch, he hardly dared avow to himself. He never could have told it to another. He sat thus in his bedroom, this noon time, for a long while, utterly beaten down and prostrate.

The window stood open, and the church clock aroused him. It was time to return to the college. He arose, bathed his aching head, and prepared to start. As he passed out of the street door he saw the clergyman's wife coming out of the opposite house carrying a letter in her hand, but scarcely noted the circumstance. The weary afternoon passed away as many had done before. Bourdichon and Co. flew May-bugs; a new and exciting game was this day invented; a train of gunpowder was laid round the desk (which, in the shape of a horseshoe, occupied one side and two ends of the room), and communicated with a little magazine of the same material placed beneath an inkstand, and at a safe distance from the nearest pupil. The train was fired, the magazine exploded, and the inkstand blown up in a manner which caused some real alarm to the professor, and a great deal of simulated terror among the class.

At night in his lodging he sat musing, heedless of the progress of time. This was the eve of the wedding. Was Raynal with her now? No, he had heard Félicité tell her husband that the bridegroom had ordered a grand dinner at the " Three Crowns." He was going to give his last bachelor's entertainment to a few choice spirits, including one or two of the gentlemen whom Polyblank had met at the memorable dinner at the château. The day had been very hot and sultry. That evening scarcely a breath of air was stirring, and as twilight set in Polyblank rose and went out, and listlessly strolled through the dark streets in his old way.

Coming in the course of his purposeless wanderings in front of the hotel in the Little Place, a stream of light poured out upon him through the open windows of a room of the first floor, from which came also the sound of loud voices and merry laughter. A small crowd of idlers had assembled in the street below, and among these for a few moments the professor took his place, until he happened to observe a woman, attracted by his dismal countenance, looking at him very hard, and by a motion directing the attention of her companion to him. Then he turned his face homewards, and slowly retraced his steps. Just upon his threshold, however, Joe caught him, excitedly, by the arm.

" Do you know what has happened?"

" No; what do you mean?"

" She's gone."

" Who?"

" The Englishwoman. Raynal's wife."

" Dead !" gasped Polyblank.

" Dead ! No," replied the other impatiently. " Gone —gone away. Got out of bed ; crept out of the house while no one was about, and has gone away."

Without speaking a word Polyblank dragged his brother across the street, and breathlessly they ascended the laundress's stairs. There they found the laundress very red and angry, and the little nurse very white and frightened. But they could furnish no very useful information. The little nurse knew only that the clergyman's wife had written some letter in French, which the sick woman had dictated in English, and that after the Englishwoman had signed it the clergyman's wife had taken it away.

" Whom was that letter for, do you think ?" asked Joe. " The baroness, I suppose ?"

The professor made no answer. Did Joe think she was strong enough to walk ? he asked presently.

" She's as weak as water," replied the other ; " but she might find strength enough for a great effort under some powerful excitement. It will kill her, though ; that's a dead certainty."

" Joe," said his brother, after a pause, " she must not go to the château. Will you come and help me to look for her ?"

" Very well," said Joe, reluctantly. " We shall get a soaking, though. There's a storm coming on."

And even as he spoke the thunder rolled and crashed overhead.

But if they could be in time to prevent the meeting between the two women, they were too late to prevent the news reaching Manon, for it had come already.

Whilst she was gathering flowers in the garden the portress appeared at the window with a letter. Manon came forward to meet her, radiant with smiles and flushes of pleasure, thinking, no doubt, it was from Raynal. A little disappointed when she glanced at the superscription, she took it in her hand and sat down in the drawing-room to read it. The sun was shining brightly without. The birds were singing. The flowers in her lap exhaled a delicious perfume. Oh, it was a happy world, and she the happiest woman in it! She smiled again as she broke the seal. Then she read her death-warrant.

CHAPTER XIX.

A WHITE FACE AT THE WINDOW.

Ma rivale est triomphante,
Elle ordonne de mon sort,
Et je me vois dans l'attente
De l'exile ou de la mort.—CAZOTTE.

It was all over. The game was played out. The world was at an end. How could she live any longer? Why should she? Without his love, what was there left worth living for? Alone as she was, he filled so large a space in her eyes that there was no room left in the universe for anything else. His love was all in all to her. It was her whole world, and beyond its boundaries lay only darkness and despair.

While yet she held the dreadful letter in her hand, she heard Madame Dubosq's footsteps coming along the passage, and, as though she were flying from before some menacing danger, she made her escape through the window to the garden. Then entering the house again by the door, she hurried up to her own room. Before she had gained it, however, she heard Madame Dubosq's voice calling to her, and Madame Dubosq's footsteps following her like Fate. What possessed the woman, that she should want to trouble her—to persecute her thus, at such a moment? Probably she wanted to consult Manon upon some point of vital importance respecting next day's marriage feast. With something of the look of a hunted fawn, the baroness turned again and fled upwards towards the attics, and entering one which was used as a lumber room, closed the door and flung herself against it, panting, giddy, and bewildered. The midday sun lay hot upon the roof, and the close atmosphere of the room stifled her. She made her way through the scattered rubbish littering the floor, and, after a struggle, dragged open the heavy shutters and let in some air. Before her was a straight row of white, silent houses, their shutters all closed, as though their inmates were asleep or dead. Over the weather-stained slates of the roofs she could see a narrow strip of ragged moorland, bounded by the blue-grey hills. Not a sound—not a sign of life. The village street was hot, dusty, and empty. Along the whole length of the arid, white road, stretching away to the right, there was not a living creature to be seen. Manon leant against the window-sill, and with trembling fingers spread out the crumpled letter. She read it once, and twice and thrice, scarcely comprehending it. Her brain seemed in a whirl. Memory failed her, and every moment she was obliged to turn back again and re-read what she had just read to help her to understand what followed. Still she could not understand. It was all so unexpected, so astounding, so horrible! Presently, it became a question with her as to who had written the letter. Had he himself? Had he done it to try her? Could it be a hoax? Was he, after all, going to marry

her to-morrow, or was it all over? All over! Merciful
heavens! could it be possible that her happiness was to
end thus? Was it possible that this piece of crumpled
paper could contain so much misery? And if it were
really true, what was to become of her? What, indeed!
She sought a solution in the white, hot, dusty silence
before her, and her thoughts travelled over the housetops
beyond the moorland, over the grey hills and far away.
Once more she began to read the letter, and then with
her chin resting on her hand she gazed intently down
upon the courtyard stones below. The house and the
street were very still, but there was a strange, faint buz-
zing noise in her ears, like the drowsy hum of mosquitoes'
wings, or the sea-murmur of a shell. As she stood thus,
all at once a horrible feeling took possession of her which
seemed to drag her down. Why not? What had she
to live for? One spring, and there was an end to all
her misery, this side of Judgment. She raised herself
up to and knelt upon the window-sill, still gazing down-
wards. Her brain grew giddy. The humming in her
ears swelled to a confused roar, midst which she seemed
to distinguish half audible words—an imperious command, perhaps a threat or passionate entreaty. A hand
was laid upon her arm, and she sprang back from the
window. With the thought that she had just been
rescued from a fearful death, a deadly sickness overcame her, and she leant against the wall and closed her
eyes

"I beg your pardon, ma'am; Madame Dubosq sent me
to look for you. Dinner is ready. Are you ill?"

"I am not ill," replied Manon with a ghastly face.
"Only—only—come away—come away."

And holding the girl's arm, she dragged her from the
room and locked the door with terrified haste; as though
she shut up there a horrible danger.

And now she must go down to dinner and Dubosq. Yes, there was the inevitable Dubosq with her customary appetite. She was even hungrier, it would seem, than usual, and was impatiently crumbling and eating her bread.

"My dear, I couldn't think what had become of you."

"I was busy."

"I have been calling for you and looking for you everywhere. You were not in your room?"

"No."

"You were upstairs, though?"

"Yes, in the attic."

"In the attic?"

"Yes, I went to look for something."

"In that dreadfully dusty place, too. If you had only asked me to help you. And you found what you wanted?"

"No."

"I will look for it for you after dinner.

"It is not worth the trouble. I don't want it now. Talk no more about it."

Would the woman never drop the subject, and leave her alone? Would she never cease chattering and pressing upon her the contents of the dreadful dishes? She tried to eat. The food choked her. She played with her knife and fork, making believe to dine, lest she should be questioned and worried. While the Dubosq was jabbering, Manon folded and refolded her napkin, examining with scrupulous care the pattern in the cloth. Anything rather than raise her eyes, for she felt that she could not bear to look upon the face before her, so intolerable in its replete contentment. Without looking up, though, Manon noted with nervous irritability the sound produced by the working of Dubosq's indefatigable mandibles, and the gluck-glucking of the wine she swallowed.

Worthy soul! she harboured no secret sorrow in her

gentle bosom. She had no anxieties for the morrow, beyond those incidental to the successful issue of the grand wedding banquet in preparation. Why should she not eat, drink, and be merry? She saw that Manon was inclined to be thoughtful and silent, and so pursued her innocent babble without pressing too persistently for replies. It was not unnatural, she thought, that the young widow should be reflective; and she improved the occasion with an axiom or two appropriate to the circumstances. Since the world began has it not often happened thus?—that there has been a deep unfathomable gulf severing the nearest and dearest, sitting side by side upon the same hearth, or laying their heads upon the same pillow? What do we all really think of one another, we who shake hands and kiss? Heaven forbid that *all* the secrets of our hearts should ever be revealed!

All at once the thought of the letter occurred to Manon. She had not got it. Had she left it in the attic? Had she dropped it on the stairs? For her life she would not have her secret known—yet, alas! it must be known soon. If she had dropped the letter on the stairs, it was perhaps even at this moment in the hands of the servants, affording food for wonder and mirth, may be, over the stew-pans in the kitchen. The blood rushed in a torrent to her face at the thought, and she cast her eyes nervously around. Yet, strange to say, mingled with her fear was so much of prostration and mental torpor, that she could not at the moment frame a reasonable pretext for leaving the table to go in search of the missing note. Would the dinner never come to a close? Mechanically she accepted the plates handed to her, and allowed the servant to remove them with the food untasted; now and then looking up wistfully at the girl, seeking from her expression to discover whether or not she was in possession of the secret.   At length, however, the coffee came.

The meal was ended.   Manon rose and waited for a favourable moment to make her escape.   Not yet, however, was her ordeal over.   The Dubosq was desirous of her opinion upon the subject of the preparations, and she must submit to the torture.   Would such and such things be better so and so, or the other way?   Manon listened with an aching heart.   A score of times the dreadful truth was on her tongue's tip; yet her heart failed her when she would have revealed it; and the unspoken words seemed to choke her.   It was only when the Dubosq had left the room on some errand that she seized the opportunity and escaped.   She went quietly upstairs, unlocked the attic door, and glanced anxiously around.   There, on the floor, by the open window, lay the crumpled letter.   She approached it trembling, but without raising her eyes to the aperture; then snatching the paper from the ground and wrestling with the shuddering horror once more creeping over her, fled precipitately.

Gaining her chamber she locked the door, flung herself upon the bed, and for the first time her grief found vent in a flood of passionate tears.   She lay with her fair hair tumbled and tangled in a confused mass upon the pillow in which her face was buried.   After a while her sobs subsided, and no other sound broke the stillness of the chamber except a low half-smothered moan wrung from her at intervals by her bitter agony.   Not a very lengthened period, however, elapsed before the Dubosq came tapping at the door.

" My dear, I want to speak to you a moment."

" Please go away," the other cried, piteously; " I'm not well; I want to be quiet."

" Oh, it was only to ask you about the sleeves

to your figured silk. I would not detain you a moment."

" Do what you like with them, only leave me alone."

" Well, don't say afterwards that you were not con-sulted," said the Dubosq, bridling. " I'm sure you'd better decide !"

" No, I leave it all to you."

" Are you very ill ? Can I do anything ?"

" No, no, dear Mogador; only let me be quiet."

At last the tormentor was gone, and she was once more alone with her grief. Her eyes were dry now. Her sorrow had given place to a sullen rage, and she paced to and fro the length of the room, as a tigress wears life away within its barred cage. She came presently to a standstill before her looking-glass, and gazed upon the face which *he* had so often said was beautiful. It was dark and swollen now—the features contorted—the lips thin and bloodless, tightly drawn and tense. An impo-tent fury possessed her. She twisted her hair in her hands, and dragged at it savagely. She clutched her throat with a strong grip; and as her fingers slowly re-leased their pressure the purple marks they left showed vividly upon her fair skin. But once again there came a tapping at the door, and crossing the room, Manon, with an angry jerk, pulled it open, and stood with lower-ing brow and flashing eyes confronting the astonished Dubosq.

" It was only to know whether you were any better, my dear !"

" Good heavens, woman," cried the other, wildly, " cannot you let me alone ?"

She slammed the door to in the good lady's face, and flung herself down upon the bed gnashing her teeth with rage. After a short interval this paroxysm passed away, and she became calmer. Then she rose slowly and began to dress herself to go out. She took little pains with her toilet. Fastening her dress, which awhile ago her wilful hands had dragged and torn, she smoothed her hair, put on her bonnet and shawl, and, opening her bed-room door, stood for a moment listening on the landing. Very carefully then she descended the stairs, her heart beating violently at every creak, traversed the passage and passed out into the garden.

As she proceeded along the path Mimi and Bibi came running towards her with soft little cries. She stooped down and raised them in turns in her arms to kiss them. A little further on Ponto forced his way through the bushes with a joyous bark. One of her horses catching sight of her over the hedge dividing the garden from the paddock, as she passed beside it to open the side gate, whinnied and trotted up to rub his warm nose against her cheek. She spoke more tenderly if possible than was her wont to these dumb friends, and then went out into the lane. Twilight was giving place to night, and in the far distance the twinkling of the lamps upon the fortification of Saint Babylas was dimly visible. She turned her face towards the town, and walked rapidly along—so rapidly that she was tired and out of breath on reaching the turn of the long, dusty road at which the crucifix stood out sharply against the darkening sky. While pausing here a moment she heard behind her the sound of horses' hoofs and wheels, and a jingling and rumbling that told her the diligence was approaching. She signalled to the driver to stop, and inquired whether there was room.

There was one vacant place inside, and she took her seat opposite to a fat peasant woman in a cap and apron, nursing a basket and bundle, and from the former supplying herself with mouthfuls of cake and bites of apple.

Two blue-bloused clod-hoppers discussed the merits of some new mode of beet-root culture.

Manon sat silently in her corner. The other occupants of the diligence were strangers to her. She seemed to listen to their conversation without hearing a word that they said ; but, lost in thought, fixed her eyes for some time so earnestly upon the the fat peasant woman's face that she relinquished her refreshment in some confusion ; while one of the agriculturists at whom she in turn also stared as steadfastly, imagined that his discourse interested her, and was thereby enticed out of his depth into a sort of rhetorical whirlpool, wherein he finally sank.

The lumbering vehicle jingled and jolted along the dusty road, and then bumped and clattered over the uneven stones in front of the town gate. It stopped at the foot of the drawbridge, and the custom-house officer thrust a lamp in at the door, which made the passengers blink like a roost of owls ; and the official lingered for a moment or two, after asking the usual questions, to make quite certain that the still white face he saw was that of the lady of Longanna. Quite unlike our pretty Manon of heretofore, was she that night. What seemed like a grey shadow rested upon her features, deepening and hardening their lines.

Hers was now a face, which seen for a moment flattened against the glass in the chemist's shop window, Coquillard took to be that of a ghost. He was—this hopeful apprentice—just then supposed to be rolling pill paste ; but though physically he was up to his elbows in pilul. rhei, he was mentally up to his eyes in the horrors of the "Two Corpses," which, with a suppressed scream at the suddenness of Manon's approach, he let fall with a flop behind the counter. Before he had time to make up his mind as to whether or not the face belonged to a visitor from the other world, its owner had glided rapidly into the shop, and now stood by his side, with a hand tightening upon his wrist.

"Wha-at is it?" he asked, all of a tremble.

"Hush! hush!" she answered, in a low tone, glancing as she spoke towards the shop parlour. "Are they in?"

"Mrs. Pomponney is at Mrs. Gobinard's. Mr. Pomponney is at the café, but I can fetch him in a moment."

"At the café; yes, I thought so. Look, here is a napoleon for you. You must keep that to buy some story books, and I want you to do me a favour. Where is Mr. Polyblank?"

"He's not at home. Mrs. Pomponney will be back directly."

"Yes, yes, to be sure. I want to have a chat with her presently. There's no one in, then?"

"No—no one," the boy answered, wondering, and a little frightened.

"You can do me a favour, then. You know the experiments Mr. Pomponney and the doctor have been trying together up there in the little room where he keeps the—where you took the basin from?"

"Ye-es."

"I want to have a peep at the apparatus. It is for the sake of—it's only because I am very curious, you know, and——"

"Let me fetch Mr. Pomponney, ma'am. I'm sure he will be glad to show you the laboratory."

"No; there's no occasion for that. We will go upstairs without him. I have a reason for not telling him that you shall know by-and-by."

"But the key?"

"The key! Haven't you got it? He put it the other

day—at least he told me he kept it in there—in that desk."

Sure enough the key was in the place she had indicated, and she took it, as she spoke, and moved towards the staircase door. "Come," she said, beckoning him, "or, stay. Give me a light and I will go alone."

The youthful Coquillard looked at her blankly. He did not quite comprehend what all this meant, and he felt very uneasy.

"I had much better fetch Mr. Pomponney."

"No, no;" and she tightened her grasp on his wrist, and pulled him in the direction of the staircase.

He regarded her with his light blue eyes wide open in terrified wonder. There was something about her, it seemed to him, at once commanding and queenly, and spectre-like and horrible. What dreadful misfortune was about to happen? he asked himself, and for a moment he had an idea of breaking from her, rushing into the street, and crying aloud for assistance. Perhaps it would have been the wisest course; but little time was allowed him for reflection. He hesitated but a moment, and in that moment the opportunity passed away. Already she was half-way up the stairs. "Bring a light," she said. "Be quick!"

He was some time fumbling with the matches and lighting a small oil-lamp, which he took from a bracket in the shop. She, however, did not wait for him, but hurried up the stairs, groping her way in the darkness, and, arriving at the laboratory door, passed her hand over it in nervous haste to find the keyhole. In spite of her hurry, though, she had not been able to effect an entrance when Coquillard came up.

"I cannot turn the key," she said. "You try. Let me hold the light."

" I can hold it."

" No, you may let it fall, or—there, I have knocked it out.   You must light it again, and I will wait for you."

He had unlocked the door before this accident occurred, and he left her standing just within the room, while he went down the flight of stairs to relight the lamp.   While thus engaged he heard the jingling of glass, and cried to her, in alarm, not to move until he came back.   He was not long gone, although he had to light a couple of matches; but when he returned he found her looking deadly pale and trembling.

"Never mind the experiments," she said abruptly. "I don't care about looking at them, after all.   Lock the door and come down again."

He did as she bade him, and followed like one in a dream.   Bidding him hastily good night, she passed out into the street, and in another moment the darkness had swallowed her up.   Young Coquillard remained behind with the lamp in his hand, his eyes and mouth wide open, amazed and confused by this strange visit.   A sudden dread crept over him when he thought she might have come and taken him thus unawares for the purpose of defeating the famous experiment—for he recollected that she seemed angry while Mr. Pomponney was descanting on that topic on the occasion of her last visit to the shop. Thereupon he went quaking to have a look at the laboratory.   To all appearance nothing had been disturbed. But she must have had some motive for going into the room—must have done something, or why was she so agitated ?   He recollected that he had heard the clinking of glass, and he cast his eyes around, wondering what reason she could possibly have for meddling with the bottles, which stood in dusty confusion.   He would have concluded that she had accidentally knocked against one of the shelves, and thus caused the noise he had heard, if it had not been for her agitation. All at once the truth burst upon him suddenly as the lightning's flash. He turned his eyes in a tremor of apprehension to a corner where a certain blue glass bottle stood. The stopper had been removed. There was a label on this bottle, on which was inscribed the single word " Poison."

CHAPTER XX.

THUNDER AND LIGHTNING.

Go back.
She has been yours through all, and you are hers;
And though you went not back, there is a bar.
That now for ever sunders me from you.—HOME.

A STORM was gathering. The day had been hot and sultry. From time to time a hollow moaning gust swept through the dark deserted streets; and now and again the pavement was spotted by large rain drops, but as yet the tempest held aloof. The storm might burst, however, as soon as it chose, and the elements rage in all their fury for what some people cared that night in the town of Saint Babylas. In a private room in Madame Gobinard's establishment was assembled a gay party of gentlemen, who had dined sumptuously at Pierre Raynal's expense, and cared not the value of a tavern toothpick for foul weather. They were choice spirits these friends of the expectant bridegroom—bons vivants and bons enfants they would have been called in the romances of their own country; in British music halls, jolly dogs.

For the most part they were young men who had seen life and were now in liquor. This was the farewell feast of a gay young bachelor, and these were familiar friends in whose congenial companionship some of his uproarious bachelorhood had been passed. You cannot be surprised then if a tinge of sadness mingled with the merriment—there were moments betwixt the cup and the lip in which regretful thoughts of the coming sacrifice would intrude unbidden, or that the voice of a jolly dog proposing the health of his host should betray a certain huskiness indicative of feelings which are said in the literature of dinner table-life to " do honour alike to the head and the heart." Loud, however were the cheers, and uproarious the acclamation, with which the other jolly dogs hailed the toast, and there was more than one moist eye and full heart in the little company.

But there are maudlin periods in everybody's drink, you scoffers may suggest ; and it is the nature of a jolly dog all the world over, in his moments of enthusiasm, to be carried away by the belief that he has feelings which do him honour, and which Providence has wisely ordained should be a source of much gratification to himself, though perhaps of little value otherwise. A very jovial feast it was, though, in spite of this passing shadow, and Pierre Raynal was voted vocally, in the English style, the jolliest of jolly good fellows. The room became very hot as the banquet drew towards a close, although the windows were wide open ; and some of the guests, with loosened vests and flushed faces, were glad enough to step out upon the balcony to breathe a little fresh air. The wine had flowed freely, as might be seen by the flushed features and heavy eyes of most of the company. The moderateur-lamps, with globes of rose-coloured glass, threw a red glow upon the scene, which, with the figures of the men, lounging in various positions, with its disordered furniture and littered table, had something of the appearance of the robbers' retreat that one is familiar with at the theatre. It was about this particular period of the evening, when the host, as sometimes happens with hosts, had slipped out of his guests' recollection, and they were enjoying themselves hugely without reference to him, that the waiter came in and whispered in Pierre Raynal's ear, handing to him at the same time a sealed letter.

" The man who brought it said you must have it at once, sir," observed Alexander, with a deprecating air. " I said you could not be disturbed, but he would not take no for an answer, and so really——"

" Very well ; I'll see whether there's any reply."

He turned the letter over carelessly in his hand, wondering what it could be about, but without feeling very much interest in the matter. He knew the writing, and was, you see, so much in the habit of receiving notes from the loved one. It does not follow that he loved her any the less because he was not dying to see what was behind the seal. There is, according to words of wisdom, a time for all things, and suppose this should be one of those crossed sheets of pretty nothings with undotted i's which she so loved to write, and he so loved to read. This surely was neither the time nor place for its perusal. Playing with the billet then for a moment or two in his fingers, he at last decided upon breaking the seal, then read :

" Come to me at once."

These were the only words, unaccompanied by any signature—without any term of endearment. He noticed, too, in some surprise, that it was written upon a sheet of his own private note paper, surmounted by his monogram, and that the envelope enclosing it was also his. What did it mean ? He rose from the table without attracting any attention, glanced round with the idea

of apologizing for absenting himself, saw he was not no-
tieed, and followed Alexander from the room.

" Where is the person who brought this letter?"

" Here, sir."

It was the landlord of the house where he lodged,
who smirked in expectation of proffered refreshment.

" Where did you get it, friend?"

" From the Baroness de Grandvilain. She wrote it
in your apartments, and is waiting for you there now."

" Waiting for me?"

" If you please, sir."

He was anything but pleased, for he had a foreboding
of evil, and felt very uneasy. One course only was open
to him. He must go at once and see what she wanted.
He therefore sent Alexander in search of his hat, bade
him tell the company that he would return in a few
moments, and hurriedly left the hotel. There was no
vehicle to carry him, but his lodgings were not further
than the next street. It was fortunate that they were
not more distant, for the storm so long threatening gave
indications that at length it was about to descend in all
its fury. The air was thick and sulphurous, and the
silence for the moment was as profound as the darkness
was intense, save where the glimmering street lamps at
intervals emitted a feeble ray.

As he reached the door, and was in the act of crossing
the threshold, a stream of blue lightning tore athwart
the sky, and for an instant the white houses on the opposite side of the street gleamed forth ghost-like, then
vanished as suddenly, while directly overhead broke a
deafening crash of thunder. He found the baroness
standing in the centre of the room, and as he approached
she remained silent and motionless, her face so white and
bloodless, she seemed as though she had been turned to stone.

14

"Manon," he said, as he advanced, "what has happened?   Speak to me, Manon.   Are you frightened by the storm?"

Whilst speaking he had reached her side, and he stretched out his arms to encircle her waist; but she shrank back from him, shuddering.

"No, no," she cried.   "Not yet—not again.   Not till you know all."

"Know all?" he repeated, with a darkening brow. Know all!   What would she say?   Had she discovered his secret, or—dreadful thought—had some pecuniary misfortune befallen her?   Nothing was certain.   Yet that could not be.   Was he upon the point of allying himself to a beggar?   No.   She must have learnt the truth.   His arms dropped slowly as she drew back. His lips, tightly compressed, seemed prepared to bar the passage to any hasty word which might rise unbidden before he was sufficiently master of himself to speak with safety.   She also was silent for a moment; and then in low tremulous tones she spoke, clasping her hands together, her white fingers twisting and tearing at one another in her strong agitation, as though she would have detracted from her mental agony by the duller sense of physical pain.

"You know, Pierre," she said, "I told you that it would kill me if anything happened to part us—that if death took you from me, I should soon follow you. Perhaps you thought that those were idle words; as I might think, probably, if I heard them spoken by some other; but oh! you would believe me if you knew what I have suffered to-day since I learnt that we must part—since I learnt that henceforth you were dead to me."

His lips quivered, and he made a motion of speaking,

but held his peace and waited for the end, and, as he did so, there was noticeable in the expression of his eyes an intense curiosity and cowering dread which might have implied that he knew the thing that was to be spoken, but wanted to learn how its discovery had come about. Without removing her eyes from his face she took from her pocket the crumpled letter that had awhile since struck her down, and handed it to him to read. His hand shook slightly as he took it from her, but his features in no way changed as he read down the page of crabbed writing; then he turned the leaf and read on slowly to the end. So very slowly, though, did he read, and so long did he linger over the last lines, that Manon could scarcely endure the torments of suspense she suffered. Yet, as she waited and watched for some sign of astonishment and indignation, and waited in vain, the foolish hope she had nursed, in spite of her reason, died slowly out, and left her despairing.

"It is true, then?" she said at last, hoarsely, "and there is an end to all."

He did not raise his eyes to her face. He still seemed to be reading the letter; at least he held it before him, probably from the same feeling which induces a criminal to delay giving the signal for the executioner's axe to fall.

"It is quite true," at length he answered, sullenly.

She pressed her hands to her face, and from her lips escaped a low, plaintive cry, such as might be wrung from a brave and delicate woman struck by a brutal hand. Even at this moment, however, a gleam of hope broke in upon her blank misery. He could not have meant to wrong her! He was not altogether to blame.

"Pierre," she said entreatingly, "tell me. You did not know she was alive when you asked me to marry you.

You deceived me; you told me nothing of your former marriage, but that was because you thought it would pain me to know you had loved her first. And yet you might, for you knew how I myself had been forced into a hateful marriage while I was quite a child—with no will of my own. Oh, Pierre, you need not have doubted my love for you, or feared that I should have doubted yours."

As she spoke she had, by almost imperceptible degrees, crept up to his side. He still doggedly avoided looking at her, and now she took his hand in hers, where it lay passive between her slender fingers, irresponsive to their eager pressure.

" Oh, Pierre," she continued, in a low tone, with a wistful longing in her tearful eyes, " you were forced into this marriage as I was, and you thought her dead?"

What struggle was going on in his mind? Was he still hesitating as to the course he should pursue? But surely that were impossible when there were only two courses to choose from—the right and the wrong. But listen when he speaks:

" I was forced into it," he said, looking up at last, " and I should have been a villain had I not married her. God only knows, though, what I have suffered since— what shame and humiliation. But I thought she was dead. I swear to Heaven I thought she was dead. I had all the particulars from Alexis d'Abligny, who brought me news from England. The whole story being, as I thought, buried with her, I knew it would only pain you to hear it, and so—I never told you."

" Oh, thank Heaven for this," she cried, and hiding her face upon his breast burst into a fit of passionate sobbing, which, for a moment, he made no effort to check, being apparently too busy with his own thoughts to notice her.

Presently, the violence of her passion subsiding, she drew away from him again, and sank into an arm-chair standing by the side of a table against which he had been leaning. There, covering her face with her hands, she sat, silent and motionless.

Without, the storm raged fitfully. The lightning ever and again lighting up the gloomy, old-fashioned room with a sudden glare in spite of the heavy curtains almost covering the windows, whilst the thunder, rolling and rumbling over head, appeared at each return to grow nearer, louder, and more threatening.

Suddenly she started up in a paroxysm of agony :— "There is but one end to this if you still love me."

He raised his hand on high and swore by Heaven that his love had in no way abated, and that he was ready to lay down his life for her.

"I believe you," she said, clinging to him, "and I know that you will think as I do. Is not life hateful to us in this misery? Why, then, longer suffer when release is so easy and so close at hand? When but a brief hour of pain will set us free, Pierre," she continued, speaking rapidly in almost a whisper. "To-day I have been sorely tempted to put an end to my life, but I struggled against the desire, and wanted to see you once again to bid you farewell. Yet, now that we have met, I ask myself should we part? See! I have got poison here. What will it matter to us what the world may say when we are gone. What is the world to us when hope is dead?"

Ah! reader, judge not this poor thing too severely. Remember she had been an actress, and had read the novels of her country, in which incidents of this nature not unfrequently find a place. Think of what she had suffered. How high her hope had soared, and to what a depth of misery she had fallen—enough to throw her mind off its balance. And, after all, do not similar scenes sometimes occur even in our land of propriety and decorum, and with persons, too, who have not trod the boards of the Châtelet Theatre? Poor Manon, we cannot excuse, but we may pity you.

She paused for his reply, and he stared in bewilderment at her white face and wild eyes, shining with a strange lustre; whilst her slender lithe fingers were clenched upon his arm in the passion of her appeal. Her bonnet was removed, and her shawl had fallen to the ground. Her light brown hair was matted on her forehead. The traces of her tears were still upon her cheeks. Never had she looked more beautiful, he thought, than at that moment; but there was something dangerous in her loveliness before which he recoiled shuddering. Hastily loosening her grasp, he broke into a loud unnatural laugh.

"You must be mad, Manon," he said. "I will take no poison. It seems we can't be married, but we need not die."

Surely these were words of wisdom; and he would have been a fool to listen to the frenzied promptings of that poor tortured heart before him. Surely she was not mad enough to think that he must put an end to his life because there was an end to their love—as though men killed themselves about such matters! Yet, mad woman as she was—desperate, passion-led, and unreasoning—she was not so utterly bewildered but that, struck by his tone, something of the truth began to dawn upon her now at last; and, at the crisis of her fate, the gilded mask slipping from the idol she had so long worshipped, revealed to her the foul imposture which it had hidden.

A bottle of brandy and some glasses stood upon the table close to his hand, and their jingle, as, in moving, he touched them, attracted his attention. He took up the bottle and twice filled a glass and emptied it. Apparently, the spirit nerved and steadied him, for, as he put the glass down again, the dark cloud passed from his brow, and he said :

" We need not despair yet, Manon, for perhaps things are not as black as they seem."

She looked at him in wonder, but made no reply.

" The marriage was solemnized in an out-of-the-way country place in England. I know for a certainty that the clergyman who performed it is dead. The clerk is a poor man, and if it were made worth his while——. Besides, I am not quite sure that the marriage was legal, for it was performed only in a Protestant church."

Yet was she silent as death. The storm for the moment seemed to have ceased. The wind was hushed. Again he poured himself out some brandy. The clinking of the glass, caused by his trembling hand, was the only sound which broke the silence reigning in the room.

" Perhaps, after all," he said at last, " perhaps she could be bought off, and if she defies us, can be defied."

It would be impossible to describe the effect which these few sentences produced on Manon. The man's coarse nature and inability to understand and appreciate the innate purity of the woman before him, had precipitated him into an irretrievable error. The shock she suffered by the disclosure of her lover's moral depravity might be compared to that sustained by the deceived votary when the Veiled Prophet bared his facial horrors to her view. It seemed as though the conviction which the last few minutes had afforded of Raynal's unworthiness, was the result of a life-long observation of his character, so clear, so certain was it. The shock was terrible—the sorrow more than she could bear.

Pressing her hands to her forehead, her white lips

moved, but she uttered no word. Perhaps Raynal thought he had convinced and conquered her, for he made as though he would take her round the waist. But in a moment she turned upon him with flashing eyes. " Do not touch me !" she cried, with mingled fierceness and contempt, as, shaking loose his hold, she moved towards the door. " There is an end to all !" and then, as he sprang towards her, she added in a cry of agony, " God forgive you !"

But at that moment, as she stood there, terrible in her beauty, the storm burst overhead with a deafening crash ; the blue lightning poured into and seemed to flood the room. The whole building rocked like a ship at sea. Then, in the moment which succeeded, were heard piercing screams, mingled with the sound of falling bricks, the hoarse shouting of men's voices, and the tramp of hurrying feet; but in the room there was silence. In the blinding glare she fancied she had seen him fall ; and now, in spite of her wrongs, a woman's instinct caused Manon to spring to the spot where he lay on his face. To turn him over and place her hand on his heart was the work of a moment, and it was an unspeakable relief to find that he lived.

Gathering her dress closely about her, she hurried downstairs, and passed out into the pouring rain, heedless of the suggestions of the women gathered about the door, frightened by the lightning's blaze, but even more affrighted by the fire they saw burning in Manon's eyes.

She was without bonnet or shawl, but was unconscious of the fact. Through the streets she hurried on, meeting no one by the way, and happily, favoured by the darkness, passed the drawbridge and the outer gate unnoticed, and found herself alone upon the marshes—alone with heaven,

out in the raging storm; alone in the world, loveless,
hopeless, sick at heart, wearied with her experience of
life, which, short as it had been, had brought so much
bitter sorrow to her. The rain descended now in torrents.
The sky above was black as ink, the marshes in some
places were already flooded, and the landmarks of the road
were fast disappearing. Yet, heedless of the danger
menacing her, she pressed onwards, her clothes saturated
and heavy with wet, her limbs trembling with the cold,
her step faltering and slow, the power of volition and
self-direction nearly gone; for brain fever was coming on,
and when the day dawned cold and ghastly over the
dreary marshes, it had her in its clutches fast.

She had just strength enough left to reach Longanna.
She felt that she must go home, though she scarcely
knew why, and crawled painfully along. The deserted
village street, in which not a soul was stirring, brought
to her mind an account she had once read of a city of the
dead, and she felt at that moment as though she were left
alone by herself in the world—the last of an accursed
race. At length, arriving at the château gate, she rang
the bell loudly. Immediately was heard the sound of
voices and of many feet within. The door opened to
show a little group of frightened women, who shrank back
in terror as their mistress appeared in their midst; bare-
headed, drenched with the rain, her flesh grey with cold,
and with dilated eyes, in which gleamed the light of
madness. She seemed to make an effort to speak, but
lacked the power, and passed on. When her hand was
on the dining-room door, Madame Dubosq, who hitherto
had been awed by Manon's appearance, caught hold of
her, exclaiming in a terrified tone:

"Not in there, madame! Not in there!"

But Manon broke from her and pushed open the door.

The blind was down, and a single candle cast a faint, yellow light upon shadowy objects. Joseph Polyblank was there, and the professor, and there was a third person. The form of a woman, over which they were bending, was stretched upon a sofa. It was Raynal's wife, who had left her bed and, in spite of the fury of the storm, made this journey to die under the roof of her whose brief dream of happiness she had for ever destroyed. When Manon came at length face to face with her rival, she stood in the presence of the dead.

CHAPTER XXI.

DRAWING TO A CLOSE.

So the dream it is fled, and the day it is done,
And my lips still murmur the name of one
Who will never come back to me !—AMELIA B. EDWARDS.

THE storm had left many traces of its progress in the streets of St. Babylas. A score of chimneys overthrown. Here and there a house partially unroofed. One wing of the old cathedral struck by lightning ; its grey stones scattered on the grass, with, grinning wry-mouthed from among them, three of the ugly faces that had ornamented its corners, carved by the monks three hundred years ago

But in the suburbs the destruction of property had been still greater, and further out on the marshes hay-stacks, out-houses, labourers' cots, entire farmsteads even, had been carried away by the flood ; while among the back lanes of Longanna the furious elements had wrought wholesale ruin. Early in the morning, clamouring at the château gates, was a mob of ragged women alter-nately crying aloud for succour, and giving utterance to shrill reproaches.

Many long faces were to be seen among the wealthier inhabitants of the town, for a vast amount of uninsured property had been destroyed by the storm, and several persons, who hitherto had been well to do, were reduced almost to penury. Some of the principal shopkeepers talked of selling their business for what it would fetch. What was the use of stopping in a place where there was no money left? Monsieur le Maire was actually seen in the Great Place running about distractedly without his hat! Later on, it was said that there had been a severe run on the bank, and subsequently the rumour was that the bank had found it necessary to suspend payments.

Those who had their wits about them, after the first moments of loud lamentation and hopeless despair, got pen, ink, and paper, and made a rough debtor and creditor account of their earthly possessions. By this process startling discoveries were made and conflicting results arrived at, the fallacy of which was afterwards attributed to mistakes in arithmetic, which perhaps were pardonable under such agitating circumstances.

Among these busy calculators was Madame Gobinard, at the "Three Crowns." In her little office, across the court-yard, her busy pen chirped merrily, but madame's face was of the gloomiest.

"Alexander!"

That sprightly domestic, somewhat languidly, responded. He, too, was indirectly a loser by the misfortune which had befallen the locality. A young lady, whom he had notions about, had an uncle who rented land in the marshes. What remained of its produce was now under water soaking. "Have you seen anything of Mr. Raynal this morning?"

"Not I, madame."

"Ask whether he has been here."

Alexander, departing gloomily to make inquiries, returned after a lapse of time with some animation observable in his deportment.

" He has not been here."

" Has any one seen him ?"

" No one.   Whether anyone will any more, is rather
uncertain."

" What do you mean ?   Has anything happened to
him ?"

" No one knows exactly.   One thing only is certain—
but there is a rumour."

Here followed the rumour in a whisper, jealously
guarded by the closed door of Madame Gobinard's office.
A little while afterwards, madame, continuing her
accounts, cast up a long addition, and frowned darkly at
the total.

To the solemn visages abounding at this period in
Saint Babylas's streets, the ruddy and joyous countenance of the great literary lion, Mr. Max, presented a
pleasing contrast, as he strolled along the shady side of
the leading thoroughfares, puffing placidly at a huge
regalia.   Little Paul, also radiant, and also provided
with a large cigar, met Mr. Max in the Little Place, close
to the door of the Café Leduc, and, hearing that he had
breakfasted, proposed that they should take a mazagran
together, and have a talk.

The coffee served, they threw themselves into easy
attitudes on the crimson velvet sofa, and Little Paul lit a
fresh cigar.

" This is an awkward affair about Raynal."

" What is it ?" asked Mr. Max.

" Oh, haven't you heard ?   I thought everybody knew
of it."

" I should like to hear, if you've no objection.   What
is it ?"

" " I know nothing for certain, mind. Be careful, please, not to quote me as an authority."

" I'll be most careful."

" It is only hearsay, mind."

" Rest assured."

" They do say, then——"

And the gentlemen laid their heads together and talked scandal under their breaths.

Later in the afternoon, Max, strolling down the street where Raynal had his lodgings, cast his eyes towards his windows, and there saw Raynal (who by this had quite recovered from the shock of the lightning) beckoning. With great presence of mind Mr. Max—wishing to avoid an interview—waved his hand, as though mistaking Raynal's meaning, and went his way, smiling brightly. Less fortunate, however, was Little Paul, also strolling in the same direction. Raynal having caught his eye beckoned to him in like fashion, and Cherami, taken off his guard, ascended to Raynal's chambers.

He found the young man very pale and haggard, and with a rather nervous manner. Would Paul smoke? he asked. No. Raynal fidgeted with a cigar-case lying upon the table. Presently he said—

" This is a bad business."

" Yes—what has happened?"

Raynal looked at him fixedly. Did he not know, then? " You received a letter, I suppose?"

" From Madame Dubosq. I hope that the baroness is not seriously ill? It was imprudent of her to be out in the storm last night."

" How did you know she was out in the storm?"

" How?—upon my word I hardly know. Some one said so—somewhere—at the café, I think."

They were talking of the affair then at the café!

" Altogether it is rather an unfortunate business," said Raynal, after a brief pause ; " but of course a day or two will set all right again. In the meantime I am bothered plaguily for a little money."

" If I could help you, my dear fellow," burst in Little Paul, with somewhat overacted heartiness, " I wouldn't require to be twice asked. But you know me. The lot of money I spend, and the precious little I earn. Hand to mouth, you know, and never a shilling in my pocket."

" Yes, yes, I know that." Here they shook hands. " Better times in store for all of us, I hope. You were talking the other day about an appointment you wished to obtain here in the public library. Have you heard any more about it ?"

" No ; there's not much chance of that, I am afraid."

" You're wrong there. I forgot to tell you yesterday I was talking to Tête about the office. It's almost a certainty that you will get it—with a little influence."

" I am awfully obliged to you old fellow." Here a little more hand-shaking. " I wish to goodness," said Little Paul, " I could manage this little money matter for you. How can it be done ?"

" Oh, that—never mind about it. Of course I did not expect you to have the money to spare. I thought, though, you might lend me your name. I know some one here who might then accommodate me—nominally for you. I should not like to ask for myself—for such a trifle."

" Well, we will see about it. When do you want the money ?"

" As soon as possible. It is only at this moment that I am pressed."

" If I bring the stamp the first thing to-morrow morn-ing, will that do ?"

" Yes ; thank you."

Then having shaken hands for the third time, the gentlemen separated, and Little Paul descended the stairs with a thoughtful countenance.

" I'll go and make inquiries for myself," he was thinking. " Supposing his statement to be true, I don't think I ought to start in debt. What is really Raynal's position? Will he ever repay me? They do say—but then who are ' they?' "

Who were they who went about spreading all kinds of strange reports regarding the postponed wedding? Who, indeed? Are there not always persons who " feel it their duty"—who " think it only right"—but " would not like it to go further," &c. &c.? At ordinary times there was quite enough chattering and tale-bearing done by the good folks of Saint Babylas; and even in these days of danger and disaster some sympathetic souls found a few spare minutes to say a word or two upon the subject of Manon's sudden illness; and you may be sure that the paucity of real facts to work upon did not in any way prejudice the inventive powers of the principal tale-bearers.

A score of reasons, each more extraordinary than the last, were ascribed as the cause of Manon's indisposition. But next day something of the real truth crept out. The exact truth did not even then transpire; but the rumours flying about the town settled down into one shape. There was something wrong about Raynal. That was why the affair had been broken off.

But when the official inquiries respecting the death of Raynal's wife took place, it was impossible that the facts of the case could any longer remain a secret.

That wondrously staid and decorous little maiden, hard

at work upon her everlasting stocking-mending, was seated at the door of her mother's house in the street of the Priests. Twilight had set in some time ago. It was nearly dark—too dark for almost any work but knitting—too dark for that, at last she came to think, and rising from her chair turned to go into the house. Her mother was out, and there was no one else indoors. It was for that reason she had taken her seat where we have found her. The mysterious disappearance of the sick lodger had made the laundress and her daughter a little nervous ; and the latter, left all alone, fancied that the passing strangers in the street would be better company than none at all.

Now, just as she was crossing the threshold to go in, a hand was laid upon her shoulder. "What makes you start so, my dear ?"

"A dark, handsome gentleman stood looking down at her—a stranger to the little nurse.

"I am not frightened," she made answer. "I did not hear you coming."

"You have an English lady stopping here ?"

"No."

"No !"

"She has gone away, we think. She went out last night."

The dark gentleman was evidently surprised and vexed by this intelligence.

"Where has she gone to ?" But on this point the little nurse could give no information. "We don't think she's coming back."

"Had she paid her rent ? Did she leave anything ?"

"There are some things upstairs."

"Is your mother or any one else at home ? Your lodger will be back presently, I think. I was to wait for her. If her room is open I had better wait there."

Seeming rather mistrustful of the handsome gentleman's intentions, the little nurse, after a momentary hesitation, lit a candle and led the way upstairs. He must have been of a very thievish disposition who would have appropriated any of the rubbish scattered about the meanly furnished apartment; but the child kept her sharp eyes fixed upon the stranger, and followed his every movement. He cast a scrutinizing glance around, and was not long before he caught sight of the old writing-case which had attracted Polyblank's attention. Glancing from it towards the little nurse and back again, he bit his moustache, and reflected for a few moments. Then with an impatient gesture strode over to the window and pulled it open.

"I'll amuse myself by looking out until she comes. You need not wait."

But she did not leave him altogether. She made no answer, but going as far as the door, left it standing wide open, and took up a position on the landing, from which she could keep a sharp look-out upon his movements.

Seeing her object, he soon called to her to come back into the room.

"How long has your lodger been with you?"

"A good long while."

"And she has a good many friends, I suppose? Why did not your mother send to them?"

"She only knew the two English gentlemen, the doctor and the professor."

"Polyblank!"

"Yes, and the wife of the English priest, who wrote a letter for her."

"Oh! she wrote, did she?"

With rather an ugly scowl for so handsome a gentle-

15

man, the stranger turned on his heel without asking any further questions, and went back to the window.

" What did that fellow want to mix himself up in the business for ?" the stranger was thinking, looking at the moment at a light in a window opposite. " It was he, I've no doubt, who wormed the secret out of her, then acquainted her with the position of affairs here, gave her all information, and urged her to write to Manon. She seems to have been very ill, if I may believe what she said in her letter. Why did they keep her alive ? They must have had some end in view. Ah, I see it now ! I can see their whole game. It was not Polyblank who wrote, but the clergyman's wife. Polyblank, instead, was trying to keep the affair dark. The scoundrel knew what would best serve his purpose. He would rather have had us married, and then turned up quietly with his little secret, and wrung a handsome annuity out of us for hush money. He must be greatly enraged at the failure of his scheme. As for me, I shall do yet: I can get a divorce. After all Manon loves me, in spite of the rage into which she put herself. She does love me ; and as long as that is the case I can do what I will with her. I have no fear on that score; but now that that woman has found me out here, the rest may follow, and then——"

His meditations were here interrupted by the sound of footsteps on the stairs, which having also caught the ear of the little nurse, she ran down to meet the new comer. For a moment Raynal stood irresolute, listening to the sound of their voices as they conversed together in hurried whispers, then sprang towards the writing-case, and with a violent effort wrenched it open. A few ragged papers, old letters, and bills met his eye, and these he tossed carelessly on one side, bestowing no more than a passing glance on them.

Then he came to a letter in an envelope, with Australian stamps upon it. While he had this in his possession the laundress entered the room, and raised her hands in astonishment on seeing how he was occupied.

" What are you doing, sir? You must not touch those papers. The police will be here directly to take possession of the effects."

He did not seem to hear her. He was still reading the letter, and as he did so, his features contracted convulsively, and the perspiration broke out in large drops upon his brow.

" Give me those papers," continued the woman.

And she made an attempt as she spoke to draw away the writing-case; but his hand tightened on it, and he held it fast whilst he still read on.

" I cannot let you touch the papers," she said. " They are under my care until the officers arrive; now that the poor woman is dead."

" Dead !" He looked up suddenly and listened with a fixed, stony expression in his eyes, as though he scarcely understood the meaning of her words.

" Yes, dead enough, poor thing; but not dead without her share of suffering. And what does the villain care ? Not a jot, I'll stake my life on it. What do men care for the misery they bring on those who are fools enough to believe in them ?"

" Where is she ?"

" At the château over there. At the château in Longanna, and it's likely enough there'll be two dead women under that roof before they have taken the poor Englishwoman away. The baroness, they say, is not likely to live out the night."

He started slightly at this news; then folding up the letter he had been holding in his hand, prepared to put

15—2

it away in the breast-pocket of his coat. The woman caught him by the arm.

"Who are you, sir, who come interfering with these things? Leave them alone. Put back that letter or I will cry for help. What's your name? Where do you come from?"

"I have more right than any one to what is here," he said, shaking himself loose from her hold on him. "The woman who is dead was my wife."

"What! then you are the man who deserted her! The wife of the English priest told me all the story not an hour ago. You are this Mr. Raynal that the baroness was going to marry! You have killed them both, then. But don't think you will go unpunished in another world, though you get off so easily in this."

While she was speaking, he turned away, with a gesture of impatience and scorn. It seemed as though the matters of which she spoke were of but trifling import by the side of some other subject occupying his thoughts.

He opened the writing-case, and again turned over the papers it contained; then once more took the letter from his pocket, to look at its date.

"If I had had money I might have kept them quiet," he muttered, half aloud. "I ought to have married her long ago. Now it's too late—unless I make one last effort. Oh, what a fool I have been to waste so much time."

He turned upon his heel without another word, and passing out of the room, began to descend the stairs. The laundress called after him:

"Are you going away like that? Have you nothing to say? Leave me your address."

"I will come back."

" When ?"

" In an hour or so. Be in no fear—you shall be paid what is owing to you."

" I did not ask for it."

" Well, well. I will return during the evening."

About an hour afterwards Raynal rang at the château gate, and was refused admission."

" Madame is too ill to see any one."

" Let her know that I am here."

" The doctor said she was not to be disturbed."

" Is the doctor here now ? Who is it ?"

" The English doctor, Mr. Peau-le-blanc."

He turned away with a half-uttered oath. They were all conspiring against him. How could he hope to struggle successfully against such odds ? He went away, but returned in a short time with a letter which he had written at a cabaret in the village. This time he asked to see Madame Dubosq, but she sent out word that she could not leave the sick lady's bedside ; so he went away, after requesting that the letter might be given to Manon, and cursed his hard fate a thousand times as he walked home across the marshes.

" And he never asked a question about the poor dead woman, lying there upstairs," the old portress thought as she looked after his retreating form. " A bad heart, that ; but he will meet with his reward. A cruel, bad man. And to think that she could love the likes of that ! Why are such men allowed to live, and go about making people miserable ?"

Some portion of the old road was under water, and he was obliged to go a long way round to avoid the flood ; so that he was exhausted and weary when at length he reached the town gate. As he was entering the Little Place he saw Mr. Tête, the mayor, and Paul Cherami,

walking along, arm and arm, talking and laughing.
What he had told Paul about the appointment was only
partly true.   Raynal had heard that there was a chance
of Paul getting it, but that it was not very likely.   Apparently the latter part of the information was incorrect.
The mayor would never be so friendly with Paul unless
the affair were as good as settled.

Raynal crossed the Place, but before he could reach
them they had separated, and gone in opposite directions.
He overtook the mayor.

"Good evening, Mr. Tête."

The mayor drew back, and coloured slightly.

"Good evening," he said, then dropping his eyes
passed on hurriedly.   It was very evident that his intention was to avoid Raynal's company.   The rumours
afloat were gaining consistence, and some of the truth
was coming to light.   Reddening deeply, Raynal entered
the Café Leduc, and on the threshold, encountering an
acquaintance he was in the habit of meeting there, was
cut again.

The lady behind the counter, too, did not accord him
the gracious smile and inclination of the head with which
she usually greeted his arrival, being at the moment remarkably busy at her needlework.   Lastly, the waiter,
at other times so ready with his proffered services, kept
his place at the other end of the room, where he was
trying a difficult side-stroke at a disengaged billiard-table,
and, when summoned, approached slowly.

Raynal glared defiantly around upon the assembled
company.   "There's not an idiot in the whole town who
does not know every pro and con, and in and out of the
cursed business," he thought ; "and this is how I am
treated ; without having had a chance given me of saying
a word in my defence.   And all this coil about that

woman! If they knew the whole truth, now, and what fear has been haunting me these two years past!"

It was clear enough that the regular customers at the Café Leduc were not anxious for Raynal's society, and when he looked to the right or to the left, he found two or three groups with heads close together, mumbling, while their eyes were fixed upon him. He rose, at last, in disgust, and strode out of the room, slamming the door to after him.

"Curse them all!" he said; "as if I wanted their sweet looks or kind wishes. I can get on well without those, I daresay."

But all the world, it would appear, was not anxious to shun him. On the contrary, there was one person, of rather a horsey exterior, who, catching sight of Raynal from the opposite side of the way, crossed over and tapped him on the shoulder.

Raynal turned a white face to meet his.

"Oh, it's you!"

"Yes, it is. I have been looking for you all day. Twice at your place, where they said you were out. Two or three times at the 'Three Crowns.' Up and down everywhere."

"You have taken a deal of trouble. What do you want?"

"I want my bill settled—that's all. Hire of saddle-horses, half-purchase money of dog-cart; good long score I've got against you, one way and another—a couple of thousand francs and more."

"You needn't be afraid; you'll get it. What makes you so pressing now?"

"It's almost time I was beginning to be so; your bills are long overdue. I can get neither principal nor interest. One need have the patience of Job."

" Dont talk so loud, if you please.   The people at the
café door can hear you."

" I'm not ashamed of what I say.   I tell no lies."

" Of course not.   Who said you did?   But you're
labouring under a mistake.   You have heard all this
nonsense they're talking about me in the town.   You've
heard, perhaps, that I had another wife alive when I was
going to marry the baroness.   Have you heard, though,
that this wife is dead?   Between ourselves, the match is
nothing like broken off.   But keep this quiet, and have
patience for a day or two more at the outside, and you
shall have every penny of your bill."

The horsey man, taken in by Raynal's truthful manner,
nodded and winked mysteriously, and took his departure,
leaving his debtor to go quietly home.   Raynal found
some letters waiting for him there from other persons
who wanted their money, and could not possibly wait
any longer.   Among these was Madame Gobinard, who
had a heavy account to settle, and would feel much
obliged if Mr. Raynal could pay her what he owed.

Even while he was engaged in the perusal of these
vexatious epistles, a loud knock came at the door.
Raynal bade the knocker enter.

It was Doctor Tominet, very red-faced, and much out
of breath, who threw himself into a chair without offering any friendly salutation, and only removing his hat
for a moment to wipe his head with a snuff-coloured silk
pocket-handkerchief.   Then putting it on again when he had
done so, he scowled defiance from beneath his broad brim.

" You expected me, I suppose?" said he, at length
breaking the silence.

" No," replied Raynal, wearily, " I was not thinking
of you; but I'm not surprised.   You, too, have come for
money, I suppose?"

" We wont waste words.   I have."

" You ean have nothing at this moment.   You are all alike ; you'll give no time and listen to no reason."

" I've listened long enough.   Besides the marriage is broken off, and you know I let you have the money only on the strength of your grand promises.   You were to have been married to-day."

" It has been put off, not broken off.   I shall be married in a week or two.   You must wait till then."

" I tell you frankly, Raynal, I don't believe it. If half what I hear is true, the affair is finished for good and all ; and even if it were not so, she'll never get better of her illness.   That vagabond quaek—that pig of an English-man—he murders every one he gets into his hands.   I would not give a big sou for her life."

" I tell you, you are mistaken. But do what you like ; I'll not eondeseend to ask for indulgenee."

" Ask or not, I'll wait no longer," eried Tominet, rising and buttoning his eoat aeross his breast.   " At noon, to-morrow, my fine fellow, if you don't let me have the money, I'll loek you up."

" Very well ; do your worst."

When Tominet was gone, Raynal loeked the door and threw himself upon the sofa.   But in a few moments he had risen again, and drawing forth the letter he had put away in his breast-poeket, read it through very slowly.

" There is nothing left but to run for it," he said, aloud, as at length he returned the paper to the plaee from whieh he had taken it.   " The game is up here, and I should be mad to remain any longer.   No ; when I shall have got the money in the morning, by the help of Cherami's name, I shall depart at onee.   A thousand franes will do."

Surely so small a sum might easily be obtained, and

there were many places in the wide world where he might live happily, out of the reach of the strong arm of the law. With this reflection our rascal ate a hearty supper, took a stiff glass of grog, and went to bed. But more than once during the long night he woke up, struggling with some imaginary foe, and once, half springing from his bed, listened, with fast-beating heart and trembling limbs, to a fancied foot-fall on the stairs.

"It's nothing," he said, leaning back, with a sigh. " I shall be glad, though, when I get away from this place. I wish now that I could have obtained the money and gone yesterday."

CHAPTER XXII.

WEARY WORK.

La parole est une sotte traduction.—NODIER.

IT would, perhaps, have been the wisest course for Raynal not to have lost sight of his friend Little Paul, after obtaining his promise of assistance, until that promise was fulfilled. The first thing, next morning, instead of making his appearance as Raynal had expected, Mr. Cherami sent a note by a messenger which contained these words :—

"My dear Raynal, I am afraid you will be vexed by what I am going to say, and yet such old friends as we are ought to be privileged to speak frankly to one another. In one word, then, I cannot assist you in the way you suggested yesterday. Had I the money in my pocket, believe me nothing in the world would have given me greater pleasure than to have lent it to you. Since we talked together, however, I have been casting up my accounts, and find to my horror I owe five times as much as I thought I did. It will be with great difficulty that I can get straight again, and it would be impossible for me to retain my appointment here if I did not do so. Under these circumstances you cannot blame me if I hesitate before incurring fresh liabilities. If, at any future time, I can be of assistance, pray ask me ; and, in the meantime, believe me to be yours very faithfully."

While Raynal was reading this letter, its writer and Mr. Max were taking their breakfast at the " Three Crowns." Mr. Max was leaving for Paris that afternoon, and the two friends had determined to drink a glass of wine together before he went away. " A very good glass of wine !" was Mr. Max's verdict on the liquor which Little Paul had generously provided upon the occasion. Mr. Max had allowed him to pay. " Our friend, Madame Gobinard, has got some good stuff stowed away in her innermost cellars. Get upon the right side of her, dear boy. I almost envy you your exile when I think how many brave bumpers you may quaff in this out-of-the-way corner, and no one else in the world a bit the wiser. Good wine is so scarce now-a-days. And sinecures, too, you rogue. How you ever managed it, is more than I can tell."

" It is not even now quite settled," said Cherami, but with a little anxiety in the tone of his voice. " There are slips 'twixt the cup and lip, you know. For instance, in the case of our friend who gave us a dinner upstairs two days ago, to celebrate a coming alliance."

" Poor devil !" said Mr. Max. " What has become of him, and what will ?"

" I didn't join him in that loan I spoke about," said Little Paul.

"You acted wisely, unless you wanted to lose the money."

"I could not see why I should get myself into difficulties on his account. After all, I am indebted to him for only a couple of dinners."

"He's a bad subject, I'm afraid; you may recollect, ever so long ago, there were some very ugly tales told of our friend. A criminal prosecution, was it not?"

"As bad as that?"

"I hardly remember the exact particulars. Now I come to think of it, though, I fancy there was no formal charge against him—only strong suspicion. It arose out of an action over there in England. Wasn't it a question of an illegal transfer of bank stock?"

"I recollect something of it, now. It was supposed that our friend made a little too free with the signature of his wife's uncle, and they would have put him into the dock for it; but, luckily for him, his uncle was missing somewhere in New Zealand, or lost at sea, or dead; and so our friend slipped through. One thing is certain, though——"

"He's a bad lot."

"Precisely. Suppose we have another bottle?"

While the two gentlemen were yet at table Raynal had called at Little Paul's lodgings, in desperate hope of persuading him, even after what he had written, to join in the bill. But Cherami was not to be found, and there was now no time to lose.

Resolved to leave no stone unturned, he visited the stable-keeper, and, with his legs crossed, lounging easily in the horsey man's arm-chair, gave a glowing account— perhaps a trifle too glowing—of his private affairs and future prospects, and concluded by soliciting a small loan. But the horsey man listened with a stolid countenance, chewing the while a tiny blade of hay; and then laughed and shook his head, and said he would rather not. Pressed for an explanation, he still shook his head and chuckled; but he would give no reason for his reluctance, so that at last Raynal went away in anger, vaguely threatening vengeance as he departed.

Half-a-dozen other persons he called on during that morning's weary ramble, but the news of the interrupted nuptials had preceded him, and wherever he showed his face he met with the same reception. Decidedly the game was well-nigh played out in Saint Babylas, and our wicked wolf must seek pastures new in search of innocent lambs.

In desperation, he even called on Tominet. The worthy doctor had partly retired from business, and had taken a little house upon the road to Longanna, at a spot which, standing on high ground, had escaped the flood. Very white walls had this little house, and very green shutters; also a garden, with very prim flower-beds, with very few flowers in them, and box borders trimmed with almost mathematical nicety. Raynal found the doctor taking a nap in his arm-chair, and he woke up, hot and savage, to ask what he wanted.

"How dare you come here? My man of business has left me only a little quarter of an hour ago. You will find yourself under lock and key, my fine fellow, before the sun goes down."

But Raynal had grown reckless.

"Lock me up at once if you want to lose your money. Here I'll stop till he comes back. Lock me up, and you will never see a sou piece of what I owe you."

Tominet, not altogether liking Raynal's tone, asked what he proposed. Then Raynal told him that although the marriage was off—(he found he was obliged to own to this much)—the baroness was inclined to pay a good round sum to induce him to give up all claim on her, return her letters, and so on. The only question was the amount. In the meantime, a few pressing debts must be paid. Would Tominet make a further advance? He could please himself—do it, or leave it alone. After all, it was only like throwing away a sprat to catch a whale. But he knew his own business, Raynal supposed; it was not for him to dictate.

The doctor listened to all this patiently. He very nearly made up his mind to let the young man have some money. Then he decided he would not, and no arguments could change his decision.

Raynal went away desperate. He had asked for and been refused a hundred francs; having sunk to that by easy degrees from a couple of thousands. How was he to get away from the place? Whom could he now apply to? Depressed by repeated disappointments he was walking moodily along, with downcast eyes, when a familiar voice called to him by name. It was the English manager, who had formed one of the company at the château dinner.

Raynal was in no humour for idle gossip, but the manager, who was on horseback, regulated his pace so as to accompany him.

" I thought you had gone back to England," Raynal said, with an expression which seemed to imply that he would have been glad had that been the case.

" I have been there and have returned; only for a couple of days, though."

" It's a long journey to make for such a short stay."

" Business, sir!—business. You have got some circus-people in the town I want to make an engagement with.

There's a trapèze fellow I mean to pick up cheap. I saw them before I went home, but had not then made up my mind to engage them. I have since thought the matter over, and have returned to see whether they will be tempted with English gold. By dealing liberally, I find one often falls over a bargain that shouldn't be lost."

This conversation began to have more interest for Raynal than it had at the commencement.

" It's a good plan, I think," said he.

" Well, I've done pretty well, I think, at most things. I've made my running rather fast of late years. One or two more lucky seasons, and I shall have put by enough to retire on."

" Ah !" sighed Raynal.

" And you, too," said the manager. " You have made a good match, if all I heard was true, and if am to believe my eyes. That was a splendid spread the baroness gave us the other day. A handsome place, too, the château ; and not the only one she has got, I understand."

" No, she has several ; also property in England. But after all——"

" Well, I suppose it will be yours in due course. It will, you know, if you manage matters properly ; but I need not tell *you* how to act. Why, you lucky dog, you ought to be the happiest man alive ; and you will be. By the way, it's coming off directly, isn't it ?"

" In a day or two."

" Yet you don't look over-joyful."

" Come, now," said Raynal, with an air of confiding frankness, " I'll tell you what's bothering me. You knew me in old times, when I was always hard up. I'm no better off now. I ought, at this moment, as you say, to be the happiest man alive ; and what do you think stands betwixt me and happiness? A paltry thousand francs. I owe that sum, and must pay it immediately—this very morning; and I have not the money. I've no one whose secresy I could rely upon, or I would try to borrow the sum; and I see nothing for it but being publicly disgraced, or exposing my poverty to the woman who loves me."

To this the manager listened very attentively; and, as he listened, the fingers of his hand were turning over the gold in his trousers pocket.

"I'd like to help you, Raynal," he said, after a moment's pause. "I think I could. I'm not quite sure. What is the latest time when the cash must be forthcoming?"

"It would be very kind of you to assist me in this little difficulty. Upon my word, I had no idea of asking *you*. In two hours' time——"

"That will do very well."

"Where?"

"At the place where I am stopping."

"An hotel?"

"Yes; the 'Three Crowns.' You know it, of course."

Raynal's heart was in his mouth. For a moment he was not sufficiently sure of himself to venture to speak. Soon, however, he asked:

"How long have you been there?"

"I came last night late, and I was out the first thing this morning."

He probably then had not been seen by Max or Little Paul. But one of them might meet him before the two hours had run out. If so, Raynal's chance of the thousand francs would not be worth much.

"By-the-bye," said the manager, "there was an Englishman at the baroness's the other day—a tutor, or a schoolmaster, or something of that sort."

" Yes."

" I want something in the translating way done. Rather particular work, with many technicalities. It struck me he would be the man to do it, and not likely to make an extravagant charge, eh ?"

" I daresay not."

" Well, I've no time to lose. It is something in connexion with the engagements I am about to make with the circus people—some papers to draw up. Tell me where I can find him, and I'll ride there at once."

" Yes, to be sure—but—but——"

" What's the difficulty ? He's a schoolmaster in the town here, isn't he ?"

" Yes."

" I understood he was here at the college."

" He is at a college. Not here, though—a long way off."

" Where ?"

" Oh, Douai, I think ; besides, it's holiday-time. You would not find him. Let me see now. I can help you with what you want, I daresay——"

" What ! do it yourself ? Do you know English well enough ?"

" No, not myself. I don't mean that ; but I can find some one. I'll go about it now."

" In two hours' time then, at the 'Three Crowns.' "

"I will be there."

Raynal felt that his case was not so hopeless after all. It seemed quite certain from the Englishman's manner, that he meant to lend the money. The only thing to be feared was that some one might enlighten him as to his actual position before the two hours had elapsed. That was not very likely, however.

Raynal called after him, "Where are you bound for now ?"

16

" The circus.   I've just been to Longanna to see one
of the company who lodges there, but he was from home.
I suppose I shall find him at the booth, on the Great
Place."

He put spurs to his horse when he had said this, and
departed at a brisk trot.   It was all right, then.   No one
at the circus was likely to allude to the broken-off marriage.   Indeed there were only two men in the town
who were likely to speak to him on the subject at all;
and it would indeed be an extraordinary mischance if he
were to meet them within the next two hours.   Nothing
could frustrate his expectations except—what happened.

The nearest road to the Great Place lay through
St. Abraham's Gate and the Street of the Priests.   In
the latter the manager met Professor Polyblank.

Yes, there he was, sure enough; not, however, at
all like the professor he had met at the table of the
Baroness de Grandvilain, for that, if he recollected
rightly, had been—anyhow towards the close of the
repast—rather a jovial gentleman, perhaps a little too
much given to classical quotation, but something of a
wag in a small way—something of a jovial soul—at any
rate a very affable gentleman, with rather distinguished
manners.   But this professor, who came shambling
towards him with a stooping gait, with an unbrushed hat,
with a sallow, haggard face and dreamy eyes, staring at
vacancy—it was difficult to recognise him, and yet the
manager pulled up short, and called, in English—

" Mr. Polyblank !"

The professor started, then turned and came towards
him.

" I beg your pardon; did you call to me, sir ?"

" To be sure.   I thought I could not be mistaken;
but Mr. Raynal said you were not in the town.   It's

holiday time, I suppose, and you have come over from
Douai ?"

" Douai !"

" You're professor there at the college, are you not ?"

" I have an appointment at the college of Saint Babylas, close at hand—in the next street."

" What the deuce made him tell me you weren't here,
I wonder? I suppose he didn't know. Luckily I've
met you, however. I suppose he wanted to do the friend
he spoke of a good turn. Well, I don't blame him ;
and he can't blame me for looking after my own interest.
Which way are you going, sir ? To see the baroness, I
suppose ?"

" N—no," stammered the professor, colouring slightly.

" You may recollect we had the pleasure of meeting
for the first time at that lady's table. You read us
some verses. Deuced clever they were too, I remember.
Are they published yet ?"

" Not yet."

" But they will be soon, I hope ? And the baroness
and Mr. Raynal. When are they to be married ?"

" Never !"

Polyblank had spoken with emphasis—indeed, in an
excited tone, with a kindling look and an angry gesture.
The other started.

" The devil they're not ! I'd like to hear some further particulars."

" Particulars ?" stammered the professor in a confused
way. " Oh, I know nothing. I heard so, that's all. I
know nothing."

" You wont say, eh ? You're right—quite right."
" But," he thought to himself, " I'll soon find some one
else who'll tell me all about it." Then added aloud :—
" I wanted to speak to you about some literary work I

16—2

think you might do for me ; have you half an hour to spare ? If so, will you call at the circus on the Great Place, and ask for me ? I should be extremely happy if I could do you a service. I owe you one." And he rode off.

When the two hours expired, Raynal presented himself at the door of the "Three Crowns," and asked for Mr. Brownsmith.

" He's not in, sir," said the chambermaid.

" I suppose he will be here directly. He appointed to meet me here at this time."

" He went out, sir, half an hour ago."

" Went out ? Well, anyhow I'll wait at the door here, so that I may see him coming."

While waiting thus, the diligence came, rolling and rumbling over the uneven stones of the Little Place, and drew up with a flourish at the hotel door. The usual crowd of idlers was already assembled in anticipation of the great event.

As usual, the nimble Alexander was at the door, ready to receive the luggage of any new comer who might feel inclined to patronize the "Three Crowns." As usual, Madame Gobinard stood in the background, ready to give a smiling welcome to the wayworn traveller. As usual, elaborate preparations were rewarded by small results. Two strangers, only, arrived by the diligence, and neither put up at the hotel.

To tell truth, judged from a British point of view, the two persons who thus arrived did not look like lucrative customers ; for one was dressed like a small English farmer, and the other wore a blue blouse and heavy hob-nailed boots. Now, it was rather strange, the one dressed like an Englishman—and his French proved him to be a native of our little island—had a sallow face, such as might belong to a dweller in a large city, who kept late hours and breathed an unwholesome atmosphere; while the man in the blouse, who was unmistakably a Frenchman, was the picture of rude health, a golden-haired, rosy-cheeked fellow, not at all like what everybody knows a Frenchman ought to be.

Raynal, lounging against the gate, was for some unaccountable reason curiously interested in these travellers.

"Who are they, I wonder?" he asked himself; and then he smiled. What were they? What could it matter to him who they were?

What, indeed!

CHAPTER XXIII.

THE COMING DANGER

My apprehensions come in crowds.
I dread the rustling of the grass;
The very shadows of the clouds
Have power to shake me as they pass.
WORDSWORTH.

AMONG the travellers in the interior of the diligence was our good friend Mr. Pomponney, who had been as far as Calais to make inquiries after the welfare of certain chemicals consigned to him by a London house, which had somehow gone astray at Customs. Upon the road he had made great friends with the two strangers, and hearing that they were coming to Saint Babylas upon business, had eagerly inquired what business it was, and listened with intense interest to such details as they thought fit to impart to him. At the same time he, too, had given all the information that lay in his power respecting the inhabitants of his native town, and altogether the journey had been a very pleasant one.

Alighting before the hotel door, Mr. Pomponney bowed in his politest manner to his fellow-travellers, and they having bowed also, the chemist took his way across the Little Place, whilst the strangers entered the booking-office in the hotel court-yard. The chemist, however, did not take his departure before he had also bowed, very respectfully, to Raynal.

"I trust that you are in good health," he said; "and Madame la Baronne de Grandvilain. I have been away from Saint Babylas since yesterday morning. I trust that neither Madame la Baronne nor yourself suffered any inconvenience from the storm."

Raynal, colouring slightly, made some hasty reply, and turned away. The eyes of several of the bystanders were fixed upon him, and a broad grin was on some of their faces.

"Here's a letter for you, sir, the English gentleman left, when he went out."

It was the nimble Alexander who spoke, at the same handing Raynal a note. The other tore it open, and read :—

"DEAR MR. RAYNAL,—Very sorry, but it wont G.
        "Yours ever truly,
                "ROBINSON BROWNSMITH."

The manager, then, had found him out, and this chance was gone with the rest. What next?

He crushed the paper in his hands and strode rapidly away. The little crowd tittered among themselves and pointed after him. The whole town knew the story now. How could he exist any longer in this hateful place? the baffled swindler thought, as he tramped onwards over the uneven paving-stones. By this time the game was well nigh over, and the reader and writer have very nearly done with Pierre Raynal's fortunes. Yet a little while, and the miserable farce will be worked out, and the unhappy rascal consigned to the outer darkness which lies beyond the words, "the end," upon our last page.

You may be sure good little Felicité was on the lookout for the return of her lord and master, as the hour approached when the diligence might be expected. Afar off he saw her peeping from the shop door, with an anxious expression which changed to one of joyous recognition as he came within the range of her vision and waved her an anticipatory kiss.

Unmindful of the presence of a would-be customer, who reached the shop door at the same moment that he crossed the threshold, Mr. Pomponney caught Felicité to his heart, and gave her a loud sounding smack on either cheek.

"Behold me, my cabbage!" the chemist said in his native tongue. "Behold me returned after a journey—but a journey! Behold me as tired as a dog, and with the hunger of a wolf." Then to the customer, whose presence he had noticed for the first time—"a journey, sir, of over ten leagues; a journey from Calais, undertaken in the course of certain negotiations relating to a consignment of goods from a foreign port."

"Yes, yes," said the customer. "I want two sous worth of rhubarb."

This order disposed of, Mr. Pomponney had leisure to dilate upon the dangers and difficulties of the journey just accomplished, and narrate at length the details of half-a-dozen interviews with the custom-house authorities, in which he, Pomponney, had got ever so much the best of everything; except that, in the end, he had got no nearer towards obtaining possession of the missing chemicals than when he started upon his voyage of inquiry.

In the middle of these histories, catching sight of Raynal just outside the shop, the circumstances of their late interview occurred to him. " Since I have returned, my dear Felicité," pursued the chemist, " I have not, I trust, neglected any opportunity of extending our business connexions with the gentry of the neighbourhood. Although, hitherto, we have enjoyed the privilege of supplying the Baroness de Grandvilain, we have not—Ah, my dear sir, this is indeed an honour ! What may I have the pleasure of serving you with ?"

These words were addressed to Manon's former lover, who had entered the door and approached the counter.

" It is merely a trifling favour I wanted to ask of you," said Raynal, easily ; and then stopping, glanced meaningly towards Felicité, as much as to say, " I should like to speak to your husband, alone."

Rightly interpreting the look, Mr. Pomponney winked mysteriously at Mrs. Pomponney, and nodded his head towards the back parlour. To this Felicité replied by a sort of appealing look which Mr. Pomponney mistook for a request to be allowed to make one at the coming conference. " My dear," said he, in a tone of mild expostulation, " Mr. Raynal and I wish to speak together, for a moment, in private. Doubtless Mr. Raynal has some matter on which he desires to confer with me. My dear, if you will allow us one moment."

On this, good little Mrs. Pomponney retired in some confusion, and left the gentlemen alone.

" If the matter upon which you wish to consult me is a professional one," began the chemist. An idea had taken possession of the worthy Pomponney. He was in the habit of prescribing in a general way for the more humble of his customers, and had achieved some small successes now and then. The news of his cases had perhaps travelled to Longanna, and he in future would displace the celebrated Tominet. It is true that his friend Joseph was anxious to obtain the position of physician in ordinary to the château, but then—All is fair in love and war; why not in physic?

"No, no," said Raynal, biting his lip in mortification. "No, no. It is not. I don't want to consult you. The merest trifle in the world. I have come out without my purse, and wanted a hundred francs, for an hour or two, till I have time to get back to the château."

The chemist's face beamed radiant. Almost better, this, than the consultation. Such confidence! so friendly!—and he opened the till. There were not more than twenty francs there, and he had about ten more in his pocket. Most likely Felicité had the money. Should he ask her? No, it would be so much better to mention the matter casually during the course of the evening. Besides, why should he want to tell his wife of every little trifle? This was strictly private business between gentlemen. There was no occasion to make a fuss about it. The Saint Babylas bank was at the next street corner. He could run there and back in a moment, and draw out the money.

"May I trouble you to take a seat, sir? One instant only. By the oddest chance, I have not as much in the till."

He was rather vexed that it should have so happened. It would have been better had Raynal not chanced to light upon the till at a moment when there was such a very small amount of capital therein deposited.

Raynal nodded assent, and taking a seat with all the

carelessness he could assume, prepared to wait for the chemist's return. But he was a long while coming. Felicité, busy with some domestic arrangements in the parlour at the back of the shop at the moment when Mr. Pomponney was departing on his errand, now peeping round the corner of the blind which half covered the window in the partition door, wondered what could have happened, and whether it were possible that the smooth-spoken, wicked gentleman in the shop could have it in his heart to bring her Hyppolite into any sort of trouble.

Meanwhile Raynal, beating his boot with the light cane he carried, and, in the old way, gnawing at his moustache, called all his patience to his aid, and waited silently. But he was doomed to meet with another disappointment.

Before the bank counter, as the chemist stood with the cheque he had just written between his fingers, who, of all persons in the world, should slap him on the shoulder but the jovial Joseph himself, looking even in better health and spirits than he ever had been.

"Pomponney," said the doctor, "it's an age since I have seen you. How are you, Pomponney?"

On Joe's side it seemed almost like a meeting between long-lost brothers; but the chemist's manner was cold and formal. Perhaps he was, too, just a little bit ashamed of his own friendly intentions a few moments ago.

"It's you, is it? How do you do, sir?"

"It's I, sure enough. This little town has not nearly seen the last of me. I'll be the making of this little town yet, if it will allow me."

The cleanly-shaven cashier smiled grimly at these words. The fame of Joseph's deeds had spread far and wide, and the great wooden-leg business was by this time historical.

Joe noticed the cashier's expression, and a sort of twist of the chemist's features, and went on. " It is not everybody in the world who has lost confidence in me, Mr. Pomponney. The results of science may sometimes be defeated by fate or chance ; but, in the long run, sir, they triumph."

" Yes, yes," said the chemist, fidgeting. This was his own style of talk, but he could not put up with it from other people.

" I have not lost all my friends, sir, think you ?" pursued the doctor, as though in answer to a question. " Some of the highest in the land, sir—some of the best families in the neighbourhood, still honour me with their confidence, I am proud to say. Lonciong nobbless— lonciong nobbless est à moi. For the rest I care nothing —backed by the Baroness de Grandvilain, whom at this present moment I have the honour to attend in her serious indisposition."

" Indisposition !" echoed the chemist. " What indisposition ?"

" Haven't you heard?" said Joseph. "My dear Mr. Pomponney, you should keep up with the times. It is true that the details relating to Mr. Raynal's ignominious dismissal are known only to a few of the members of her household, and to the medical adviser, who of course is, as it were, one of the family ; but the broken-off marriage is now the town's talk."

Mr. Pomponney crushed the cheque between his fingers, and turned pale.

" Is this true ?" he asked, looking despairingly towards the cashier. This gentleman, with a shrug of the shoulders, which seemed to say, " Understand, I am in no way responsible for what every one says," replied, " Every one says so."

Mr. Pomponney sank into a chair, and wiped his face with his pocket-handkerchief.

"Thank Heaven, I heard of it in time!" he exclaimed aloud; and then, as the other two regarded him curiously, he pulled himself together as best he could, saying, "I—I might have done something I should have been sorry for."

Joe and the banker's clerk still regarded him with fixed attention, but could make nothing of his words. Indeed, he might have kept his secret easily, had it not been too large for him, and forced its way out, as it were against his will.

"The villain!" he exclaimed; "he might have ruined me. The atrocious miscreant!"

"What! Raynal has been trying to borrow of you?" cried Joe, springing readily at this conclusion, which seemed to him a very natural one, and just what would occur under the circumstances.

"He has tried to do so, sir," replied Mr. Pomponney, rising. "He took advantage of my temporary absence from the town, and consequent ignorance of recent events, and in the most dastardly and hypocritical manner, endeavoured to—to——"

Here Mr. Pomponney's feelings got the better of him, and he sank back once more, and wiped his head.

"Was it a large sum he wanted?" asked Joe.

The chemist squeezed the paper more tightly in his hand. "A considerable amount, sir," he replied. "Perhaps not enough to utterly ruin me had I lost it, but more than I should have liked to lose—much more—much more!"

There was a disagreeable smirk upon the doctor's face; for the truth is, Joe, when he laid his hand upon the chemist's shoulder, had looked over it at the cheque he was filling up.

" You've had a lucky escape, sir," said he. " I'm very happy I was the humble instrument of your preservation."

Outside the bank door again, Mr. Pomponney glanced rather uneasily in the direction of his shop. It must be confessed that the task before him was not a very pleasant one. Raynal had not asked for a large sum of money. It is true that, large or small, Mr. Pomponney was perfectly justified in resisting any attempt at imposition; but then, after all, was he quite certain that Raynal's case was as hopeless as was represented? Supposing Raynal was " a good man," as the phrase goes, and Pomponney, by refusing him, made him his enemy for life.

Half-way down the street he had a good mind to go back and draw the money from the bank. Joe was still there, however, and would he not see through that little fiction about the largeness of the amount. In reality, Joe would have done nothing of the kind, but Mr. Pomponney's conscience made a coward of him, and he dared not face his old friend.

As he approached the shop, he gazed fixedly at the upper windows, in the vague hope of seeing his Felicité. If he were only fortunate enough to do so, he might, by some signal, attract her attention, call her out, and send her back again with a message to the enemy.

" You've only got to tell him so and so." He was rehearsing the words he would say to Felicité if he luckily caught sight of her. It is the way that people put it who employ others to do their dirty work. " You've only such and such a thing to do. Just say so and so, and don't put up with any of his nonsense."

Thus our Pomponney could see quite plainly that it would be the easiest thing in the world for anybody else but himself to put this fellow Raynal off, and that most decidedly somebody else ought to do it. While, however, he was thus reflecting, time rolled on, and it was ridiculous to think that he could much longer delay the evil moment; but just when he was screwing up his courage to go in and brazen the affair out, he caught sight of Professor Polyblank approaching in the distance from the direction in which he had himself come, and, taking refuge in an archway, waited confidently for his arrival. What better scapegoat could he have chosen?

The professor came towards him with that uncertain hesitating gait which was peculiar to him. "What a poor beggar that fellow looks!" thought Mr. Pomponney. "Really, scarcely a creditable inmate of one's establishment. We must see, presently, when things have shaken down a little, whether we cannot make some change for the better, Mr. Polyblank!"

The professor started, looked about vaguely, and at last came towards him.

"You're going in, I think?"

"Yes."

"You might undertake a trifling commission for me if you have no objection; and I have a little confidence to make to you which I should hesitate to make to any one with whom I was not upon terms of close intimacy. Your long residence under my roof may, however, to some extent, justify the exception I make in your favour."

Polyblank smiled and bowed, wondering what he ought to say, and what unexpected piece of good fortune was in store for him.

"The fact is, then," continued Mr. Pomponney, "that man Raynal, who was to have married the Baroness de Grandvilain, has just come to try and swindle me out of a hundred francs. I don't want to see the fellow. Indeed, I would rather not. I might forget myself, and do what I shouldn't like to do; and I thought if you would tell him for me——"

But here the worthy chemist was interrupted by the strange expression of the professor's face, and by the sudden laying of a heavy hand on his (the chemist's) shoulder. Turning quickly, he found Raynal behind him with a threatening expression of countenance.

"He need tell me nothing," said the subject of the chemist's discourse. "I've heard all I want to hear. Don't let me hear you say half as much again, or I'll break your neck for you."

There was something so threatening in the young man's tone and gesture as he uttered these words, that Mr. Pomponney could not refrain from staggering back a pace or two, and raising his arm as though to ward off an expected blow. The blow not coming, Mr. Pomponney gained courage to say:

"We want no blustering here, sir, if you please. We want nothing of that kind!"

Raynal stepped up to him with set teeth and a savage look about his eyes. "What have you got to say to me?" he asked.

But it would have appeared that the chemist had little to say under these circumstances, and was only too anxious to place a safe distance between himself and his assailant. In endeavouring to do this he lost his balance over some projecting brickwork, and assumed a sitting posture upon a little mound of cabbage-leaves and other refuse. Here Raynal left him, and strode away with a contemptuous smile.

"You see, sir," said the chemist, still maintaining his position among the cabbage-leaves, but waving his hands with something of the old grand style; "you see

the sort of ruffian I have to deal with.   I hardly know
how I refrained from chastising him as he deserved."

Without pausing to inquire into the chemist's motives
for this singular forbearance on his part, Polyblank
hurried after Raynal, and overtook him in a quiet by-
street.   Raynal heard footsteps behind him, and turned
to see with whom he had to deal.

"Can I speak to you a moment?" asked the professor.

The other with a bad grace stopped to listen.   He was
in a sullen rage, and had lost patience with the game he
had hitherto played so perseveringly.   Every chance was
gone by this time ; the mask might as well be dropped,
for there was now but little need of it.   Why, then, be
civil to this schoolmaster fellow ?   What use could he
be of ?   What did he want, except it was to scoff at
him, now that he was down?

"You will, I hope, believe me when I say that it is
not idle curiosity that prompts me to inquire into your
affairs.   From what Mr. Pomponney said just now, I
learnt that you were in want of a small sum of money.
I am not aware whether after—whether, under the circumstances—that is to say, whether you mean to continue to reside in the town.   I thought that in the case
of your going, I might——.   But I trust that you will
take this in a friendly spirit, as it is meant."

Had Polyblank himself been begging for the money
he could not have blushed and stammered more hopelessly, and to most other persons his meaning would
hardly have been intelligible.   In this case, however,
there was no occasion for waste of words.

There was a small wine-shop close at hand, which
chanced at the moment to be empty, and here they
talked the business over.   Half-an-hour afterwards, at

the Saint Babylas bank Raynal presented a cheque for a hundred francs, which bore the signature of Peter Polyblank. By an odd chance, Joseph, who had called in again to make some inquiry, was present when the payment was made.

"That's your brother, isn't it?" asked the cashier, when Raynal had gone, showing the cheque, as he spoke, to the jovial Joseph.

"There's no doubt about that," said Joe; and, to himself, he added, "What made him do this, I wonder?" But the cause of the payment was not what most interested the professor's vivacious relative.

"He banks, does he?" said Mr. Joseph, as he sauntered towards his café. "He's been making a nice little thing of it lately, one way and another. Well, I'm glad he has; I'm sure I don't grudge him a two-sous piece, but I don't see why he need be quite so close about it. It isn't what I should have expected from him. It isn't altogether brotherly."

Raynal, then, had at last got sufficient money to enable him to leave the town. The sum was small enough, and would but carry him a short way on the journey he was about to undertake, for there was no safety for him, he thought, until he should have placed the broad Atlantic betwixt him and the threatening danger.

But without this money he could not have stirred, for during the last two days he had been almost penniless. At any rate, now he could make a start, and destroy the traces if pursuers were already on his track. To get down to the sea-coast and over to England was the object he had first in view. The place where they wanted him most was the last place they would think it

17

likely to find him, and there he might be safe for awhile, until he could raise some money through a channel in which he felt pretty certain of success, and then take a passage for America.

At any rate, he could get away from this hateful town, where every hand was raised against him. In three hours, at most, the diligence would start for Calais, and he determined that he would go by it. Three hours! that was not a very long time to pass away. Three hours, and he would see the end of these accursed streets, in which he had walked so many weary miles and suffered such humiliation these two days past. Three hours, and danger would be left behind.

CHAPTER XXIV

EXIT.

Mony a one for him makes mane,
But nane sall ken where he is gane ;
O'er his white banes, when they are bare,
The wind sall blaw for evermair,—*The Twa Corbies*.

THERE had been so much to talk about in Saint Babylas during the last few days, it was surely no wonder if two insignificant travellers by the diligence attracted but a small share of public attention. A long while afterwards, when strange events had taken place, and had found their record in the pages of the local *Gazette*, this carelessness was not a little regretted in certain circles, and there were not wanting those—Pomponney, you may be pretty sure, among the number—who made belief always to have had some inkling of the truth, and to have put this and that together, and formed their own conclusions.

The only impediment these persons found to gaining universal credence lay in the difficulty of accounting for their previous total silence upon the subject.

In justice to the less clever ones, who might have seen so much and yet saw nothing—who had every opportunity afforded them of gathering interesting details, but gathered none, it ought to be fairly stated, at once, that there really was nothing whatever at all peculiar about the appearance of either of the travellers, and that had you not suspected that they wore a mask and were not what they seemed, they were as uninteresting a couple as you could well meet with in a long day's march.

In the official list of passengers by the diligence were recorded the names of Brown of England and Camus of Dijon, and they were both agriculturists. Mr. Pomponney at least knew this much: they had come to Saint Babylas upon business, and that business had something to do with the cultivation of beet-root—still more vaguely described, at the time as "something about beet-root."

Whatever the something might be, however, it would appear that there was no immediate hurry in the business; and when they had made certain little arrangements in the diligence office, Brown and Camus thrust their hands into their pockets and went out strolling. Without making any inquiry as to the whereabouts of any particular locality, they strolled in what seemed quite a purposeless sort of way up one street and down another, every now and then coming to a stand-still to stare about them, and then strolling on again; and surely no one in the world could have looked as if he knew less what he was about, and where he wanted to go to, than Brown of England— unless, indeed, it were Camus of Dijon.

Such very common-place and uninteresting loafers were they however, that nobody but a skittle-sharper would have been the least likely to trouble himself with speculations upon their account ; and as no such disreputable gentry existed in the good town of Saint Babylas, Brown and Camus were allowed to stroll unheeded, and strolled on. But in the course of their wanderings they came to that street in which Raynal's lodgings were situated, and, halting before the door, Camus of Dijon said—

"This is it."

"Will you go in ?" asked Brown of England.

" I think I will," said Camus, in a dreamy sort of way. " Will you stop out here ?"

" I might as well," said Brown, in an absent manner. " If you want me, perhaps you'll whistle."

Left to himself, Brown of England lounged against the house-side, and hummed a popular street tune of his native land. An extra uprightness about Mr. Brown's bearing would have inclined a stranger to suppose that, some time or other, he must have been in the army ; but there was also that peculiar kind of angularity in his movements which a close observer may generally detect about an English policeman when he has assumed private clothes by way of disguise. But he had such an innocent sort of face, it was really like doubting the existence of truth in any shape to believe that its owner could mean mischief.

Presently there was a light quick step audible in the courtyard, and in another moment Camus was standing by Brown's side ; but it was not at all the same Camus who had left him a moment ago. There were still the light curly locks and ruddy cheeks, but there was an anxious, half-scared look about the eyes that seemed to say that something was amiss.

" What's wrong ?"

" I hardly know as yet. I hope we're not too late."

" Too late ?   The devil !"

So excited was Brown of England at the intelligence his friend had brought him, it was no wonder that he broke out into his native tongue; breaking out at the same time into a cold perspiration, and wiping his face with a coloured cotton pocket-handkerchief.

" Come along," said Camus ; " we've wasted too much time as it is.   If we had not had the misfortune to listen to that fool in the diligence we should have known all about it long ago."

Not at all like the two slouching rustics of five minutes since were Brown and Camus, as they walked briskly away, talking together in low, earnest tones.   A while afterwards, however, with their old manner on them, they were making inquiries at the diligence office.   Were there any more places vacant for the conveyance to start two hours hence from the " Three Crowns ?"   All had been taken but one.   The three seats in the coupé in the name of Brown.   In the interior, Guenillon, Grelet, Merlot, &c.

Camus glanced over the man's shoulder and read the names upon the list.   There was a note against one :—

" François to get up at the cabaret at Longanna."

" Is Mr. François a resident of Longanna?" asked Brown.

" There may be more than one François in the village. The name is common enough."

" To be sure.   You might have seen him, though, when he came to book his place."

" Ah !   However, I didn't.   Let me see now how that was.   He sent some one here to book it for him."

" Didn't you know the some one ?"

" No, I didn't."

" There may be four or five hundred Françoises in the village," said Brown of England ; " but I have a sort of conviction that's the gentleman we're looking after."

" If it is, we shall find him without much trouble. In the meantime, let us go on with our inquiries."

A hundred and one questions, pertinent and impertinent, did our travellers ask in all quarters of the town before they seemed to have obtained the information of which they were in search, and several miles had they tramped before eventually they turned their faces towards Longanna, at which place they had concluded they would find they person of whom they were in quest.

Alone by themselves upon the marshes, a wondrous change came over these persevering pedestrians. They were no longer Brown of England and Camus of Dijon, nor were there, as hitherto, to be found in their talk any of those frequent allusions to trade and husbandry which had been so adroitly introduced into their conversation whilst making their inquiries in the town. They differed from agriculturalists in general in this respect, that they were only reapers, not sowers, and it was out of other peoples' crops that they made now and then a moderate harvest. Ugly crops were these, springing up for the most part in over-crowded cities, in crooked lanes, blind alleys, and back slums—rank and weedy crops of no advantage to any one in the world, except to the Brown and Camus brotherhood, who made their selections from time to time when there were any particular weeds made themselves conspicuous among the rest and required to be rooted out and laid by in strong stone boxes, specially designed for their safe keeping.

An hour before the time the diligence was expected to pass through the village, the proprietor of the solitary cabaret stood at the door of his establishment and gazed despondingly down the long white road before him.

" It seems to me," he thought, " it's going to rain again. I suppose we shall be washed away altogether before we've done. Well, if we are, what odds ?—everybody's money is under water as it is. The question is, Will it ever come to the surface again ? In the meanwhile, these are not the times to give credit. Bah ! how cold it has turned. I might as well go in and shut the door for all the custom I am likely to get to-night."

But in this last idea he was wrong, for at that moment two of the villagers were plodding heavily down the street with the intention of dropping in to talk over their grievances while they drank a jug of beer ; and hardly had they taken their seats before a third appeared upon the threshold. Not long afterwards a couple of bagmen, fatigued by a long and somewhat profitless journey round some of the neighbouring villages, came in, called for drink, lit their pipes, and cursed their luck ; then called for more drink, and, in a miserable sort of way, seemed to be enjoying themselves pretty well, all things considered.

After these a small farmer from a flooded barn on the marshes, very despondent indeed, called for neat brandy. Then a dark, handsome gentleman, at whom the customers looked shily from the corners of their eyes, drawing each other's attention to him by nudges, and nods and winks. He also called for brandy, and sat apart, biting his moustache meditatively.

Undoubtedly times were bad, and the spirits of the customers at a low ebb, but they drank fairly, and what more could be desired ? Perhaps the cabaret keeper was inclined to be unusally down-hearted this particular evening, for although undoubtedly he had been doing a much better trade during the last half-hour, and making larger profits than he had done any other half-hour the last six months past, he looked around with a gloomy brow, and shook his head and sighed.

After all, things were not as they used to be. Would they ever be in the old state again? Not likely. Would he ever again play another game at cards with such jolly dogs as had patronized his cabaret in those happy days before the manufactory was burnt down, and the village flooded? Would there ever be such parties of dominoes —such merry drinking bouts, all at the expense of the jolly dogs, and very much to mine host's advantage? No chance of it. Why, there were no jolly dogs left above water in a circuit of three leagues—that he felt certain of—nor any but long faces and black looks likely to be found among his customers. But here, again, was the cabaret-keeper labouring under a wrong impression; for again the door was thrown open—this time to give entrance to a couple of strangers; the first as jolly a dog, to all appearances, as ever wore boot leather, who introduced himself with a " Salut, messieurs, mesdames, la compagnie!" although the only lady present was a little girl of eleven years of age, the cabaretier's daughter.

" Un joli brin de femmelôte," he told her father they would call her down in his part of the country, which curiously enough was the cabaret keeper's country also. Upon the strength of this extraordinary coincidence, the jolly stranger and he shook hands very warmly, and the jolly stranger, right off, ordered a bottle of wine, which he said there was just time to drink before the diligence might be expected.

" Ah, and another too," said the landlord. " Will

you have the kindness to be seated, gentlemen, pendant que je vais aveindre la fine bouteille ?"

At this phrase the brave Dijonnais laughed merrily, saying he was glad to see mine host had not forgotten his mother tongue ; but with regard to sitting down, there were plenty of seats disengaged, though no vacant table, unless the strangers were to share that at present occupied by the dark, handsome gentleman, who sat apart. However, why not ? The table was a large one, and the meditative gentleman bowed a gracious consent to the request for his permission ; indeed, he could not do otherwise, for Mr. Camus of Dijon had such a persuasive way with him.

The landlord was not long before he returned from his cellar, carrying a bottle very carefully in a little basket, and as carefully uncorking it, saying, as he filled his guests' glasses, " Vous me direz des nouvelles de ce vinot; il n'y en a pas de pareil au pays."

It was a good bottle of wine, Mr. Camus protested, and loudly smacked his lips as he held a glass aloft between his eye and the flaming candle.

"And your friend," said the landlord, greedy for praise ; "what does he say to it ?"

The friend said, " Très bong." He was an Englishman, Mr. Camus explained ; a gentleman with great experience in agriculture, who had come over with him from England to make some inquiries respecting the cultivation of beet-root. It seemed from what Mr. Camus said that beet sugar was now largely imported into England, but that the consumption thereof by the English people could be almost doubled, and an enormous fortune made by proper management. The question was, ought the sugar to be manufactured in France or in England ? Again, could the difficulty and expense of shipping be avoided by growing the beet-root in England, and could this be done as cheaply as over here?

These matters Mr. Camus and his friend Mr. Brown of England had gone into thoroughly, and had come to certain conclusions which at that moment they were not at liberty to divulge. Mr. Brown had come over to pick up a few wrinkles, and those wrinkles had been picked up, and Mr. Brown had got them in his head, and meant to turn them to account in due season.

Mr. Camus had, it would appear, not only got his wrinkles in his head, but on the outside too, for at times he had a haggard, thoughtful look, which made him appear old and wise. Upon these occasions, when the crows' feet round his eyes were most conspicuous, it was difficult to account for his beardless chin and luxuriant locks, but when he laughed and showed his white teeth, he was quite boyish.

There was a rickety old cuckoo clock in one corner of the room, which Mr. Camus alluded to as the " dindelle," and, by this, it wanted at least a quarter of an hour of the time the diligence might be expected.

" But they are never punctual, I suppose ?" said Mr. Camus.

" Never, by any chance," the landlord responded.

" There is time, then, for another bottle ?"

" Plenty."

" As long as we're not hurried," said Camus, " ça me fait trop aller de guingoi."

When the landlord was gone, Brown and Camus began to talk English, and of the two perhaps Camus talked the language best.

" I suppose our friend is right in what he says about the time," observed the native of Dijon.

" I suppose he wont much care, as long as there is

time to uncork the bottle and make us dub up for
it."

"I suppose not. It is to be hoped, though, the diligence will get in to an hour or so of the time they state,
or we shall lose the boat."

"There'll be the deuce to pay if we do that, and our
friends all waiting to meet us."

"It's no use to ask any questions of these boors. I
wonder, now, if this gentleman could tell us?"

"If we only knew whether there was another boat to
England later in the day. In that case, you see——"

"But the gentleman wont know anything about the
English boats. Everybody isn't always wanting to go
over to England."

"To be sure; that did not strike me. I fancied at
first the gentleman was English."

It was the dark, handsome gentleman, sitting at the
other end of the table, who was the subject of these remarks; and who, by the rising colour in his face, seemed
to be sufficiently acquainted with the language they were
speaking to know that they had reference to him. As
Mr. Brown, too, was staring at him with all his eyes, it
was scarcely possible any longer to remain silent.

"There is a boat to-morrow about noon," he said.
"You will have plenty of time to catch that."

"Ah! you are English, then?" cried Mr. Brown, delighted at the discovery of a compatriot.

"Well, no."

"No! You surprise me. But you have lived there a
long time, no doubt. You must have lived there, to pick
up so good an accent."

It must be owned there was nothing very extraordinary
about his English, and the meditative gentleman listened
a little doubtfully to this praise, and fixed his eyes

steadfastly upon Mr. Brown's face.   Let the term of his
residence upon the other side of the Channel have been long
or short, he seemed to have picked up some of the insular
prejudice.   He mistrusted strangers, and might have
taken Mr. Brown for a swell-mobsman, with designs upon
his pocket.

"I lived there for a short time," he said, and here
would have dropped the subject and backed out of further
conversation; but Mr. Camus came to his friend's rescue.

"A splendid country, sir," cried he.   "Some lovely
spots in it.   Some rich land, nobly cultivated.   You may
have heard, sir, my friend and I have been making some
inquiries hereabouts, respecting the cultivation of beet-
root?"

The gentleman, yawning slightly, replied without the
slightest show of interest, that he thought he had heard
something of the kind, but was not listening attentively.

"Yes, sir," pursued Mr. Camus, nothing daunted;
"and that brought us into this neighbourhood, though I
must confess we have met with a little disappointment—
from a strange cause, too.   You see, a lady living in
these parts, the Baroness de Grandvilain she's called——"

The meditative gentleman's eyes turned quickly towards him at the sound of this name.

"That's it," put in Mr. Brown, with a knowing smile.

"This baroness, then, we are told, was to have been
married to some fellow or other, and——"

The landlord had returned by this time with the
second bottle.

"I've been rather slow," said he.   "My light went
out.   I was afraid of shaking the wine.   You'll find it
worth waiting for, I hope."

"And the diligence?"

"No fear of that for another ten minutes."

"That's well. I have five minutes' talk to get through with this gentleman before then. As I was saying—— Here, landlord, another glass. You will drink with us, sir, I hope? Come, it will do you no harm before your journey."

"I did not say I was going a journey."

"Did you not? I guessed it, then. What put it in my head—— But as I was saying—this baroness was to have been married to a Mr. ——, Mr. ——? What was it, Brown?"

"Mr. François. Was not that what they told us?"

The meditative gentleman changed colour.

"Why, what put that in your head, mon fieu? How you talk! It was Lenord, or a name much like it. However, this gentleman knows what it was, no doubt, if he lives hereabouts. A better bottle than the last, my brave; the best I've tasted, too, since last Christmas time, one night when we were merry-making at my father-in-law's, and were singing. Do you know this song, little miss?

> J'ai ouy chanter le rossignô
> Qui chantait un chant si nouveau,
>   Si bon, si beau,
>   Si résonneau,
> Il m'y rompait la tête,
>   Tant il prêchait
>   Et caquetait ;
> A donc pris ma houlette,
> Pour aller voir Naulet.

What are the other verses, little miss? And this diligence, is it never coming?"

During this time the meditative gentleman had been meditating, with his hand covering the lower part of his face, and his eyes half hidden by the brim of his hat, pulled low down over his brow. When the song came to an end, he broke silence, this time speaking in French.

"You did not finish what you were saying about the

Baroness de Grandvilain.   What had her marriage to do with your inquiries?"

"Ah, to be sure.   I forgot what I was talking about. On a great deal of the baroness's land round hereabouts beet-root is cultivated, and we wished to ask a lot of questions of her bailiff, if she has one.   Do you know, sir?"

" I believe not ; I don't know."

" Well, so they seemed to say ; and that the land was all let out, and that it was a sort of companion, a middle-aged lady living with her, who managed about the rents with the farmers."

" I believe so."

" This baroness, from what they say, I should take to be an easy-going sort of person—easily deceived?"

" Perhaps."

" But quite young, I am told, and wonderfully pretty, and rich too.   She has a fine estate over there, in England.   It was her English man of business who gave us a letter of introduction.   But this diligence—is it never coming?"

The landlord had been standing outside the house for the last two or three minutes, and he came in as Camus spoke to say that it was close at hand.

The meditative gentleman rose and walked towards the door.   Mr. Brown drew out his purse and settled the account.   The rumble of the diligence wheels was now audible, at most a hundred yards off.   In a few moments more it had drawn up, with much jingling, jolting, and bumping, in front of the cabaret door.   The people who had been drinking inside came trooping out to see the sight ; and one of the farmers recognising a friend upon the roof, called out to him loudly, as though he had been on the top of a mountain, and he bawled back again louder still. The driver, too, was bawling something to the landlord, and the conductor, adjusting a twisted strap in the harness, bawled loudest of all, by way of quieting the restive horses.

As the meditative gentleman stood by the side of the door, the only silent person in the assemblage, his face wore even a more thoughtful expression than it had done any time during his interview with Mr. Camus of Dijon. Was it possible that he was meditating flight? If so, why stop so long to think about it? Why not run and think afterwards? Oh, if he had only known how precious was every moment, and that the danger from which he was flying was creeping stealthily upon him, to have him, in a few brief seconds of time, tight within its iron clutch?

A hand was laid upon his arm—Camus of Dijon! "You have got a place in the inside. You must ride with us instead, in the coupé."

"Thank you. I prefer the other place."

"And we prefer your company."

"What do you mean?"

"Don't speak so loud, or we shall be noticed. There is no occasion for a scene. I always avoid that sort of thing when it is possible. Suppose we speak English? You can't begin to practise too soon. You will want all your knowledge of the tongue over there for your defence."

"I don't understand," the other said, faintly.

"Yes, yes, you do," replied Camus, with a persuasive smile. "You wont give us any trouble, I am sure; besides"—and here his voice altered to a harsh, grating tone, at which the hearer shuddered—"besides, we are two to one, Pierre Raynal, and you are our prisoner."

As Raynal turned towards him, another hand grasped

his other arm. He stood now between Brown and Camus, each holding him tightly. The precious moment was gone for ever. All chance of escape was lost.

"Let us get into our seats," said Camus. " I took three places, as I made pretty sure we should ride toge- ther. It was almost a pity you wasted your money on a place in the interior. However, it cannot be helped."

"I will get up first," said Brown. "Mr. Raynal can come next, and you follow. I have the bracelets in my pocket; but we have no need of those, sir, I think. I dare say we shall get on very pleasantly—considering."

Without making any answer Raynal took his place between the two police officers, to whom, as the dili- gence started, the landlord standing at the door waved an affectionate adieu. As they rumbled onwards his voice was faintly heard above the clatter, bidding them bon voyage. In this cry, the farmers, villagers and bag- men joined in chorus, and to them Camus waved his hand in reply.

"Be of good heart, sir," he said, turning towards Raynal. " Who knows ? You may get through with flying colours. There are so many quibbles and quirks in your laws over there—so many loopholes to slip through. Besides, every one is innocent until he is found guilty. Eh, Charley ?"

Here he whom we have known as Brown of England, smiled grimly. It may have been possible that he knew more than he thought fit to say upon the subject of Raynal's chances. Some time afterwards, talking the matter over with a friend, he remarked, " We should hardly have taken the trouble we did to catch him, if the case had not been tolerably straightforward."

Camus, whom the wine had, perhaps, inclined towards conversation, went on to inform his prisoner that he need be under no apprehension upon the score of the legality of his capture, as all the necessary formalities had been most carefully attended to. The person known by the name of Brown carried in his pocket a warrant issued by a London magistrate for his (Raynal's) apprehension, which instrument was presently exhibited, and its validity fully attested by the signatures it bore.

The person of the name of Camus carried another instrument, of French origin, entitling him to be his prisoner's custodian as far as Calais, when he would be handed over to the safe keeping of the other officer, and taken by him to London.

" But," he concluded, " there need be nothing unpleasant between gentlemen. Of course, if you tried to escape it would be useless ; but you are too much of a gentleman to attempt such a thing ; therefore, as my worth friend here just now observed, there is no occasion for the darbies."

Raynal, gazing fixedly into the darkness in front, paid no heed to this talk, and scarcely comprehended the meaning of a word that was uttered. One thing only he understood : the game was played out. All hope was over—the last chance gone. After all his schemes, and struggles, and agony of mind, he had failed at last ; and soon the gaol gates would close upon him, and God only knew how many weary years of his life be ground out within its pitiless walls.

Half stunned by the suddenness with which the capture had been made, he was as yet scarcely able to realize the full extent of the misfortune that had befallen him. In a few hours' time, in the loneliness and grave-like silence of his cell, he would have time to think ; but now everything seemed like a dream.

The sound of the voices of the landlord and his guests

18

died away in the distance. Lights flashed in the windows of a house here and there as the diligence passed, and now and then a door opened, showing the ruddy glow of the fire within. At a street corner the light of the lamps upon the diligence fell on the faces of a group of men standing there; now they had reached the château, which stood out black and silent against the black-blue sky; now it was past, and now they had reached the end of the village, and were out in the open country beyond.

A cold and clammy mist hung over the marsh land and the dreary waste of water, covering a broad space farther than the eye could reach. The horses, in a cloud of steam, floundered onwards through the thick mud, and every five minutes seemed to be coming to a stand-still, and giving up the business for a bad job. Then, urged on again by shrill cries and guttural oaths from the driver, they floundered forward once more.

The marshes past, came a high hill to mount, with a steep descent upon the other side; in the performance of which the diligence zigzagged from side to side of the road, turning corners with a dangerous roll, like a ship in a rough sea. Down in the valley below they came then on a sleeping village, with a church tower and a churchyard, with glimpses of white wooden crosses as the lamps lit them up in passing. A hard-sleeping village it seemed, in which the heavy clattering and lumbering of the clumsy vehicle woke up only one solitary dog, that gave out half-a-dozen barks of sharp remonstrance, and subsided into silence again with a long whine.

Beyond this a broken country, and a never-ending road, with a straggling row of lime trees on either side. Another village then, and then the same road stretching across more marsh land; then another village, and so on through the night. At times, if such a supposition were not too monstrous, one might almost have imagined that Brown of England was guilty of snatching half-a-dozen winks of sleep at frequent intervals; but Camus was always wide awake, and generally smoking. Did Raynal slumber also? If so, it was with his eyes open. Yet he could hardly be awake—be alive to what was passing around. It was like the face of one who walks in his sleep—blank, meaningless, with dull and heavy eyes, stonily fixed upon vacancy.

When day broke they were still rumbling onwards, now over a dreary barren country, yielding scanty crops of reedy grass, relieved at long distances by poor crops of wheat and rye, and fields of peas and beans. Coming to a halt in a quaint old fortified town, with moss-grown streets and crumbling walls and dilapidated battlements, Brown and Camus got down, helping their prisoner to alight also, and offered him some refreshment. He refused to eat, but took a long draught of cold brandy-and-water, while the policemen solaced themselves with cold pâté and ale. Then the coachman called them back to their places, and they started once more. But, as yet, the journey was only two-thirds done, and there seemed to be but little chance of their reaching Calais in time for the morning boat.

As though in a dream he heard the two men discussing the probabilities pro and con, but took no interest in the matter. What did it signify to him whether it was that boat, or the next, or any one? As before, they were rumbling and jolting along the same endless lime-tree bounded road, and the same flat land and stagnant ditches lay right and left of them. The same melancholy villages coming every now and then; a couple of lean dogs yelping after them in one, in another a grey-headed idiot running before the horses' heads, and jabbering and

18—2

waving aloft his cap. A churchyard crowded with wooden crosses, on which the withered wreaths were thickly piled. The ruin of a castle, one wall only left; a score of wind-mills, only one at work; still the same long road, and the marsh land again; but with a faint salt flavour in the breeze blowing across it, which told that the sea was now not far off.

At last the sea itself, the crowd of shipping, the busy harbour and deadly-lively streets of Calais; and now Mr. Camus's part of the journey was drawing to a close. Some weary hours yet to pass away, however, before the right boat started, and these passed in a private room of an hotel, the windows of which overlooked a sunless court-yard, much like what might be found in an English gaol, Mr. Brown remarked.

Here, as they waited, the twilight gave place to dark-ness. The lights twinkled upon the harbour. Dusky forms moved to and fro in the obscurity, hauling heavy ropes and rattling chains. Men shouting from the shore were shouted to by others from the boats, and now and then angry discussions were carried on in shrill tones,—men and women screaming together; the men screaming the loudest.

The boat was alongside now, and they could go on board for an hour before it would start. That hour gone by, Mr. Camus had taken leave of his friend Brown and the prisoner, and stood leaning over a wooden railing, looking after them as the boat receded from the shore. A white wistful face looked out towards him from the deck of the steamer for a moment, and in another moment the darkness gathered over it, and Raynal's features faded from his sight, as their owner here fades from this history. With the punishment awaiting him at his dreary journey's end we have nothing to do, nor with the details of his future life.

A wretched life, surely; with glimpses of fleeting happiness; mayhap moments of forgetfulness found in drink. He was a rogue, a thief, a coward. He deserved his fate, you must allow; but did all the world think so? Oh, how he had been loved by one pure, unselfish heart! And now that she lay at death's-door, was that love quite dead within her breast? Who shall say? There are some loves so enduring, no cruel outrage, no heartless neglect, can thoroughly crush them out.

CHAPTER XXV

ONLY ANOTHER FAILURE.

> Il fût sage et savant; puis, comme tout s'achève,
> Quand son âge eut atteint un siècle révolu,
> Il part pour le ciel, en nous léguant ce rêve,
> Car il avait rêvé ce que vous avez lu.
>
> *L'écolier d'Aubantal.*

ONE evening, some weeks after these events, Professor Polybank was rather surprised to receive a visit from his brother Joe. It was not very often that the doctor made a call, for he generally had so much important business on his hands, he really had no time to waste in that way. How was it, then, that this evening was an exception to the general rule? If you will have it, Mr. Joseph had a particular reason for calling. If you insist on further details, he wanted to borrow a couple of napoleons.

Now, if the truth must be told respecting past transactions, there had been some few other napoleons borrowed from time to time, which had not been, strictly speaking, repaid at the time agreed upon for that purpose. Indeed, many of them had not been repaid without some considerable delay—perhaps, if we stick closely to facts,

two-thirds of them had not been repaid at all. At least
so it appeared from the testimony of some rough memo-
randa on the subject in the professor's pocket-book. To
the best of Joe's recollection, they had all been returned
long ago, with the exception of one solitary napoleon;
but then Joe kept no accounts.

"I never did," he said, when speaking on the subject.
"Perhaps I ought. It isn't fair to either of us to be
so careless. But of course you're right, Peter; you're
always right in these matters. You've head enough for
both of us, you have."

The subject had then been dropped, and no subsequent
allusion had been made to the balance for some weeks
past. The brothers had not met very frequently. Peter
had had so many other things to think about, he had
forgotten Joe's little debt, as he had many others of
Joseph's contracting, long ago.

When the door opened, however, he thought to himself, "Joe's come to pay me." Surely this was one of the
wildest notions that ever entered the professor's head;
and his head was now and then a rare storehouse for
wild notions generally.

"Why, Peter!"

"It's you, Joe, is it?"

"It's I, Peter. How are you getting on, by this time?"

"It is rather a long time since I saw you, Joe," said
the professor, thoughtfully. "It's a good long time;
isn't it a month?"

"Lord bless you!" cried Joe, who knew it was five
weeks at least, "not half that time; it's a good many
days, though."

"Some days are very long," said the elder brother,
wearily. "I dare say it's as you say, Joe. I lose count
of time now and then. My life is rather monotonous."

" I couldn't plod myself," cried Joe, heartily; " but you are made of different stuff. How long have you been in ? What's that you're doing ?"

He alluded to an elaborate apparatus intended to boil water, upon the arrangement of which the professor, with his cuffs turned back, was very busily engaged, getting his fingers very dirty in the process.

" I'm going to boil some water," he said.

" For grog ?"

" No, for tea."

Joe looked at him with a pitying smile. It struck our doctor that his relative thus occupied presented a somewhat mean and insignificant spectacle. The apparatus was of tin, much blackened by smoke, and with the sides slightly battered in by long use and careless packing. It was of a complicated make, and formed of several pieces, some of which fitted loosely, and fell apart, if great care were not used in holding them together when lifted; other stuck so tightly that the jerking out of the hot water was inevitable when it became necessary to part them.

As the adjustment of the series of tin pots of which this famous machine was composed required much nicety and precision, the professor put on his spectacles to the work, and, as has been already recorded, turned up his cuffs. It seemed to Joe that all this was very paltry, but he did not chafe impatiently as he sat watching the tedious operation. " Poor Peter," he thought; " this is the way he has pottered his life away. It was so when we were boys together. He used to sew his own shirt-buttons on, and he blubbered if there was a blot in his copy-book. I would drop a great splutter of ink between the pages, and squeeze them together. We used to call that making a black beetle. Lord, what a fellow I used to be for larks !"

There are some larks which are not nearly such good fun for the larkee as the larker; and this was perhaps the style that Joe had gone in for. Sometimes he would appeal to his brother Peter, saying—

" Do you recollect the fun we had at old Bagstock's? These young brutes here at the college often put me in mind of the tricks I used to play there."

At this Peter smiled grimly. He had never been remarkable for either fun or tricks. Quite early in life, before he had had time to be a boy, he had been obliged to be a man. Before he had any chance of having that fling which youth is proverbially entitled to, it was necessary that he should be serious. Before he was half old enough to leave off learning lessons himself, he was teaching other boys their lessons, to earn his own bread.

Somehow it was not the same with Joe, about whom fate willed it otherwise. Joe was adopted, and had his schooling paid for, like a gentleman. He also had means found him to learn the medical profession. He learnt a good deal besides at this period, and saw much life— only just managing to crawl through the examination when the time came, but still crawling through somehow, just as well as if he had worked hard all the while.

" I am not one of your humdrum sort," he would say to his brother.

" No, Joe," Peter would reply.

" I like to go ahead—to go right at a thing—to get past it—to get away!" he would continue, rather vaguely, but with great enthusiasm.

" Yes, Joe," said Peter.

In those days there was a deep and genuine admiration dwelling in Peter's heart for his dashing brother. He had some feeble aspirations of his own, but somehow the time never seemed to arrive when the neccessary projects for their fulfilment could be put into execution. Sometimes he began to doubt, too, whether the time ever would come ; but he thoroughly believed in Joe. There was no doubt—there really could be no doubt about Joseph. He must turn out something wonderful. Everybody said he would. It was, indeed, the most suprising thing in the world that after all he didn't.

" That's rather a long job, isn't it?" asked Joe, when he had watched the progress of the great tin pot trick for rather more than ten minutes, and there was still no sign of boiling water.

" It's done fast enough usually," replied his brother. " The thing's a little out of order."

" I should think it was, a little," said Joe.

The professor went on with the operation, and Joe still regarded him with the same smile of pity. Methylated spirits were required in the working of the apparatus, and to-day an extra quantity was necessary. A small bottle which he had just emptied stood upon the table, but there was a larger bottle—Peter had bought a large quantity, in order to get it cheaper—in the portmanteau. To get at this it was necessary to take out first a number of articles lying on the top of it ; and among these was a packet of manuscript tied together with a piece of string.

The professor laid this on the table near to where his brother was sitting ; and Joe, for want of some other occupation, drew it towards him, and examined the first page.

" Why, what's this, Peter?"

" That—oh, nothing. Let me put it back."

" All right—all right. I wont hurt it. It looks like Latin verses—something you've been copying."

" They're not copied. Give them to me, and I'll put them away again. They're only some things I have done from time to time, when I have had a few spare moments."

Joe did not feel much interested.

" I suppose that water will boil some time before Christmas. I shan't be very sorry, either."

" Will you have some tea with me?"

" I'm not a very good hand at tea. I find it disagrees with me rather. I suppose you've no brandy."

" I have a little gin."

" I don't much care for French gin; however, I'll take some to show I'm not prejudiced."

The professor brought forth the liquor, and Joe, mixing himself a strong glass, drank it without any wry faces, and presently mixed another. Meanwhile Peter, having brought the working of the apparatus to a successful issue, made his tea, and sat down to it.

" And what has brought you here?" he asked, at last.

Joe looked a little confused. It had been his intention not to waste much more time before he came to the point; but this was not the proper way of coming to it. He felt hurt, too, at being suspected of an interested motive.

" What should have brought me? That's not a very nice way of putting it. You think I can't come to see you unless I want something." Then, to himself he thought, " I'll see before I go if there's a better chance of breaking it to him. If not, I'll drop him a line from the café. Perhaps, after all, that will be the best way. Something might occur of a sudden nature. I shall be able to decide what it's to be later on."

" I did not mean to say that, Joe," said his brother, seeing him sitting silent and gloomy. " I did not mean to hurt your feelings. Tell me how you're getting on. Have they—is that affair—that Jean Gin business——"

" Yes—yes, there's an end of that. You need not rake it up, Peter. That's not very kind of you."

" No ; I beg your pardon. I didn't mean to talk about that. You're getting on well, I hope."

" Pretty well. I'm not doing such a great deal at present; but I shall make my way, I expect, in spite of my enemies."

" I feel sure of that, if—if you're steady, Joe."

" What do you call steady ? You don't suppose I'm to go on grinding away as some fellows do, making a penny out of their pills, and twopence out of their draughts ? Do you suppose anybody ever achieves greatness, now-a-days, by the old-fashioned plodding, humdrum course, that was good enough for our great-grandmothers?"

" I can't say," said the professor, who hardly followed his brother's argument.

" You and I are different, Peter," continued the doctor. " You're slow and sure. Well, perhaps you're right. The tortoise won the race, you know, because he stuck to it. It's not a bad thing, mind you, that sticking business, as long as you stick to something worth sticking to."

" Some of us have not much choice, Joe. I should like to change my calling if I could make a living some easier way."

" I wonder now you never tried," said Joe, leaning back to have a good look at his relative, and regarding him in quite a different light from that which he had always viewed him in before. " Did you never have a notion of anything else ?"

" Perhaps I have sometimes," said the other. He was leaning his head upon his hand, and tracing figures in the dregs of his teacup.

" Do you know now, Peter, it's a most extraordinary thing, but I have never looked upon you otherwise than in the scholastic line. I couldn't picture you any other way than teaching the young idea. You've always seemed to be working away so tremendously hard. It wouldn't be like you if you weren't doing it."

" I have worked rather hard, Joe, in my time. I wish I could afford to rest a little."

" You've not saved enough to be able to drop it, I suppose."

" Drop what ?"

" Enough to live upon, I mean."

The elder brother rose angrily.

" You know better than that, Joe," he said. " I might have saved something, but I need not tell you where my savings have gone. Do you think that because I work hard, I make much money ? You are very much mistaken if you do. No, Joe ; I am afraid I shall never be rich enough to take my ease. I have a few pounds put away, but only a very few—enough to pay for my medicine if I am taken ill some day, or for my funeral."

Joe was silent for a time. Then an idea occurred to him.

" Just tell me over again what you said about those verses. What did you mean to do with them ?"

" Oh, never mind them. I had an idea once ; but I am afraid I could not find a market. It's not the right sort of thing. Taste is so changed now-a-days. It has left me behind. I don't think I am very practical."

" I don't know that," said Joe. " I should rather like to have a look at the verses. Let me have some more hot water. This gin stuff is not so bad as it might be. You've got no tobacco, I suppose? Well, never mind ; let's look at the verses. Read some of them."

" You wont care for them, Joe," said the professor. " I don't think they are your sort."

" What do you mean by my sort?" asked Joe, indignantly. " Do you suppose I am not capable of appreciating them? It seems to me that a book of Latin verses, odes, and epigrams, and that sort of thing, would be exactly what would take. There can't be much of the same style."

" I don't think they are altogether bad, Joe," said Peter, blushing a little, and nervously fingering the loose pages of the manuscript. " One or two of them, I really believe, are not at all bad."

" I daresay they are all of them very good," replied Joe. " I don't see why they shouldn't be. Let me hear you read a little."

Poor professor, he was only human! Of course he read, without much further pressing, some of the celebrated verses which he had read that day of the dinner at the château. When warmed to his work, he even carried his reading to an unnecessary length, and Joe, unobserved, yawned prodigiously; also, unobserved, he took another glass of hot grog.

" They're extraordinary," said Joe. " Why, we should be acting like fools to let them lie here, waste."

" What can we do with them, Joe."

Joe reflected.

" There must be persons who would buy this sort of thing. London would be the best place, I should think. But in Paris there must be houses where they print the classics. It's worth the journey."

" That was what occurred to me," said Peter. " But I'm afraid I shall hardly make the journey pay."

" How so?"

" Well, you see," replied Peter, after a moment's hesitation, "I don't think I'm quite what's called a good man of business."

"Well, perhaps not," said Joe. Then in a while he
added—"Look here, Peter, I'm no author, you know,
but I can talk a little. It will be holiday time directly;
suppose we were to go to Paris together?"

"That would be rather expensive, if nothing came of
it," said the professor; "besides I'm not quite sure that
I shall get any holidays. From what Roustoubique says,
I fancy he wants me to remain in charge of the pupils
who don't go home."

"But you wont stand it!" cried Joe, indignantly.
"It's infamous!"

"How am I to help it?" asked the professor, with a
faint smile.

"How?" repeated Joe. "By publishing your book;
by making a name for yourself; by being independent of
such a paltry tyrant."

Peter leant his head upon his hand, and thought it over.
It was a tempting bait, and the more he thought of it the
more he liked the notion. Joe was in no hurry, but went
on with his grog.

"It comes to this," said he at last, "if you're game
to venture a matter of sixty francs, I might run up to
Paris and see what can be done. However, it's for you
to decide. I don't like the notion of the stuff being
wasted, and I can't help thinking that you might make
a nice little thing out of it if we manage matters properly."

"There's no knowing. I have a great opinion of your
judgment, Joseph, though you must allow you sometimes
blunder a little."

"Well, everybody does that, I suppose," said Joseph;
"and some people's blunders are smaller than others'
because they aim at such petty results. If I had not a
soul above blue pills and black draughts, I daresay I

should not go very far wrong; but you'll find some of these days, that by some stroke of genius—the awfullest fluke, everybody will call it—I shall very quietly make my fortune."

"I believe you, Joe," said the professor; "and you shall try what you can do with the book; and understand, before you set about the business, that half whatever we make is yours."

"Oh, that's all right enough," said Joe; "we are not likely to quarrel." As Peter was writing out a cheque for sixty francs, Joe mentioned that little matter of the two napoleons, which amount was added to the other; and Joe presently took his departure, in high spirits and full of bright hopes of the future.

The Parisian publishers must have been among the most dilatory persons in the world, for Joe was away a whole week before he could get an answer from the first, and then he merely said that he had not time that moment to go into the matter. At the cheapest of Parisian hotels the charges for living are such as tax a slender purse severely, and then Joe had a certain character to keep up, and some treating to do, which greatly added to the expense. When he had been a fortnight in the gay capital he yet had not succeeded in the object which had brought him thither; but he had learnt one or two things. This was one of them : It was a much better plan to publish your book yourself, if your book were a good one and likely to sell. The difference in the profits under this system was enormous. As to the expense, some credit could be obtained, and with a matter of seven or eight hundred francs really magnificent results might be arrived at.

All this was as clear as day, and with the aid of the

first four rules of arithmetic you might work the sum out as easily as Joe did. We know already that there was a little balance in the St. Babylas Bank standing to the credit of Peter Polyblank. Some days after the receipt of Joe's communication a large portion of this accumulated capital found its way to Paris, and the professor waited in great anxiety for tidings respecting its disposal. It arrived safely. Joe wrote at once to acknowledge the receipt, promising to write again next day.

That evening, feeling a little restless, Peter went to the Café Leduc, in the Little Place—a most unusual proceeding on his part.

Two or three of the fastest among the St. Babylasians were sitting at the next table, and loudly disputing about horses and odds. Their noise disturbed our good friend, who was trying to read the newspaper. "I wish they would be a little more quiet," he thought. "I'm sure the Paris races do not interest me, and I don't want to hear anything about them."

Poor innocent, he had no notion how much better it would have been for him if "Cora Pearl" had come in first.

When three days had elapsed, and no tidings had arrived either of Joe or the money, the poor professor could no longer bear the suspense, and sent an urgent letter, threatening to come himself to Paris if he did not hear by return of post. This elicited a reply from Joe to the effect that he was coming back—and, sure enough, next day he came.

When the professor arrived at his lodging that evening Joe received him in a dramatic attitude. "Don't speak to me," he cried, "don't speak to me, Peter!—I'm an infernal scoundrel."

This beginning was certainly not encouraging; but it prepared the professor for what was to come. It seemed that Joe was managing the literary business capitally—that everything was going on in a highly satisfactory way, very convincing details of which were introduced into Joe's narrative at this point. Nothing could have been better, in fact, only unfortunately the doctor fell in with a sporting friend, who persuaded him to go to the races. Here he had secret information imparted to him relative to a " dead certainty." Surely no mortal man, under like circumstances, could have resisted the temptation. It is true that, strictly speaking, the money was not Joe's, but that made the opportunity none the less tempting. The only thing to be regretted was that the dead certainty was not as certain as it might have been.

" Where's the manuscript ?" asked Peter, when he had somewhat recovered from the first shock.

At this question Joe was confused.

" Upon my soul," he said, " I don't know how to look you in the face." The professor's lips moved, but he could utter no word. What was coming next ?

" You see, I was in such a state after that race came off, and I found what a fool I had been. I was nearly mad, and set to drinking raw brandy by the tumbler-full, not knowing what I was about. The end of it was——"

" Well, well," said the professor, impatiently.

" The end of it was I got my pockets turned inside out."

" Do you mean to say you have lost the manuscript ?" cried Peter, aghast.

" No, no; hang it, not as bad as that; it's only just

19

a little torn, and I think some of the brutes must have trodden on it."

The manuscript here produced had certainly the appearance of having been walked upon, and when examined several pages were found to be wanting.

That night the professor re-read a large portion of what was left, and, tying it up very carefully, put it back into the tattered old portmanteau with a weary sigh. "Perhaps it might have failed," he said to himself. "Perhaps what has happened is for the best. Some of the verses do seem to want touching up a little. I'll put them away for a time, until I feel a little more inclined to revise them. I'm not in the humour just at present."

With this reflection he put away the work which might or might not have made his name immortal; and when again he looked at it he had other projects in view, and after but a cursory glance at the first page or two, condemned it as rubbish; it has therefore never been printed, nor, indeed, has any other work from the same pen. Perhaps it is fortunate that we do not carry all our grand designs into execution, for if we did the laurel would not bear leaves sufficient for all of us.

CHAPTER XXVI.

GOOD-BYE AND GOOD LUCK.

And so, weak heart, good-bye!
When that day comes you will remember me,
Thinking it might have been, but may not be ;
And so, good-bye ! good-bye !—DONALDSON.

" FELICITE," said Mr. Pomponney, "you will see."

" I am glad of it," snapped Felicité, "for it's almost time I did."

She had had a hard day's work, had that poor little wife of the prophetic Hyppolite. She had been scrubbing and scouring, and things had gone wrong with her. Hyppolite, meanwhile, had rolled his pill paste, dispensed his pennyworths of pharmacerie, discussed the events of the day with his customers, lectured the youthful Coquillard upon sins generally, but more particularly the sins of youth combined with inordinate appetite; smoked his pipe, drank his half cup, played his " partie " at the Café Leduc, and returned home, thinking himself a mighty fine fellow. As usual, he was prophetic, and this time it was the quickly-approaching and inevitable downfall of the Polyblank brothers, upon which he was oracular. When, however, the meek Felicité thus responded, it for the first time occurred to Hyppolite that his prophetic fame was on the totter. But he was prudent, and refrained from questioning. Therefore, turning over on his pillow, he went to sleep without another word. Just at this moment, by the way, it did not seem to require the powers of a Zadkiel to predict the downfall of the professor, for he had fallen already. Indeed, that very day he had received his dismissal from the Imperial College. In this result the machinations of the Bourdichon band had culminated. There had been dreadful doings in the professor's class during the last month, and, on a small scale, a sort of insurrection. One day Roustoubique being summoned away on business, at the same time that one of the masters was away on account of severe illness, the professor's services were called into request—(he now did all the extra dirty work)—as usher, after his duties as class master were over.

The news spread like wildfire that the Poulet Blanc was to take charge of the réfectoire, and of a study during play hours. Instantly the heads of Bourdichon's band were laid together, and a plan of action decided upon. Secret countersigns and watchwords were adopted. A whistle being absolutely necessary, Bardajos occupied the hour devoted to the professor's class to its manufacture. In the dining-room they found Mr. Polyblank's dinner set out at the end of the table, in the place usually occupied by the absent study-master. It was a Friday. There was sorrel soup, after which a dish of haricot beans and boiled eggs. Two eggs were served to the professor, which were hastily appropriated by a couple of young gentlemen before Mr. Polyblank had observed them. Having finished as much as he could get through of the soup, he began to eat the haricots, when Master Bardajos, who had not been quick enough to steal the dish, asked the professor how it was he had not got any eggs?

" I don't know," replied Polyblank, simply.

" Don't you stand it. You ask for them," urged Bardajos. Therefore, calling a garçon, the professor asked why the eggs had not been supplied to him?

" They were," said the servant, looking about with a puzzled air; and he went off to consult with one of his fellows who had helped to lay the tables. A noisy consultation ensued, with much gesticulation, ending with the servant's expressed opinion that one of the young gentlemen must have taken the eggs.

" Search them, sir," he suggested.

" What would be the use of searching us, now we have eaten our dinner?" said the youngest Moineau. Then, opening his mouth, he added, " Can you see your egg, sir?"

At this piece of impertinence the other young gentlemen laughed boisterously, and the professor gave the youngest Moineau an hour's retenue.

" That's your fault, you sneak," said the youngest

Moineau, punching Bardajos in the ribs with his elbow.

" Is it ?" retorted Bardajos, maliciously hitting him upon the pocket where the stolen eggs were.

Meanwhile, the professor and the servants were going round the table searching the pupils. Presently it came to the turn of Moincau the younger, who would not be searched.

" Empty your pockets, sir," said the professor.

" I shan't."

" Empty your pockets."

" Empty them yourself."

So the professor, in a rage, thrust his hand into the pocket containing the broken eggs, but immediately withdrew it, amidst general laughter. But Moineau the younger for this offence was led away to the dungeon, and then, the dinner being at an end, the others were marched out into the playground. For some time the scholars amused themselves by pelting the professor with small pebbles, and keeping him in a lively state of excitement by calling out his name in tones of deep distress from remote parts of the yard, when he was walking in an opposite direction. When the play hour was half over, Bourdichon called Pepinet on one side.

" I'll tell you something," said he, " if you'll swear not to split."

" What is it ?"

" Do you swear ?"

" Yes, I swear."

" There is a loose plank in the palings between this and the Proviseur's garden. We can squeeze through, and have a feast of gooseberries."

" Come on, then."

At the palings they met the eldest Moineau, who was

also sworn in, and all three crept through the hole. A few minutes afterwards Bardajos's head appeared at the opening.

" Go back !" shouted the others.

" I've as much right here as you have."

The noise brought the professor to the spot, and after a spirited chase the three fast young gentlemen were captured, and led away to the dungeon, where Moineau was discovered asleep, but, awakening, was highly delighted at the notion of company. The prisoners were each to copy two thousand lines of La Fontaine, and had brought with them pens, ink, and paper, the pens being ingeniously tied together in such a way that five copies of the same line could be written at once with the same amount of trouble that is ordinarily taken in writing one. But a very short time was thus occupied, the young gentlemen soon abandoning their exercises in favour of sports and pastimes. A target being drawn upon a piece of paper and fastened to the wall, paper wings were attached to the pens, which were thus transformed into darts. Then sides were chosen, and a match commenced. When they were weary of this sport they fell to quarrelling, and thus passed away another hour or so. The twilight was setting in, and it was already too dark to see to write.

" Hallo, you others, look here !" said Bourdichon. He had found a loose plank in the floor of the dungeon ; for this dungeon (cachot), in spite of its terrible name, was a first-floor room over a sort of out-house, attached to the infirmary, the entrance to which was from the street.

" What say you to breaking through and escaping ?" said Bourdichon.

The other young gentlemen were easily persuaded, and they chose names appropriate to the work in hand.

" I'll be Cartouche."

" And I Vidocq."

" And I Macaire."

" But, I say, what am I to be ?" asked Pepinet.

" Oh, as for you," responded the other young gentlemen, " you needn't be anything."

Master Bourdichon meanwhile was examining the floor. Very soon he had pulled up the plank. Then one of the young gentlemen broke a hole through the lath and plaster with his feet, and the band went down on their hands and knees and peered cautiously through the aperture. It was pitch dark down below, and had an awful look.

" What are we to do next ?" asked Cartouche.

" Put down Pepinet as an experiment," suggested some other celebrated malefactor, but Pepinet raised a dismal howl at the proposition. When he was silent again, a strange noise was heard from below—the shaking of a chain and a ferocious snort. Evidently some wild animal was there. Perhaps it might get up at them through the hole.

" Let's put down Pepinet," once more suggested the French Jack Sheppard.

" Hush, I tell you," cried Bourdichon ; and then, with a loud laugh, " why it's only a donkey." And in another minute he was forcing his way down the hole.

" I can drop on his back," he said ; but in this scheme he was foiled by the sudden giving way of treacherous laths. At the same moment the stable door opened, and the donkey's owner rushing in, a fight took place, followed by the capture of four celebrated prison breakers, afterwards to be led round to the college gate and handed back to the door-porter, with some trifling loss of dignity Surely, never had the unhappy professor spent such a day since he entered the walls. As he looked at his list of punishments he dreaded to think what Roustoubique would say to those fearful affairs of the gooseberries and the donkey. But alas! the worst had yet to come. Roustoubique was not to return till next day, and poor Polyblank had been prevailed upon to pass the night in the college, and was to sleep in the absent usher's bed. This part of his task he most dreaded.

For the last hour or so his youthful charges had been extremely quiet. It was a calm before a storm. Whispers full of sinister import circulated round the study, and winks of evil meaning were from time to time exchanged. Nothing of importance, however, took place until all were in bed, when something in the shape of a panic was occasioned by a rumour that the lid had come off the youngest Moineau's "gentle" box, and that the happy family were crawling at large. Tidings of this disaster reaching Polyblank, the reptiles were chased, caught, and ejected through the window After which the other young gentlemen were able to go to sleep in safety. Presently, all was still. The professor, worn out with fatigue, closed his eyes and dozed.

This was the moment chosen by the arch-conspirators. Bourdichon and Bardajos, rising stealthily, crept on hands and knees down either side of the dormitory. They were passing from bed to bed awakening the band. Like shadows from the grave then stole forth the trusty ones, gathering together the shoes of the slumbering virtuous. Then all got noiselessly back into bed, and Bourdichon and Bardajos turned off the gas at each end of the room. A signal was to be given by Bardajos. There was a moment of intense suspense, and then his whistle sounded loud and shrill, and simultaneously twenty pairs of bluchers were hurled at the head of the devoted school-master, whose bed they covered. Awakening from his sleep, and supposing his life to be in danger, he bounded on to the floor and shouted for help. Next moment he received a heavy thump on the back from a bolster. Before he could recover himself, he got another on the stomach. Then one on the head, then one in the face. Fighting his way through his assailants he reached the door, opened it and rushed into the passage shouting for assistance. It was the worst thing he could have done, for next moment the door was shut upon him, and his efforts to force it open again were met by shouts of derisive laughter.

There, in his shirt, the unhappy victim stood when the porter, a couple of grinning garçons, and Roustoubique himself, who had returned unexpectedly, came upstairs. At first they all roared with laughter at Polyblank's woful figure. Then set about forcing the door. The riot being quelled, and some of the ringleaders dragged away and locked up, with a threat of expulsion next day hanging over them, Roustoubique turned fiercely upon the professor.

"Dress yourself, you fool," he said, "and go home. I don't want you here."

Polyblank went home without any reply. He found the door locked.

"We thought you were not coming, sir," said Felicité, from a window.

"Yes, yes, I know," replied the professor, in an impatient tone. "Please open the door."

She was surprised at the tone of his voice, and came downstairs in a hurry. "Has anything happened?" she asked.

" Happened?   No."

He passed upstairs hastily, and closed his door.   He could not trust himself to speak.   Shame and rage were tearing at his heart.

" What a despicable wretch I was," he muttered, betwixt his clenched teeth.   " Why didn't I knock him down? why didn't I? why didn't I?"

Alas! his life through he had always, until too late, left the right thing unsaid and the right thing undone. There came a timid knock at the door: it was Felicité. She was the only friend he had found in this hateful place, and he now was treating her with rudeness.   She would sympathize with him, but he turned his back on her.   Often, before, he had so acted towards others who would have helped him; and they had thought him insensible to kindness because his awkward tongue could not speak the few proper words of thanks.

" Mr. Polyblank," said Felicité, entering the room and laying her hand upon the professor's shoulder, almost caressingly, " I am sure you are in great trouble.   Do let me share it with you.   How can I be of service?   I and my husband will gladly help you if we can."

This was a fib, as far as Hyppolite was concerned. He prophesied a person's rise or fall, but did not trouble himself about helping in either direction.

" You are very good to me, madame," said the professor. " I am rather unlucky, I think, and I'm not sure that I am quite fitted for my business."

" It is a very hard, and a very weary, wearing business," said Felicité; " and I should have thought that a gentleman knowing so much (she had a prodigious notion of Polyblank's learning) might do much better."

" I wish I knew how," responded the professor, with a sigh.   " I should like to find out that."

" Then I think I can tell you," exclaimed Felicité, in great excitement. " The librarianship of the public library is vacant. My husband is connected with the museum, and he shall try and make some interest for you. One of Baroness de Grandvilain's friends has the gift of the place, so of course she will use her influence in your behalf. Is she well enough for you to ask her ?"

She was still very ill, he answered, and if she were well he would not ask, because——But while trying to tell the reason his voice broke suddenly. Then again was good little Felicité's hand laid upon his shoulder, and she bade him in a low, soft tone never to mind, for he need not trouble himself to tell her. Of course she knew all about it! As if such a bungler as Polyblank could keep such a secret. The ice broken, he told her all that he had suffered. How he had hoped—how he was a fool for hoping, where his love was so hopeless. And to this she replied with words of gentleness and comfort.

Ah! how is it that women always have some consolation to impart in such cases, when we men can only sit silent, or, speaking, speak beside the mark ? Never, for some months, had Polyblank slept so soundly as he did that night; nor arisen as he did next morning—so hopeful of the future. Mr. Pomponney, urged on by that good wife of his, really went vigorously into the library business, and was very successful. He got several promises of support, and, with a letter of introduction, the professor set out to see Mr. Cherami, in whose gift the place was.

" Cherami," he repeated to himself, as he walked along. He fancied he knew the name, but could not recollect to whom it belonged. But he was not long in doubt. On entering the room he found himself in the presence of the Little Paul, from whom he took the famous Latin verses that night at the Café Leduc. With a slight blush

Polyblank presented his memorial, and stated the case. Little Paul listened, twirling his moustache; and when the professor had finished, he said :—"I regret to say, the place is already filled;" and then in a sort of half bantering tone continued—

"It were a pity, though, for a gentleman of your literary attainments to bury himself in an out-of-the-way hole and corner such as this wretched little Saint Babylas. On the contrary, go elsewhere, my dear sir, and become famous."

The professor cowered a moment under the blow; and then, an unwonted spirit possessing him, he retorted—

"You, though, sir, who are already half famous, are content to subside ignobly."

"Ah, yes, my case is different," replied the other, though with less confidence.

"It is," said Polyblank, with flashing eyes. "I will go, as you suggest. It is perhaps the hand of fate that urges me onward. A few years hence, may be, I may have made my name and earned my niche, whilst you lie forgotten in your unmarked grave. Who knows. Good morning."

And with this burst he went his away, striding proudly down the street, as though he had achieved a glorious victory; while Little Paul, ridiculous as it may seem, felt somehow strangely humbled and uncomfortable, left sitting there in his crimson velvet chair. However, the time for the statue or bust just indirectly alluded to had not yet arrived, and Polyblank had his living to seek. Well, he was not, he thought, likely to get anything to do in France, but he would return to his own country, and try his hand at a new trade.

"I can't mend boots," said the professor, with rather

a painful smile, contemplating, as he spoke, his old botched-up half-Wellingtons, " or I should have tried my hand at that long ago. But surely I can do something that a poor gentleman may do; and if I can't, why I'll hide away somewhere, and die in the dark. At any rate, with Heaven's help, I'll never degrade myself again."

There was some money due to him for his services at the college, and he rightly thought that it would be poor false pride not to go and get it ; therefore he went to the college and asked for Mr. Roustoubique. The Proviseur was in his own room, the porter said ; and Mr. Polyblank went in search of of him. The room, however, was empty, but seeing the Proviseur's hat upon the table, Polyblank sat down to wait. He sat by the table, and carelessly noticed an open letter lying there signed by the " Recteur," a superior officer, under whose control were Mr. Roustonbique and the Proviseurs of the other colleges associated with the University of France. Glancing from this letter, his eyes fell on half a sheet of paper lying by its side, on which the ink was not yet dry. Now, the name of the recteur was Constant, and on this piece of paper somebody, it would seem, had been imitating Mr. Constant's signature ; for there was it written, more than a score of times. The door opened, and Roustoubique hurried in. Polyblank rose to meet him.

" Hallo !" cried the Proviseur, starting slightly, and changing colour. " So it's you, is it, come at last ? A pretty time of day, too, I must say."

" I am not aware that there was any hour fixed for my visit, replied Polyblank, coldly.

" Oh, indeed, cried the other, taking his seat at the table. " That's what you thought, ch ? Then in future, allow me to tell you——"

" Allow me to tell you, sir, that my future does not concern you," said Polyblank. " You dismissed me last night, you must remember, and I am my own master now."

Roustoubique's eyes and mouth opened with surprise.

" You—you are going away, are you ?"

" Certainly. You told me to do so."

" Oh, very well—very well. As you like. Of course, you know your own business best. I hope you'll find a good place, and that they'll be better pleased with you there than I have been. Why I have kept you so long I don't know. Why I have kept you. I say—did you take a paper just now off this table ?"

Mr. Roustoubique had been fidgeting about all the while he had been talking, and feeling in his pockets, and looking on the table and on the floor; and he now asked the question, because Polyblank was thoughtlessly twisting a piece of paper in his hand. He had, in fact, in his absent way, possessed himself of those signatures which Mr. Roustoubique had been scribbling. Now, strangely enough, when Roustoubique recognised the half-sheet, and snatched at it eagerly, the truth flashed at once upon Polyblank, and he knew that he had to deal with a rogue. Holding the paper tightly, he laid his hand upon the desk, and, looking Roustoubique full in the face, said :—" Shall I tell you what I think of you ?" The colour left the Proviseur's cheeks, and his white lips moved, but he spoke not. There was something unusual in Polyblank's voice and manner, which, from the first moment, Roustoubique had noticed with steadily increasing dread. The worm was going to turn upon him at last.

The Proviseur was in a mortal fright when he found Polyblank's eyes thus fixed sternly upon him, but he could make no reply.

"I'll tell you what I think of you," said Polyblank. "You are a knave!"

"How dare you address such language to me?" cried Roustoubique finding his voice at last, though it was rather a weak one. "How dare you? I've a good mind —I'll ring the bell."

"Don't send for a witness," cried the other, seizing him by the arm, "or by Heaven I'll beat you before his face. Give me, sir, what is due to me, and I will depart. Give me my money, and you shall have your paper back. Only be quick, and let me get out of this into honest air where I can breathe."

In quite a pitiful, whining way, Roustoubique besought the ex-professor to be calm and reasonable, and not to talk so loud, begging him to believe that he (Roustoubique) would always be a friend to him; but he was so completely thrown off his guard that he could not pretend to any virtuous indignation. With unsteady hand he unlocked a drawer and produced some gold and silver— a paltry sum it was; and Polyblank somewhat disdainfully thrust it into his pocket without counting the pieces. Then having given a receipt, and handed back the paper, he turned to go. He paused, however, at the door, and said—

"You have treated me very badly, Mr. Roustoubique. I might, at any rate, oblige you to give me a good testimonial, but I do not require one. I intend to give up teaching."

"I hope you will do well," said Roustoubique, with a sickly smile.

"I hope so;" and Polyblank went downstairs and turned his back upon the Imperial College of Saint Babylas for ever.

And now there remained little else for him to do but
repack that battered old portmanteau, in which he had
brought his few chattels into the town some months ago,
and take his departure.   He went back to the chemist's
with the altered gait which since his interview with Little
Paul, he seemed to have unconsciously assumed.   Seeing
him coming along thus, with an unusual glow on his face
and sparkle in his eye, and actually swinging his walking-
stick with quite a reckless sort of air, little Felicité at
once concluded that he had obtained the vacant librarianship in search of which he had set out ; and Pomponney
had actually opened his mouth with the intention of observing that such was the result he had always anticipated,
but Polyblank held up his hand and gravely shook his head.

"No, my dear madam," he said, "I've failed again,
and so I'm going back to England."

He did not look in her face as he spoke, and so he did
not see the tears well up in her eyes ; but he took her
hand in his, and gently pressed it as he thanked her—
still with averted look—for her kindness to him.   Then,
less fearful of himself, he held out his hand to Hyppolite,
who had been mixing medicines for dear life during the
last sixty seconds, and who responded to this farewell
greeting with the alacrity that some worthy creatures
never fail to manifest at the hour of parting.   Polyblank
went upstairs, and gathered up his books and papers, and
began very elaborately to fold up and stow away his
other coat; but a sudden fit of impatience seizing him,
he gathered up his two or three rags and tatters, and
odds and ends, and flung them carelessly into the portmanteau.   He felt a little nervous about further leave-
taking; but, though he owed nothing for rent, having
always paid in advance, he had yet to settle a few trifles
in the way of housekeeping.

This done, and, once more, good-bye said, he walked slowly towards the "Three Crowns"—Coquillard, forced into the service by Felicité, carrying the portmanteau under protest, and taking it out of its edges against such house-sides and door-steps as he could conveniently knock it against, by the way. The diligence for Calais left at eight o'clock in the evening, and he had determined to dine at the public table, as he had done upon the day of his arrival. Therefore, having bespoken a place in the diligence, and requested Alexander to keep him a seat at the table, he had only one duty to perform, which was to see his brother Joe, and make arrangements for the future.

In this matter he felt some slight degree of awkwardness ; for—strange as it might appear in the case of one less familiar with the vicissitudes of fortunes—Joe was at that identical moment in flourishing circumstances. Yes, Joe had once more fallen on his feet ; and was indeed so much a rising man, just at this time, that the recognition of a needy and threadbare relative would necessarily be, to some extent, inconvenient. If this book, instead of being the record of the sufferings of Professor Polyblank, had been the history of the triumphs of the jovial Joseph, the few facts now about to be related might have filled many chapters with curious and improving details. Suffice it, however, to say, that after that little knock-kneed failure, Joe's patients having dwindled down to 0— for even those whom he used to physic gratis fought shy of him, and sought the advice of the cheapest of the opposition doctors—he gave himself up to several weeks of dissipation, with the determination of leading a roaring life as long as his means lasted. His means being limited, the life he led grew necessarily less and less roaring after the first few days.

20

Up to that time, although public opinion was against
him, he had kept his appointment as medical attendant
to the Imperial College ; but at last he managed to lose
it.   He had an original theory with respect to tooth-
drawing, and having the mouths of the college pupils at
his disposal, it occurred to him, one unlucky day, that
he would avail himself of that circumstance for the purpose of experimentalizing.   That fatal morning, while
Joseph's hand was in, two-and-twenty young gentlemen
lost a grinder each.   You can easily conceive how loud
were the lamentations which ensued, and how the suf-
ferers wailed and gnashed the teeth which remained to
them.   Next day the account of this proceeding raised
feelings of indignation in the homes of the pupils.   Some
parents wrote and protested.   Other parents protested
personally.   Some threatened to take their sons from
the college.   Some did take their sons away.   Roustoubique, who long had been pining for such a chance,
wrote a full, true, and particular account of the whole
affair to the authorities, and Joseph was dismissed.

It might be supposed that this would have had a depressing effect on our medical enthusiast.   On the contrary, he swaggered about the streets, and in and out of
the café, as though the town belonged to him.   As his
money disappeared, it is possible that he was, to some
extent, liable to the imputation of forcing his company
upon those who would and could pay for him.   The
worthy Leduc, in those days, did not appear over-anxious
to enjoy Mr. Joseph's patronage, and more than once
hinted as much ; but Joe was not to be easily routed.
He stood his ground, in spite of frowns and cold
shoulders ; and at length, when quite at his worst, he
made the acquaintance of an elderly stranger, who played
a game of billiards with him one day, treated him to a

glass of absinthe, and, four-and-twenty hours afterwards, offered him a medical appointment worth between three and four hundred per annum.

After all, there is nothing astonishing in Joe's luck. Such things happen every day, and like windfalls are always dropping into some one's outstretched hands, though some of us, for all that, may stretch out our hands a very long while before we catch anything. Joseph had come into his good luck about a week before the period at which this history has now arrived, and had borrowed money from his new friend, and purchased dazzling raiment. It was quite natural, therefore, that, meeting his brother on the sunny side of Imperial-street, he should remark upon the professor's shabby appearance.

"My dear Peter," he said, "you'll never rise. Somehow you wont do it. It's no good trying to pull you up with one, if you will pull back."

A few days before Joe's stroke of luck, he, in a casual way, having called upon the schoolmaster to raise a small loan, had referred to some mysterious investment that he had made, which, as he had termed it, would probably turn up trumps. After the stroke of luck, Polyblank made some inquiries about the investment, and was surprised to hear Joe say that he was sorry he had touched it, as matters had turned out; but he had got the thing on his hands, and could not get rid of it again. This, at the time, was rather vague talk; but the professor was soon to learn the truth.

This last afternoon in Saint Babylas, Polyblank, as has been related, after booking his place, and engaging himself for the table d'hôte, went out in quest of Joe. The doctor was not to be found, and, after a fruitless search, the professor walked back towards the hotel. What should he do for an hour or two? he asked himself.

Supposing, for the last time, he walked across the marshes, and took a stealthy peep at the old garden where he had spent so many happy hours? He would not go into the house. He had thought the matter over, and decided not to do so. There was no occasion for him to pay a farewell visit, under the circumstances. At any rate, no more was required of him by the strictest rules of etiquette than to leave his card at the gate, with P.P.C. in the corner. During the last month he had called several times at the château to make inquiries about the sick lady, but had always been told that she was too unwell to see anybody. No doubt he would be told so now, were he to call. She evidently did not want to see him. The sight of him would perhaps distress her. But there could be no harm in taking a last look at the garden. She would never know it, and it would be a great pleasure to him.

With this determination, therefore, he stepped forth briskly along the high road. He had gone about half the distance, when he saw a hackney carriage coming towards him, and, when even with it, a female voice with which he was acquainted called to him by name. He approached the carriage door, and saw with some surprise that the vehicle contained Madame Dubosq and his brother Joseph.

"Peter," said the Dubosq, to Mr. Polyblank's unbounded astonishment, and he, coming within reach, found his neck suddenly encircled by the Dubosq's fair arm, whilst at the same time a chaste salute was imprinted (by reason of his jerking his head at the critical moment) between his nose and his left eye.

"Peter," said the lady, "you must not mind my calling you so *now*. After what has occurred, Joseph must allow there can be no oeeasion for further concealment."

Mr. Polyblank, staring very hard, was silent.

" Joseph," continued the lady, " would rather that our union had been kept quiet a little while longer, but events have now proved to him that the person upon whom he had depended was not to be depended upon."

As she spoke she cast a triumphant glance towards the doctor, whose aspect, strange to say, was anything but joyous; and, all at once, it dawned upon the professor that he had got a new relation.

" I must repeat," continued the lady, " although Joseph was of a contrary opinion, that that person's generosity was not to be relied upon. It is true, as I have over and over again observed to Joseph, that she flings her money about like dirt upon dirt; but the really deserving, as I have frequently pointed out to Joseph, she too often allows to go unrewarded."

As Mr. Polyblank saw that the time had now arrived when he must positively say something, he said, "Indeed !"

" By keeping our union a secret, as Joseph suggested, and by delicate inquiry ascertaining what this person felt inclined to—in fact, at what amount, to speak plainly, she estimated the worth of the best years of a life sacrificed to her interests, we should, as it were, have grounds to go upon."

" Yes, of course, you know," broke in Joseph, whose face was very red indeed, as he spoke. " She having said that my wife would not be forgotten, we wanted to know, you see, Peter, how far she was going to be remembered."

Mr. Polyblank, finding that the time had once more arrived when he must again break silence, repeated his former venture, and said, " Indeed !"

" Yes, Peter," cried the lady, eagerly, " and I had agreed with Joseph that our union should remain concealed for some time longer; but the baroness having become aware of the fact, we have, as I tell Joseph, only discovered a little sooner than we otherwise should have done, to what extent the generosity of—of that person was to be depended on."

The lady stopping here, the professor looked inquiringly from one to the other, wondering whether any further communications were about to be made to him; and finding there was not, he said, hesitatingly, "So you are married?"

He was upon the eve of saying that they were old enough to know their own minds, but caught himself in time. For the life of him, though, he could not stammer out any of the words of congratulation customary under such circumstances; nor indeed did Joseph's appearance, which was very much like that of a fatted calf upon its way to sacrifice, warrant him in indulging in ardent felicitations.

"You see, Peter," continued the lady, "Joseph's appointment insures him a handsome income. A medical man is so much better married; and I hope," she added playfully, "we have not been imprudent."

To this the professor somewhat lugubriously responded that he hoped so too.

"Well," said the lady, after a rather awkward pause, "we must be getting on. Good-bye."

"Good-bye," said Polyblank; and it then occurred to him, for the first time, that Joseph knew nothing of his departure. It was not, though, he thought, the most convenient opportunity for making the communication. He therefore shook hands with them both, and promised Joe that he would write to him in a few days. As the carriage rolled away in the distance, he stood watching it with a gloomy face. Joseph was having another start in life. Would he do well this time? Would he and his wife live happily together? Somehow, take her all together, Polyblank could not help thinking that she was, without exception, the most disagreeable woman he had ever known. Presently, with a sigh, he turned and walked on slowly towards the château.

It was the last he ever saw of this promising couple.

CHAPTER XXVII.

POLYBLANK'S LAST MISTAKE.

Mais notre ancre à nous !
Pauvre petit chasse-marée,
Tient au fond si fort—si fort amareé,
Qu'il nous faut haler—haler—coup sur coup :
Hissa—ho ! hissa !—hissa ! hissoué !
DE LA LANDELLE.

BEFORE very long, Polyblank had reached the garden wall of the château, and came to a halt before that weak place in the fence over which, long ago, he had climbed surreptitiously to lie in the shade of the old trees by the water-side. Mounting now upon the palings, he peeped about and listened. He could see no one. All was still. He would venture. Since he had met Joseph and his wife, he felt more than ever convinced that he must not pay the baroness a visit. From what little he had heard of the story of Joseph's marriage, he was very certain some petty meanness had been perpetrated. He knew very well that Joseph's honour could not be relied upon. He knew, also, that when such a woman as Joe's wife likes to be mean, she can be very mean indeed. Most likely they had wrung some money from the young baroness, and she, in giving it, had told them never to darken her doors again. If he were now to call, he argued, she might think that he, too, had come a-begging. Perhaps she would offer him alms!

Then he could not help reflecting how all whom she befriended seemed to turn upon her; and he wondered whether, now that the Dubosq had gone, she was alone in the château without a friend. Since Raynal had left the town, she had never been seen abroad. Polyblank knew that she had been dangerously ill. He wondered whether she was much changed. He would have given a great deal to have caught one fleeting glimpse of her. Ah! what would he not have given, could he have lived over again one of those dear old evenings now gone for ever!

Thinking thus, he climbed cautiously over the palings, and walked slowly through the shrubbery to the water-side. As he walked he crushed the dead leaves lying thick upon the ground. It was the first day of winter, and a cold wind coming across the bleak marsh land sighed mournfully on the naked branches of the trees. The water ebbed slowly past, as it had done in the old time; but somehow it seemed now to make the scene very sad and dreary. There was the old place where he had been disturbed at his pic-nic, when she came rustling through the bushes. Oh! how long ago it all seemed! Why, at that time he was sanguine about his success at the college. Joseph had not yet arrived. He had not known what it was to feel the misery that he felt at this moment. Well! he had been alone in the world many years before this. Why should he all at once find the old loneliness more lonely? Some persons tottering on the very grave's brink are ready to begin life again quite hopefully. Joseph's was one of these sanguine natures. Why should he despair? He was going back to England—to that England which, according to some of its most persistent exiles, is ever dear to them—yes, to that dear old country, where some hundreds of waifs and strays starve and die annually without being particularly missed or regretted. But such was not to be his case. Had he not made up his mind, whilst striding through the streets of Saint Babylas that morning, that he was to be successful? No doubt of it; though just now he could not recollect exactly how it was to come about. Now he was standing on the spot where first he fell a-dreaming. Yes, this was where he sat when he heard the rustle of her silk dress; and there was—*the rustle now.*

He had not time to reach the fence. He had not time to hide. She had caught sight of him from the garden, and came towards him with her hands stretched forth, in the old way, and with something of the old smile lighting up a poor little wasted face; so pale and sad, he could scarcely have sworn to its ownership had it not been for the familiar sound of the gentle voice.

"Dear Mr. Polyblank, I am so glad to see you. I have been so long wondering why you did not come."

He had forgotten all about his fancied ill-treatment. He had forgotten that he had to begin the world again. He had forgotten that there was any world beyond the château boundaries, when at once these words recalled him.

"I have called several times," he said, "but they told me I could not see you."

"I never heard of it. I thought you had never been here since that night. They should not have sent you away. I gave directions that I was to be told if you came; but I suppose your brother's wife did not wish you to see me."

He said no more, for he could easily understand that

they had desired to keep him at a distance while their
schemes were hatching. Walking silently by Manon's side
on their way to the house he thought this over, and also
thought that it was time to be going back to the "Three
Crowns," and yet he did not make any attempt to go.

Presently Manon said :—" I have been very unhappy
here, and I am going away. I have been so very unhappy since we last met, that I have thought sometimes
my heart would break, and that I should die. Perhaps
my heart is broken," she said, looking up at him with a
sad smile; "but I am still living, you see. Yes, I am
alive: but do you know I am quite alone in the world?
I am hardly twenty yet, and I have lost my father and
mother, my husband, and—and I have seen a great deal
of trouble. You, too, Mr. Polyblank, have told me that
you have no friends or relations alive but your brother,
and your life also has been hard. Now I thought——"

She paused here, plucking a flower and dreamily
parting its leaves. With a violently throbbing heart he
listened and waited, his eyes fixed on her face—so beautiful in its pale sadness—his ears greedily drinking in her
softly spoken words.

" Now I thought," she continued, "that I had yet one
friend—not a very old one, perhaps, but one who, I fancied,
was sincere, and that one was you——"

The words rose half uttered to his lips,—If she could
only believe how sincere he was—how his love had grown
from day to day—how she was all in all to him——how—
but she went on speaking, all unconscious of his agitation.

" So I have been thinking what a weary life yours
must be at that college, if the accounts which I have had
of it are true; and that I could offer you a happy home
if you would accept it."

"If," he repeated, the blood rushing in a tumultuous torrent to his face.

"I have often told you," she said, "that I have a good deal of property in England. Now I am thinking of going over there to live. Will you come with me as my agent, to manage my estate and take care of my money for me, for I am not fit to look after my own affairs?"

Just for one moment he stood silent and motionless, while the blood flowed back from his face to his heart, the beating of which seemed for that moment to stop. One moment more, and he saw the full extent of the miserable mistake he was upon the very eve of making. She did not love him; but, kindhearted and generous as she ever had been, she offered him now a handsome income, which he felt was intended to be a provision for him for life. And should he refuse the offer, because it fell short of the mad folly he had conceived a while ago? All in a moment this occurred to him; and in that brief space he also saw the extent of the vast gulf dividing him from the idol he had worshipped. Yes, there she stood, young, lovely, rich, with the smiling world at her feet. Here he stood, a poor plodding, careworn creature—not formed to be a hero of romance, though possessing qualities which such heroes would frequently be the better for sharing.

And would the gulf between them ever lessen, now that the days of anxious, grinding poverty were passed? Would he ever rise to something higher, nobler—more worthy of her? As he bowed his head to kiss her hand, he prayed to Heaven that such might be the case.

And thus she at twenty and he at thirty began the world again. And was his life happy? And did she marry him in the end? Ah! good reader, we have all of us our own ideas of happiness. Make Manon and the poor professor happy according to your own notion. One fact, however, must be recorded by the writer before this book be brought to a close, and it is this :—Here ended the sufferings of Professor Polyblank.

THE END.

ERLESMERE:
OR, CONTRASTS OF CHARACTER.

BY L. S. LAVENU.

"'Erlesmere belongs to the same class of novels as the stories of Miss Young, 'The Heir of Redclyffe,' &c., nor is it inferior to them in ability and in the exhibition of internal conflict, though the incidents are more stormy. There are many passages of extraordinary force; tragic circumstances being revealed in momentary flashes of dramatic force."—*Press.*

FLORENCE TEMPLAR.
BY MRS. F. VIDAL.

"'Florence Templar' is a tale of love, pride, and passion. There is no little power shown in the manner of presenting the high-minded Florence. The story as a whole is very good."—*Examiner.*

"Graceful and very interesting, with considerable artistic skill."—*National Review.*

"A good story of English life, interesting in its details, and told with liveliness and spirit."--*Literary Gazette.*

HEIRESS OF BLACKBURNFOOT.
By author of "A Life's Love."

"We heartily commend this story to the attention of our readers for its power, simplicity, and truth. None can read its impressive record without interest, and few without improvement."

BEYMINSTRE.
By the Author of "Lena," "King's Cope," &c.

"We have still some good novel writers left, and among them is the author of 'Beyminstre.' The conduct of the story is excellent. Many of the subordinate parts are highly comic: an air of nature and life breathes through the whole. It is a work of unusual merit."—*Satur-day Review.*

"There are admirable points in this novel, and great breadth of humour in the comic scenes. 'Beyminstre' is beyond all comparison the best work by the author."—*Daily News.*

NANETTE AND HER LOVERS.
BY TALBOT GWYNNE.

"We do not remember to have met with so perfect a work of literary art as 'Nanette' for many a long day; or one in which every character is so thoroughly worked out in so short a space, and the interest concentrated with so much effect and truthfulness."--*Britannia.*

HIGHLAND LASSIES.
BY ERICK MACKENZIE.

"'Highland Lassies' deserves to be a successful novel, for it is one of the most spirited and amusing we have read for a long time. The interest is sustained without flagging to the very last page."

7

STANDARD AUTHORS.

ONE SHILLING.

Fcap. 8vo, with Illustrated Cover, and well printed on good paper.

WHEN ORDERING, THE NUMBERS ONLY NEED BE GIVEN.